DARRYL ANKA

SHARDS
OF A
SHATTERED MIRROR

BOOK II
· NOCTURNAL ·

"Shards of a Shattered Mirror Book II: Nocturnal," by Darryl Anka. ISBN 978-1-951985-42-4 (softcover), 978-1-951985-43-1 (eBook).

Published 2017 by Virtualbookworm.com Publishing Inc., P.O. Box 9949, College Station, TX 77842, US. ©2020, Darryl Anka.

Table of Contents

Chapter One:

THOOK

"By the time of the Landing, seven hundred years ago, the humans of Earth had discovered evidence of life on a few of the other planets and moons in their solar system through their telescopes, space probes, and other scientific instruments. Although it was simple life – bacteria, lichen, and the like – it proved life would arise wherever it could gain even the most tenuous foothold. After the introduction of Hybrid technology, the galaxy opened up for humanity and even the most optimistic and imaginative among us marveled at the diverse, alien multitudes that populated the stars. One of the most unique species we encountered was the Thook."

"A Child's Guide to the Galaxy"
by Jacaranda Florus & Ander Garza

*

THOOK, A WORLD SLIGHTLY LARGER THAN EARTH, occupied an orbit in the habitable zone around a red dwarf star that twenty-first century astronomers called Kepler 186f, but Thook's inhabitants named it Os'ek, which means "Red Eye," long before the founding of ancient Egypt and Mesopotamia. It was circled by three diminutive moons that swept around the planet at varying speeds, acting like a giant cosmic clock, with the innermost moon as the second hand, while the middle moon ticked off the minutes and the outer moon languidly counted the hours.

Os'ek was many times dimmer and cooler than Earth's sun, so Thook was only as far from its parent star as Mercury was from Sol and whipped around Os'ek in only one hundred thirty Earth days.

The most disconcerting thing for a visitor from Earth wasn't the brevity of the Thook year, but the length of its days and nights. Being so close to its ruddy star, Thook was almost gravitationally locked and, although one hemisphere didn't permanently face Os'ek, the planet rotated slowly on its axis only ten times in every orbit, which meant there were thirteen days in a Thook year, making each day and each night six and a half Earth days long.

With thirteen days between sunrises and a year less than one-third of Earth's, life on Thook was an odd mix of sluggishness and speed that played havoc with the human biological clock and made most visitors feel like they were getting nowhere fast.

However, Thook's orbital anomaly wasn't the strangest thing about the planet. The inhabitants, also known as Thook, were far stranger.

At first glance, the Thook were no more or less alien than any other non-human denizen from one of the Interstellar Alliance's many exotic planets. They had extremely large round eyes, ranging in color from the palest yellow to deep crimson while their waxy skin varied from bone white to a milky blue. They were tall and very thin, with long arms and legs that made them seem to be walking on stilts and possessed voluminous rib cages that enclosed tri-lobed lungs.

For most visitors, that first glance was often their last, because the Thook exhibited the unexpected quality of being absolutely forgettable. Not to say that they weren't fascinating people, for they were intelligent, engaging and very advanced, both socially and technologically, in addition to being one of the most powerfully telepathic races in the galaxy.

But the neural frequency at which their telepathy operated had the bizarre effect on all non-Thook of wiping a person's short-term memory. As long as someone was in direct eye contact with a

Thook, everything was normal, but as soon as the person looked away, all memory of the conversation, the interaction, and the individual Thook evaporated from that person's mind, as though the meeting had never taken place.

Humans, most Hybrids and other extraterrestrials had to rely on recordings or symbolic objects to remember that they had interacted with the Thook at all. A visitor, walking down the streets of a city on Thook, would have the dream-like experience of seeing individual Thook appearing and vanishing like phantoms as they made and then broke eye contact with those who passed by. It was like moving through a ghostly realm where the only things that remained solid were the tall, cathedral-arched buildings of vibrantly colored nano-glass that comprised the majority of the structures on the planet.

Sylvania Rousseau navigated the wide glass walkways of Tek'pan'tek, the planet's capital city. She was wrapped in a cold-weather nano-cloak, for under Os'ek's weak light, it never rose above thirty-three degrees Fahrenheit anywhere on Thook and, during the week-long nights, the temperature could plunge to minus eighty. Fortunately, Thook's thick atmosphere, plus its nearly nonexistent axis tilt and subsequent lack of seasons, helped to sustain an equilibrium that distributed warmth around the planet and prevented the temperature from plunging even lower.

The dark-eyed Nocturnal spied a blue-tinted building marked by a particular symbol in the Thook's complex alphabet of circles, crescents, and dots that matched the insignia she carried in her gloved hand. She entered and made her way down a semi-transparent glass hallway that enhanced the spectral effect of the ephemeral Thook workers that occupied the various chambers.

Sylvania placed her hand on the entry door to a large chamber at the end of the hall. It opened like the petals of a large flower to admit her. The door closed behind her and she slowly turned in a circle to search for the chamber's occupant.

"Thannik? Are you here?"

"This way," Thannik's disembodied voice responded.

Sylvania turned toward the fluttery voice and, as she faced the Thook's expressive burnt-orange eyes, he took on solid form in her mind.

"Sometimes, I wish I had your ability to make people forget me," she said wistfully.

"I can't imagine anyone could forget you, Sylvania," Thannik said graciously. "How long has it been?"

Sylvania balked at a painful memory. "Our last recording was dated just after Killian left. I was still pregnant with Poppy."

"Oh, how thoughtless of me to remind you," Thannik said. He cast his eyes downward and, in doing so, vanished from Sylvania's awareness. She turned around the room again as though she'd just arrived.

"Thannik? Are you here?"

"Over here," Thannik's voice fluttered.

Sylvania turned and Thannik appeared. "Sometimes, I wish I had your ability to make people forget me," she said again, thinking it was the first time.

"No one could forget you, Sylvania," Thannik repeated for her sake. "What can I do for you?"

"You can help me disappear."

Thannik stared at her, careful not to look away this time. "You're in danger?"

"The Alliance is in danger. But if I go away, the danger may be diminished, especially for my daughter."

"What danger?" the Thook pressed.

Sylvania shook her head. "I won't make you a target."

Thannik pondered her request. "You wouldn't be safe on Thook," he said. "All non-Thook stand out here."

"Take me to whatever world you believe would be safest," Sylvania said, "where I'd be hardest to find. Don't tell me what world or where it is. If anyone comes looking, then even if they could force you to tell them, they won't remember what you said as long as you make sure it's not recorded."

"Not to worry. I have experience with this." Thannik fluttered the Thook equivalent of a chuckle. *"Esh'tek ka Thook ya'ben."*

"What?"

"An old saying. All secrets flock to Thook."

*

Poppy and Willa, both having recently turned fourteen, sat on the grey stones of the castle ruins at the Rock of Cashel. Their hilltop perch afforded them a panoramic view of the surrounding Irish countryside, now etched with the black skeletons of bare trees that signaled the approach of winter. Though the overall temperature of the Earth was higher than in centuries past, it could still get chilly in the northern territories.

"Please help me find her," Poppy pleaded.

"You once told me this was a place where secrets were safe," Willa reminded Poppy. "Now you're asking me to betray your mother's secret."

"Emotional distance is one thing," Poppy countered. "But physical distance . . . to never see her again? She abandoned me!"

"She didn't abandon you, she's trying to keep you safe," Willa said.

"I'm not afraid of . . . what's that awful grey girl's name?"

"Xanthes. You should be afraid," Willa said. "If she has the Mark, the Anu gene like me, there's no telling what she's capable of."

"How can she have the Mark if she's from another planet?" Poppy sniffed.

"Holly says that long ago, the Anu probably traveled to many worlds besides Earth."

Poppy turned away, stared out over the grassy fields that were slowly fading from emerald green to muted celery. She shivered in the crisp afternoon air and wrapped her shawl tighter around her shoulders. "What does she want with my mother? Why does she want to kill me?"

"Psychological warfare, so Holly says," Willa stated, her mood darkening. "She hurts me by hurting my friends."

Willa gazed out at a mass of slate-colored clouds that swiftly approached from the horizon. Though there wouldn't be snow, winter storms could still deliver a chilling rain. "We should go."

Poppy didn't budge. "What if Mom's isolation is exactly what Xanthes wants? If she's alone, we can't protect her."

"True," Willa agreed, "but she'd need to find Sylvania first. It's a big galaxy."

Poppy turned her sad eyes to Willa. "If you can find Mom with your abilities, then Xanthes can too. We need to find her first."

The traumatic memory of her telepathic encounter with Xanthes pierced Willa's mind like a needle. She raised a hand to her head. Even the memory of the psychic attack was disturbing enough to make her dizzy.

"You okay?" Poppy said, concerned she'd pushed too hard.

Willa nodded as the dizziness passed. "It's been three months since she and I linked minds and I still . . ." She took a deep, cleansing breath of cool air to ground her senses. "If it hadn't been for Holly's help and Ashleen's Kenning, I might not have been able to break the bond. To be honest, I still feel a connection between us."

Poppy frowned. "What are you saying?"

"If I use my abilities to find your mother, Xanthes might sense her location through me."

Desperate as she was, Poppy realized Willa was right and gave a resigned nod.

"Come on," Willa said as she hopped down from the low wall. "Maybe we can think of another way to find her."

Poppy nodded more thoughtfully. "Like Sapphire Smith."

"Who?"

"A character in an old story."

"Those ancient detective novels you like?"

"Yeah. Smith always says no one can completely disappear. No matter how hard they try, they always leave a clue."

Poppy's words bounced around in Willa's mind. "Completely disappear…"

Willa jumped down from the wall. "I think I know where your mother went. Come on."

"Where are we going?"

"I don't need powers to do some old-fashioned detective work," Willa said.

Poppy slid off the stones and, as the first drops of rain fell, she followed Willa toward the Shaddok that would transport them back to Port Dublin in the blink of an eye.

*

The towering triskelion of the Mitsuyama starship factory rose into the crystal blue sky against the dramatic backdrop of the Italian Alps, one of the few remaining places on Earth that still wore a delicate cloak of white in winter.

The memory-metal and nano-glass torus of the factory's hub was nestled in the mountains above the picturesque village of Bellagio and commanded a stunning view of Lake Como.

Kale Ashgrove stood on the main factory floor and admired the sleek new star cruiser that would replace the ship he lost in the Maelstrom. The memory of being stranded in space for nearly a year with his brave and resourceful crew, and their subsequent torture and death at the hands of the Archon's cruel interrogators, still haunted him.

"She's a beauty, no?"

Kale was grateful for the interruption as he turned to face Figuero "Fig" Rigoletto, the chief designer of Mitsuyama's starships. Fig was a diminutive human with a ready smile, a shock of close-

7

cropped white hair, and a luxuriant moustache that lent him the appearance of a modern-day Geppetto. His brown eyes sparkled with humor and shone with unbridled passion for his work, which he considered more art than science.

"Stunning," Kale admitted. "Your finest work yet, Fig. I'm honored to receive such a masterpiece."

"A person who appreciates fine art will always be close to my heart," Fig said in a warm Mediterranean accent that made all who met him feel welcome.

He turned Kale's attention back to the gleaming starship. "She has the latest Q-jump engine and the most advanced AI interface, along with a few special features I designed just for you," Fig said with a wink.

"Thank you. It'll be good to feel the freedom of space again," Kale replied, somewhat wistfully.

Fig's eyes filled with empathy and his bushy moustache drooped as his smile faded. "I was very sad to hear about your crew. I'm sorry."

Kale nodded his thanks, too choked up to speak.

Fig gave him a pat on the arm and quickly changed the subject. "Is there anything else you'd like me to add?"

"At some point, it may be necessary to add weapons," Kale said, though he hated the very idea of doing so.

Fig nodded sadly. "I understand. The Council briefed me on the situation. I built interfaces into the hull for such devices." He pointed to two rings of covered ports near the front and rear of the ship. "Here and here." With a deep sigh, Fig returned to his jolly self. "What will you name her?"

Kale slid his gaze along the smooth hull. "I'm not sure. I'll discuss it with the computer."

Fig nodded his approval. "She's fully installed and active if you'd like to have a conversation."

"She?"

"You can let the computer decide that, if you wish," Fig said. "You know where to find me." Fig headed across the factory floor to attend to some alien customers, his smile warm as fresh-baked cookies. "And how may I help you fine folks today?"

Kale brushed away any lingering hesitation and walked up the ramp to the ship's open airlock. He entered the main cabin and was immediately taken with Fig's simple, yet stunning design of the nano-glass monitors, sleek control panels, and integrated pilot's seat. Everything was done in shades of cool crystalline blues and whites with a few critical-system features that stood out in bold red accents. The deck was composed of neutral-gray hexagonal artificial gravity plates. Readouts scrolled across the monitors in electric blue letters and symbols. Small, clear sensor blisters were placed in the ceiling and walls to allow the ship's computer to see, hear, and gather information on the starship's internal condition, as well as allow it to form a neural interface with the pilot.

Kale sank into the comfortable folds of the pilot's seat. It immediately conformed to the biometrics of his body.

"Nice to meet you," the computer said in an androgynous voice.

"And you. My name's Kale Ashgrove."

"My construction designation is AI-X-1300, but you may assign a name to me if you wish."

Kale took a few minutes to think it through. "How do you feel about Elowen?" he said, his voice low and thick with emotion.

"Judging by the stress markers in your voice, this is the name of someone you know . . . or knew?"

Kale wondered if choosing that name would be wise. "She . . . she was the pilot on my previous ship. She died."

"I'm sorry," the computer said with all the sympathy its emotion simulation routine could muster. "If you wish to honor her memory, I'd be happy to carry her name."

"Yes. I'd like that," Kale said. "Thank you."

"Thank you, Elowen," the computer prompted.

Despite his grief, Kale managed a soft smile. "Thank you, Elowen. Should we proceed with the neural interface?"

"I never interface on the first date," the computer jokingly replied in Elowen's voice.

Kale was taken aback. "You sound just like her."

"I accessed her records, her personality profile, and daily logs. If you'd prefer I use a different personality . . ."

"No . . . no, that's okay," Kale said.

"I'm ready to interface when you are, Kale. May I call you Kale?"

"Yes. Please. I'm ready."

A scanning light snapped on above the main console. A beam shot out and reflected in Kale's eyes. After a moment, the light switched off. "Interface complete," Elowen said. "Was it good for you?"

Kale laughed. "You definitely have her sense of humor. Promise me something."

"As long as it doesn't conflict with my ethics subroutine."

"If any Orions come aboard, you'll call me Captain Ashgrove. Kale's a slang word in their culture that means --"

"Fig uploaded your full report. Your dignity is safe with me," Elowen promised. "You watch my back and I'll watch yours."

Fig poked his head into the cabin from the airlock.

"How are you two getting along?"

Kale smiled. "Looks like the beginning of a beautiful friendship."

"I love that movie!" Elowen squeaked like a giddy schoolgirl.

Kale frowned. "You just came online. When did you have a chance to access the classic film archives?"

"Just now, when you referred to the film," Elowen beamed.

"Just now?"

"Yes. I watched it twice. Took me a whole three-hundredths of a second."

Kale's broad smile told Fig that the pairing was a perfect match.

*

Xanthes sat cross-legged on the floor of her dark-stone meditation chamber, eyes closed, in the center of a circle inlaid with burnished copper symbols.

Uzza, her aged Sensate mentor, stood to one side, a walking stick in one gnarled hand, his shrouded gaze fixed on his seventeen-year-old apprentice.

Under his dedicated guidance, along with the aid of a powerful potion, Xanthes stretched her arcane senses beyond the Maelstrom's borders as she searched for clues to the whereabouts of her father's spies on Earth.

The Archon had received no intelligence reports from them and grew increasingly impatient to launch his conquest of the rich worlds within the Interstellar Alliance.

Though she'd never say so out loud, Xanthes had thought it extremely foolish for her father's interrogators to kill Captain Ashgrove's entire crew in their search for information, especially in light of Ashgrove's rescue by the Resistance, despite the efforts of the guards to recapture their prized prisoner.

The hapless guards on duty that day had all been summarily slaughtered, their bodies dumped in the rendering vats, and processed into the nutrient slurry used to feed the Archon's genetically-engineered army of Splicers.

The events that claimed the lives of Koro and Haldane, as well as Gant's infiltration of the Black League, began to unfold in Xanthes's mind. Very soon, she knew her powers would be strong enough to uncover the League's secret base, but that would not be today. Her pale eyes flickered open as she emerged from her trance.

Uzza cocked his craggy face in her direction. "You were successful?"

"Yes," Xanthes said as she rose to her feet. "The potion worked well. Once Elowen, our little puppet, arrives on Earth, I will be able to see and hear through her eyes and ears."

"Your powers have grown considerably over the past few cycles," Uzza remarked with a hint of pride.

"Had they not, you wouldn't be alive to gloat about the effectiveness of your training," Xanthes reminded him.

"I live to serve," Uzza said with a slight bow.

Xanthes gave the expected reply as she made for the door. "And you serve to live."

Once he was sure his pupil was gone, Uzza tapped the nine inlaid copper symbols in a specific order with his walking stick. The holographic image of Zaduga, the elder leader of the Sensate Order, appeared in the air over the center of the circle.

The Elder's grey face was darker than Uzza's and lined like old leather. An unholy fire burned in his pale eyes that warned of the immense power contained in his deceptively frail frame. Zaduga's stiff, high-necked black tunic held him ramrod straight like an iron statue. His greeting issued from the lipless slit of his downturned mouth.

"Never-ending are the Nine."

"Never-ending," Uzza said, completing the ritual exchange.

"What do you have to report?"

"My apprentice's powers will soon surpass our own, Zaduga. She suspects nothing of the minute adjustments I make to the potion that will bind her to the Order," the Sensate informed his superior.

"Well done," Zaduga said, his greedy eyes aglow. "We've waited for generations for the ancient gene to appear in one of Overlords. You'll be well rewarded once the Archon and his minions become our willing servants."

"I live to serve," Uzza said with his usual bow.

"No," Zaduga corrected him. "We live to rule."

"Never-ending are the Nine," Uzza offered in agreement.

"Never-ending," Zaduga confirmed.

Uzza tapped the hologram off as his mouth cracked into a satisfied smile.

The next day, after the storm, the air was cool and fresh. Willa sat on a flat boulder on the bank of a gurgling river deep within the grove a few miles from her home. A tall, majestic Yew tree at her back dappled her ruddy locks with shade while the late-afternoon sun warmed her shoulders. She opened her Cryptic senses to the forest. A light breeze rustled the leaves and filled her nostrils with the rich musk of the damp earth and green moss that carpeted the riverbank.

She closed her eyes and allowed a vision to coalesce in her mind. She saw the complex system of entangled tree roots and fungal filaments deep underground that formed the mycelial network between the trees.

The longer she focused, the clearer the vision became, until she could even perceive the flow of water, nutrients, and electrical impulses that passed from tree to tree as they fed and communicated with each other.

Willa began to feel connected to the forest network, as if she'd grown roots that spread out in all directions from where she sat. As her thoughts adjusted to the languid time scale of the trees, she could hear their veiled whispers, and her mind filled with the stories they shared of the myriad happenings in and around the forest.

She was privy to the comings and goings of every bird, animal, and insect that made their homes among the branches and ferns. She could follow the trail of the underground network for many miles to the great oak tree that supported the gleaming sphere of her nano-glass home in its thick, twisting branches.

She sensed her mother inside their cozy Nest as she tended to her beloved hydroponic garden and even inhaled the herbs' fragrant responses to Lily's tender ministrations.

An image of the shape-shifting Pooka, Rusalka, in his typical configuration as a large, red-eyed hare, pushed into Willa's awareness and she realized the trees were whispering of the Elemental's approach.

"Good afternoon, Rusalka," Willa said without opening her eyes.

The Pooka frowned as he emerged from the woods and made himself at home on a moss-encrusted log. "There'll be no sneaking up on you from now on, I suppose," the Pooka grumped.

"It's your own fault for secretly forcing a Kenning on me," she teased. The truth was, she was grateful for the Pooka's subterfuge. If it hadn't been for the Kenning that amplified Willa's burgeoning abilities, she would have succumbed to Xanthes's telepathic attack at the Quorum Lodge.

She opened her eyes. "It's been months. Where have you been?"

"Busy," Rusalka said curtly. "You caused quite a stir among the Elementals, you know, what with your reversal of time and the Orion spies and everything."

"I'm curious," Willa continued, "exactly what did the Kenning do to me?"

"It was Queen Ashleen that did it," the Pooka protested.

"I'm not blaming you. I just need to understand it."

"Of course, of course," Rusalka said, smoothing his ruffled fur. He turned his ruby eyes to her. "Do you ken what we are . . . the true nature of Elementals?"

"Nature spirits," Willa stated as if it was obvious.

"That's a child's answer," the Pooka scolded.

"Okay, you're mean nature spirits," she teased.

"It's important that you understand," Rusalka said. "Your life might depend on it. All our lives might."

"Sorry. You were saying?"

"We're not spirits in the classic sense. We're more like . . ." The Pooka searched for the proper metaphor. "The clay of consciousness."

"That's very poetic," Willa said, "but not very helpful."

Rusalka's furry face scrunched in concentration. "Think of the moisture in the air. When it gets cold, the moisture condenses and forms pools of water. Colder still and the water becomes ice."

"I follow you so far," Willa said, not following him at all.

"All things have an energy field, what humans used to call an aura. You, me, the trees, even the rocks; in fact, the whole Earth has such a field."

"Go on," Willa encouraged.

"That field is like the moisture in the air, but it has an intelligence. Under the right conditions, it can condense, if you will, and patterns form within it. The patterns can further crystallize into various shapes, some very fluid and some more solid."

"You're saying that Elementals are like frozen expressions of Earth's intelligence, sculptures formed from the clay of the collective consciousness, so to speak," Willa said, struggling to wrap her mind around the concept.

"Yes! Exactly!" the Pooka said, excited that he was getting through to her. "But because we're all just patterns in that field, we're more fluid than you. We can soften our shape, change our patterns, express ourselves in different ways. We're not stuck in one form, like you."

"What's this got to do with the Kenning?"

"The Kenning links you to the field in the same way Elementals are linked. It's what you witnessed in the Enclave. We're connected to one another and now you're connected to us. You can draw power from the entire collective when you need to, from the energy of the Earth itself," the Pooka exclaimed, his eyes bright.

"So, I'll be able to shapeshift like you, disappear and appear like you, know the things you know," Willa whispered in awe, her imagination opening to the possibilities.

"Well, you still have to learn to call upon it at will and control it. That's where your Mastery training comes in. Otherwise, that much power could overload you, burn out your nervous system and fry your cells."

"Oh. Great. Thanks for the warning."

"Don't worry, you can do it," Rusalka said. "I have confidence in you."

"I may have to borrow some of yours," Willa said, surprised by the Pooka's faith in her abilities.

The background whispers of the trees grew louder in Willa's mind and pulled her attention to one side.

The mysterious red fox that seemed to be spying on Willa had returned. It sat on a boulder far upstream from them, its russet fur catching the last rays of the setting sun. The fox's caramel-colored eyes were locked on Willa and the Pooka.

"Do you see that fox?" Willa whispered. "It keeps showing up at odd moments but always runs away when I try to follow."

"I think you know it's not just an ordinary fox," Rusalka said, his red eyes returning the fox's steady gaze. "I sense that's a Shapeshifter… and something more that I can't fathom."

"Can you tell who it is?"

"No. Whoever it is can hide their true identity from me. Not an easy thing to do," the Pooka said, unsettled by the Shapeshifter's power. "But I don't sense that it means us any harm."

As if to demonstrate the Pooka's assurance, the fox trotted off into the woods.

Willa and Rusalka sat in silence, thinking the fox might return, but their only company was the rushing river and the rustling leaves of the surrounding trees. Willa turned her attention to the golden sunset.

"I should get home."

Rusalka hopped off his log as Willa rose from her rock.

"Thank you," she said with genuine appreciation.

Rusalka gave her a respectful nod and scampered into the woods.

Willa ran her hands over the trunks of the Yew trees as she passed by them and felt a deeper connection to the forest than she ever had before.

"Where do you think you're going, girl?"

The hollow voice froze the blood in Willa's veins. It was a voice that she knew all too well. She turned and stood in the ghostly glow of Belladonna the Banshee.

"Belladonna," Willa said with a smile, trying her best to act like this was a pleasant surprise. "I haven't forgotten my promise to you."

"It's been months!" the Banshee howled as her eyes flashed fire.

"I know, but I'm only just learning to control my powers. I still don't even know why you're affected by me. Maybe it's the Anu gene, maybe it's something else altogether."

Belladonna floated in the air, mulling over Willa's words.

"Well, in the meantime, the least you could do is let me feel the earth beneath my feet," the Banshee opined.

Willa didn't enjoy the sensation of the Banshee's ethereal form passing through her body, but she steeled herself and nodded her consent. Belladonna floated toward and through her and, upon emerging, began to solidify. The old Sage touched gently down upon the ground and sunk her feet in the loamy soil with a deep sigh of pleasure.

"No matter how many times I remember the feel of the world, the memories pale in comparison with the physical sensations." She turned her sad eyes to Willa. "Thank you."

"I only wish I knew how to make it permanent," Willa said.

"It's enough that I know you'll try," Belladonna said, her mood lightening. "I'm sorry I get impatient with you. Three hundred years is a long time to be trapped between life and death." Belladonna's smile faded, her eyes darkened. "Perhaps…"

Willa felt a great wave of fear as her heightened senses tapped into Belladonna's unspoken thought.

"No. Don't ask me to do that. I couldn't."

"If I die while I'm physical, like any mortal, I'll be free to enter the spirit realm. I won't be trapped as a Banshee any longer."

"No," Willa protested, feeling sicker by the moment.

"I'm not asking you to kill me," Belladonna said, "only to bring me the means to do it myself. It would be a mercy!"

"No! I'll find a way to make you whole, permanently. You'll live a long life and die naturally, when it's your time."

"Willa, don't you see? It's way past my time." As she spoke, Belladonna's body began to float upward and transformed back into the incorporeal Banshee.

"I'll find a way! I promise! I won't give up if you won't," Willa said.

Belladonna's features softened as she felt Willa's conviction. She nodded and vanished.

Willa let out a sigh, hoping with all her heart that it was a promise she could keep.

*

Willa reached the edge of the Yew grove and was about to cross the field toward home when a small Luminaria globe floated through the air and hovered a foot in front of her. Holly's face appeared in the sphere.

"Hello, Willa," Holly said.

Holly rarely used this method of contact and it gave Willa pause. "Is everything okay?"

"Not to worry," Holly assured her. "I just need your attendance."

"Where are you?"

"The Luminaria will lead you," Holly said with a smile, then disappeared from the globe. The crystalline sphere glowed like a tiny moon and Willa followed the beacon as it floated back into the forest.

As Willa made her way through the trees, her Cryptic senses were flooded with joy from each and every Yew, Oak, and Ash that she passed. An air of celebration resonated among the trees, and Willa's heart swelled with appreciation for the connection she shared with the majestic flora that surrounded her. She wiped tears of gratitude from her eyes as she followed the Luminaria into a large, circular clearing.

The globe dimmed and floated over to Holly. It alighted in her outstretched hand and shrunk to a small bead, which Holly tucked into a pocket in her snow-white tunic. Willa was surprised to see her parents, Lily and River, as well as Poppy, all standing next to Holly with proud smiles. Rose and Lilac Larkspur, the twin Cryptics from the Quorum, were also in attendance. They beheld Willa with their enigmatic, lavender eyes. Reserved smiles graced their smooth, porcelain features.

"What's happening?" Willa wondered aloud.

"Welcome to your Ascension Ceremony," Holly said.

"My what?"

"Your graduation, silly," Poppy said unceremoniously.

Holly strode over to Willa and placed a hand on her apprentice's shoulder. "You've completed your training with honor. The Ascension Ceremony confirms you as a full-fledged Cryptic. Each level of Mastery that you complete will mark the occasion with a similar ceremony."

Willa was nearly overwhelmed by the pride that radiated from Holly. She looked over at her mother and father and sensed the same pride emanating from their tear-filled eyes. She caught a smile and a wink from Poppy and a slight bow of respect from the Larkspur twins. She turned her attention back to Holly.

"What do I do?"

Holly knelt on one knee; a glance at Willa invited her to do the same. Holly placed one palm on the ground. Willa mirrored the move.

"Project your mind deep underground. Call to the fungal network that connects all the roots of the trees into a single entity. Open your heart and allow the forest to feel your joy."

Willa closed her eyes. Her breath fell into a steady rhythm as she slipped into a Cryptic trance. Holly closed her eyes as well as the Larkspur twins. They joined Willa in her communion with nature.

The gathering was wrapped in sacred silence for several heartbeats. Slowly, the earth began to push upward around the edge of the clearing as a circle of large, reddish-tan Scotch Bonnet mushrooms grew before everyone's eyes and formed a magical Faery Ring. Tiny Elemental Faeries, known as the Tylwyth Teg, appeared on top of the bell-shaped mushroom caps. They twirled and danced in the air on gossamer wings, then vanished like soap bubbles.

Holly and Willa stood and admired the Faery Ring. Holly removed a small, wooden ring from another pocket. It was inlaid with a deep green Malachite stone in the shape of a triangle. Holly took Willa's left hand in hers and slipped the ring on her student's little finger.

"The wood is from the branch of a fallen Yew tree that has given itself back to the Earth. The Malachite stone mirrors the green of the forest. The triangle is the symbol of the Cryptic and connects land, sea, and air and all the things of nature. You are now one of us, Willa Hillicrissing, and you've earned the right to be known throughout the land as an honored member of the Northern Quorum Lodge."

Although Willa had never seen Holly wear a ring before, it was on her finger now and identical to the one she had bestowed upon her apprentice.

Holly caught the look. "Those who walk the path of Mastery don't always wear their badges of honor, except during Ascension Ceremonies. However, I feel it would be appropriate for you to wear it whenever you wish, as a reminder of the Mark within you."

Willa stared at the ring and nodded, tears in her eyes.

Holly nodded to the rest of the gathering. Lily, River, and Poppy all joined Willa and wrapped her in heartfelt hugs. Rose and Lilac remained at a respectful distance, but their smiles were as wide as Holly's.

Chapter Two:
DARKNESS

"The beginning of wisdom is to know you know nothing. To know nothing is to know the unknowable. To know the unknowable is to explore the Great Mystery. To explore the Great Mystery is to discover what is worth knowing. All things worth knowing are hidden in Mystery. All secrets are shrouded in darkness. But I do not live in the darkness, the darkness, and the secrets, live within me."

Nocturnal Mantra
by Nightshade the Nocturnal

*

THE ISLE OF MAN, a mere thirty-two miles long and fourteen miles wide, rested in the Irish Sea between Northern Ireland and Britain.

The lush, green countryside spread out from Snaefell, the island's single mountain, that topped out just above two thousand feet.

The fields around the roofless ruins of Peel Castle were dotted with four-horned Loaghtan sheep that lazily grazed on the tall grass while a large, bob-tailed Manx cat with orange, black, and white fur lounged within the sandstone remnants of the castle's cathedral.

Holly stood within the ruined cathedral's chancel and gazed out through the tall, narrow window arches at the pink-tinted clouds that floated above the setting sun.

The cool timbre of Selene's voice cut through Holly's serenity. "Why in Nightshade's name did you ask to meet in this forlorn place?"

Holly turned to meet Selene's pitch-black gaze. "Two reasons. One is nostalgic and the other, symbolic."

Selene raised an impatient eyebrow.

"Our apprenticeship began here," Holly continued, mildly annoyed that she had to remind Selene of such an obvious fact.

"I'm well aware of that," snapped the Nocturnal, "just as you know that I prefer not to dwell on the past."

Holly sighed. "The symbolic reason for meeting here is . . ." Her brief hesitation betrayed Holly's misgivings, but she forced herself to continue. "I'm asking you to continue Willa's training."

For once, Selene was speechless. Holly took a moment to enjoy the Nocturnal's stunned expression.

"Me?" Selene blurted with uncharacteristic surprise.

"I'll still be involved," the Cryptic assured her, "but I can't take her to the next level."

"You'd have the necessary skills if you hadn't abandoned your training," Selene admonished.

"I abandoned nothing," Holly replied firmly. "I simply prefer to remain a Cryptic. Willa needs to go further if there's any chance she can help repel the coming invasion."

"Of course," Selene said, "but surely the combined powers of all on the path of Mastery, along with Willa's gifts, can stave off the attack."

"I'm not so sure. The grey girl's abilities are formidable. She grows stronger with time and if there are more like her . . ."

Selene gazed out through the archway at the darkening sky. Her Nocturnal vision allowed her to perceive patterns of energy in the sky and even in the castle stones. This was the tenuous veil that separated one parallel reality from another and allowed Nocturnals to siphon information from those alternate timelines.

However, try as she might, Selene wasn't able to parse her Great Grandmother Belladonna's formula for becoming a Wraith, no matter how many parallel versions of Earth she scanned. Selene contemplated Holly's dire warning and turned back to her silver-haired colleague.

"I'll sponsor Willa, guide her in becoming a Nocturnal, but only on my terms."

Holly stepped closer to Selene and lowered her voice, although there was no one within earshot aside from the Manx cat. "I know there's something you want from Willa," Holly said. "I don't know what it is and Willa won't tell me. I'll respect your privacy, Selene, but I want to be very clear. If you put your agenda ahead of Willa's wellbeing or put her in danger, I'll petition the Quorum for your immediate expulsion."

"I'm not the heartless monster you think I am, Holly."

"Maybe not, but your ambition has a monstrous appetite and I'm afraid it might swallow you, and Willa, whole."

"Thank you for your concern," Selene said without a hint of warmth. "Have Willa meet me at Mystery's north gate after morning meal."

Selene turned and left through the crumbling arch at the far end of the cathedral.

The Manx cat rose, stretched, strolled over to Holly and transformed back into Variabilis. "Are you sure this is wise?" the dour Shapeshifter said, his obsidian eyes locked on Selene's receding silhouette.

"Not in the least," Holly admitted. "But if Willa can handle Selene, she might fare better against Xanthes."

"Not a very kind comparison," Variabilis said with a dry smile.

Though her face betrayed no emotion, Holly's heart sank at the knowledge of what her young apprentice was about to endure under the Nocturnal Order's intense regimen.

"Kindness," said Holly, "could get Willa killed."

Willa and Poppy sat in a booth near the crackling hearth in the Stargazer Inn. The setting sun threw long shadows across Marrowbone Bridge outside the bay window. Water dripped from the eaves: the echo of an earlier storm. They drank cups of spiced cider and passed the time counting how many doppelgangers that Stargazer, the inn's shapeshifting owner, had split herself into in order to serve the throng of thirsty customers. There were fifteen duplicates at last count.

"Are you sure he got the message?" Poppy asked anxiously.

"He'll be here," Willa assured her, "I'm sure his training just went long."

No sooner had Willa spoken than Rowan Ashgrove's strapping silhouette filled the doorway. He spotted them and made his way over to their table. Rowan had always been handsome, but now that he'd turned eighteen, he'd taken on a mature air that attracted more than a few glances from the town's females and quite a few males as well. As he sat, Willa's Cryptic ring caught Rowan's eye.

"Congratulations."

Willa blushed and smiled. "Thanks."

Rowan's allure wasn't lost on either girl, but a nudge from Poppy brought Willa's attention back to the matter of Poppy's missing mother.

However, before either girl could speak, one of Stargazer's doppelgangers sidled up to Rowan, her voice a silken purr. "Hey, Row, haven't seen you 'round here lately."

"Hi, Star. Training… you know," Rowan said.

Star playfully bumped his shoulder with her hip. "If you're going to be a First Contact Specialist, you should have more contact with the folks here first before you go galavantin' off to other planets. What can I get you?"

"Cider, please," Rowan said, trying not to blush.

"You got it. Need a refill, girls?"

Willa and Poppy shook their heads, hoping Star would hurry away. Star favored Rowan with a flirtatious smile as she went to fill his order.

Poppy whispered to Willa, "I thought she had a thing for that Sage."

Willa pointed to another of Star's dopplegangers serving a group at another table. "That's the one with eyes for Alder."

Poppy squinted at the double. "How can you tell?"

"Women's intuition," Willa said with a smug smile.

Poppy scowled. "Guess you found a good use for that Mark of yours," she teased.

Rowan cleared his throat to get their attention. "So, why am I here?"

A look from Poppy told Willa to start the conversation. "We need your help but it has to be a secret."

"You can't tell anyone!" Poppy added a little too loudly.

Willa frowned at her. "Yeah, that's what 'secret' means. Keep your voice down."

"Sorry."

Rowan regarded the nervous girls. "Why do I get the feeling you're going to get me into trouble?"

"It's about my mother," Poppy whispered.

"We think we know where she went," Willa added. "We need you to find her, convince her that she's safer on Earth than running away to another world. We can defend her here."

"I don't know. If you can't find her with your abilities, what makes you think anyone else could?"

"That's the problem," Willa said. "If I use my abilities, Xanthes will sense Sylvania's location through her connection to me. We need to do this the old-fashioned way."

"You want me to track her down?"

Star chose that moment to deliver Rowan's cider. "Such sad faces. I know what'll cheer you all up — three fat slices of Aurellian butter cake!"

25

Willa perked up. "Aurellian butter cake?"

Poppy elbowed Willa in the ribs. "Focus."

"We'll share one slice," Rowan said.

"Ever the diplomat," Star said and went to fetch the delicacy.

Poppy turned back to Rowan. "You took a ship from Andromeda Spaceport and went to rescue your father without permission. You're… what's the word?"

"An idiot?" Rowan offered.

"Resourceful," Willa said. "Stealthy."

"You remember how well that worked out, right? Thorn and I were lucky to make it back alive. Dennik was the one who rescued my father. Why don't you ask him?"

"He's in the Sirius system to testify in Gant's trial," Willa reminded him.

"Oh, right. Look, there must be someone who'd make a better detective than I would," Rowan said.

Willa placed her hand on his arm. "We want to keep this in the family. We know you. We trust you."

"Please," said Poppy with the biggest puppy-dog eyes she could muster.

Rowan mulled it over. "Okay, I'll look into it. No promises, though. If your mother doesn't want to be found, I might as well try to catch my own shadow. Where do I start?"

Willa lowered her voice. "Thook."

Rowan's expressive eyes shifted back and forth between Willa and Poppy, searching for any sign this was a joke. "You're serious. If the Thook are willing to help Sylvania disappear, she's as good as gone."

Star deposited the butter cake on the table, glanced at everyone's glum expressions. They all averted her eyes. "Goodness, the tension's thicker than Morovian pudding. What's got you all so flustered?"

Poppy's jaw clenched. "It's private."

"Anythin' I can do to help?" Star said.

"It's not something you can solve with butter cake," Poppy said.

"Wait a minute," Willa said as an idea took shape in her eyes. "How many dopplegangers can you split into?"

"Gotten as high as fifty," Star said with pride.

Rowan frowned. "What's that got to do with --"

"Fifty detectives are better than one," Willa said. "Especially if they're all the same person."

Star raised a curious eyebrow. "What are you talkin' about?"

"Your splitting skill is rare but, as a Shapeshifter, you can take on the characteristics of those you mirror, correct?"

"Of course. Wouldn't be much of a Shapeshifter if I couldn't," Star assured her.

Willa smiled, pleased with the plan blossoming in her mischievous mind. "Ever been to Thook?"

"Would I remember if I had?"

"My point exactly," Willa exclaimed to Star's puzzled expression.

"Do your parents know about this plan of yours?" Rowan asked.

Willa frowned at him. "What part of 'secret' don't you understand?"

*

Xanthes cast her dark eyes on the gleaming hull of the newly-built escape pod within her secret, underground factory. Sanja Vet, a violet-skinned alien from the planet Tet, and Xanthes' personal lead Tech, flicked her bright red eyes to and fro as she pointed out the pod's features.

"We have finally integrated enough of the Earther's technology into this pod to ensure it will cross the Maelstrom without adverse effect, my Lady."

"About time," Xanthes huffed, "it's taken you nearly a year!"

"Many apologies, my Lady. Bridging the differences between our tech and theirs was most challenging."

"You're sure this will do the job?"

"Beyond a doubt, my Lady. Your... 'passenger' will survive the journey intact. I guarantee it."

"With your life?"

"Of course, my Lady. I live to serve," Sanja said with a deep bow.

Xanthes returned the traditional response. "And you serve to live. You're sure my father knows nothing of this craft?"

"No one but us, my Lady. I have seen to the silence of the tech team."

"Very well. Replace them as soon as possible. There must be no leaks. And bring me the passenger."

"Yes, my Lady," Sanja said as she bowed out of the chamber.

Xanthes scrutinized the pod, proud of what she was able to accomplish. The tough outer shell was an alloy of titanium-boron-aluminum in a graphene and nano-glass matrix. The small, but powerful hyper-light engine had minimal Q-jump abilities, but it only required a short burst to punch through the electromagnetic Maelstrom that shredded ordinary starships. Xanthes nodded her approval. This tough little pod and its occupant would be the opening gambit in her plan to dominate Earth and the other worlds of the Interstellar Alliance and rule in the Archon's stead.

Sanja returned with Elowen Koa in tow. Kale Ashgrove's former pilot, at first a prisoner and now a willing, programmed puppet under Xanthes' control, stood at attention, her one good eye focused on her master.

Xanthes waved a hand, dismissing Sanja, and after a series of bows, the small alien was gone.

"What do you think of your new command, Captain Koa?"

A semblance of life crept into Elowen's eye. "It should do the job," she admitted, her voice flat.

"You're clear on your story?" Xanthes said.

"I was tortured for months until I managed to seduce a sympathetic guard who found me attractive. It's not something I'm proud of but I did what I had to do to survive. The guard, Captain Vontash, gave me a paralytic drug that made me appear dead. He hid me in a processing factory until he could secure an experimental escape pod and, after disabling one of the Archon's tracking satellites, he set me on a course for the Maelstrom. However, Vontash's plan was discovered and, just before the pod launched, I watched him die holding the other guards at bay until I could escape. I made it through the Maelstrom and activated the pod's distress beacon."

"And your mission?"

"To reunite with my former Captain, Kale Ashgrove, to rejoin Earth's society, to regain my former security clearance, and to return to Xos with detailed intel on Interstellar Alliance weapons, defensive systems, access codes, advanced materials, and tech schematics, as well as search for any weaknesses that would leave them open to invasion."

"Excellent," Xanthes said. "You're ready to return to Earth."

"No," Elowen said.

"No?" Xanthes was taken aback by the refusal.

"I have no recent signs of abuse."

Xanthes was impressed. "Good point." Xanthes delivered a blinding right cross to Elowen's jaw and another to her eye socket. She grabbed Elowen's left hand, slapped her hand palm down on a nearby steel table, picked up a metal globe of Xos and brought it down hard, breaking two of Elowen's fingers. Through it all, Elowen barely flinched. She rose to her full height and calmly looked at her bloody, battered face in the escape pod's reflective hull.

"Now I'm ready," Elowen said.

*

Selene led Willa through the narrow streets of Mystery, a small village nestled near the Dark Hedges, a tunnel of tall Beech trees that arched over a well-worn forest path. The byways and squat buildings of Mystery, erected three hundred years ago, were built entirely of black marble.

The fine hairs on Willa's neck stood at attention as she followed her new sponsor past the crypt-like dwellings. If it wasn't for fleeting glimpses of a few Nocturnal denizens silhouetted behind thin, fire-lit obsidian windows, Willa would have sworn the town was a necropolis, inhabited only by corpses and the spirits of the dead.

Selene glanced back at her charge, impatient. "Keep up."

Willa quickened her pace as they approached a black, stepped pyramid that rose a hundred feet above the city at its Stygian heart. They entered a long, square tunnel cut into the pyramid's base. Once inside, Willa found herself bathed in the blue-green glow that emanated from large cabochons of Ye Ming Zhu stones set into the dark, marble walls.

"What is this place?"

Selene's response was hushed, almost reverent. "The Fulcrum. The lodge of the Nocturnals."

"I thought the Quorum Lodge --"

"A Cryptic's place is in nature. When necessary, we all use the Quorum Lodge for certain meetings or rituals. However, Nocturnals, Shapeshifters, and Sages have their own lodges. I believe Wraiths do as well." Selene took note of the Cryptic ring on Willa's finger. "Don't think it will be as easy to earn a Nocturnal ring as it was to get that one."

Willa narrowed her eyes at Selene. She would normally return the insult, but thought better of it as they moved deeper within the eerie pyramid.

They passed rows of hallways with square silver doors set a foot deep into the tunnel walls. Each door was engraved with an intricate "Flower-of-Life" symbol that gleamed in the cool, azure light.

Selene answered Willa's unspoken question. "Quarters and meditation chambers."

Willa wasn't thrilled at the thought of being entombed within a claustrophobic stone alcove like some Medieval monk. "This is where my training will happen?"

"Here and other places within Mystery. First, however, each new student must be brought before the head of the order to formally receive permission to enter the Second Level of Mastery. If she has the slightest doubt about your level of commitment..." Selene let the thought trail off, her meaning already clear.

They entered a large, vaulted chamber, its four walls angled inward, mirroring the pyramid's stepped exterior. Large, polished spheres of Ye Ming Zhu sat on black marble pedestals in each corner, flooding the chamber with aquamarine light.

Hundreds of clear nano-glass marbles rested in dimples on the stone shelves that circumnavigated the room, interrupted only by the four tunnel entrances that allowed access to the inner sanctum.

Selene stopped before a square dais in the chamber's center. A simple cube of black marble served as the only seat. It was occupied by Sequoia, a hauntingly beautiful woman in snow-white garments: a shocking contrast to the room, her cinnamon skin, and her all-black hair and eyes. She sat so still, Willa wondered if she was looking at a statue instead of a living being. The illusion was quickly dispelled by the silvery voice that issued from the statue's generous lips.

"Despite the look on your face, dear girl, I am quite real."

"Are you a Wraith?" Willa asked.

Sequoia laughed. "I'm as solid as you are." Her obsidian eyes flickered to Selene for a heartbeat. "Though there are those among our kind who are a bit too eager to claim the silver mantle of spirit."

Selene ignored the comment and gestured to Willa, whose golden eyes remained riveted on the radiant woman.

"May I present Willa Hillicrissing. Willa, this is Sequoia August Moon, the Provost of our order."

Willa just stared at the Provost until Selene gave her a sharp nudge with her elbow. "What did I teach you?"

31

Willa collected her wits and gave Sequoia a respectful bow of her head. She uttered the traditional greeting. "May your light reveal my shadow."

"And in the shadow, may you find your light," Sequoia said. She stepped down from the dais with supernatural grace and stopped less than a foot in front of Willa. Her inky gaze reflected pinpoints of azure light from the room's glowing stones. Willa silently hoped Sequoia would mistake her immobility for courage instead of the cold fear that froze her feet to the floor.

"So," Sequoia whispered, "I'm told you possess the Mark."

Willa desperately wanted to be anywhere else other than locked in Sequoia's sepulchral chamber but she dared not move a muscle.

"Speak up, girl!" Selene chided.

"That's what everyone seems to think," Willa finally managed through dry lips.

"And what do you think?" Sequoia said, genuinely curious.

"I think people expect too much of me."

Sequoia held Willa's gaze for a few heartbeats before allowing a faint smile of approval. "We shall see." She turned to Selene. "Show her to her chamber. Let her rest. Her training begins at moonrise."

"As you wish, Provost." Selene bowed her head, eyeballed Willa until she did the same, then led her nervous student from the chamber. Willa chanced a brief glance back at Sequoia. The Provost had turned away, her attention already focused on other matters.

A moment after Willa left the room, Sequoia gestured toward the far tunnel. Opal Deserette, a Nocturnal only three years older than Willa, emerged from the shadows. "What did you sense from her?" Sequoia asked her young apprentice.

Opal took a moment to gather her thoughts. "She's... definitely different," she said with caution.

Sequoia smiled. "You can do better than that."

Opal exhaled and focused. "I sense she's been through a Kenning."

"Very good. If she truly has the Mark and her abilities have been accelerated by a Kenning, what does that make Willa?"

"Unpredictable," Opal responded.

"Yes," Sequoia agreed. "It also means she has the potential to become the most powerful Nocturnal in the world, or…"

Opal waited until she was about to burst. "Or?"

"Or the most dangerous one. Which is why I'm assigning you to keep an eye on her through her training."

"Me?" Opal sputtered. "I'm just an apprentice."

"Willa won't need your skills," Sequoia said. "She'll need a friend."

*

Willa surveyed her private chamber. The walls, floor and ceiling were fashioned from the same grey-veined black marble as every other building in Mystery. Illumination was provided by a single greenish-blue stone set into the ceiling. On one side of the room, a cushioned pad covered a long marble slab, forming a simple bed. An alcove was cut into the opposite wall and was fitted with a desk, a chair and a shelf that held a single nano-glass bead.

"Homey," Willa muttered. She crossed to the desk and tapped the nano-bead. It expanded into a floating flat screen that displayed a detailed map of Mystery. A tiny blue dot glowed in one section of the central pyramid, which Willa assumed was her chamber's location.

A soft chime drew her attention to the door. Willa tapped the screen back to a bead. She searched for a control to open the door but the walls were blank.

Opal's voice filtered through the door from the hallway. "Just place your palm anywhere on the door."

Willa complied and the door slid smoothly into the wall. Willa regarded the young Nocturnal, who offered a disarming smile.

"Hello. I'm Opal. Opal Deserette."

"Willa Hillicrissing."

"Am I interrupting?"

Willa gestured to her Spartan quarters. "As you can see, I'm quite busy."

"Oh. I can come back later."

Willa threw Opal a look. "I'm kidding. Please come in."

Opal entered and the door slid shut. "Sorry, it's hard to tell since most of our day is spent in meditation."

"Sounds fascinating," Willa said, trying to be polite.

"Oh, it is!" Opal chirped. "Tapping into one's parables is incredibly illuminating."

"Parables?"

"Shorthand for parallel probable realities. It's an amazing experience."

"I'll take your word for it," Willa said.

Opal was puzzled. "But I heard you already saw a few of your parables during your first Divinorum. Isn't that true?"

"I certainly hope not," Willa said.

Opal nodded as she recalled some of her own less-than-pleasant experiences with Divinorum. "You didn't like what you saw."

"Terror, destruction, death… what's not to like?"

"I'm sorry, I didn't mean --"

Willa waved off the apology. "It's okay. I shouldn't burden you with my problems."

"What are friends for?"

Willa's senses went on alert; her golden eyes narrowed in mild suspicion. "Is that why you're here? To be my friend? Let me guess, you're the Provost's eyes and ears."

Opal was taken aback by Willa's sharp tone. "The Provost watches over all her charges," she stammered.

"But I merit special attention, don't I? That's why she sent her own apprentice to 'sister' me?"

"How did you know?"

"Didn't she tell you? I have the bloody Mark!"

"She mentioned it. I've heard stories but I don't really know what that means. Are you some sort of Seer?"

Willa slumped onto the bed, her eyes welling. "Yeah, one who sees things she doesn't want to see."

Silence hung in the air. Opal regarded Willa's tear-filled eyes. "We don't have to be friends," she said softly, "but we don't have to be enemies either. I'll leave you to your thoughts." Opal turned toward the door.

"Don't go," Willa said.

Opal stopped and waited.

Willa collected herself. "I... could use a friend."

Opal sat beside Willa. "To be honest, so could I. The training is hard and I haven't seen my family in over a year."

"What? Why?"

"Mystery is more like a monastery than a village. The rituals require months of dedication and outsiders aren't allowed," Opal admitted, her own dark eyes moist. "It takes a heavy toll." A realization blossomed into a sad smile. "The Provost probably wants us to be friends as much for me as for you."

Despite her misgivings, Willa felt sorry for Opal. "Okay, tell you what, we can be kith."

Opal wiped her eyes on her tunic sleeve. "What's that?"

"Sort of like kin. It's a word for old friends who've just met. My mentor Holly taught it to me."

Opal smiled. "Kith. I like it. Is there some ritual that crystallizes the bond?"

"You Nocturnals and your rituals. It just is when you say that it is."

Opal extended her hand. "Then we are kith."

Willa shook her hand as the door chimed. Willa placed her palm on the silver surface. The door slid open. Selene's dark silhouette was backlit by the hall's soft blue light.

"It's moments to moonrise. Time to begin your training."

35

Chapter Three:
TRIBUNAL

"Centuries before the Landing of the Hybrids on Earth, the Nommos beings from the Sirius star system discovered our planet on their travels through space. After the indigenous humans got used to their amphibious, salamander-like appearance, and stopped believing that the aliens were gods, the Nommos established peaceful relations with the tribes they encountered and shared their knowledge of agriculture, math, astronomy, and other sciences with humanity.

After humans evolved further and developed the ability to travel to the stars, they once again encountered the Nommos in the Sirius system, which in their language is called Siskeen. In honor of our shared history, in recognition of their refined sense of justice, and in gratitude for what the Nommos bequeathed to our ancestors, it was agreed that the Nommos Tribunal would decide all matters of interstellar law. While various federations existed among the stars before humanity spread into space, this union was the beginning of the Interstellar Alliance that we know today."

From the forward to "A Brief History of Interstellar Law"
By Dr. Hadrian Maxon & Dr. October Zaragoza

*

THE HONORABLE ORINGA KALA was immersed up to his mint-tinted eyeballs in his private meditation pool where he'd been for the past three cycles. Even his junior aides, who were used to the judge's eccentric behavior, were beginning to worry. Oringa paid them no mind. He continued to breath oxygen through his slick, blue skin as he contemplated the gravity of the trial over which he was about to preside. His usually composed mind found it hard to accept the circumstances of the case: *Murder! In an Alliance Council Chamber, no less! Unthinkable!* Yet, it had happened in front of dozens of witnesses, including the venerable Brahma Kamal, head of the First Contact Council on Earth. "Unthinkable!" he said out loud as a fizz of small bubbles escaped his wide, rubbery lips.

Oringa sighed, releasing more bubbles, and decided it was time to confer with his fellow Tribunal members since the trial was slated for the next cycle. Oringa rose from the pool, flicked the last drops of water from his salamander-like tail and stepped into a clear nano-glass tube. He was showered with a glistening gel that kept his amphibious skin moist when not submerged in water. He tapped a panel on the glass wall and was immediately wrapped in a delicate, black and white rubberized garment that sealed in the gel and displayed the three-lobed insignia that marked him as head of the Tribunal.

Oringa always regarded the emblem with a touch of irony for, while it afforded him the sacred honor that came with the office, it also demanded the burdensome task of acting as tie-breaker when his fellow judges were split in their opinions, which was often.

"Ah, well," he mused, "such is the nature of the beast."

Oringa was as fond of quoting human sayings as he was fond of humans themselves. Being a much older race than *homo sapiens*, the Nommos often felt an almost parental affinity for the descendants of those they had visited so long ago when humans had no technology beyond stone tools and fire. Oringa knew that humans often felt patronized by the outdated attitude so he kept the feeling to himself. Still, he was proud of humanity's accomplishments and closely followed Earth's progress as humans and Hybrids expanded out among the stars. Except that now, mankind's travels had opened a Pandora's Box of sorts. Stories of the Maelstrom, the

Black League, and Kale Ashgrove's capture and torture by the Archon were spreading throughout the Alliance faster than the speed of light. Not to mention that the encounter with the Orions led directly to the shocking murder that was the reason for the upcoming trial.

Equally disturbing, Oringa was hearing rumors of growing concern on several worlds about what to do should the Orions manage to adapt Alliance tech into their ships and successfully cross the Maelstrom. Some planetary governments were in favor of retaining solidarity among the Alliance members, others were entertaining secession so the full force of their defensive systems would be used to protect their planets instead of being spread thin throughout one hundred fifty star systems. Such polarized views, should they gain momentum, could cause a serious rift in the Alliance.

Oringa put these thoughts in the back of his tri-lobed brain for the time being and tapped a button on the wall. The voice of an aide issued through a small speaker. "Yes, Magister Kala?"

"Please ask Masters Oannu and Yadroon to join me in my chambers at mid-bright."

"Right away, Magister."

Oringa went to a cabinet set into the wall and made sure he had a full bottle of Salvian Mist. If he knew his fellow Magisters, it was going to be a long meeting.

*

The stars shone over a complex of domed dwellings on the outskirts of Port Dublin. Inside one dome, Gant paced as Variabilis stood against a wall, his black eyes mirroring Gant's every move.

"I'm relieved to finally get a chance to plead my case," Gant grumbled, "But I don't understand why it took so long for the Tribunal to schedule it."

"The Alliance is made up of one hundred fifty worlds. There were hundreds of cases ahead of yours," Variabilis said. "Perhaps if Brahma Kamal had assigned the case to a local court... but they would've passed it along to the Tribunal anyway, considering the serious nature of your crime."

"Even though I dealt the traitor nothing less than he deserved, in the eyes of your laws, it's still murder," Gant said in frustration.

"Well, one way or another, it'll be over soon," Variabilis added.

Gant stopped pacing. "You still don't trust me, do you, even after all this time."

"Don't take it personally," said the Shapeshifter. "There are those in the Alliance who don't trust my kind, nor any on the path of Mastery. As a result, we don't often let our guard down."

"It's no wonder," Gant said, "you can hide behind a thousand faces, take the shape of ordinary objects. I wish we had some of you in the Black League. You'd make excellent spies."

"Unfortunately, if your Archon invades Earth, it may come to that."

"Your estrangement from those who fear you... is that why you live in that isolated tower in the middle of nowhere?"

Variabilis narrowed his eyes. "I think you should be more concerned with where you might wind up."

"Your people already told me that the Alliance doesn't have a death penalty, so as long as I'm alive..."

Variabilis allowed a ghost of a smile. "There are worse things than death."

Gant tried to fathom if Variabilis was joking, then decided humor wasn't in the Shapeshifter's nature. "What do you mean? Where might the Tribunal send me?"

"If you're found guilty, you could wind up working in a recycling factory on a remote moon for the rest of your life, or worse, in a Balabog hatchery."

"That doesn't sound so bad," Gant said.

"Have you ever smelled a Balabog? You'll be purging your lunch on a daily basis."

It was Gant's turn to eye Variabilis with suspicion.

"Relax," the Shapeshifter said. "You're not an Alliance citizen. Most likely, the Tribunal will simply banish you."

Gant blinked in confusion. "You mean, send me back to Xos?" Gant pondered the paradox. "But, if that's the likely outcome whether or not I'm found guilty, why not just release me into the Black League's custody? Why the trial?"

"The law's the law. Protocol must be followed. An example must be made. Justice must be done. Take your pick," Variabilis said.

Gant found the Shapeshifter's apathy surprising. "You don't approve?"

"Make no mistake, I support the Alliance in every way. Well, most of the time. It's just that Shapeshifters are solitary creatures. We don't have much use for the ways of others."

Gant felt his frustration rising. "So, you're saying I've watched Earth's moon complete nine orbits from the windows of this prison, sweated the outcome of the trial, been cut off from everyone except my keepers and put up with you... for *nothing?*"

Variabilis shrugged. "Like I said, rules are rules."

"You know what you can do with your damn rules!" Gant shot back.

"You might still wind up with the Balabogs," the Shapeshifter offered as if it was a consolation.

"And you wonder why people don't like you," Gant fumed.

Variabilis chuckled. "I'm perfectly aware of why they don't."

A chime interrupted them. Variabilis pulled a nano-bead from his tunic pocket. It chimed again. "It's time to transport you to the Tribunal."

Gant's bluster faded. "How far did you say Sirius is from Earth?"

"Eight and a half light-years. We'll be there within the hour."

Gant put on a stoic face and nodded. "Let's get this over with."

*

Willa sat outside Mystery's pyramid in the center of a large round dais of black marble. Thin lines and arcane symbols of gleaming silver were inlaid into the stone in intricate patterns that reminded Willa of an ancient stone calendar she once saw in a museum. Thirteen blocks of black marble surrounded the dais, each with an angled facet polished to a mirror finish that reflected Willa's image in the bright moonlight.

A ghostly white, female Hybrid exited from a windowless marble structure several dozen yards from the dais. She was thin and completely hairless; even her eyebrows were absent. Her large eyes were blank white orbs without pupils. Though blind, she walked straight toward the dais. Her eerie appearance made Willa think of a walking corpse, which reinforced her comparison of Mystery to a city of the dead.

The mysterious woman wore a long, loose tunic of gray silk with a high Mandarin collar and soft, dark gray knee-high moccasins. As she passed between the reflecting stones, Willa saw that she held a small silver cup in her skeletal fingers. The pungent smell of Divinorum reached Willa long before the woman did. She flickered between apprehension and exhilaration as she wondered if the Nocturnal ritual would be different than her Cryptic rite of passage.

Selene, dressed in all black as usual, entered the dais from the opposite side. Willa noticed a silver band on her ring finger. It bore the crescent moon sigil of the Nocturnals. Both women sat on marble blocks to Willa's left and right. Selene spoke in the same reverent tone she used when she introduced the Provost.

"This is Moonstone, our Divinorum Master."

Moonstone's reedy voice echoed in Willa's mind though her thin lips never moved. The strangest thing about it was that it sounded like several voices speaking in unison. *"The voices you're hearing belong to versions of me in five different alternate realities, including this one."*

"You're telepathic!" Willa blurted, caught by surprise.

A slight frown creased Moonstone's alabaster features. "Don't speak, just think and feel."

Slightly embarrassed, Willa sent a thought. *"Sorry, I didn't mean to be so --"*

"Obvious?" The voices said with a hint of humor.

Willa was fascinated by the implications. *"I know that Nocturnals tap into parallel realities, but I never thought you could communicate with your..."* She searched for an appropriate word.

"We call them counterparts," Moonstone explained. *"Communication is the first step toward becoming a Shapeshifter, but that's a lesson for another mentor. For the moment, the five versions of 'me' can help link you to four other versions of you. Five is the usual number most can handle, though it can vary. As a Nocturnal, you'll be able to share knowledge, experience, and advice with them as they will be able to do with you. The voices will be your constant companions."* She said. *"Besides, from what I understand of the current situation, you're going to need all the advice you can get."*

Willa turned to Selene and spoke. "The voices are always with you?"

"It's something we don't share with outsiders," Selene said.

"That explains a lot," Willa remarked.

Selene bristled. "Having the Mark doesn't give you leave to be rude!"

"Sorry, did I say that out loud?"

Selene released an exasperated sigh and fixed her gaze on Moonstone. "You've got your work cut out for you, Master."

Moonstone smiled. "I recall another Initiate who was quite full of herself," she said out loud.

Willa sent a thought to the Divinorum Master. *"How do you know your thoughts from a counterpart's? Doesn't it get confusing?"*

"The thoughts are yours, just from different perspectives. You'd probably have most of those thoughts on your own eventually, but this method saves time."

Clarity came in a flash. *"You're amplifying the brain's natural capacity to function like a quantum computer and access multiple dimensions of information simultaneously!"* Willa said.

Moonstone nodded and focused her telepathy for Willa alone. *"If only more Initiates caught on as quickly as you. Of course, I would never say that out loud."*

Selene frowned when she sensed she was being left out of the conversation. Moonstone caught her look.

"Some things are for the Initiate alone," the voices said in Selene's mind. *"You know that better than anyone."*

Selene acquiesced with a grudging nod.

Moonstone held the silver cup out to Willa. *"Shall we begin?"*

Willa took the cup, along with a deep breath, drank the Divinorum, closed her eyes and awaited the inevitable rush. She had imbibed Argus's Divinorum thirteen times throughout her Cryptic training. There was something different about this brew.

Willa opened her eyes. The infinite plain was under her feet as usual, but instead of being engulfed by the titanic crystal sphere that always appeared on the horizon, the sky was a domed mosaic of scintillating shards. Willa felt a strange tingling in her feet. She looked down, astonished to see her feet and legs transform into a spreading network of tree roots. They burrowed deep into the semi-transparent plain, anchoring Willa like a great oak.

Her torso stretched upward like a tree trunk and her arms and fingers extended into hundreds of branches, each of which connected with a different sky-shard. The shards reflected a multitude of angles of Willa's face like an infinite hall of mirrors. Some were identical in appearance, some were similar and many were so different it took Willa a moment to realize they were alternate versions of her in parallel realities.

Silver streams of energy flowed from each shard down Willa's branches, transforming her into a tree of light. Hundreds of whispered voices flooded her mind and lulled her into a dream-like trance as they repeated a hypnotic mantra in unison.

"We are many and one. We are shards of a shattered mirror; facets of a multi-dimensional crystal of consciousness. We are your counterparts and you are ours. We are you and you are us. We are many and one."

As the mantra repeated, Willa looked deeply into the eyes of each counterpart. Some were still the innocent girl of thirteen before she began her Cryptic journey. Some were old and wise. Many were full-fledged Cryptics, Nocturnals, Shapeshifters, Sages and even a few were ghostly Wraiths.

But one...

One shard grew closer than the others. The counterpart had white hair, gray skin and eyes almost as pale as Moonstone's. Xanthes's voice rose above the rest, full of malice. The energy from her shard turned reddish-black and cracked Willa's branches as it coursed through the tree.

"We are one, we are one, we are one!"

Willa's tree writhed in agony as the dark energy forced its way into her mind. Her trunk became translucent, her heart glowed crimson and beat so fast it threatened to burst.

"We are one! We are one! We are one!"

Willa screamed as her tree split all the way down the trunk and shattered into a thousand splinters. The dark energy cracked the plain like glass and burned through Willa's roots.

Willa's scream was cut short as she snapped from the nightmarish vision. She still sat in the center of the dais, flanked by Moonstone and Selene. Both showed deep concern.

"What happened?" Selene said.

It took a moment for Willa to gather her wits. "I saw the grey girl."

"What?"

"Xanthes. I saw her in one of the shards. She took control of the vision."

Selene shook her head in denial. "That's impossible!"

Willa turned to Moonstone who was solemn as a statue. "It can't be true, can it?"

Moonstone spoke aloud, her reedy voice a dagger in Willa's heart. "Divinorum doesn't lie."

"But that means…"

"Xanthes is one of your counterparts," Moonstone said.

"How is that possible?" Selene demanded. "Counterparts only exist in parallel realities!"

"How indeed," Moonstone mused. "We must convene the Nocturnal Council and consult with all our own counterparts." She turned to Willa. "Until we find an answer, your training is suspended." Moonstone rose and returned to her windowless lair. Willa felt a chill pass through her heart as she pondered the meaning of her horrifying vision.

*

The circular Sirius Tribunal Chamber was capped by a spiral dome that gleamed like mother of pearl.

Oringa occupied the center seat behind a curved table on an elevated dais, flanked by his two judiciary colleagues, Oannu and Yadroon, who wore similar rubberized garments emblazoned with the official tribunal crest. The triad of judges oversaw thirteen jurors from a variety of worlds, including a human and a Hybrid from Earth.

Dennik sat on Gant's left and Variabilis was on Gant's right at a curved table in the center of the room. Since this was an official occasion, Variabilis wore a copper ring on the middle finger of his left hand. A gaggle of alien spectators filled the gallery that ringed the chamber. They filled the air with muted conversation in a dozen languages.

Gant leaned over to Dennik, his voice low. "Where's your friend Gar?"

"I sent him on an important errand," Dennik replied in the same hushed tone.

Before Gant could inquire further, Oringa tapped a blue dot on the table. A reverberating gong called the gathering to attention.

"I call this Tribunal to order in the tenth cycle of A'roon in the nine thousandth passage of No'at. The case before us involves an off-world and non-Alliance individual charged with the ancient crime of murder."

Murmurs rippled through the crowd at the unusual pronouncement. A look from Oringa restored the silence.

"Who speaks for this person?" Oringa said, his liquid eyes leveled at Gant.

Variabilis rose and honored the judges with a slight bow. "I do, Magistrate."

Gant turned to the Shapeshifter in shock. "You?"

"I hold an advanced degree in Interstellar Law," Variabilis said softly before once again facing the Tribunal.

"How do you speak to the charge?" Oringa said.

"Not guilty," the Shapeshifter said with confidence.

"On what grounds?"

"Rule fifty-four."

The three judges raised their brow ridges in unison as the spectators once more exploded into a cacophony of chatter. This time, Oringa was vocal. "Silence!"

The crowd was hushed. Oringa cast his gaze back to Variabilis.

"That rule hasn't been used in over two passages and never in the case of murder," said the Magistrate.

"Nevertheless," Variabilis said, "the rule is as active now as it was in the trial of Tev Beyo."

Oringa glanced at his fellow Magistrates. They each nodded their acceptance.

"Very well. We must discuss this. Tribunal will resume in two micro-cycles." Oringa tapped the gong, then rose and entered his chambers, followed by the other two judges.

The jurors entered their chamber as the spectator gallery resumed their conversational babble.

Dennik leaned forward as Variabilis sat down. "What's rule fifty-four?"

"And who's Tev Beyo?" Gant added.

"The Interstellar Alliance shall respect all cultural and religious customs of its member worlds, even where such customs conflict with the laws that govern the Alliance as a whole," Variabilis said. "The Tev Beyo trial extended that protection to citizens of non-member worlds who commit crimes within Alliance jurisdiction."

Dennik digested the rule's meaning. "You want to convince the Tribunal that killing Haldane was allowed by Gant's *religious* beliefs?"

"Or his cultural imperative," Variabilis acknowledged.

"You think the Tribunal will believe that?" Gant said with a hint of hope.

"Rule fifty-four exists because there are some truly unusual customs in a lot of the civilizations that make up the Alliance. It clearly creates a gaping loophole that I'm happy to walk through, but without that flexibility in the law, the Alliance would quickly fall apart," Variabilis said.

"And I thought you didn't like me," Gant said with a smile.

"I don't," admitted the Shapeshifter. "Fortunately for you, Dennik's your character witness, not me."

Gant frowned. "Then why are you here?"

"Because whether I like you or not, the law says that the advocate most familiar with the case must defend the accused. My opinion notwithstanding, you're entitled to the best possible defense."

Wheels turned in Gant's mind. Perhaps he didn't need the Alliance or the Black League to kill the Archon. With the right plan and a little guile, this single Shapeshifter might do the trick.

*

Rowan sat in a public square in the center of Thoria, the capital city of Thook. He wore his pilot's jacket against the frigid night air and passed the time watching the ghostly apparitions of passing Thook fade in and out of his consciousness as they entered and exited his line of sight. The Contact Initiate insignia on his shoulders told the inhabitants he was here on business and thus, no one gave Rowan a second glance.

Rowan's solitude was broken by the approach of fifty identical Thook. As the throng grew closer, their numbers dwindled and coalesced into a single being. The tall, round-eyed alien held out a nano-bead and Rowan took it without breaking eye contact.

"I recorded all the conversations since I'll forget them once I turn back into myself," Star said while still in the shape of a Thook.

"Any luck?" Rowan said hopefully.

"Not sure. One said he heard that a local named Thannik had a female human friend from Earth who visited now and then."

Rowan sighed. "I suppose a small lead is better than no lead at all."

"Tell the bead to start playing recording thirty-seven before I shift or you'll forget we had this conversation," Star suggested. "Give it a fifteen-second delay."

He did so and the Thook shifted back into Star. Rowan blinked as though he'd lost his train of thought. He focused on Star, who appeared equally confused.

"Any luck?" Rowan repeated.

The bead glowed to life and the playback clicked on before Star could answer. "Playback of recording thirty-seven..."

*

Captain Bryony Bracken, head of Earth's rescue patrol, was on a return course through the solar system in her scout ship. She had just crossed Saturn's orbit when her sensors picked up an Alliance distress signal. She zeroed in on it and discovered a small ship that looked like an escape pod. Her computer recognized the engine's frequency signature as a Q-jump drive so Captain Bracken naturally assumed it must have come from an Alliance ship. However, a quick sensor-sweep revealed no other ships within a hundred thousand klicks. She tapped her com as she approached the pod.

"This is Captain Bracken of the Solar Rescue Ship *Protector*. Do you copy?"

There was a crackle of static, followed by Elowen's panicked plea. "Yes, yes, I copy! Please hurry and get me out of here! I think the self-destruct has accidentally been activated!"

"What's the countdown?"

"I'm not sure, some of the systems are compromised," Elowen said. "I may only have minutes!"

"On my way!" Bracken replied. Her ship's cargo airlock was large enough to hold the pod with room to spare. Bryony opened the outer hatch and expertly maneuvered the *Protector* backward until the pod was swallowed by the cargo hold. She closed the outer hatch, pressurized the chamber and hurried to the inner hatch. She hit the door control the instant the readout was green and hurried inside.

Elowen pounded on the quartz window, her muffled voice thick with fear. "The hatch is stuck! Please hurry!"

Captain Bracken grabbed a laser torch from her equipment locker and cut through the pod's lock assembly. She yanked the hatch open and Elowen scrambled from the pod.

"Get to the cockpit!" Bracken said.

Elowen ran from the cargo hold, Bracken on her heels. They cleared the inner hatch and Bracken sealed it, then slapped the outer hatch control. It opened and the escape pod blew out into space in the explosive rush of air. The Captain closed the outer hatch seconds before the pod detonated in a blinding flash. Dozens of small fragments peppered the Protector's force field but did no damage.

Bryony and Elowen exhaled with relief. The Captain turned and was shocked as she finally got a good look at the scars that covered one of Elowen's eyes and the cuts and bruises on her face.

"Who are you?" Bracken said. "What happened to you?"

"My name's Elowen Koa."

Bryony's lavender eyes widened in surprise. "We thought you were dead!"

"If you hadn't come along, I would be. Thank you for --" she said a split second before she passed out.

*

Rowan carried the nano-bead as he and Star followed the recorded directions supplied by the Thook that Star interviewed.

"Follow the lighted path to the crystal monument. Look for the structure with the faceted blue spires across the Zocalo and enter the center passage. When you come to the first chamber, call out to Thannik and he will answer."

They arrived in the chamber where Sylvania held her secret meeting with her Thook contact.

"Thannik! We're friends of Sylvania Rousseau. We need to talk," Rowan announced to the seemingly empty room.

Thannik faded into their awareness as he stepped into their line of sight. Star stood as close as she could to Rowan so neither would break eye contact with the towering alien. It wasn't lost on Rowan that Star enjoyed the intimate contact, but he kept his focus on the Thook.

"I am Thannik."

"I'm Rowan and this is Star. We know Sylvania sought you out so you could hide her from danger."

"If you know that," the Thook said in his warbly voice, "then why bring danger to her by seeking her out?"

"Her daughter sent us. She's young and feels abandoned by her mother. We believe Sylvania will be safer surrounded by family and friends."

"Sylvania thought otherwise. I must respect her wish," Thannik replied.

Rowan fought to retain eye contact with the reluctant Thook. "I don't think you understand what she's up against. It's likely the threat will find her no matter how far she runs. At least with us, she has a chance."

"I think that deep down, you agree with us," Star interjected.

Thannik hesitated, slightly startled. "What makes you say that?"

"You could break eye contact anytime you want and walk away and we'd never know you were here or that we had this conversation," Star said. "But you haven't."

"I can't betray her trust," Thannik said. "She would never forgive me."

"If anything happens to her, neither will I," Rowan promised.

Rowan and Star could tell the Thook's mind was searching for any way he could help them without breaking his promise to Sylvania. Though it seemed nearly impossible, Thannik's large eyes suddenly got larger as an epiphany struck like lightning.

"I think I know a way to help you," said the Thook.

Chapter Four:

COUNTERPART

"The existence of parallel realities was first theorized on Earth by physicists in the early Twentieth Century. However, earlier versions of the multiverse were proposed by Buddhist, Greek, and other ancient philosophers thousands of years before modern science. Of course, many civilizations in other star systems discovered the existence of alternate realities long before Earth humans conceived of the concept, but it wasn't until the creation of Divinorum by our Hybrid ancestors that the denizens of one parallel reality could extend their senses and communicate with the inhabitants of another."

Excerpt from "Reflections on Reality"
by Rio Amaryllis, Divinorum Master

*

The First Contact Council was in full session. The venerated chamber was filled with delegates from every member world in the Alliance as well as the heads of every Lodge on each planet that was home to Cryptics, Nocturnals, Shapeshifters, and Sages. Wraiths, being exceedingly rare and not well understood, were conspicuously absent.

Willa sat with Holly, Selene, Sequoia, and Moonstone in a section of the gallery reserved for those who had important business with the Council.

Lily and River Hillicrissing sat in the spectator section along with Poppy, Kale, Thorn Ashgrove, and Alder Redwood, the Sage who had taken a keen interest in Willa ever since it was revealed that she possessed the Mark. While Alder often wore bejeweled rings, the gold one on his left index finger was emblazoned with an inlaid circle of blue Lapis, the sigil of a Sage. Argus, the Sasquatch Divinorum Master, sat next to Alder in a large seat designed to hold his enormous bulk.

Kale glanced over at the group of young First Contact Initiates whose attendance was mandatory at all official Council sessions. He turned and whispered to Thorn.

"Where's your brother?"

"I haven't seen him for a few days. I assumed he was busy with his training."

Kale couldn't shake the feeling that something was wrong. "It's not like Rowan to miss an official session."

At that moment, a nano-glass security robot strode down the aisle and stopped before Kale. The robot held out a black nano-bead in its slender fingertips. "Message for you, Master Ashgrove."

Kale hesitated as all eyes in the aisle focused on the bead. Everyone knew that black beads carried urgent news or even secret messages which were keyed only to the person receiving them. Kale took the bead and the robot headed off. He stuck the bead in his ear, listened to the message, then rose from his seat.

"Is everything okay?" Thorn said, hoping his father would share the message.

"I'll be back soon as I can," Kale said and hurried out without another word.

The others eyed Thorn for information, but all he could do was shrug.

A rising buzz of chatter from the gathering drew everyone's surprised gaze to Rusalka, and Ashleen, who had just entered the chamber and took seats slightly removed from the rest of the crowd. It was highly unusual for Elementals to attend any Alliance functions and most aliens within the Alliance had never encountered such beings before.

Willa caught Rusalka's ruby glance and gave a respectful nod. The Pooka nodded back and whispered something to Ashleen. The Pooka Queen's pink eyes found Willa for a heartbeat, then flickered to Selene, who sat in the spectator gallery.

Selene caught the disapproving look, then trained her gaze on Brahma as he brought the session to order.

"Honored ambassadors, we've called you to this emergency session to hear new information that may prove vital to the survival of every world in the Alliance."

The crowd murmured in anticipation. Brahma turned his attention to Willa, Holly, and Sequoia.

"Allow me to introduce Willa Hillicrissing and her mentors, the heads of the Cryptic and Nocturnal Lodges on Earth, Masters Holly Cotton and Sequoia August Moon. She is also attended by Selene Nymphaea, her Nocturnal sponsor and Malvania Moonstone, their Divinorum Master."

Willa cast a glance at the Divinorum Master, surprised to learn she had a first name. Brahma's soothing voice coaxed Willa's attention back to his large, ice-blue eyes.

"Some of you are familiar with the fact that Willa possesses the Mark, a rare gene that can be traced back hundreds of thousands of years to the Anu race that had a hand in creating Earth humans and, by extension, our Hybrid society. What most of you may not know is that the Mark endows our young Initiate with special abilities enhanced by both her Mastery training as well as an Elemental Kenning."

Dozens of faces riveted on the two Pookas, who did their best to ignore the looks of astonishment and disbelief. To those familiar with Earth's nature spirits, it was unheard of that any being other than an Elemental would be allowed to experience a Kenning.

"However," Brahma continued, "that's not the reason for this gathering. As you've all been briefed, the Alliance has become the target of a relentlessly aggressive empire ruled by a ruthless entity called the Archon. Last year, through the capture of one of our ships and its crew, he came into possession of Alliance technology, which he plans to use to subjugate our people and vastly extend his empire's reach."

Thorn felt a mild flush of embarrassment, knowing it was his father's ship that Brahma was referring to. Willa's father placed a supportive hand on Thorn's shoulder to remind him that everyone knew it wasn't Kale's fault. Thorn allowed himself a gentle smile and nodded his understanding.

Brahma let the gravity of his words sink in, then turned his attention to Willa. "But our Initiate has discovered some new information. Something quite startling. Something we believed to be impossible."

While most weren't conscious of it, nearly everyone was leaning forward on the edge of their seats as Brahma spelled it out.

"During a recent Divinorum ritual, Willa had a vision that shattered everything we thought we knew about parallel realities. The Five Levels of Mastery proved that we can tap into them, mirror those realities, even communicate from a higher plane of consciousness with the counterparts who occupy those alternate realities. But never have we imagined that we could physically cross into those other realities, nor that our counterparts could cross into ours… until now."

The gathering exploded in a cacophony of alien languages. Some delegates jumped to their feet, their pods, their tentacles, all clamoring for attention. Those that had the presence of mind to switch on their vocal translators shouted their opinions.

"Impossible!"

"Your data must be flawed!"

"Where's your proof?"

Brahma raised his hands in a plea for order. "Friends, please, allow me to explain." Despite his request, the crowd's concerns escalated.

Willa couldn't take any more. She stood and shouted in an amplified voice that shook the chamber with the power of an angry goddess.

"Listen to me!"

The gathering plunged into stunned silence.

Holly reached out to calm her protégé. "Willa --"

"No!" Willa pulled away and strode to the center of the chamber. "None of you get to be more scared or outraged than me! I'm the one this is happening to. If I can deal with it, then so can you!"

Embarrassed by their outbursts and shamed by a fourteen-year-old, the crowd settled back in their seats. Willa glanced over at Brahma, who urged her to continue with a nod.

Willa took a deep breath. "When the Divinorum revealed that the grey girl, Xanthes, was my counterpart, something else made sense. As you know, Koro, who came through the Maelstrom with the others from Xos, committed suicide. His last words were 'look to the stars.' As a pilot, he knew the stars of his home world. I realized what he saw when he came to Earth, what his mind couldn't accept... what drove him mad. He saw that the stars were the same in our sky as they were in his, an impossibility if you've traveled over a thousand light years to another world."

There were a few hushed mumblings but they quickly stopped as Willa leveled her golden gaze at the crowd.

"I believe the Maelstrom isn't just some electromagnetic anomaly," Willa said. "It's a portal that connects our universe with the Archon's parallel universe."

Several spectators exchanged concerned looks as the implications sank in.

"My connection with Xanthes is so strong and our stars are the same as hers because I *am* her. Why do we share the same language? Because Earth and Xos are the same world in two different realities!"

*

The Port Dublin Medical Facility was a gleaming glass sphere, filled with state-of-the-art re-gen machines, nano-glass robots, and AI terminals that performed everything from emergency surgery to administrative functions. A few humans, Hybrids, and aliens comprised a minimal staff of living beings who provided a natural, relaxed bedside manner that made the patients feel more at ease.

Elowen Koa rested in a re-gen bed in a private suite. An energy beam had repaired her cuts and bruises and was quickly regenerating her lost eye. The beam snapped off and the projector slid back into its wall alcove.

Hyacinth, a Hybrid med-tech, entered the room with a broad smile. "How are you feeling?"

"Much better," Elowen said. "Almost like my old self."

"Wonderful. Feel up to seeing a visitor?"

Elowen nodded and the med-tech gestured for Kale to enter. She patted Elowen's hand. "I'll leave you to it." Hyacinth left and closed the door to give Kale and Elowen some privacy.

Kale pulled up a chair alongside the bed. Neither said a word, but the look they exchanged spoke volumes about the ordeal each had suffered under the Archon's cruel torture. Kale wiped a tear off his cheek and took Elowen's hand.

"I thought they killed you."

Elowen swallowed hard at the memory. "They did. They kept resuscitating me, over and over, so they could torture more intel out of me." She turned her face away as tears of shame welled in her eyes. "I told them everything, Captain. I wasn't strong enough. I'm so sorry."

Kale gently turned her chin back to face him. "No one could've resisted their mind probe." He offered her a sad smile. "What's the ancient expression? I sang like a canary. I'm just grateful you're alive. They told me how you escaped."

"The pod was the first step in adapting our tech to their ships. I'm afraid it won't take them long to outfit their entire fleet," Elowen said.

"You can brief the Council later," Kale said. "Right now, you need to rest and regain your strength."

Elowen's mood darkened. "I'm not sure the Council trusts me."

"What do you mean? Why wouldn't they?"

"It's nothing anyone's said, but my nurse... did you notice? She's a telepath."

"Medical personnel are chosen for their empathic abilities," Kale reminded her.

"Empathy, yes. Telepathy, not normally. It's subtle, but I can sense her probing my mind now and then. I think they believe I might've been turned. That I'm some kind of spy," she fretted.

"I'll talk to the Council," Kale vowed. "You've been through too much for them to treat you like anything less than a hero."

Elowen smiled and squeezed his hand in gratitude. "Thank you, Captain."

"Get some rest. You'll be back in a pilot's seat in no time." Kale rose, then paused at the door. "I... named my new ship after you."

"Thank you, Captain, I'm truly touched. But, seeing as how I'm alive..."

"I'll change it to something more appropriate," Kale said.

"May I suggest we keep the name Sagittarius? She was a good ship."

Kale smiled. "Sagittarius, it is." He exited, his spirits light.

Elowen's eyes remained fixed on the door as it slid shut behind him. Her grateful smile dissolved into a blank stare as her programmed personality switched off.

*

Sylvania Rousseau wasn't herself. She hadn't been herself for quite some time, thanks to the memory wipe.

The Thook Mind Masters had done their job well, telepathically erasing and replacing Sylvania's memories, including her own identity. The process had taken three months, not that Sylvania remembered any of it. As far as she was concerned, she was, and always had been Brandelyn Esperanza.

If anyone had asked, although no one ever did, Brandelyn would have told them she was born and raised right here in Vasko, a small town of a hundred thousand souls on the planet Tavanna, a world on the outskirts of the Alliance.

She would also have been able to recall her mother and father, memories of growing up on the shore of Lake Umar, and when her parents accidentally died in an avalanche while climbing Mount Kastavar. None of these memories were real but that wouldn't matter to the inhabitants of Vasko, since every citizen's identity was an elaborate work of fiction.

Each morning on her way to market, Brandelyn would greet her neighbor Turso, a man who had no idea who he used to be. Or Brandelyn would have a friendly chat with Ullock, a female alien who owned the local flower shop and had no clue she had a brother on a planet just five light years away.

The history of the town and everyone who lived there had been meticulously crafted with great artistry by the Thook. Their telepathic programming automatically adjusted to allow for new arrivals to blend in as though they'd always lived there and been known by all for many years.

Vasko was a city of the vanished, with thousands of buried stories of how and why each person came to live there and, because the Thook had created Vasko, the town's true nature was the best-kept secret in the Alliance.

When Thannik had told Sylvania how he could help her disappear so Xanthes would never be able to find her, she struggled with the pain of knowing she would forget Poppy and that her daughter would never know what happened to her mother.

Although heartbroken, Sylvania believed it was the only way to keep Poppy safe.

As Brandelyn, she had a good life as a popular artist and had no knowledge of Nocturnals, let alone that she had been one, or any memories of Earth.

However, as the saying goes, all good things must come to an end and, despite the Thook's best-laid plans, the peace and tranquility of Vasko was about to be shattered beyond repair.

*

Oringa and his fellow Magisters took their seats in the Tribunal chamber and tapped the gong that called the gathering to order.

"Will the accused please stand," Oringa said. It was clear to those among the spectators who could read the expression on the amphibian's face that Oringa was still unsettled by the nature of the case.

Gant stood, as did Variabilis and Dennik. Gant glanced at his advocate for any clue as to which way the judges might lean, but the Shapeshifter's expression was unreadable as stone. Gant braced himself for the worst and faced the three judges.

Oringa received final nods from Oannu and Yadroon. He stood. His liquid eyes glided over the gallery and rested on Gant.

"It is the ruling of the Tribunal to honor Rule Fifty-Four of the Interstellar Code." The gallery began to buzz but hushed as Oringa raised a hand for silence. "In keeping with that decision, we hereby banish the accused in perpetuity. You will have three standard Earth days to get your affairs in order, at which time you will be escorted to the border of Alliance space. Should the accused enter our territory again at any point in the future, he will be subject to immediate arrest and incarceration for the remainder of his natural life. The Tribunal rests."

Oringa tapped the blue button. The gong sounded the end of the proceedings and the three judges retired to their respective chambers amid the buzz of the crowd.

Gant turned to Variabilis. "That's it?"

"That's it," the Shapeshifter said.

"Thank you."

Variabilis waved the sentiment away. "As I said, just doing my job."

Dennik clapped Gant on the shoulder. "Looks like you're free to join the League."

"I vow to do everything in my power to help you defeat the Archon," Gant said. That part was true, of course. Gant knew that the more he could tell the truth, the less Dennik would suspect Gant's desire to rule in the Archon's place. He eyeballed Variabilis and smiled. "In fact, I've been working on a plan."

The Shapeshifter returned a deadpan stare. Though he couldn't read Gant's mind, he was dead certain that something sinister lurked behind that cunning smile.

*

Xos-Asura, Archon of the Empire, sat in his aerie atop the Citadel. A steel-suited guard, the one who brought Elowen Koa to Xanthes in secret, stood at attention to one side as the Archon's daughter entered the inner sanctum. Her eyes flickered to the guard as she passed him. Xanthes stopped a few feet before her father and bowed. "You summoned me, Father?"

"I was never prouder of you than on the day you slit your treasonous mother's throat," the Archon said, his voice dripping with venom. "Only to find that you take after her."

Xanthes glanced at the guard again. It was clear her gaze made him nervous. She turned her full attention back to Xos-Asura.

"How have I betrayed you, Father?"

SHARDS OF A SHATTERED MIRROR

"I've been informed that you resuscitated a female prisoner, programmed her, and released her without my knowledge," the Archon said.

"A surprise, Father. My witching senses showed me that the spies you sent to Earth had failed. The female I sent in their stead is undetectable as our puppet. She is known to them and has access to valuable intel. I can see and hear what she sees and hears. I simply wanted to make sure the subterfuge would work before I told you about her," Xanthes said with unwavering confidence.

The Archon narrowed his cold eyes. He wasn't fool enough to believe his conniving daughter. She was, after all, an Overlord and one personally trained by the powerful Sensates. Nevertheless, she would still be useful in his plan to conquer the vast, rich territories within the Alliance.

Xos-Asura summoned the guard to his side with a gesture. "You are to be rewarded for revealing Xanthes's hidden plan to me."

The guard bowed his head in gratitude. "Thank you, My Lord."

"I also sentence you to death for betraying my daughter."

"My... my Lord?"

The Archon slid a blade from a concealed slot in the arm of his chair and slit the guard's throat quick as a striking serpent. The guard dropped to his knees, grabbed his throat, eyes wide in shock as blood gushed from the wound, staining his armor.

"Your reward is a quick death."

The guard collapsed on the stone floor as life drained from him.

The Archon wiped the blade on his garment sleeve and slid it back into its compartment. He fixed his gaze on Xanthes, whose expression never changed. She had the good sense to remain silent.

"One of the interesting things we learned in our interrogation of the prisoners is that the name of their planet... Earth... also means soil," the Archon said. "I applaud your ambition, but if you keep a secret from me again, rather than rule the Earth, you'll be buried on it."

"I live to serve," Xanthes said, her head bowed.

"And you serve to live," the Archon replied. "Report to me the instant you have any intel from your spy." Xos-Asura glanced at the guard's bloody corpse. "And send someone to clean up this mess."

Xanthes bowed again and left the chamber, her gait measured and calm. Inside, Xanthes was seething, not only because her plan had been exposed, but also because her father had deprived her of the pleasure of torturing the disloyal guard.

*

Alarra and Brim were in the same blue nano-glass quarters where Brim, Dennik, Koro, and Gar had been housed when they first arrived on Earth. Though the trip through the Maelstrom to fetch Alarra had been harrowing, the Alliance had provided Dennik with a small starship reinforced against the anomaly's powerful electromagnetic tides. The ship's computer had also been programmed to self-destruct should it fall into the Archon's hands.

Alarra thanked the stars that they had made it across the Empire's territory without encountering any of their patrol ships, and that she was now safe on this world called Earth along with her husband and her son. Of course, Dennik was now with Gant at his trial in the Sirius system, but she knew they'd be reunited soon.

Alarra and Brim had been assigned an escort, *a pleasant euphemism for a guard*, Alarra thought, and the escort had been kind enough to show them some of the wonders of this verdant planet. They'd only been back for an hour or so, and had just finished a sumptuous midday meal when there was a knock on their door.

Brim opened it to find Willa, more somber than Brim had ever seen her before. Of course, their ubiquitous escort was also just outside the door.

"Willa! It's wonderful to see you," Brim said as he stood aside. "Please, come in."

Willa entered and Brim shut the door. "I want you to meet my mother, Alarra. Mother, this is Willa Hillicrissing."

Alarra gave a slight bow of her head and Willa did the same.

"My son has told me a lot about you. I'm pleased to finally meet you in person."

"Thank you for rescuing my friend's father," Willa said. "We owe you and your husband a great debt."

"The debt is paid in full by the generosity your world has shown us, and your willingness to help us in our fight against the Archon," Alarra said graciously.

"I wish we could have met in less desperate times," Willa added. "I've come to tell you something I've discovered about our two worlds. Something that won't be easy to hear."

"Will it help us defeat the Empire?"

Willa pondered the question. "I'm not sure. I suppose it's possible."

There was an irresistible smile in Alarra's emerald eyes. "Then whatever you have to say will be welcome."

*

Gar ambled through the streets of the town of Sintra near Port Lisbon in Portugal. Gant had been forthcoming in telling Dennik and Gar that Haldane had left his ship in one of the underwater caves that pockmarked the shoreline, but couldn't recall the exact location. Gar had been searching along the coast for the past three days with no luck.

Of course, the search would've gone much faster if he'd asked the locals for help, but Dennik had given him strict orders to keep his search a secret. As such, Gar had to pretend he was an off-world oceanographer taking measurements of coastal erosion to compare with rising sea levels on his home world.

Gar wasn't happy with the charade but he understood the need for it. The computer aboard Haldane's ship might reveal valuable intel in its files about his mission. There might even be a clue as to whether Gant had truly been ignorant of Haldane's duplicity, though Gant's willingness to help Gar find the ship probably meant there was nothing incriminating in the files.

Gar waved to Daria Dos Santos, a bubbly Portuguese woman he'd gotten to know because she rented compact electromagnetic submersibles to tourists and locals from her dive shop at the end of one of the many docks that lined the beach.

"Olá, Daria," Gar said.

"Olá, Senhor Gar! Your sub awaits," she said as she cleaned the nano-glass hull.

"Obrigado," Gar responded as he tossed his equipment into the transparent sphere. "I'll be a few hours as usual today."

"No problem, Senhor. Take your time. It's a slow day."

Gar slid into the pilot's seat. Daria sealed the round glass hatch and, as Gar's gnarled fingers glided over the controls, the sub slipped into the ocean and dove beneath the waves.

The submersible's electromagnetic engines extended like pontoons on either side of the cockpit bubble. Each was a hollow tube that generated a corkscrew vortex of water that shot out the back of the tube and propelled the sub through the underwater landscape in relative silence.

Several large caves were lit by beams of sunlight that stabbed down through holes eroded in the domed ceilings. Many of the largest caverns had small, hidden beaches within them where gentle waves lapped upon sandy shores.

Schools of silvery Sea Bream, Red Mullet, and tiny Cuttlefish swam past the sub as Gar scanned a series of cave entrances with searchlight and sensors. Gar wondered if the oceans of Xos had once been home to such a rich variety of sea life. A thousand years of occupation by the Empire had turned Xos into a planet-sized factory that consumed and polluted every natural resource to build the ships and weapons required to maintain a stranglehold on twenty subjugated worlds.

In the solitude of the sub, Gar's memories drifted back to the day he joined the Black League to break free from the Archon's tyranny. The Resistance had won several battles but they were still very far from winning the war.

Three hours passed as Gar floated through the ocean. His sensors registered nothing more than fish or crabs in the caves. He was about to turn back when he spotted a cluster of Dogfish sharks circling near the entrance of a distant cave. Daria had briefed Gar on the sub's database, which contained files on dozens of local species. Gar recalled that some sharks were able to detect magnetic fields and used them to navigate through the murky depths. But they were also often attracted to magnetic anomalies. Gar knew that starships, even with their systems on minimal power, could still generate a detectable magnetic field.

Gar piloted the sub through the loose gathering of sharks and entered the cave. Within seconds, he surfaced in a vast, domed cavern. Haldane's ship rested on a sandy outcrop. Its spear-shaped hull glinted in a single ray of sunlight that shone through a gap in the craggy ceiling.

He maneuvered the sub to within a few yards of the shore and tapped a control. A large tube of nano-glass extended from the hatch and formed an airlock tunnel. Micro pumps rapidly evacuated the seawater and the hatch opened like an iris. Gar crawled through the airlock, jumped down into the shallow water and waded to the small beach that surrounded the starship. The sound of waves rushing through the network of water-carved tunnels echoed within the cavern as the salt air filled Gar's lungs.

He scanned Haldane's craft with a portable sensor, well aware that Empire ships were often booby-trapped to prevent the Resistance from hijacking them. Nothing unusual registered on his readout. Gar cautiously approached the ship's outer airlock door. He took a small magnetic tool from his equipment bag and detached a cover plate in the hull. Gar checked the exposed circuitry and, with a practiced hand, reconfigured the control blocks. The outer door slid open with a gust of stale, pressurized air.

Gar took another moment to examine the dimly-lit airlock interior, then stepped inside and shut the door. He opened the inner door and headed down the central corridor to the compact bridge without encountering any surprises.

Indicators showed the craft was maintaining minimal life support with back-up batteries. The ship's computer was dormant but snapped on with a single touch on the main control console.

Gar knew that any sensitive files would be protected by sophisticated encryptions that would take time to decode. He plugged a small, portable power source into a port and, with his magnetic tool, unlocked and removed the entire computer core.

Gar carried the core back to the sub, retracted his airlock tunnel, sealed the hatch and sank beneath the surface. He didn't know if he and Dennik would find anything of value within the files, but it revitalized the old soldier to be on a mission once again.

*

Alarra and Brim sat around the table with Willa, sipping juice and trying to wrap their minds around what she'd told them.

"Xos is an alternate version of Earth," Alarra said.

"Yes," Willa said.

"In an alternate universe," Brim added.

"Yes."

Alarra began to feel dizzy. "Do we all have… what did you call them?"

"Counterparts. Yes, thousands, maybe millions of them in different parallel realities."

Brim exchanged a glance with his mother. It was clear they were thinking the same thing. Brim took the initiative. "So, if Xanthes is your counterpart on Xos, does that mean my mother and I have --"

Willa nodded. "Probably, although they might not be on Earth at the moment."

Alarra stood and paced as she gathered her thoughts. "If the Maelstrom is truly a door between our two universes, maybe we can find a way to close it so the Archon can't invade your reality."

"I've been thinking about that," Willa said, "but there's a problem."

"What kind of problem?" Brim said.

It was Willa's turn to pace. "You told me that the Empire controls twenty star systems, right?"

Alarra nodded.

"Why not more?"

"The Maelstrom, whatever it is, created an enormous bubble of energy, many light-years in diameter. It encloses the Empire, prevents it from expanding. The 'skin' of the bubble is impenetrable. The Maelstrom is its weakest point but, as you know, you risk your life passing through it without your advanced tech."

"But the Archon and the Overlords didn't come from any of the planets in the Empire so the bubble didn't always exist," Willa said.

"I suppose not," Alarra acknowledged. "But the Overlords arrived nearly a thousand years ago. The bubble was discovered three hundred years ago, but there's no way to know when it first appeared."

"You said there was a problem," Brim interjected.

"It's possible that if we somehow manage to destroy the Maelstrom, the bubble would pop, so to speak. This universe would be safe, but --"

"But the Archon would be free to conquer more worlds in our universe!" Alarra said, alarmed at the grim prospect.

Brim saw the flip side. "But if we don't destroy it --"

"Then the invasion of our universe is inevitable," Willa said. "I've seen it in the shards."

Alarra understood. "Yes, Brim told me you have this... Mark?"

"It could give me the ability to defeat the Archon's army," Willa said. "However, I can sense that Xanthes has the Mark, too."

"Some in the League have spoken of her witching ways. I always hoped they were false rumors, created to spread fear within the Resistance," Alarra said, downcast at the news.

"Don't give up," Willa said, as much to bolster her own confidence as well as to lighten Alarra's and Brim's mood. "The Divinorum visions show me what *might* happen, not necessarily what *will* happen. There are still many possible outcomes."

Brim wasn't completely convinced. "You *know* there are, or you *hope* there are?"

Willa gave it some thought. "If there are an infinite number of parallel realities, then there are likely several where the Alliance is at war with the Empire. There has to be at least one where the Archon is defeated. For all we know, it could be this one. It might not seem like much to hang our hopes on, but one chance may be all we need."

*

Rowan and Star stood in a domed, crystalline chamber. Each facet emanated a spectrum of slowly undulating blues, lavenders, and soft pinks. Nearby, a floating Luminaria globe reflected the changing colors in its glassy surface.

Five Thook stood before Rowan and Star in a semi-circle, their large, round eyes fixed on the two of them. Thorasta, the Mind Master in the center, spoke in a soothing, melodious voice.

"Are you seeking a new life among the vanished?"

"No," Rowan answered as his nano-bead recorded the exchange. "We seek one of the vanished."

"We're not at liberty to share that information," said the orange-eyed Mind Master on Thorasta's left.

"We aren't asking you to break your trust," Star said. "We understand that most of the vanished have instructed you never to reveal their identities or their whereabouts. But are there any who didn't make that specific request?"

69

"Those who vanish do not wish to be found," Thorasta said.

"For most, yes," Rowan said, "but we've been told there are some who asked for a new identity to help heal mental trauma or certain psychological conditions."

"True," Thorasta said with some hesitation.

Rowan pressed on. "In those cases, they're not hiding. They hope to rejoin their families and friends one day, yes?"

Thorasta nodded slightly, careful not to break eye contact. "Yes, but even if they didn't ask us to hide their new identities from their loved ones, they're still entitled to privacy where outsiders are concerned."

"Unless a family member gives their consent," Star said.

"That would be an exception," Thorasta agreed.

"May we use your Luminaria?" Rowan said.

A red-eyed Mind Master gestured toward the globe and the Luminaria floated to the center of the room and hung in mid-air. Rowan tapped the sphere in a distinct pattern. Within seconds, Poppy's face filled the crystal ball.

"Poppy, listen carefully. Star and I are with the Thook Mind Masters. They're willing to tell us where Sylvania is if we can explain her psychological condition."

Poppy realized Rowan was attempting to enlist her in some plan. "Okay," she said cautiously.

Rowan continued before the Thook could suspect he was improvising. "The med-techs said that Xanthes's violent telepathic attack on your mother caused an extreme psychological reaction. If I remember correctly, they diagnosed her as being mentally and emotionally damaged and suffering from paranoid delusions."

"That's right," Poppy said, going along with the charade.

Rowan addressed Thorasta. "The telepathic attack has skewed Sylvania's judgment, made her believe she needed to change her identity. Her daughter is asking for her to be returned to Earth so we can help her recover from her trauma."

"May we ask who perpetrated this unconscionable attack on your mother? Does it have anything to do with the outsiders sequestered on Earth?"

Poppy's eyes flickered to Rowan, uncertain what she should say.

"That's a long story," Rowan offered, hoping that would end the conversation.

Thorasta smiled, "No one here is in a hurry."

Chapter Five:
A CRACK IN THE SKY

"What, from our perspective, may appear to be an anomaly, from another point of view may be the norm. We should never assume that something is truly impossible. Quite often, all it takes is a small shift in the status quo and suddenly, what seemed impossible a moment ago becomes the new status quo."

"The Book of Paradox"
by Sassafras the Sage

*

BRANDELYN SAT ON THE GRASSY HILLSIDE near her home and gazed up at the stars. The night was cool but not chilly and Tavanna's two small moons were only just appearing on the horizon. For some reason she couldn't fathom, Brandelyn always wound up staring at one particular distant star. She's asked a neighbor who was an astronomer if it had a name and he labeled it "Sol." Brandelyn always felt a strange longing when she looked at the star and wondered if it shone on any inhabited planets and, if so, what those people might be like.

While Tavanna's level of technology allowed the population to live in comfort, for some reason they never seemed interested in developing space travel. Brandelyn also felt no need to travel among the stars, yet still found it odd that nobody on the entire planet was driven to explore the universe in any way other than via their ground-based telescopes. Thoughts like these were fleeting and Brandelyn's mind always seemed to gravitate back to less philosophical matters. It was her turn to prepare the evening meal that was a weekly tradition with several close neighbors. She was wavering back and forth between caramel pudding and spice-berry tarts for dessert when a flash of light caught her eyes and drew her attention back to the stars.

At first, Brandelyn couldn't make sense of what she saw. The luminous burst made her think someone was shooting off fireworks, except the lines of light that spread out from the center became jagged cracks as though the sky was made of glass. The cracks bent counter-clockwise as the sky and all the stars began to spin like fireflies caught in a whirlpool of black water.

Brandelyn felt light-headed as she watched the impossible phenomenon expand across the vault of the sky. With a cold shock, she realized she was floating a few inches above the grass, along with dozens of small rocks, leaves, twigs and anything else that wasn't anchored to the ground. Nearby tree branches creaked like old floorboards as they bent upward, caught in the irresistible gravitational pull of the glowing whirlpool.

The clock bell in the tower at the center of the town rang out, although it was tinny and out of tune as the sound was distorted by the gravity waves that stirred the atmosphere. A titanic thunderclap rattled Brandelyn's teeth as she and the surrounding debris thudded back on the ground after the initial gravity surge passed. She remained lying in the grass as her unblinking eyes beheld the bone-chilling spectacle of the new-born Maelstrom that dominated the night sky.

*

Rowan and Star waited patiently for the Mind Masters to return after their deliberation.

"You think Thannik's idea will work?" said Star.

Thorasta entered the chamber alone. As soon as she made eye contact with Rowan, she became visible to his senses.

"We're about to find out," he said.

Star moved closer to share Rowan's line of sight and the Thook rippled into her awareness as well. Though the Thook were usually hard to read, Thorasta was clearly concerned. Rowan started his recorder.

"Something's happened," Thorasta said without preamble. "The Vanished, including your friend, are in mortal danger." She handed Rowan a nano-bead. "Here are the coordinates of the planet Tavanna, where Sylvania is. Her pseudonym is Brandelyn Esperanza. She lives in the town of Vasko. We're in the process of mounting a rescue, but we don't have enough ships."

"A rescue? From what?" Star said, unaware she had tightened her grip on Rowan's arm.

"Another Maelstrom has appeared near Tavanna. It's slowly tearing the planet apart. Satellite sensors have registered several massive quakes. Many villages are in ruins."

Rowan absorbed the dire news. "Another Maelstrom? How many people are on Tavanna?"

"Nearly a million," Thorasta said. "We can't possibly evacuate them all in time! We've contacted the Alliance Council and asked for every available ship but I fear it won't be enough."

"Then we'll save as many as we can," Rowan said.

Thorasta nodded and tapped Rowan's recorder. "Playback in five seconds," she said, then broke eye contact and vanished from the Hybrids' senses. Rowan and Star stared blankly at the wall for a moment, then focused as Thorasta's voice issued from the recorder. "Something's happened…"

*

Willa was in her Nocturnal chamber, deep in meditation. Her eyes snapped open and she cried out in pain, as though a thousand electrified needles suddenly penetrated her flesh. Mercifully, the paralyzing sensation passed quickly, though it left her reeling. As she regained her composure, a vision of the new Maelstrom exploded in her mind.

"No. That's impossible!" she cried. Willa rose, slapped her palm against the door and fled from the chamber. Willa ran down the corridor, turned a corner and collided with Opal.

"Ow!"

Willa and Opal rubbed their heads. "Sorry! But something horrible has happened! I need to talk with Sequoia!"

"She was called to an emergency meeting on Andromeda Spaceport," Opal said. "Something about a rescue mission. I didn't catch the details."

"I had a vision," Willa said, still shaking. "There's another Maelstrom!"

Opal was stunned. "What? Where?"

Willa fell into a thousand-yard stare as the vision returned. A terrifying scene of Tavanna being shattered into rubble flooded her mind and set her brain on fire. She cried out in pain.

Opal grabbed Willa's shoulders to steady her. "Willa! What's happening?"

The vision passed. Willa braced herself against the wall. The cool marble felt soothing against her skin. She nodded to Opal as her strength returned. "I'm okay."

Opal kept one hand on Willa's arm, despite her assurances.

Willa drew a deep breath and stood. "I need a star map."

"Come with me," Opal said as she hurried toward a side hall.

Willa followed the young Nocturnal and they entered Sequoia's private chambers.

"Are you sure we should be here?" Willa said, her voice low as though the walls might take exception to their presence.

"Of course. I'm the Provost's personal aide," Opal said. She went to a marble shelf holding dozens of nano-beads and plucked one from the center. She tapped a pattern on it. The bead floated up and opened into a large screen that displayed every star system within the Alliance and several systems beyond its jurisdiction.

Willa studied the map and double-tapped a section on the upper left that was marked in red. It enlarged and revealed a blinking icon at its center.

"This is the Orion Triangle and that..." she pointed to the blinking symbol, "that's the first Maelstrom." She scanned the stars with her enhanced senses. A system at the very edge of Alliance territory illuminated in her vision. "The second Maelstrom is there. The nearby system isn't supposed to be inhabited, but it is. That's where the rescue mission is going."

Opal was puzzled. "A secret planet within the Alliance?"

Willa continued to stare at the map. "Not anymore. Let's go."

Willa tapped the screen. It shrank back into a bead and settled into its dimple on the stone shelf. Willa headed for the hallway.

"Where are we going?" Opal said as she followed Willa out.

"To find Moonstone. I need a stronger draft of Divinorum."

They turned the corner into the hall and stopped as Selene blocked their path.

"What are you both up to?" she demanded.

"We need to find the Provost and Moonstone," Willa said. "Another Maelstrom has appeared."

Selene could sense Willa's anxiety and the pounding of her heart. "I know, but it's crucial that we resume your training."

Willa moved around Selene and continued down the hall, followed by Opal. "Yes, immediately! I need more Divinorum."

"Not so fast," Selene said. "You haven't fully integrated what you experienced in your Initiation ritual."

"But --"

Selene cut off Willa's protest with a gesture. "You may be the best hope the Alliance has of defeating the Archon, but don't let it go to your head. I'm still your sponsor. You're not ready for another draft of Divinorum until I say you're ready, is that understood?"

Selene turned to Opal. "Go about your duties."

Opal bowed her head. "Yes, Doyenne." She hurried down the hall.

Selene cast her obsidian gaze back on Willa and gestured in the opposite direction. "Your chamber. Now."

Willa stood her ground. "But there are lives --"

Selene cut her off again, but this time, in an uncharacteristically gentle tone. "I understand that lives are in danger. The Provost and the Contact Council are handling it. If you don't take the time to properly integrate your Divinorum experiences, you won't be ready when the real danger comes."

Willa fought the urge to argue. She reluctantly saw Selene's point and walked back to her room with the Nocturnal close behind her.

*

Xanthes cried out in pain and collapsed on the stone floor of her chamber. She clutched her temples and writhed in agony as her guard rushed to her aid.

"What is it, my Lady?" the guard said as he knelt beside her, at a loss for how to help. He tapped the com on his wrist. "Med-tech to the Lady's chambers --"

Xanthes gripped his arm. "No!" The pain had stopped but left Xanthes in shock. She caught her breath as the guard tried to help her to her feet. She brushed him off, angry and embarrassed to appear weak.

Uzza entered the chamber, looking like he'd seen a ghost. He fixed his icy gaze on the guard. "Leave us!" he hissed.

The guard bowed and hurried out. Uzza regarded his pupil as she steadied herself against a wall.

"So, you felt it, too."

"Felt what?" she spat back. "What in the name of the Elder Gods was that?"

"The Sensate Order believes it's a rupture in space," Uzza said.

Xanthes frowned. "A second Maelstrom?"

"Possibly."

"Where?"

Uzza shook his head. "That's unclear. The Order seems unable to pinpoint its location. It's not within the Empire. The rupture isn't even registering on satellite sensors. However, it may not be beyond your reach, my Lady."

Fear flickered in her pale eyes. "I'm not about to open my mind to that thing a second time!"

"I believe the worst is over. What we sensed was likely the initial subspace shock wave. Even now, I can feel the energy settling," Uzza said.

Xanthes cautiously extended her senses. "Yes, you're right."

Uzza waved his gnarled hand toward the meditation circle on the floor.

Xanthes hesitated, but her curiosity was far stronger than her fear. She nodded, sat in the center of the circle and closed her eyes.

*

Willa sat on her bed, eyes closed, deep in meditation as Selene stood nearby.

"The first four counterparts you saw in your Initiation will likely be the ones you'll bond with," Selene said. "See them again in your mind's eye. Call them to you."

Willa let the images return. Two of her counterparts were so similar to her, she could've been staring into two different mirrors. The third was old enough that hints of grey were streaked through her fox-colored locks. The fourth was a few years older than Willa, with all-black eyes. The counterpart's skin shifted to a fine pattern of tiny blue scales that rippled like leaves in a slight breeze: A Shapeshifter.

"I see them," she informed Selene.

"Good. Now quiet your own inner voice and search for their thoughts."

Willa took a breath and exhaled. She recalled what Holly had taught her about listening to the trees and hoped the same technique would work with her counterparts. Her thoughts faded, her mind went silent. But instead of hearing the faint whispers of her counterparts' thoughts, her senses were rocked once again by the churning rumble and blinding light of the second Maelstrom.

Willa's body went rigid. Her eyes snapped open to reveal inky black orbs like Selene's. Her head tilted back and her gaze became fixed, as she locked on the Maelstrom with her inner sight.

Selene was alarmed. "Willa? Willa, can you hear me?"

Willa was oblivious to her mentor's presence, her every sense focused on the Maelstrom's destruction of Tavanna. As she had done once before, when she saved Thorn from Brim's deadly blade, Willa's powers rippled outward, engulfed the second Maelstrom and altered the flow of time.

She tried to reverse the anomaly but, drenched in sweat from the strain, the best she could do was slow the Maelstrom so it appeared almost frozen. The Alliance ships would be able to rescue Tavanna's denizens. Somewhere in the deepest recesses of her mind, Willa saw the irony: She had to stop time to give the rescue squad more time to complete their task.

However, the link between her and the anomaly was a two-way street. As Willa reached out with her amplified powers, she simultaneously received flashes of Xanthes, Poppy's mother Sylvania, and horrifying images of her mother and father and all her friends lying dead in the dirt as Port Dublin was devoured by flames and Mystery lay in ruins.

Selene grabbed Willa's shoulders and shook her, frightened by her lack of response. "Willa! Willa, what's happening? Answer me!"

Willa broke from her trance. Her black, Nocturnal eyes reverted to their golden hue.

Selene realized her heart had been racing. She took a breath and forced herself to relax. "Are you okay?"

Willa nodded, still disoriented. "When I connected to my counterparts, I suddenly had the power to control the Maelstrom."

"What did you do?" Selene asked, not sure she wanted to hear the answer.

"I slowed it down, nearly froze it in time, long enough to evacuate the population from the nearby planet." She lapsed into silence but Selene extended her senses toward Willa.

"There's something else, isn't there?" she said.

The door chimed, interrupting Willa before she could answer. She palmed the door open to find Sequoia and Opal in the hall. They entered.

"I just returned from Andromeda," Sequoia said. "We received word that the rescue operation will succeed because the new Maelstrom... well, let's just say it's suddenly cooperating somehow." Sequoia fixed her eyes on Willa. "Was that you're doing?"

Willa nodded.

"What else were you about to tell me, Willa?" Selene prompted.

Willa knew it was pointless to keep the rest of her vision secret. "As I grow stronger, so does Xanthes. The connection between us is like some kind of conduit that amplifies both of our powers."

"It couldn't be helped," Sequoia said. "If it wasn't for you, all those people would have died. The Contact Council will definitely have a talk with the Thook about their little secret, though," she added with disapproval.

"More important than that," Selene interjected, "is why a second Maelstrom has appeared. If the first one connects our universe to another, what parallel reality will the second one lead to? We need to know why this is happening."

"Agreed," Sequoia said. "Willa, please get some rest. When you feel up to it, join me in my chamber." Sequoia signaled Selene to leave as well. She hesitated but understood the Provost's request when she saw Opal move to Willa's side. Selene left with Sequoia. The silver door closed.

"What does Doyenne Nymphaea want from you?" Opal asked.

"What do you mean?" Willa said, knowing exactly what Opal meant.

"Don't be coy. I know her. She's different with you."

"I can't talk about it," Willa said as she rose to her feet.

Opal sat on the bed and peered into Willa's butterscotch eyes. "Aren't you carrying enough on your shoulders? I can tell you need to talk about it with someone. Let me take some of the weight."

Willa shook her head. "That's kind, but I made a promise. I haven't even told my family."

"Well, if you need an ear…"

Willa smiled. "I'll have the voices in my head call the voices in yours."

Opal laughed. She placed a supportive hand on Willa's shoulder. "Remember, I'm here for you."

Willa nodded her appreciation. Opal stood, palmed the door and left the chamber.

Willa squeezed her eyes shut and tried in vain to expunge the vision of her dead family and friends. She opened her eyes, moist with tears and wiped them away as she stood and left the room.

*

Xanthes was locked in a trance inside her meditation circle. With each intake of breath, she felt the witching power grow stronger until the spot on her forehead between her eyes burned like molten iron. Sweat glistened on her grey skin. Her heart thumped against her breastbone; her ears rang. Just as she felt her head was about to split, her vision exploded out into the cosmos faster than light.

She saw the second Maelstrom churning against the stars, the planet Tavanna being torn asunder in its gravitational grasp. As she watched the destruction unfold, Xanthes felt a familiar echo in the deepest recesses of her mind. Another mind reached out from the darkness and penetrated the heart of the Maelstrom. The whirlpool of energy ground to a halt. Mountainous masses that had been ripped from the surface of the planet were suddenly fixed in space as time itself froze.

"Willa!" Xanthes cried out as she snapped from her trance.

Uzza went to her side. "The Earth girl?"

Her mind raced as Xanthes scrambled to her feet and paced. "I felt her power touch the second Maelstrom. She stopped it dead!"

"That's not possible," her mentor said.

Xanthes turned on him, her eyes fierce. "You doubt my word?"

"No, my Lady, I simply meant --"

Xanthes waved him to silence. "She stopped time! Do you understand? She's far more powerful than we imagined!" Xanthes closed her eyes as she parsed what her senses had shown her. She opened her eyes; struggled to put the pieces together. "There's something else. Something she knows about us. About our connection, but…"

"What?" Uzza pushed.

Xanthes shook it off. "It doesn't make sense."

"If I may, my Lady, perhaps we should consult the head of my order?"

"Fine," Xanthes said, still troubled. "But after what I just saw, how can I possibly defeat her?"

"The way it's always been done," Uzza said. "You find your enemy's weakness and exploit it."

Xanthes's confidence slowly returned as she took his meaning. "Her family. Her friends."

Uzza nodded. "You placed a spy among her people. Rooting out their tech secrets is one thing, but demoralizing them is far worse. Use your powers, pull your puppet's strings, create a diversion. While the Earth girl's attention is elsewhere, kill everyone she loves."

*

Aside from Rowan and Star in the cockpit, Rowan's ship *Corvus* held forty passengers, Sylvania among them, though in her mind she was still Brandelyn. Quarters were tight and Brandelyn squeezed her way up to the cockpit, not only to thank Rowan for the rescue, but also to find a measure of breathing room.

"Excuse me, but may I ask where we're going?" Brandelyn said as she positioned herself behind Star's co-pilot seat.

"A planet called Thook," Rowan responded.

"Is that where you're from?"

"No. My home world is called Earth."

"Does everyone on Thook and Earth have ships like this one?"

"Not everyone has their own, but there are large transports that can take groups of people wherever they'd like to go," he said.

"And you're both a part of this… what did you call it? The Alliance?"

"Yes. And so are you," he said cautiously.

"Then why don't we have ships of our own?" Brandelyn said.

Star glanced at Rowan and spun her seat around to face Brandelyn. "Here, sit. See how it feels," she said, changing the subject.

"Oh, I couldn't," Brandelyn protested. "Could I?"

Star rose and offered the chair. Brandelyn smiled and plopped herself down. She gazed at the data streaming across the main view screen along with its display of stars.

"It doesn't feel, or look like we're moving," she remarked, somewhat disappointed.

"The ship has artificial gravity plating," Star explained.

Brandelyn was impressed. "Remarkable."

"We're far enough from the Maelstrom… that's what we call the anomaly… to make our first Q-jump," Rowan said. "Corvus, please initiate when ready."

"Initiating jump in three, two, one, mark," the computer said.

The engine hummed with power. The stars distorted on the view screen and collapsed into a circular rainbow of light, then expanded again to reveal a different set of constellations. Brandelyn felt a strange queasiness in her stomach but it quickly settled.

"What just happened?" she asked.

"We just jumped thirty light years," Rowan said with a smile.

Brandelyn gazed at the stellar display, then locked her maple brown eyes on Rowan. "I'll ask again, if we belong to this Alliance of yours, why do you have this technology and my people don't?"

"That's a long story," Rowan said. "A *very* long story. There's someone on Thook who can explain it better than I can."

Brandelyn spun her seat halfway around so she could see both Rowan and Star. Her brow furrowed as she studied their faces.

"What?" Star said.

"You both seem so familiar," Brandelyn said, her mind searching for a memory that wasn't there. "But we can't have met before."

Star threw a nervous glance at Rowan who turned to face his curious passenger. "My name's Rowan. Rowan Ashgrove. This is Star. What's your name?"

"Brandelyn Esperanza."

Rowan extended his hand. "Pleased to meet you."

Brandelyn couldn't shake the feeling that she knew Rowan and Star but, though she struggled to clear the fog in her mind, she failed to dredge up any memory of having met them before. She gave up and shook Rowan's hand. "Very pleased to meet you. Thank you both for rescuing us."

"I'm just happy we made it in time," he said.

Brandelyn rose and gave the chair back to Star. "How soon will we arrive at…"

"Thook. Within the hour. Please tell your friends they'll be well taken care of. The Alliance will find new homes for all of you," Rowan pledged.

Brandelyn nodded her gratitude and went back to the main cabin to share the good news. Rowan turned to Star, his voice low.

"The Maelstrom should've torn that planet to shreds long before we got there," he said. "I sense Willa's hand in this."

"If she's grown that powerful, maybe we have a chance against the Empire after all," Star said hopefully.

"Maybe," Rowan parroted, but secretly, he was more worried about what kind of toll the effort had taken on Willa. He pushed the thought down and turned to the computer. "Initiate the next jump, Corvus."

"Initiating jump in three, two, one, mark."

The display of stars collapsed once again and the ship bounded across the void.

*

Zaduga, the wizened head of the Sensate Order, sat stiff-backed in his carved, ironwood chair. Uzza and Xanthes stood before him in his circular stone chamber. Xanthes's pale eyes took in the bizarre assemblage of occult objects that filled the alcoves and niches set into the rough-hewn walls. A row of ancient, red, leather-bound books held the collective knowledge of the Sensates going back several thousand years. Xanthes had heard of these rare tomes but few outside the Order had ever laid eyes on them.

Aside from the Archon, no others in the Empire, not even the Overlords, were feared or granted the respect given to the head of the Sensate Order. His influence and loyalty to the Archon kept power struggles among the Overlords to a minimum. In addition, the Sensate Order's knowledge of genetics allowed Xos-Asura to maintain his legion of Splicers: One million genetically enhanced and utterly obedient soldiers that patrolled the Empire and quelled rebellions with ruthless efficiency.

Such knowledge also led the Order to discover the ancient Anu gene that gave the Archon's daughter her unusual powers. Xanthes knew that Uzza had been grooming her to join the Order. She also knew that her unique abilities, when properly enhanced, would make Zaduga and the Sensates more powerful than the Archon and all the Overlords combined. If there was one thing Xanthes knew deep in her bones, it was the putrid scent of unbridled ambition. Zaduga and Uzza stank of it. No matter. She had sensed their secret plan to control her long ago and, when the right time came, she would turn the tables on them and take Zaduga's place as head of the Sensates, as well as usurp her father's throne: a two-pronged coup. Once the worlds of the Alliance were annexed, she'd be more powerful than any Archon in history.

"Shall we begin, my Lady?" Zaduga said.

Xanthes nodded and stepped closer to him. Zaduga reached out with one gaunt arm and placed his gnarled, grey fingers on her forehead. He closed his eyes and allowed flashes of her vision to flow like electricity along his neural pathways and deep into his brain. It took every ounce of self-control to remain stoic as the Maelstrom's power assaulted his senses. Zaduga marveled at the girl's ability to survive the mental onslaught with her sanity intact. It also gave him pause: *are we truly be able to control her?* He would have to proceed cautiously, lest she foil their plan.

Willa's image flickered through his mind like an elusive ghost, along with a flash of insight that forced Zaduga to retract his hand as though he'd been burned. His ashen eyes snapped open.

The Sensate rose from his chair and hurried over to the leather books. He plucked one from the shelf and searched through the delicate parchment pages.

Uzza had never seen his aged mentor move so quickly. "My Lord?" he queried.

Zaduga kept silent until he found what he was looking for. He scanned the arcane writing, then closed the book with a decisive clap. He gently replaced the volume and turned toward Uzza and Xanthes, his lined face etched with disbelief.

Uzza allowed a moment of silence before he ventured a guess. "You understand the connection between the Earth girl and our Lady?"

Zaduga slowly nodded. "There's a very old theory that suggests our universe isn't the only one. That many other universes exist as well."

"What are you talking about?" Xanthes said. "How can there be other universes?"

"A simple analogy would be different communications channels," Zaduga began. "They can overlap and interpenetrate one another and still deliver discreet information due to the different frequencies they operate on. The theory states that many universes overlap our own, but remain separate and invisible to our senses because they exist on different frequencies."

"Interesting as that may be for our techs, what's that got to do with my connection to Willa?" Xanthes said impatiently.

"You and the Earth girl don't live in the same universe. I believe the Maelstrom isn't merely a magnetic anomaly. It's a tunnel between our universe and hers."

Xanthes focused her witching senses on Zaduga. "What aren't you telling me?"

Zaduga met her gaze squarely. "My Lady, hard as this may be to accept, you and the Earth girl... the reason for your connection to each other... you and she are the same person in two different realities."

Xanthes stared at the aged Sensate and wondered if he'd gone insane. He continued to stare at her in earnest as if he could make her understand by sheer force of will. Though it troubled her to admit it, Xanthes could tell that Zaduga was dead serious and most likely telling the truth.

"You're saying I'm her and she's me."

"According to the theory, we may have alternate versions of ourselves in each universe. That's not all. I sense that you're feeding off each other's power," Zaduga explained.

Xanthes puzzled it out in her mind. "Like we're each tapping into the power of both universes instead of just one."

"Yes," Zaduga said.

Uzza approached his pupil. "Then, if you're evenly matched, it's more critical than ever that we tip the balance of power in your favor, my Lady, and the sooner, the better. You must send a message to your spy."

Xanthes understood. She gave Zaduga a faint bow of her head. "Thank you, Master Sensate. You've done the Empire a great service."

Zaduga bowed more formally. "I live to serve, my Lady."

Xanthes left the chamber without the standard reply -- an unprecedented sign of respect.

Uzza smiled at his mentor. "Never-ending are the Nine," he said softly as he followed Xanthes out.

"Never-ending," Zaduga replied. The plan to use the Archon's daughter for their own gain had to work. Zaduga imagined it wouldn't be long before Xanthes sat in her father's place. Zaduga would have to muster all his arcane abilities to make sure that, when the time came, she would bend to the Sensate's will.

Chapter Six:
SYNCHRONICITY

"Long ago, the word 'coincidence' meant something accidental. Although two events appeared to be related, it was believed the relationship was nothing more than an illusion; a random statistical anomaly. Of course, we now understand that there are no true accidents; that everything is an orchestration unfolding from a higher plane of consciousness in perfect timing. In other words, synchronicity is simply a space-time demonstration that everything is interconnected; that everything is one."

"The Book of Paradox"
By Sassafras the Sage

*

SYLVANIA AWOKE ON A SOFT PALLET of nano-sponge designed to support her body in complete comfort. Her all-black Nocturnal eyes blinked at the iridescent reflections from the crystalline walls of the Thook memory chamber. She sat up and glanced around at the empty room.

"Hello?"

Thorasta stepped into her line of sight and appeared out of thin air. "Ah, good, you're awake."

"Who are you? Where am I?" Sylvania said, somewhat disoriented.

"Don't worry, you're safe," the Mind Master said in a calm voice. "My name is Thorasta. Your friends will explain everything."

"My friends?"

Thorasta stepped away and vanished from Sylvania's senses. A moment later, Rowan and Star entered the chamber sporting cautious smiles.

"Hello," Rowan said. "Do you remember me?"

Sylvania sat up, her brow furrowed in concentration. "You're... one of Kale Ashgrove's sons. Thorn... no... Rowan."

"That's right. This is Star."

Sylvania cocked her head, the memory a bit vague. "Star... as in Stargazer?"

Star nodded and split into twins. "The one and only." She blended back into one.

Sylvania went cold as her memory flooded back with a shock. "Wait! What are you doing here? How did you find me?"

"Willa and Poppy had a hunch --"

Sylvania got off the pallet in a flash. "My daughter! I came here to protect her! By finding me you've put her in great danger!"

Rowan raised his hands to calm her. "Let us explain."

Sylvania paced, her mood desperate. "I came here so the Thook could hide me, send me somewhere that horrid grey girl can't use me to hurt Poppy."

"They did," Rowan said. "But you were in danger. We had to bring you back."

"What are you talking about? I just got here."

"No," Star said. "You've been gone for nearly a year."

"What?"

Rowan gestured to the pallet. "Please. It's a long story."

"A very long story," added Star.

Sylvania radiated skepticism.

"Please," Rowan said with his irresistible smile.

Poppy's mother sat on the pallet and crossed her arms. "This better be a damn good story."

*

Andromeda Spaceport floated high above Earth, its massive ring of docking bays topped by the squat mushroom that contained the command and control center as well as the science labs.

Willa sat at a conference table in a room adjacent to the Deep Space Phenomena Lab along with Holly, Selene, and the Hybrid head of astronomy, Jacaranda Florus. The eight-pointed star tattoo on her shaved head was slightly distorted by furrows of concern. Ander Garza, Jacaranda's human friend and fellow astronomer, entered the room in a hurry.

"Sorry I'm late," he said as he took the empty seat next to Jacaranda. "Things are crazy around here since that second Maelstrom showed up."

"That's why we're meeting. Willa's noticed something curious about it," Jacaranda said. She spoke to the air. "Ocularis, please display a star map with both anomalies."

"They're displayed in red," the station's computer announced as the holographic map sprang into being above the table.

Jacaranda turned to Willa. "Please show Ander what you discovered. Feel free to have Ocularis assist you."

"When I saw the second Maelstrom in my Divinorum vision, I also sensed something odd about its location." As most people instinctively did, Willa lifted her head slightly to speak to Ocularis. Though everyone knew it wasn't necessary, it somehow felt rude not to address the sentient computer's floating orb camera directly, as if it was another person in the room.

"Ocularis, please display the distance from both anomalies to Earth," Willa said.

Lines of light immediately appeared between Earth's blue dot and the two red dots of the Maelstroms. Readouts indicated the distance of both anomalies as one- thousand-five-hundred light-years.

"The distances are identical," Ander said, stating the obvious. "What are the chances of that?"

"It can't be a mere coincidence," Jacaranda said.

"It's not," Willa agreed. "Ocularis, please display the distance between the two Maelstroms."

Another line appeared, linking the two red dots. The distance read two-thousand-six-hundred light-years.

Ander perked up. "Wait. Based on axes of fifteen hundred light-years, that's exactly the base length of an equilateral triangle."

"Yes," Willa concurred. "Ocularis, please draw an equilateral triangle with those dimensions."

The triangle appeared on the map and Willa pointed to the apex on the opposite side of Earth, exactly fifteen hundred light-years distant. "I predict that a third Maelstrom will appear here."

Everyone in the room stared at the glowing triangle and the empty space Willa had pointed to.

Holly turned to Willa. "Do you know when?"

Willa shook her head. "No, but I sense it won't be long."

"At least there are no inhabited planets near that location," Jacaranda said with relief. "Ocularis, can you hypothesize what could be causing these phenomena?"

"The only other energy pattern in my database that matches the Maelstrom's signature is the one generated by Shapeshifters and Sages when they alter their form or that of the reality around them. However, although the patterns are similar, the frequency in the Maelstrom is much higher. I don't have sufficient data on Wraiths to do a full comparison, but I can extrapolate that the shift from Sage to Wraith would generate the same frequency as the anomaly."

Selene was skeptical. "Are you saying the Maelstroms are a side effect of Sages who successfully transform into Wraiths?"

"I cannot prove it, but it fits all the present data as the most likely hypothesis," the computer responded. "A spectral analysis of the single recording in Alliance memory banks of a Sage transforming into a Wraith contains subspace frequencies, identical to those in the Maelstroms."

Willa and Selene exchanged a furtive glance. The astronomers didn't catch it, but Holly's senses read the look like a book. She addressed Jacaranda and Ander.

"Would you give us the room for a moment?"

"Certainly," Jacaranda said. She and Ander stood and exited. The door slid shut.

"Ocularis, please provide privacy mode," Holly said.

"Privacy mode on." A glowing button appeared on the tabletop. "Please tap the control to restore normal recording." The computer's camera light switched off.

Selene broke the awkward silence that followed. "I know what you're thinking, Holly."

"No, Selene, I don't think you do because I've never wanted to punch someone before." She gestured at Willa. "That's what you want from her, isn't it? You want her to use her abilities to learn the formula that will transform you into a Wraith. You don't even want to go through the Shapeshifter and Sage levels first, do you?"

"Don't judge me!" Selene snapped. "You don't even want to become a Nocturnal. You're perfectly content talking to the trees and those meddling Nature Spirits! You don't know the effort it takes… the struggle it's been to get this far!"

"Selene, the Mastery is a calling, not a race," Holly said, trying to be diplomatic.

Selene stood and peered down at Holly and Willa. "The Earth, the entire Alliance is about to be invaded! We need all the advantages we can get!"

Willa stood, her mood defiant. "You heard the computer. If you become a Wraith, you might create more ruptures. You said it yourself, we're already in danger of being attacked from one parallel reality. Who knows what might come through other portals!"

Selene ignored her, her ire focused on Holly. "We can't rely on one 'special' girl to save us! We have to take the risk!"

Holly stood between Willa and Selene. "That's not your decision!"

"It is if no one else has the courage to make it!" Selene stormed out of the room. Holly and Willa stared at the door. Neither spoke until Holly calmed herself and took her seat. Willa sat as well, more because she felt weak in the knees.

"Are you going to report her to the Council?" Willa said.

"She'll be tossed out of Mystery and stripped of her powers," Holly said. "She'd never be able to become a Cryptic again let alone a Wraith. I'm not ready to go that far, unless she forces my hand."

Willa was stunned. "I didn't know that was possible."

"It's not something we talk about until it's warranted. It takes a Sage and a special draft of Divinorum, but yes, it can be done," Holly said with genuine sadness. "I probably shouldn't have told you that, but these are... unusual times." Holly stood. "I need to meditate on this and seek counsel from the Quorum."

"If it's okay with you, I'd like to sit here a while."

Holly nodded and left. Willa knew there was no love lost between Holly and Selene at the best of times, but it was doubly disturbing to feel the conflicting energy that was now widening the fracture between them. She sensed that fracture might spread, not only between the various lodges of Mastery but throughout the Alliance, making it an easier target for the Archon and his ambitious daughter. Willa couldn't help wondering if her growing powers were making things better or worse.

She glanced down at the glowing button on the tabletop and tapped it. The light on the computer's camera orb came back to life.

"Privacy mode terminated," Ocularis said. "How may I be of service?"

Willa weighed her options and came to a decision. "I need to borrow a ship."

*

94

"I've come to love this mint tea," Alarra said as she set the tray of steaming cups on the table. "We have nothing so fresh in the League."

Dennik, Brim, and Gar savored the aroma as Alarra took her seat. Variabilis set his cup aside and continued tinkering with the computer core that Gar had retrieved from Haldane's hidden ship.

"So, Gant will return to our universe with us? I still can't get used to saying that," Alarra mused. "It's strange to think we're in a different reality."

"Strangeness is the normal state of existence," Variabilis said. "Regarding Gant, I don't trust him and neither should you."

"He saved my father," Brim said.

"I and my fellow Shapeshifter saved your father," Variabilis reminded him. "We suspected Gant and Haldane from the start and clearly, we were right to do so."

Brim sat back in his chair. "Just because Haldane was a spy --"

"Let's not forget Koro," Gar said, cutting Brim off. "A traitor in our midst. I agree with Variabilis. We can't be too careful."

"We'll keep a close watch on him," Dennik said. "Tighten security measures in the League."

Alarra sipped her tea. "This plan of his --"

"Right!" Brim jumped in, "why would Gant come up with a plan to defeat the Archon if he wasn't on our side?"

"We have an old saying, Brim," the Shapeshifter said. "Nature abhors a vacuum. I suspect Gant wants to fill it."

"Possibly," Alarra said, "but will his plan work?"

"Yes, it could work, although I think we might need more than one of my kind to carry it out. As I told Gant, we're a solitary bunch and don't easily get caught up in other people's affairs."

"But this isn't just about our universe," Dennik said. "Your Alliance is in danger as well."

"I'm just saying the Council may have another strategy. There are nearly a hundred fifty worlds in the Alliance. No matter how powerful the Archon and his army may be, they can't attack but a fraction of them at once. If they spread themselves too thin, we might defeat them," Variabilis said.

"At what cost?" Dennik said. "Millions would die in such a war. Wouldn't it be better to take the fight to them with a small army of Shapeshifting infiltrators?"

"Perhaps," Variabilis admitted. "But Gant's plan doesn't guarantee success. Even though Shapeshifters can take on some of the qualities of those they mimic, we don't possess the Mark that makes Willa and Xanthes so powerful. If the Archon's daughter senses the plan, we'll fail, no matter how stealthy we are, and we'll also lose the element of surprise. Far as Willa can tell, the Archon doesn't know Shapeshifters exist yet."

"Granted, there are risks either way," Alarra said. "We'll discuss it further but please know that we're grateful for your help thus far."

"No problem." Variabilis finished with the computer core and set it in the center of the table. "I added a vocal interface, so you can just ask it what you want to know."

Gar leaned forward, eager to interrogate the machine. "What can you tell us about Gant?"

"There are no files in core memory of an individual named Gant," the computer responded in a matter-of-fact tone. Gar sat back, frustrated. "Great. All that for nothing."

"Perhaps a different approach," Variabilis suggested. "Computer, access your sensor logs. How many individuals did you record on the ship during the most recent trip?"

"Two."

"Do you have sensor readings on them?"

"Yes."

"Provide details."

"The pilot is Haldane Ket. In service to the Empire for twenty cycles. Sensor readings include blood pressure, respiration rate, genetic integrity --"

"Stop," Variabilis said. "Explain genetic integrity."

"Scans determine if an individual's general health matches their genetic norm."

"Are you saying you know Haldane's genetic code?"

"Yes."

Variabilis looked at the others around the table, then continued to question the computer. "Did your scans include the genetic code of the second individual?"

"Yes."

Variabilis pulled a nano-bead from his pocket and held it next to the computer's remote access terminal. "Download that information to this device."

"Download complete," the computer said.

"Why do you want that?" Dennik said with a puzzled frown.

"I need to check out a hunch," Variabilis said as he rose from his seat. The Shapeshifter headed out the door as four confused faces watched him go.

*

Five hundred years ago, a large asteroid was captured by Earth's gravity and, after some minor adjustments to Earth's tides and weather patterns that lasted over a decade, the asteroid entered a gravitationally-locked orbit between Earth and the Moon. With its faster orbit and a large crater that had the appearance of an eye, it sped around the Earth like a watchful guardian and was unanimously dubbed The Sentinel.

*

Willa walked down the spaceport corridor that led to the scout ship bay. She stopped outside the bay airlock door and waited until a couple of crimson-scaled Shinzai aliens walked past her and headed down a side hall. The coast clear, she faced the coded keypad set into the reflective wall.

"Ocularis, override the access code and open the bay doors."

"You are not cleared to use a scout ship," the computer said.

Willa closed her eyes and concentrated. "Do it," she said.

The code numbers flickered across the screen and the airlock doors slid open with a soft hiss of equalizing air.

"Now erase any record of my presence here." The keypad went blank. Willa entered and doors slid shut behind her.

Willa surveyed the row of scout ships in their berths and chose a sleek black one. She used her powers once again to get Ocularis to open the coded hatch and release the docking clamps without any of it registering on the control boards in the command center.

Willa buckled into the pilot's seat and brought the view screens to life. "Activate autopilot," she commanded. The control console lit up and the engine hummed its readiness. "Set coordinates for the Sentinel Moon. Open the outer airlock. Proceed at one-tenth sublight."

The gleaming scout ship slipped from its berth and approached the outer airlock doors just as they parted. Willa and the ship sped into space and angled toward the Sentinel moon. Willa's fingers flew over the ship's console as she plotted a course straight for the Sentinel's eye.

*

Ensconced in Andromeda's command center, Vas-Basso, a pink-skinned alien with four prehensile limbs and an equal number of iridescent eyes, saw Willa's scout ship on one of the dozens of screens that fed information to the controllers. Vas tapped the com-link and engaged his translator.

"Scout seventy-seven, do you copy?"

Vas was met with silence. He tried to hail the ship several more times to no avail.

"Commander Erebus!" Vas-Basso's translator barked for attention.

Commander Ivy Erebus, a regal-looking Hybrid in a crisp, white Alliance uniform, focused her large, pale green eyes on the controller.

"What is it, Vas?"

"External sensors just picked up scout ship seventy-seven leaving the station!"

"On whose authorization code?"

"None, Commander. All codes were bypassed without a single warning on my console," the alien squeaked. "The ship's not responding to my hails, either."

"Send a patrol ship after it," Erebus ordered. "Tell them to tractor it if they have to but get that ship back in its dock and find out who's flying it!"

"Yes, Commander!"

*

Willa was almost to the Sentinel Moon when her ship's com link beeped for attention. She tapped the control and was greeted by the measured voice of Captain Bracken.

"Scout seventy-seven, this is Captain Bracken of the patrol fleet. Who am I addressing?"

"Hello, Captain, it's Willa Hillicrissing."

The silence of outer space filled the cabin for several heartbeats.

"What are you doing, Willa?"

"Something that only I can do, Captain."

"I must insist you return to Andromeda Spaceport immediately," Bracken said. "If you refuse, I'll be forced to use my command code to take over your controls."

"You can try, but it won't work," Willa said.

There were another few moments of silence as Willa sensed the Captain's attempt to make good on her threat. The scout ship sped onward, impervious to outside interference.

"Willa, why are you doing this? You're putting yourself in danger. Please turn back," Bracken pleaded.

"The fate of the Alliance is on my shoulders, Captain. I've refused to believe it... tried to shrug it off. I see now that it's my destiny, my mission. I can't avoid it any longer."

"What are you talking about?"

"Please tell my mother and father I'm doing this for them... for everyone," Willa said, her gaze fixed on a plan only she could see.

"Willa, where are you going?"

"To face my fear." Willa cut off the com-link. "Prepare for Q-jump," she instructed the computer.

"Q-jump ready," the ship said.

"Increase speed to one-quarter sub-light. Maintain course," Willa said.

"Present course will impact Sentinel," the computer reported. "Altering course to avoid --"

"Override!" Willa said. "Maintain course."

The Sentinel grew larger on the scout's view screen as the ship shot directly toward the eye.

*

Captain Bracken watched on her screen as the stolen scout ship sped toward the asteroid moon. She tried her com-link again. "What the hell are you doing, Willa? You've got to veer off!"

The scout ship plummeted into the deep crater and, for a moment, the crater rim blocked Bracken's sensors. A split second later, her screens were washed out by the blinding flash of an impact on the crater floor.

"Willa!"

Moments later, Bracken piloted her patrol ship over the crater. Her heart sank as she scanned the new, molten crater that formed a glowing pupil in the center of the eye. Her sensors revealed hundreds of shards of smoldering metal embedded in the crater wall and in the atomized dust cloud that rose up into space: the remnants of the scout craft.

"Willa, what have you done?"

Stunned, Captain Bracken floated over the cooling crater. She dreaded the task she knew would fall to her: telling Willa's family and friends that she was gone. Her com-link beeped. The Captain hesitated, then tapped her control to receive the message.

"Andromeda Command to Captain Bracken. Report."

Bracken squeezed her eyes shut and took a deep breath. She opened them, wiped away a tear and steadied her voice. "This is Bracken. Scout ship seventy-seven is down. I repeat, scout seventy-seven is down."

*

Scout ship seventy-seven popped back into normal space just beyond the Centauri system, four-and-a-half light-years from Earth. Willa checked her readouts. Everything appeared to be operating within acceptable levels. She let out a sigh of relief. Jettisoning the sub-light power core and jumping a split second before it exploded on the asteroid was a risky plan but it had worked. With any luck, Captain Bracken would report that Willa and the scout ship had been vaporized. She hated to break her parents' hearts, allowing them to believe she was dead, but it was the only way to carry out her self-imposed mission without interference.

"Patch into the Q-jump drive to power the sub-light engines," Willa said to the computer.

"Q-jump capacity will be reduced by fifty percent," the computer said. "Maximum jump range will be down to ten light-years with a fifteen-minute recharge between jumps. Sub-light engines will operate at one-quarter capacity."

"It's okay," Willa said, "I'm in no hurry. Initiate the patch and report when you're ready to make the next jump."

"Copy," the computer responded as it carried out its orders.

*

Rowan's ship was on the final approach to Andromeda Spaceport. All the survivors from Tavanna had disembarked on Thook save Sylvania, who sat in a passenger seat behind Star as Rowan piloted them homeward.

"We sent a message to Poppy," Rowan said. "She'll be at the station when we arrive."

"Don't get me wrong," Sylvania said, "I'll be happy to see my daughter, but I'm still not sure this is the best thing for her."

"We're here for you, Syl. Strength in numbers," Star said with a smile.

"Please don't call me that. Human children used to tease me and call me 'Silly' when I was a kid."

Star's smile faded. "Sorry, Doyenne Rousseau. I meant no disrespect."

"Sylvania's fine. After all, you did save my life."

Star's smile returned. "Sylvania, then."

Though grateful for Rowan's rescue, Sylvania was still skeptical as to whether or not she and her daughter were truly safe from Xanthes. As one of the rare humans to become a Nocturnal, Sylvania knew she was on a slippery mental slope. Without Hybrid genetics, she would never be as powerful as the other Nocturnals, no matter how much Divinorum she took, which meant she'd likely never become a Shapeshifter or a Sage. Connecting to her parallel-reality counterparts and sorting through their voices often made her lose touch with her reality. She kept a tight grasp on her emotions so she wouldn't get caught up in a life that wasn't hers. It made her appear cold and distant at times, which hurt Poppy, but if she relaxed, Xanthes's mental assaults could force Sylvania to do her bidding, a possibility that would be far more dangerous for her daughter.

However, now that she knew she'd been living under an assumed identity for nearly a year, and knowing what happened to Tavanna, she realized that path was closed to her. Perhaps Rowan and Star were right. Maybe Poppy's friend Willa could use her powers to help Sylvania strengthen her resistance to Xanthes's influence.

She was still running various options through her mind as Rowan's ship docked in its berth at the Spaceport. As the three of them emerged from the airlock, Poppy ran to her mother and held her in a hug so tight, Sylvania had trouble catching her breath.

"I'm so sorry, my darling, for what I've put you through," she said as she held Poppy's tear-stained face in her hands. Poppy released a series of heart-breaking sobs, unable to speak. Tears flowed down her cheeks and onto her mother's palms.

"It's okay, Poppy, I'm here now. I'll never leave you again, I promise."

Poppy looked at her mother's smile; at Rowan's and Star's tender expressions at their reunion. "You haven't heard..." she managed between sobs.

"Heard what?" Rowan said as his smile faded.

"Willa's gone!" Poppy pressed her face against Sylvania's breast, her body wracked with sorrow as Sylvania wrapped her in a comforting hug.

Sylvania knelt and took her daughter by the shoulders. "What do you mean, gone?"

Poppy rubbed at her eyes, barely able to see. "She stole a ship. She lost control and crashed on the Sentinel Moon!"

Rowan and Star were stunned. "Are you certain?" Rowan pressed in disbelief.

"A patrol ship saw it happen. She's gone forever!" Poppy broke down in tears again. Sylvania held her close.

Rowan guided Sylvania and Poppy to a bench in the waiting area near the airlock and sat next to the mother and her bereft daughter. Star stood nearby to give them some space.

"Poppy," Rowan began as gently as he could, "do you know why Willa would steal a ship or where she was going?"

Poppy just shook her head, at a loss.

Rowan rubbed Poppy's back and stood. He turned to Star. "Something about this is off. I need to find answers."

"I'll come with you," Star said.

Rowan nodded, grateful for the company. He turned to Sylvania. "Will you be alright?"

Sylvania nodded. "Please let us know what you find out."

"Thank you," Poppy said in a small voice. "Thank you for finding my mother."

Rowan kept a tight lid on the storm of emotions swirling within him. He gave Poppy a quick nod and hurried out with Star.

*

Scout ship seventy-seven floated in space a hundred thousand klicks from the original Maelstrom. Even at this distance, the anomaly filled Willa's view screen. With her Q-jump and sub-light engines compromised, it had taken her a day and a half and nearly one-hundred-fifty jumps to travel fifteen hundred light-years when, with full power, it would normally only have taken just over four hours. Thankfully, all scout ships were stocked with a week's supply of rations and a food printer in the event of an emergency. Willa nibbled on a nut-based protein bar as she pondered her next move.

She finished her snack, closed her eyes and took several deep breaths. Willa stretched her senses into the Maelstrom and, with some trial and error, deduced the safest route through the churning gravitational turbulence.

Willa opened her eyes and entered the course on the control console.

"Computer, take the Q-jump engines offline. Route all power except life support and sub-light engines to the shields. Follow the course I've laid in at maximum speed."

"Initiating command," the computer said. The scout ship bolted toward the Maelstrom at one-quarter the speed of light and entered its rotating maw. Willa concentrated as hard as she could to slow down the powerful currents within the anomaly as she had done with the Maelstrom at Tavanna, but despite her best efforts, the ship was still hit hard by gravity waves and electromagnetic discharges that nearly buckled the hull.

Moments seemed like an eternity, but the ship finally broke through the portal and entered the alternate universe at high speed. Willa brought power back to her control console and the Q-jump engines and allowed the ship to continue on sheer momentum. She scanned the area and didn't slow down until she found an asteroid field within jumping distance.

She ordered the computer to jump the ship into the field and she landed on the largest chunk of rock she could find. Willa hoped the asteroid would conceal her from the Archon's patrol ships should their sensors happen to glance her way.

She released a marble-sized sensor probe into space as an early warning system against any unwanted company and settled in for the long haul. She'd have to use her powers very cautiously so Xanthes wouldn't sense her presence. Once she had a viable plan, Willa would draw the Archon's daughter from her well-protected inner sanctum and make sure that Xanthes would never threaten anyone again.

*

Holly, Kale, and Thorn sat around the nano-glass dining table in the Nest with Willa's parents, Lily and River. The mood was somber. Though their plates and bowls were full of aromatic vegetables, no one had touched a thing.

Lily, ever the gracious host who always put others before herself, looked up from her plate and felt the dark clouds hanging over the heads of her guests. There were tears in Thorn's eyes as well as River's.

"Everyone… please eat."

The others emerged from their trances and picked at their food in silence. Lily tried to set an example by eating a mushroom but was too choked up to swallow. She covered her eyes with her palms and sobbed. River rubbed her back but the gesture brought little comfort.

"My little girl," Lily cried. "Why would she do this? It doesn't make sense!"

A sleeping thought awoke in Holly's mind. "No, it doesn't, does it?"

"The Nocturnals are responsible," Thorn said, his tone bitter. "They probably pushed her too hard. She wasn't ready."

"I'm sure that's not the case," Kale said.

"No, I don't think so, either," Holly added.

"What are you saying," River prodded.

Holly took a moment to double-check her Cryptic senses. "I think Willa is alive."

"But the patrol Captain --"

"I know what she said," Holly countered, "but I still feel connected to Willa and not just because she's in my heart."

"How can we be sure you're not just sensing her spirit?" Lily said.

"I thought only Wraiths could do that," Kale said.

"Some Sensitives can talk to spirits as well," River added. He looked at Holly. "Is that among your gifts?"

Holly wanted to give River and Lily hope, but she could only shake her head in silence.

Thorn brightened. "Then let's talk to a Wraith."

"Good luck finding one," Holly said. "They're elusive at the best of times. Last I heard, there are only seven in the whole world and the location of their lodge is a well-guarded secret." She paused as a thought crossed her mind: *There would've been eight if Belladonna had succeeded.*

Thorn wasn't ready to give up. "What about the Pookas? Can't they talk to spirits? They would know if Willa's crossed over, wouldn't they?"

"They're Nature Spirits," Holly said. "It's not the same thing."

Thorn turned to River. "Well, what about those Sensitives, then? Where can we find one?"

"We may not need to," Holly said, following her earlier thought.

Lily turned her liquid eyes to Holly. "What do you mean?"

"Belladonna."

"The Banshee? This is no time for jokes," River said.

Holly pressed on. "She bridges the worlds of the living and the dead. She might know if Willa's alive or in spirit."

Kale was more than a little surprised. "You can talk to a Banshee?"

Holly nodded. "Willa spoke with her often." She turned her gaze back to Lily. "It's worth a try."

Lily clasped River's hand and nodded, a glint of hope in her eyes.

*

Variabilis entered the medical sector within Andromeda Spaceport's science ring. He stared at a glowing map of the extensive complex that was displayed in the ring's hub.

"May I help you find someone?" said Ocularis.

"Doctor Velika Policarpo."

"Please follow the blue line to section forty-seven."

A glowing blue line appeared in the nano-glass floor and snaked through the corridors to the left.

Variabilis thanked the computer and made his way down the labyrinthine hallways that led to his quarry.

A chime sounded as the Shapeshifter entered the medical lab in section forty-seven. Velika, a strikingly beautiful alien the color of persimmon, sat at a lab bench. She turned her warm, almond-shaped eyes toward the door.

"Can I help --" Her broad smile turned to a frown as she beheld her guest. "Variabilis. What the hell are you doing here?"

The Shapeshifter maintained his composure, despite the Doctor's venom. "Velika. It's good to see you."

"Oh, I see. You've gone insane. The psychiatric ward is down on level ten. Goodbye."

"This is important," Variabilis added.

Velika narrowed her gaze at him. "Do I need to call security?"

"How many times do I have to say that I didn't know it was your sister?"

"Oh, because all Kerrithani look alike to you?" Velika spat back.

"You're identical twins! She pretended to be you. I'm a Shapeshifter, not a mind reader. Your problem is with her, not me. But this is no time to argue. The Alliance is facing imminent danger and I need your help."

Velika was taken aback. "What danger? What the hell are you talking about?"

"Last year, two bodies were brought to this station and put in stasis under high security," Variabilis said. "You know who I'm talking about?"

Velika nodded. "The suicide and the murder victim. There have been rumors…"

Velika sat in her chair as she put the pieces together. She lowered her voice. "Rumors that there might be an invasion. You're saying this is connected?"

Variabilis nodded.

"I wondered why Commander Erebus secured their files under Need-To-Know."

"Well, there's something I need to know. Will your security clearance get us into that section?"

"Us? You're out of your mind."

"Alright, then, just you." Variabilis pulled the nano-bead from his pocket. "I need you to compare their DNA profiles to the one on this bead."

Velika thought it through. "Yes, I have clearance. But if they check the logs, see what information I accessed, there'll be questions I can't answer. I could lose my job."

"You're right. I don't want to get you in trouble. I'm sorry, I shouldn't have come. And... I'm sorry about the thing with Variel. I guess I should have known you would never talk about your sister the way she talked about you... pretending she was you, talking about her... but I guess really talking about you, of course. Well, you get the idea."

"What? What did she say about me?"

"I don't want to cause any more bad blood between you. Sorry to have bothered you, Velika. I'll be going now. Take care." Variabilis headed for the door. Velika went to him, grabbed his arm and spun him around.

"You can't leave it like that! If you want me to believe you really didn't know you were sleeping with Variel, then tell me what she said about me."

"Well, technically, she was talking about herself --"

"Tell me!"

Variabilis let out a resigned sigh. "She said you were as cold as the cadavers in your morgue. That you'd never have a real relationship because you prefer the dead to the living."

Velika struggled to keep her temper in check. "That little --"

Variabilis gently removed her hand from his arm. "I've said too much. I should go." He passed through the door.

"Vari..."

Variabilis stopped in the hall. Turned his black eyes back to her.

"I'm sorry."

"I'm sorry, too."

"Maybe, when the danger's passed, we could..."

Variabilis gave her a curt nod. "Maybe." He headed down the corridor as Velika added one more regret to a very long list.

Chapter Seven:
BRIDGES

"The concept of parallel realities took time for human society to absorb. Even today, hundreds of years after the theory was first proposed, most people still think of alternate universes as being somewhere 'out there,' as opposed to the truth that all realities reside at, and are accessible from, every point in existence.

Put another way, everything exists 'here and now' in a sort of overlapping holographic matrix, separated only by a difference in frequency."

Excerpt from the introduction to the
"First Interstellar Symposium on the
Physics of Parallel Realities" in 2205
by Dr. Indra Balakrishna

*

WILLA SAT IN THE PILOT'S SEAT of her stolen scout ship as she extended her senses to explore various probable outcomes of her plan to defeat Xanthes.

Now and then, she glanced at the readouts on her console from the remote probe to make sure no ships were approaching her position. A display of star coordinates on one screen caught her attention. Something about them seemed oddly familiar.

"Computer, what star systems are being displayed on screen three?"

The computer highlighted each star as it went through the list. "Deneb, Vega, Altair --"

"Stop," Willa said. "Display a star map that contains the second Maelstrom."

The map appeared. Just as on the map in Sequoia's chamber, the second Maelstrom was indicated by a pulsing red dot. Willa frowned, momentarily puzzled until a realization hit her like a lightning bolt.

"Computer, show me my location."

A pulsing blue dot appeared very close to the second Maelstrom. Willa's stomach lurched as she grasped that the asteroid she was using for cover was a remnant of Tavanna! Somehow, after entering the original Maelstrom, her ship had been transported over two thousand light-years and had exited from the second anomaly. The two portals were linked!

Willa wasn't in Xanthes's reality at all. She'd merely traveled through some sort of subspace tunnel to another part of *her* universe. Several disturbing thoughts ran through her mind: if both Maelstroms were, in effect, now "one-way streets," then while the Archon's armies could enter Willa's universe, there was no longer any way to enter his. That also meant that Dennik and the others from that reality were stranded.

Willa refused to accept that conclusion. There must be a way to punch through. Perhaps manipulating the ship's energy shields to emit a different frequency that was more compatible with the Archon's alternate universe, or finding a different pathway through the Maelstrom, or...

Willa sifted through a dozen possibilities before she realized she couldn't solve the problem from where she was. She'd have to return to Mystery and imbibe another draft of Divinorum in the hope that her enhanced senses, combined with suggestions from her five counterparts, would produce a solution. So much for her plan to defeat Xanthes! She also dreaded facing her family and friends after putting them through the ordeal of her "death," not to mention the reprimand she'd get for stealing an Alliance scout ship, but she saw no other choice.

"Computer. Plot a course for Earth and initiate a jump."

"Copy," the computer said. Within seconds, the ship took the first of many jumps toward home.

*

Velika walked down the med-lab corridor to the stasis morgue. She scanned her access card outside the morgue door. A blue beam shot out and read her vitals: retina, pattern, heartbeat, respiration, and genetic code. The door slid open as cameras recorded her entry.

She strolled down the aisle between several stasis pods until she came to the ones that held Koro's and Haldane's remains. She pulled a nano-bead from her lab coat pocket, tapped the controls on the two pods, and downloaded the genetic codes for both corpses. Velika pocketed the bead, returned the pod controls to normal and left the morgue.

She passed Doctor Sharoon, a female Nommos med-tech, on her way to the elevator tube and exchanged a brief nod. She entered the elevator and descended to the docking bay ring.

The elevator door on the docking bay level opened and, instead of Velika, the female Nommos emerged and went to the nearby security office. The amphibious alien handed Velika's access card to one of the robots that monitored activity on the space station.

"Doctor Policarpo must have dropped her security card. I found it in the elevator."

The robot took it in its flexible, memory-metal fingers. "Thank you, Doctor Sharoon. I'll see that it's returned to her."

The Nommos headed down the corridor and turned a corner, careful to note which way the hall cameras pointed. When the alien reached a blind spot, it shifted back into Variabilis. The Shapeshifter punched a code on the airlock keypad, entered the docking bay, boarded his well-used ship, and headed back to Earth.

*

Alder Redwood stood at the foot of Marrowbone Bridge, dressed in somber tones of grey and black. His gloved hands rested on the small silver skull that capped the top of his dark, ironwood cane. He offered a respectful bow of his head as Holly, Lily, River, Kale, and Thorn approached him. Alder's all-black eyes reflected their determined faces.

"This is not a good idea," said the Sage.

"That may be," Lily said, "but I have to know our daughter's fate."

"Are you able to sense her presence?" Holly inquired of the Sage.

"Only in the same manner as you," Alder said. "She's either alive or in spirit. Both are just as real to me."

"Then you'll forgive us if we continue on our way," Lily said. She clasped River's hand and walked around the Sage.

Alder called after her. "I assumed you'd say that. I'm here to help."

"How?" River said.

Alder sauntered up to them. "Regardless of Belladonna's relationship with your daughter, Banshees aren't exactly known for being chatty. Perhaps my abilities might encourage her to be more forthcoming."

"Fine," Lily agreed as she turned and headed over the bridge toward the forest. Alder and the rest followed, though no one looked forward to confronting the angry apparition.

As the group passed through the streets of Port Dublin, many of the townspeople offered them bows of respect. Word of Willa's death had spread throughout the village. Lily and River quietly nodded their thanks, but Lily found their sorrowful expressions excruciating. Each pair of sad eyes, whether human, Hybrid or alien, felt like nails in Willa's coffin. Lily felt hope drain from her heart the closer they got to the forest's edge.

She stopped. River turned to her.

"Lily?"

"Maybe Alder was right," she whispered. "Maybe this isn't such a good idea."

Holly walked up to her. "Trust your instincts, Lily. What does your heart say?"

"That I'm afraid to find the answer."

"Me, too," Holly said softly. "But it's far better than the agony of not knowing."

Lily gave Holly a grateful nod. She and River headed down the forest path, the others not far behind. It was dusk by the time they reached the heart of the forest where Belladonna's old stone cottage was encased in vines and the roots of a large, ancient Yew tree. Alder and Holly signaled for the others to hang back as they cautiously approached the Banshee's haunt.

"Belladonna, are you here?" Alder called out. "May we speak with you?" The Sage was met with silence.

Holly stepped forward. "We need your help. It's about Willa."

After a moment, the air started to chill. The hairs rose on the back of Kale's and Thorn's necks. The soft evening music of crickets and birdsong ceased and the rustle of wind-blown leaves died.

Belladonna's diaphanous form emerged from the cottage and floated in the air before them. Her glowing eyes flashed like an approaching thunderstorm. "What news of Willa? I sense she's no longer on this world."

Lily went to Holly's side, her eyes pleading. "Please, I'm Lily, Willa's mother. We fear she may be dead. Is it within your power to know if she lives or is in spirit?"

"Dead?" Belladonna turned a shade paler than usual. "Then I'm truly cursed to spend eternity this way."

"This isn't about you," Alder said. He aimed his cane at Belladonna, his face stern. "I compel you to tell us what we wish to know!"

The Banshee regarded the Sage with undisguised disdain. "Don't be a fool! I'm not some simple Nature Spirit to be ordered about. I'm shackled to the bridge between life and death. My fate is sealed and I'm well beyond your reach."

"We're only asking if you can sense where my daughter is," Lily said. "She means something to you as well, does she not?"

Belladonna softened as she beheld Lily's tear-filled eyes. "She does."

The Banshee closed her eyes, rose high into the air and reached out with her preternatural senses. The group watched her with anticipation. Finally, after several long minutes, Belladonna opened her eyes, floated back down, and hovered just above the forest floor. Her expression was odd, even for her. She remained silent until Alder's patience wore out.

"Well?" the Sage said.

"My senses tell me she's alive, but..."

"But..." River prompted.

Belladonna lifted her hollow gaze to Lily. "She's crossed to another reality."

Lily's breath caught in her throat. "Then, you're saying she's alive in spirit... that she's dead?"

"No," the Banshee said. "She hasn't entered the realm of spirit, but neither is she alive in this world."

"Oh, no," Holly said under her breath as the truth hit her.

Lily turned to her. "What?"

"She means Willa's crossed into another universe."

Kale immediately understood. "She went through the Maelstrom, to the Archon's universe!"

Lily was horrified. "What? Why would she --"

"To face Xanthes," Holly said, "before she becomes too powerful for Willa to defeat."

"At least she's alive," Thorn offered.

Alder looked at the boy. "But for how long?"

Belladonna floated closer to them. Alder's hackles went up, but the Banshee ignored him. "For Willa's sake and mine, please bring her back. She's the only hope I have of ever returning to the world of the living."

Belladonna vanished like a wisp of smoke and Alder relaxed. "Lot of good I did," he fumed.

"I'm going after Willa," River vowed.

"Not alone," Kale said. "I'm coming with you. We'll take my new ship."

"Are you both mad?" Lily scolded. "What if Willa's been captured, or worse!"

"We'll take Dennik and his team," Kale said. "He got me out, he can help us rescue Willa."

"That's not nearly enough," Holly cautioned them.

Alder shook his head. "I'm sorry to be blunt, but the Alliance isn't going to send an armada to rescue one headstrong child, even if it is Willa."

"Willa is the Black League's best hope for defeating the Archon. They'd risk everything to save her," Kale said, "assuming she's actually in trouble."

"If there's trouble, our daughter will be in the middle of it," Lily said, her grief replaced by anger.

"So, what do we do?" Thorn said, growing more concerned by the second.

Holly headed back toward town.

"Where are you going?" Alder said.

Holly answered without looking back. "I have a better plan."

*

Rowan's ship hovered over the newly formed crater at the center of the Sentinel Moon's eye. A sensor beam swept over the jagged moonscape.

Inside the control cabin, Star looked over Rowan's shoulder as he studied the readout on his console. "Are you sure?"

"I ran the analysis five times," he said. "There's not enough debris to be a whole scout ship. Besides, the sensors found none of the alloys that would've made up the ship's hull." Rowan tapped a control. A block of data expanded on his screen. He studied it for a moment, then laughed.

"What's funny?" Star demanded.

"That clever little imp," he said with a smile. "This data can only mean one thing."

"You going to share?"

"Willa must've jettisoned her sub-light engine core. Probably Q-jumped just as the explosion blinded the patrol ship's sensors."

"So, she's alive?" Star said hopefully.

Rowan nodded, relieved. "The question is, where did she go?" Star had a chilling thought. "You don't think..."

Rowan dreaded the implication. "It's what I would do. Why wait for the enemy to invade when you can take the fight to them instead?"

"But she's alone," Star protested.

"Not if we go after her," Rowan said.

"You're as crazy as she is! At least she has powers. What can we do?"

"You're a Shapeshifter," Rowan replied. "If Willa's been captured, you can infiltrate, pretend to be the Archon's guards, get her out of there."

Star considered Rowan's plan. "You think that would work?"

"Do you?" he said.

Star thought it through for less than a heartbeat before her mischievous side took control. "Oh, what the hell, why not?"

Rowan smiled and turned to his console. "Corvus, send a message and our sensor data to Andromeda Command and Willa's family that we have proof she didn't crash on Sentinel. Then plot a course for the original Maelstrom. Maximum jump."

"Message sent, course laid in," the computer said. "Q-jump in five, four, three, two, one..."

*

Velika headed to an analysis lab on Andromeda Spaceport and searched her lab coat pockets for her security card to gain entry.

"Excuse me, Doctor Policarpo." She turned to see the docking bay security robot approach with her security card in its outstretched hand. "It appears you dropped this."

She took the card. "Where did you find it?"

"Doctor Sharoon turned it in. She said she found it in the elevator tube."

"Sharoon, huh? Thanks." The robot went back the way it came. Velika turned on her heel and hurried down the hall to one of the other labs. She entered to find the Nommos med-tech hard at work at his computer station.

"Doctor Sharoon..."

The Nommos looked up from her task. "Doctor Policarpo. To what do I owe the pleasure?" she said in her light, aquatic timbre.

Velika held up her card. "Did you find this and turn it in to Security?"

"No. I haven't left the med-lab all day."

Velika's blood boiled. "Variabilis! You son-of-a --"

Sharoon's liquid eyes filled with concern. "Are you okay?"

"Never mind. It's nothing." Velika turned and stormed from the lab.

*

119

Variabilis flew up to his mountain tower's entrance in the form of a large hawk. He shifted back to his Hybrid form inside the main chamber and walked to the computer in his study. He placed the nano-bead with the genetic information in the dimple on his desk.

"Computer, analyze the three genetic codes on file and report any anomalies or similarities."

"Analysis complete," the computer said a fraction of a second later. "Two of the codes are familial."

"Which two? Familial how?"

"File 876405 dash 342: labeled Gant and file 876405 dash 344: labeled Koro. Ninety-nine-point-eight percent probability of a fraternal connection."

Variabilis let the information sink in. *Koro, the Archon's spy in the Resistance, was Gant's brother!*

*

A day and a half, a hundred fifty jumps, and five protein bars later, Willa's scout ship approached Andromeda Spaceport. Her com-link beeped. She'd gone over what she would say a hundred times in her head but now that she was here, her prepared speech felt wholly inadequate. She steeled herself and tapped the com. Before she could utter a word, the station Commander's stern voice filled her ears.

"This is Commander Erebus of Andromeda Station. Please identify yourself!"

"This is Willa... Willa Hillicrissing from Port Dublin. Listen, I'm really sorry --"

"Where did you get that ship?" Erebus demanded, cutting her off.

"Berth seventy-seven," Willa said, confused by the Commander's question.

An uncomfortably long silence made Willa wonder of she'd lost the connection.

"Stay where you are," Erebus finally said. "We're sending two patrol ships to escort you to docking bay twelve."

"Copy," Willa said, her confusion deepening. She'd once overheard Rowan explaining to Thorn that docking bays one through thirteen were for receiving ships from planets that didn't belong to the Alliance so they could be screened by security.

As promised, two patrol ships emerged from the station and flanked the scout ship. The familiar voice of Captain Bracken issued from Willa's com panel.

"Please shut your engines and brace for tractor link," Bracken warned.

Willa quickly complied. Tractor beams shot out from each patrol ship, firmly locking the scout ship between them. Their thrusters flared to life and they towed the scout ship into the station's docking bay. The large airlock doors closed and the bay pressurized.

Willa took a deep breath and exited through the scout ship's airlock to find Captain Bracken and two gleaming, nano-glass security robots waiting for her.

Willa tried to lighten the mood. "Captain Bracken, I presume?"

Bracken's eyes narrowed. "You know me?"

Willa's senses advised caution. "Listen, I'm sorry about my little trick --"

"Trick? I don't know what you're talking about. Follow me, please," Bracken said. Her tone made it clear that it wasn't a request.

Willa obeyed and looked back over her shoulder as the robots followed them both down a corridor and into a large elevator that lifted them to the command deck.

Bracken escorted Willa to a small, brightly-illuminated white room that only contained two nano-glass chairs on either side of an equally-transparent table. There was no mistaking the sparse trappings of an interrogation chamber. Willa realized she must be in more trouble than she thought.

"May I please call my mother and father?" she asked Captain Bracken. "I need to let them know I'm okay."

"Wait here," Bracken said and left. Willa saw that the two robots remained in the corridor to guard the door as it slid shut and locked.

Willa sat down and closed her eyes. She expanded her senses and listened for any snippets of conversation that might shed light on her situation. Her bubble of awareness penetrated the walls of the command center. Willa honed in on an exchange between Commander Erebus and Brahma Kamal over the com-link.

Willa wondered why the Commander would be talking with the head of the Contact Council about Willa's case but she set that question aside and focused on their conversation.

"It can't be Willa Hillicrissing," Erebus said to Brahma. "And it makes no sense that this person, whoever she is, would try to impersonate her."

"I'll contact her family," Brahma said over the com. "Perhaps they can be of some help clearing this up."

"Very well," Erebus agreed. "Meanwhile, I'll have a chat with our 'guest' to see what I can learn."

Willa withdrew her sense bubble as she realized her mistake. Her ruse had worked – they thought she was dead! No wonder they suspected her of being an imposter. Most likely, they believed she was a Shapeshifter of some sort. Perhaps they feared this was an attempt by the Archon to infiltrate the Alliance. She had to convince the Commander that she hadn't died.

No sooner had Willa put the pieces together than Commander Erebus entered the room. The robot sentries entered with her and stood on either side of the door.

Willa stood. "Commander, I can explain!"

Erebus waved her back to her seat and took the chair across from Willa. "Please enlighten me," she said as her pale jade eyes sized Willa up.

"I *am* Willa Hillicrissing. I only faked my death! Go on, ask me something only I would know."

Erebus gave Willa an odd look. "You're not making sense. What do you mean you faked your death?"

"I flew the scout ship toward Sentinel on purpose, jettisoned my sub-light engine core and jumped clear at the last second before it exploded. I didn't crash," Willa said.

"Scout ship seventy-seven..."

"Yes, the ship I stole," Willa said. Her senses went on high alert. Something was terribly wrong but she couldn't put her finger on it.

"Well, you see, that's a problem," Erebus said, still eyeing Willa. "Scout ship seventy-seven was never stolen. It's still in its berth, right where it belongs."

"But... your patrol ships just towed it into the docking bay."

"They towed a ship that looks identical, but it's not our scout ship," Erebus informed her. She watched Willa more closely to see what she would make of that information.

Willa sat very still, her mind racing, at a loss for words. She cleared her throat. "Commander, please call my family in Port Dublin. They'll straighten this out."

"We have," Erebus said. "They'll be here within the hour."

Willa should have been relieved at the news, but her senses remained wary. Suddenly, her counterparts' voices filled her head with dire whispers.

"You don't belong here!"

"You've got to go!"

"You've got to get off the station!"

"Run!"

Willa shut her eyes and silenced the voices, afraid they'd send her into a panic.

Erebus frowned. "Are you alright?"

Willa opened her eyes. "May I have some water, please?"

Erebus nodded to one of the robots. It went to the wall and, at a touch of its finger, a slot opened and produced a glass of water. The robot took it, handed it to Willa, then resumed its position by the door. She sipped the water slowly, using the time to think.

The Commander's com-link beeped. "This is Erebus."

A tech engineer responded. "Please come to docking bay twelve, Commander. There's something you should see."

"On my way," Erebus said. She eyed Willa and aimed a thumb at the robots. "You need anything, ask them." She rose and left the room.

Willa stared at the unmoving robots. "Take me to my ship?"

The robot that gave her the water responded in its emotionless voice. "It's good to know you have a sense of humor. According to my analysis of the situation, you're going to need it."

Willa crossed her arms and slumped in her chair. She toyed with the idea of using her powers to alter the robots' programming, then decided that putting her parents at ease and finding out why everyone was acting so strangely was more important than escaping, at least for the moment.

A chill passed through Willa as one of her counterparts broke through and brought a disturbing realization into focus.

Willa! You don't belong here!

Willa sat upright, her mind reeling.

"No one here is acting strange! I'm the stranger! This isn't my universe!"

*

The version of Elowen Koa that belonged to this second universe walked down the corridor that led to the docking bays on this alternate Andromeda Spaceport. Her flight bag was in hand. Other pilots and station personnel she passed greeted her with smiles.

"Welcome back, Lieutenant."

"Great to see you, El."

Though Elowen Two nodded her thanks and returned their smiles, her brainwashed mind was focused on a single task. She didn't know the reason why, but she'd heard that Willa's family was about to dock at the station. As the version of Xanthes in this universe had commanded, Elowen Two would eliminate everyone near and dear to Willa and perhaps, with luck, find and eliminate Willa herself.

Elowen Two's flight bag contained a few small power cells, nothing that would trip the station's sensors on their own but, with Elowen Two's tech knowledge, she'd altered the circuitry to make them unstable. It would be simple to attach them to the docking bay's power systems to create a powerful bomb and make it look like an accidental overload.

She slipped into docking bay thirty-three and nonchalantly walked past the maintenance crew to the monitoring room. Though they weren't her targets, she knew the blast would also take them and the sensors out so there would be no witnesses or recordings of her arrival in the bay.

Elowen Two slid the door shut and got to work quickly since she knew the crew chief would be there soon. She opened the airlock pressure control panels and replaced the normal cells with her doctored ones. As soon as the ship docked and the bay was pressurized, the bomb would explode, taking out the entire dock, the ship and everyone on board as well as a sizeable portion of the adjacent corridor. All incriminating evidence would be blown into space.

Once her task was completed, she replaced the panel covers and left the bay as calmly as she had entered. The ship was due to dock in fifteen minutes, more than enough time for Elowen Two to reach the safety of her quarters on the opposite side of the station.

She walked down the corridor and stood before the doors to the conveyor pod that would transport her to the station's habitat sector. The pod arrived and Chatterbox, a slender, lemon-yellow alien in a tech uniform, stepped into the corridor. His real name was practically unpronounceable and, due to his penchant for spreading rumors, he quickly earned the nickname and found no offense in it.

"Chatterbox!" Elowen Two said, surprised to run into him.

"Elowen! Happy you're back on your feet."

"Glad to be back," she said, trying to be conversational while she kept an eye on a nearby wall chronometer.

"I hear you had quite the harrowing experience," the alien said, his voice low.

"If you don't mind, I'd rather not talk about it."

"Of course, of course," Chatterbox said. "So, how do you Earthers say it? Getting back on the saddle?"

"That expression's a few hundred years out of date," Elowen Two said with a smile, "but yes, I'll be in the pilot's seat again soon."

"Excellent, excellent!" Chatterbox bobbed his crested head with approval.

"Well, I must be going --"

"Say, have you heard what's going on up on the command deck?" Chatterbox said with conspiratorial enthusiasm.

"Uh, no. I've been out of the loop lately."

"Of course, of course. Well, Jessie told Umbria who told Scatterwonk who told Veena who told me that Commander Erebus thinks the Archon planted a spy on the station."

A cold shiver of adrenaline shot through Elowen Two as she went on alert. She knew the Commander had her under surveillance while she recovered in the medical facility in case she'd been turned by the Archon's torturers, but Xanthes's programming was deep and Elowen Two had been cleared by the hospital telepaths. Were they still watching her anyway?

"What else have you heard?" she ventured.

"All I know is that it's a female Hybrid…"

"And?" Elowen prodded, impatient with Chatterbox's melodramatic pauses.

126

"And that she's being interrogated as we speak," Chatterbox finished.

Elowen Two was mildly relieved. She wasn't a suspect. But she was also confused. *Did Xanthes plant a second spy on Earth in case I failed?*

"Do you know who it is?" she asked Chatterbox.

"Well, far be it from me to spread unfounded rumors..."

"Uh-huh..."

"Word is the spy might be a Shapeshifter. Tried to impersonate Willa Hillicrissing if you can believe that," Chatterbox whispered. "But you didn't hear that from me," he said with a wink.

"It's our secret," Elowen Two said with another glance at the chronometer. Willa's family would be docking within three minutes. She'd have to figure out who the prisoner was later. "Listen, I've got to go. Nice chatting with you."

"Always a pleasure," Chatterbox said with a bob of his crest.

Elowen Two stepped into the pod. It carried her away as Chatterbox headed down the corridor toward the docking bays. She deeply regretted that her friend would be killed in the blast but, though she desperately wanted to go back and warn him, Xanthes's programming held her in its unbreakable grip. Elowen Two was grateful there was no one else in the pod to witness the tears that streamed down her face.

*

Commander Erebus and Zev Bukowski, the tech engineer, watched the sensor playback on the screen in Willa One's stolen ship in bay twelve. It showed the jettisoned sub-light core and recorded her last-minute jump as well as Willa's entry into, and exit from, the two Maelstroms.

"Seems our guest was telling the truth, Commander," Zev said. "I find no evidence the data's been tampered with."

"Then she's good at covering her tracks," Erebus said. "She can't be who she says she is." Her com-link interrupted their conversation.

Vas-Basso's agitated voice leaped from the communicator. "Commander!"

"What is it?"

"We just received a warning to evacuate docking bay thirty-three. There's a bomb threat!"

"A warning from whom?" Erebus said.

"From the ship that was about to dock there," Vas-Basso said.

"Do it!" Erebus ordered. "Divert that ship to the Command docking bay. Seal the airlocks in section three on decks five, six and seven! Alert Med-Bay to prepare for possible casualties!"

"Yes, sir!" Vas-Basso chirped and cut the link.

"If I may, Commander, who's on that ship?" Zev said.

"Hopefully, someone who can answer all our questions," the Commander said as she hurried from the docking bay.

She took the closest lift up to the Command Deck and gestured for two security robots to join her. They followed her down the corridor as they matched her brisk pace.

The transport ship entered the Commander's docking bay and slipped into the berth next to Erebus's sleek corvette starship. The security airlock sealed, the bay pressurized and Erebus entered, the robots on her heels. She waited as the transport ship's outer hatch opened like an iris.

Three people walked down the docking ramp: Lily, River, and a second Willa Hillicrissing.

"You evacuated bay thirty-three?" Willa Two asked before Erebus could speak.

"We've sealed off the entire section," the Commander assured her.

"You'll find the bomb in the pressurization control panels," Willa Two said.

"If that's the case, those enhanced powers of yours just saved a lot of lives," Erebus said with gratitude. "Do you know who's responsible?"

"No, which is odd," Willa Two said. "It's like there's a mental shield around the person. But I'll figure it out."

"Is this why you asked us here?" Lily Two said.

"No, there's another reason. Please follow me."

The dopplegangers of Willa, Lily, and River followed the Commander and the robots from the bay. Willa Two sensed something very strange, but couldn't quite sort it out. One of her Counterpart's voices whispered in her head.

"You're already here!"

"What are you talking about?" Willa Two responded telepathically.

"She's one of us!" the voice informed her.

"You're the same but different," another voice added.

The enigmatic comment made no sense to Willa Two. She moved the voices to the back of her mind, curious to see where Erebus was leading them.

*

Willa One was still in the interrogation room, getting more impatient by the second. She glared at her robot guards. "Will someone please tell me what I'm doing here?"

"The Commander is on her way," one of the robots said.

The door slid open. Erebus entered.

"It's about time," Willa One said, miffed.

Erebus gestured to one of the guard robots. "Tag her."

The robot reached Willa in two steps and, in a split second, tattooed a circular symbol on the back of her hand.

"Hey!" Willa One protested as she yanked her hand back. "What's that for?"

"So that we can tell you apart," Erebus said.

129

"What are you talking about?"

Lily Two and River Two stepped into the room. They stared at Willa One and stayed near the door. Willa One jumped to her feet with joy.

"Mom! Dad! I'm so sorry I put you through --"

Willa One stopped dead in mid-sentence as the second Willa entered between her parents, her golden eyes fixed on her mirror image.

"Care to change your story?" the Commander said to the first Willa.

Both girls expanded their senses simultaneously. They peered deep into each other's souls as information about one another poured into their minds. They stopped and shared an astonished smile.

"She's telling the truth!" said Willa Two.

"What the hell are you two talking about?" the Commander shouted.

Willa Two turned to Erebus. "She's my counterpart from a parallel universe."

"What? That's impossible!"

"Or so we thought," Willa Two said.

Erebus threw a blank stare at Willa Two's parents. They simply shrugged.

"Our daughter has already done several impossible things," Lily Two said. "What's one more?"

"The Maelstroms," Willa One said. "They're not just magnetic anomalies. They're portals between parallel realities."

The Commander looked at both Willas.

They each gave Erebus the same mischievous smile.

Chapter Eight:
POWER PLAY

"A chess master from the Twentieth Century once said, 'When you see a good move, look for a better one.' It would be wise to employ this approach in the game of Tactics as well as in the game of life."

Excerpt from "Tactics"
by Winona Sixkiller Smith

*

THE ELOWEN OF WILLA Two's universe paced in her quarters. Something was wrong. The bomb should have gone off by now. If station security was on to her, she had better leave immediately before being arrested. She could go into hiding and come up with another plan. Maybe this is why Xanthes sent a second spy. She knew Elowen would fail. Or maybe that was the plan all along. Elowen would be caught and take the blame. The Alliance would drop its guard so the second spy could attack with impunity.

But the other spy, if that's what she was, was already in custody. It was she that had failed, not Elowen. Yet the bomb hadn't exploded so maybe they both failed. The conundrum drove Elowen Two mad. She had to find out what was happening, but quietly. If she wasn't a suspect yet, she must be careful not to draw attention to herself.

Elowen Two realized she had another problem. She'd been careful not to leave prints or DNA on the doctored power cells.

However, the bay cams must have recorded her, not to mention that the maintenance crew had seen her in the docking bay and Chatterbox had encountered her on that deck. Now that the bay sensors and personnel wouldn't be destroyed, she'd never be safe unless she eliminated the sensor data and the eyewitnesses.

It was only a matter of time before security teams started questioning the crew in their hunt for suspects. Elowen Two had to think fast. Her mind replayed every moment from her arrival on Andromeda to rigging the bomb to talking with Chatterbox to...

She suddenly remembered something Chatterbox told her about a rumor. That the spy in custody had impersonated Willa and was thus suspected to be a Shapeshifter. That was it! If anyone suspected Elowen, she could claim that a Shapeshifter had impersonated her as well. They were known to be loners, even outsiders, who sometimes skirted the edge of the law. *A conspiracy of Shapeshifters!* Elowen Two nodded at the thought.

Elowen Two worked out the details of her alibi in her mind. She realized that an even better way to convince everyone would be to frame one of the Shapeshifters on the station. Maybe even kill one and claim self-defense. That would make sense. If a Shapeshifter had planned to frame her, they would also want to eliminate her as a loose end; probably make her death look like an accident. She'd say she was lucky to get the upper hand and kill her attacker. Then she'd be a hero. No one would suspect her of a thing.

There were two parts to Elowen's plan. First, she'd float her story of a rogue Shapeshifter to Chatterbox. It was exactly the kind of juicy rumor he couldn't help but spread throughout the station. Second, she'd plant a few doctored power cells in some Shapeshifter's quarters when they were on duty. Then, all she'd need to do is lie in wait for the unsuspecting Shapeshifter and take him or her out.

Her plan in place, Elowen Two tapped a code into her com. "Elowen to Chatterbox. Can you please come to my quarters? It's urgent."

Chatterbox responded quickly. "Elowen? What's wrong?"

"I'll tell you when you get here. Please hurry, I may be in danger."

"Of course, of course. On my way," Chatterbox said.

Elowen Two ended the link. She had about five minutes before Chatterbox arrived to practice looking very frightened.

*

Willa One and Willa Two sat across from each other in the main room of a large suite on the station where Willa Two's family had been quartered. The alternate Lily and River sat nearby along with Erebus as the two girls chatted.

"So, some things are the same as in my reality, and some things are different," Willa One said.

"Apparently," Willa Two concurred. "For example, I never stole a ship to go fight Xanthes. Based on the fact that you were transported to my reality, I don't know if I would've wound up in your reality, Xanthes's reality, or an entirely different universe."

"Were you thinking of stealing a ship?" Lily Two asked her daughter.

Willa Two gave her mother a sheepish grin and pointed at Willa One. "Maybe I got it from her."

"Hey!" Willa One protested.

Lily Two looked squarely at Willa One. "Then I'm very glad there's a difference between you two."

"When I emerged from the second Maelstrom, there was an asteroid debris field," Willa One said.

Willa Two nodded. "The remains of the planet Tavanna."

"Were you able to save the people there?"

Willa Two shook her head. "There weren't any people on Tavanna."

"Another difference between your 'verse and mine," said Willa One. "We need to figure out how the Maelstroms work, or I may never get back home."

"My science team is analyzing the sensor data from your ship," Erebus Two said. "Hopefully, it will provide an answer."

"Maybe you shouldn't go back," Willa Two suggested, "at least, not yet."

"What are you saying?" River Two said with a frown. "Remember that her own mother and father think she's dead."

"That's right," Lily Two said. "I'd be beside myself if the situation were reversed."

"I know," Willa Two continued, "but with the two of us here, we have a much better chance of defeating Xanthes. Our Xanthes, I mean."

"True," said Willa One. "Then, if we figure out a way for me to get back to my reality…"

"I could come with you and help you defeat your Xanthes!" Willa Two said, excited by the idea.

Lily Two shook her head. "Neither of you will be fighting either Xanthes on your own and that's final!"

"Mom!" Willa One and Two said simultaneously. They looked at each other and laughed. Lily and River glared at them.

"Sorry," Willa One said.

Erebus Two stood and leveled her gaze at the girls. "I have to get back to the Command Center. You two want to work together? Use your abilities to figure out who planted that bomb. Contact me the moment you have a lead. Do not look for the saboteur on your own, is that clear?"

Both girls nodded in unison.

The Commander gave them a final look of warning, nodded to Lily and River and took her leave.

Although Shapeshifters had a reputation for being aloof, and it was true that most preferred to live solitary lives, that was not the case for some of them, Encantado Two included. Though he was something of a recluse in Willa One's universe, the Encantado who lived in the second universe was an extremely social being.

He lived and worked on Andromeda Spaceport and served a very special purpose. New alien civilizations that were considering joining the Alliance often sent Ambassadors and their families to spend time on the station while negotiations were underway. It could take months before other members of their society were permitted to arrive in greater numbers, so many of the liaisons often felt isolated and lonely.

Encantado Two and other shape-shifting "familiars" as they were unofficially called, could take on the appearance of those species and make them feel more at home. Encantado Two enjoyed his job, especially when the Ambassadors and their families felt comfortable enough to invite him to their quarters and share stories of their home worlds with him over a sumptuous evening meal.

The Shapeshifter left his quarters for just such a rendezvous. Elowen Two, dressed in a repair tech uniform and wearing a respirator that covered half her face, watched him go from an adjacent corridor, then headed toward his room, tool case firmly in her gloved hand. She stood before the hall cam and held up an ID badge close to the lens.

"We're doing a maintenance check on all sensors due to the incident in bay thirty-three," she said to the lens. "Authorization Zeta-Delta-Zero-Zero-Nine-Sierra."

"Approved," said Ocularis.

Elowen Two reached up and switched the camera off. She attached a small remote-control disc on the wall behind the camera so she could turn it off again at will if necessary. She turned, grabbed a tool from her kit and quickly removed the panel that covered the door lock to Encantado's quarters. She made a slight adjustment to the circuit blocks and the door slid open. Elowen Two entered and shut the door.

She looked around. The room was pretty Spartan though it contained all the normal comforts. A large view port looked out onto the stars. Elowen grabbed a chair, stood on it, and popped the vent cover off the air filter above the view port. She pulled a few doctored power cells from her kit, hid them in the vent duct, then replaced the cover.

Elowen was careful to put the chair back exactly where she found it. She left the room, readjusted the door lock, and switched the hall camera back on. She stopped by the tech supply lockers, returned the "borrowed" uniform, respirator, and badge and headed toward her quarters.

All she had to do now was wait for the Shapeshifter to return.

*

Holly entered the Quorum Lodge on Earth One. Argus, the towering Divinorum Master, was stirring a fresh batch of the vision-inducing brew. Lily, River, Alder, Kale, and Thorn entered as well, but kept a respectful distance from the sasquatch. Holly went straight up to Argus as he added a pinch of dried Talus leaves to the mix.

"Argus, we need your help," Holly said without preamble.

"Divinorum not ready," the giant said in his deep rumble.

"We don't need Divinorum," she said, "we need…" Holly glanced back to make sure the others were out of earshot, then lowered her voice to a whisper. "We need your special talent."

Argus's eyes shifted to the group to make sure they hadn't overheard Holly. "That is secret!" he said as quietly as possible, which wasn't very quiet at all. "Shared that with you as friend."

"After I figured it out," Holly reminded him.

Argus grumbled in embarrassment. "You gave word not to tell."

136

"I haven't told anyone. You can do it in private. No one else needs to know," Holly said to calm him.

"What I need do?" Argus said.

"Find Willa."

Argus raised his furry brows. "Willa lost?"

"Sort of," Holly said. "Let's go into the anteroom and I'll explain."

Argus nodded his shaggy head and lumbered toward the back room. Holly turned to the group as she followed him.

"Wait here."

*

Xanthes and Uzza stood before Zaduga once again.

"She feels more powerful than ever!" Xanthes railed. "You both told me we were evenly matched!"

Zaduga and Uzza exchanged a glance, both troubled by Xanthes's outburst. "Allow me to see what I can discern, my Lady," Zaduga said. The elder Sensate closed his eyes and pushed his senses to the limit as he searched for Willa's presence. He found her and felt Willa's unbelievable power flow into his mind. Zaduga could barely maintain his connection. He withdrew from his trance, gathered his wits and turned to Xanthes.

"Impossible! Her power has doubled!"

"How?" Uzza said, unnerved by his Mentor's reaction.

"Let me think," Zaduga said. Xanthes's pale eyes smoldered as she watched the Sensate pace around the chamber for several minutes.

"You're trying my patience, old man," she said. "Perhaps I and my father would be better served by someone younger."

"Youth and experience are mutually exclusive," Zaduga responded. "I need to conjure a Simulacrum."

"Master, it's been years since you performed the ritual. Perhaps I should --"

Zaduga's hand lashed out. His eyes flashed with energy. Uzza flew backwards across the room and slammed against the stone wall, pinned by an unseen force. "Do you also doubt my abilities, Uzza?"

"Forgive me, Master," Uzza said, straining to speak, "I meant no disrespect!"

Zaduga released Uzza from his grip and turned to Xanthes as Uzza recovered.

"I'll have the answers you need by nightfall, my Lady," said Zaduga.

Xanthes knew that her abilities would soon be greater than Zaduga's, but she was nevertheless impressed by his prowess. She nodded, turned and left the chamber.

Zaduga went to Uzza, who bowed his head at the Elder Sensate's approach.

"Prepare the vision brew," Zaduga said. "Make certain it's a strong draft."

*

Willa One and Willa Two were both deep in meditation as Willa Two's parents waited patiently nearby. Lily sipped from a cup of jasmine tea while River studied a copy of the sensor readouts from Willa One's scout ship on his tablet.

The girls magnified the links to their parallel counterparts, who also opened their senses to their own counterparts and so on, until the web of communication extended to more than six thousand alternate universes.

Their combined abilities shielded both Willas from intrusion by any version of Xanthes, but it took extra effort to locate a universe in which the saboteur had already been identified.

The girls received the answer with a shock of recognition: Elowen, Kale's pilot, had been brainwashed by Xanthes! No wonder Willa Two couldn't breach the mental shield that protected the saboteur.

They telepathically thanked their counterparts and emerged from the shared trance.

"Any luck?" Lily Two said.

"It's Elowen Koa," said Willa One.

"We need to inform the Commander," Willa Two added.

Lily nodded and went to the com-link on the room's control panel. As she brought Erebus up to speed, River remained focused on his tablet.

"I think I understand why you wound up here," he said to Willa One, "and how you can get back to your universe."

"That's great!" Willa One beamed.

"It's just a theory," he added.

"Father, what is it?" Willa Two coaxed.

"Well, there's a small problem."

Lily rejoined the girls as River collected his thoughts.

"Keeping us in suspense isn't going to solve it," Lily said.

"You need a third Maelstrom to do it," River said, reluctant to deliver the bad news.

"You call that a small problem?" Willa One said. Her hope started to fade. River expanded his tablet so everyone could see the diagram he had created.

"Look, I think the anomalies are linked in a specific way, like the nodes of a circuit," he began. He simplified the diagram to a dot surrounded by a large circle. "The dot is the first Maelstrom. The circle is the universe it connects to," he said. "As long as there was only a single anomaly, it led to one alternate universe."

"And back again," said Willa One.

"Yes," River nodded. He added a second dot and a circle that overlapped the first one, creating a *vesica piscis*. "However, when the second Maelstrom opened, it created an energy link between the first alternate 'verse and our own. The flow of energy carried your ship here."

Willa Two studied the diagram. "So, entering Maelstrom one takes you to universe two..."

"Right," River said as he added a third dot and a circle that overlapped the first two in a triad formation.

"I see!" Willa One exclaimed. "The circuit's triangular. Portal one leads to 'verse two, portal two leads to 'verse three, and portal three leads back to 'verse one. My universe!"

"Exactly," River said. "But --"

"But how do you create a third Maelstrom," Lily reflected.

"That's the problem," River said. He turned to Willa One. "You said you thought the anomalies came into being because Sages turned into Wraiths?"

"It's the best theory we could come up with in my universe," she admitted.

"It's possible," Willa Two added. "My mentor once told me that bridging the physical and spirit realms while still alive could tear holes in the fabric of space-time."

River nodded. "That's as good a description of the Maelstroms as any."

Lily voiced what everyone was thinking. "So, we have to wait for a Sage to become a Wraith before a third Maelstrom will appear?"

"Maybe not," Willa One said. "The shift from Sage to Wraith has the same frequency as the anomalies. We calculated where the third Maelstrom should appear. Maybe, with enough energy at the right frequency, we can coax one to open."

Lily's eyes went wide. "That sounds extremely dangerous. Give the data to the techs and let them handle it. The two of you aren't going anywhere near a Maelstrom until we know it's safe."

Willa One glanced at Lily. "You know, you're not *my* mother."

"I am while you're in my universe. I'm sure your mother would do the same for my daughter if the situation was reversed," Lily said. Her look told the girls it was pointless to argue.

Willa One suddenly blanched. "Oh, no!"

"What is it?" Willa Two said.

"If the Elowen in this universe tried to kill you and your parents…"

"Remember, events in our universe don't necessarily happen in yours," River Two said trying to sound hopeful.

"I can't take that chance. I've got to get home!"

*

Corvus, Rowan's ship, emerged from the second Maelstrom just as Willa's scout ship had done. Except this time, three patrol ships, led by Captain Bracken of universe two, waited just beyond the reach of the anomaly's gravitational grip.

Bracken's voice filtered through the com in Rowan's cabin. "This is Captain Bracken of the Interstellar Alliance. Please identify yourself."

Rowan and Star shared a puzzled frown.

"A trick?" Star said.

Rowan checked his console. "Their ID codes check out. Maybe the Maelstrom spit us back out?"

Star glanced at the navigational readout. "I don't know. The stars look a bit out of place."

Bracken was insistent. "I repeat, please identify yourself."

Rowan took a breath and tapped his com. "This is Captain Ashgrove of the Alliance ship *Corvus* out of Andromeda Spaceport."

There was a long pause before Bracken responded. "Kale Ashgrove?"

"Rowan. Kale's my father."

"I see," Bracken said. "I'm sorry to inform you that you're no longer in your original universe."

"Yeah, we were beginning to ken that," Star responded.

"You don't understand," Bracken said. "You're not in Xanthes's universe, either."

It was Rowan's and Star's turn to take a long pause.

"Would you please repeat that?" Rowan said.

"You heard correctly, Captain. The Maelstrom transported you to an alternate version of your universe. Earth, Andromeda Spaceport, the Interstellar Alliance are all here, but they're not the ones you know. Even your Willa Hillicrissing is here. Please follow me to the Spaceport. Everything will be explained," Bracken assured him.

Rowan cut the com and turned to Star. "If this is a trap, it's a strange one. Why make up such a story?"

Rowan double-checked the navigational display, then tapped the com back on.

"Okay," he said to Bracken, "lead the way."

Bracken opened a channel to the other two patrol ships. "Remain here in case any other 'guests' show up."

Bracken's ship headed away from the Maelstrom at one-tenth sub-light and jumped toward the spaceport, followed by *Corvus*. The two remaining patrol ships flanked the Maelstrom, ready for anything.

*

Elowen Two stood in a corridor hub and logged a request on a display screen for simulator training as part of her recovery regimen. It also happened to be the hub that Encantado Two would use to return to his quarters.

A nano-glass data stick hung from Elowen's utility belt. It was standard issue for all pilots, so no one would suspect she'd hacked the program that would allow her to transform the blunt stick into a long, sharp needle when she tapped in her code.

By now, Chatterbox would have spread the rumor that Elowen suspected a Shapeshifter of being the saboteur. She would tell security that Encantado tried to stab her with the needle, but that she got the upper hand and killed him in self-defense. The security team would find the doctored power cells in his quarters and Elowen would finally be beyond suspicion. When the Shapeshifter approached, she would remotely knock out the hall security cam and, if questioned, say that Encantado had done it.

She heard footsteps approaching from a side corridor and prepared to put her plan into motion. A tall figure entered the hub. To Elowen's surprise, it was her lemon-yellow alien friend, a small toolkit in one of his six-fingered hands.

"Chatterbox. Still working at this hour?"

"Everyone's on high alert until the saboteur is caught. Security wants me to double-check all the sensors on this deck," Chatterbox said.

Elowen Two glanced down the hall at the camera across from Encantado's quarters. If Chatterbox found the remote off-switch she'd stuck on the camera, her plan would fail. "Let me help," she offered. "It'll go twice as fast that way."

"I appreciate it," the alien said with a bow of his crested head, "but I'm under strict orders to do it myself. You know how security is."

"Right. Sure. No problem," Elowen said. "See you later, then." She headed down the hall toward Encantado's quarters, hoping to snatch the remote before Chatterbox found it.

"Oh, I almost forgot!" Chatterbox said.

Elowen Two stopped and reluctantly turned back, trying not to look suspicious. "What?"

Chatterbox approached and lowered his voice as he always did when about to share a juicy rumor. "You know how you suspected that a Shapeshifter might be the saboteur?"

"Yes," Elowen said with caution.

"Well, you didn't hear this from me, but Parvin told Phillipa who told Ruby who told Quibbick who told me that Parvin saw Encantado sneaking around docking bay thirty-three yesterday."

"Really?" Elowen Two said, surprised by the coincidence.

"You think it could be him?" Chatterbox pressed.

Elowen Two nodded. This fit perfectly into her plan. "I do," she said.

"You sound very certain," Chatterbox said. "Have you heard something about him?"

"Well, you didn't hear it from me," Elowen began.

"Of course, of course," Chatterbox nodded, eager for the gossip.

"Someone said they saw me near bay thirty-three when I know I was somewhere else on the station," she whispered. "Then, a few minutes later, they saw Encantado in the same corridor heading in the opposite direction. I think he took my appearance so he could frame me for the explosion."

"You mean when I spoke to you yesterday, that was really him?" the alien gasped.

"I think so," she said.

"Well, he certainly fooled me," Chatterbox said. "However, you're not fooling anyone."

Elowen Two blinked in confusion. "Excuse me?"

Three security robots suddenly emerged from the adjacent corridors and surrounded Elowen. She froze and stared at Chatterbox.

"What's going on?"

Chatterbox shifted his form. Within a few seconds, Encantado Two stood before Elowen. He went to the camera outside his quarters and grabbed the remote disc. "Looking for this?"

"I don't understand," Elowen Two protested. "Are you suggesting that I'm the saboteur?"

"I'm not 'suggesting' anything," he said, his all-black eyes leveled at her. "It was Willa who figured it out. And you just confirmed it with that crazy story you made up about me." He turned to the security robots. "Take her to holding."

The robots closed in on Elowen and escorted her down the hall toward the security offices.

Encantado tapped a com-link on his arm. "We have her."

*

Sylvania and Poppy sat in the cozy living room of their cottage on Earth One. The night was unusually cool, so Poppy lit a small fire in the stone hearth. Sylvania nursed a glass of Elderberry wine laced with a dash of cinnamon, a treat she allowed herself on special occasions.

"It's so strange," she said to Poppy, who sat on the floor and stoked the fire. "I don't remember being this Brandelyn person, yet I feel that I'm not my usual self, either."

"No offense, Mother," Poppy said, "but I like you better this way. Don't get me wrong, I missed you terribly, but whatever the Thook did to create that other personality has… I don't know… softened you."

"Poor darling. Becoming a human Nocturnal was so difficult for me, and I needed so much focus, it took me further and further away from just being your mother. I'm so sorry."

Poppy cocked her head as she looked at her mother. "You know, you've never told me why you took that path."

Sylvania took another sip of wine as she searched her feelings, something she wasn't used to doing. "To be honest, I suppose I've always been a bit jealous of Hybrids and their abilities."

"Why? Humans can do all sorts of amazing things, too."

"I know, but…" Sylvania paused as she recalled an unpleasant memory. "When I was about your age, my best friend was a Hybrid. We were like you and Willa. Her name was Odessa. Odessa Diamond." Sylvania let out a soft chuckle. "You know the old phrase, 'diamond in the rough?' People used to say she was the diamond and I was the rough."

"That's not very nice," Poppy said.

"I got teased a lot when I was young so, in defiance, I learned to wear the nicknames like badges of honor," Sylvania said with pride. "After that, I was a lot like you, always getting into mischief."

"You? That's hard to believe."

"I know, and I'm sorry I've kept that part of myself from you. It's just that, when I decided I should be able to do whatever a Hybrid could do, I became..."

Poppy couldn't resist the jab. "Obsessed?"

Sylvania's frown was tempered by a smile. "Very serious. So, when Odessa chose the path of Mastery, I wasn't about to be outdone. I jumped right in with both feet."

"That must've been..."

"Rough?"

Poppy smiled. "Yeah."

"It was. It took months before I could even find a mentor willing to teach me," Sylvania said as she recalled how hurt she was at the time. "They weren't unkind, it was just that no one thought I could go very far, or handle the Divinorum."

"How did you? It's specifically brewed to work with Hybrid genes," Poppy said.

Sylvania leaned forward and lowered her voice in pretense of sharing a secret. "The key is persistence. After you throw up the first twenty times, your body adapts."

Poppy threw her a skeptical look. "You're funnier than you used to be."

Sylvania smiled, finished her wine and reached for Poppy's hand. "I know I may never master Shapeshifter or Sage, and I may not even be a decent Nocturnal, but I promise from now on to be the best mother I can be."

Poppy stood and threw her arms around her mother in a heart-melting hug that brought tears to Sylvania's eyes. She sniffed as Poppy stepped back.

"You really are a new person," Poppy said as she wiped a tear from Sylvania's cheek. Her mood changed as a thought crossed her mind. "Is it because you started on the path to Mastery while you were pregnant with me that I have my "lucky" sense at Hexes?"

"Possibly," Sylvania said, mildly surprised she hadn't made that connection before. She suddenly felt slightly dizzy and held her head.

"Are you okay?" Poppy said.

"It's been a while since I've had Elderberry wine. I'll just take a short nap, I'm sure I'll be fine." Sylvania kissed Poppy on the cheek and made her way upstairs to her room. Poppy touched the spot on her cheek like she'd been kissed by an angel.

Sylvania closed her door, laid down on her bed and was soon fast asleep. Her calm, rhythmic breathing slowly shifted to starts and pants; her eyes shifted back and forth under closed lids; her brow furrowed as she struggled against an encroaching nightmare.

"There you are!" Xanthes's telepathic voice echoed in her mind. *"I've been searching for you!"*

Sylvania's head tossed on her pillow as she mumbled in her sleep. "No... no..."

"You sought to open doors to other universes, to connect and commune with the versions of you in those realities, but your mind is weak!"

"Go away," Sylvania whispered. She struggled to wake up but felt herself being pulled deeper into the dream. "Leave me alone!"

"You're not like the others, the ones who seek the mysteries of the night. You're more like me!" Xanthes shouted with malevolent glee. *"I can teach you the witching way, I can make you strong!"*

"I'm nothing like you!" Sylvania gasped.

"Oh, but you are! Face the truth! You haven't been hiding from me. You've been hiding from yourself!"

Sylvania tossed back and forth like an animal caught in a trap. Her face was drenched in sweat. Her heart pounded in her ears, like ocean waves thundering against a rocky shore. Her lips were pinched tight, her teeth clenched so hard they threatened to break. *"Let me go! Please! I beg you!"* she screamed in her mind.

"Show the ones who said you could never amount to anything! Let me in and I'll show them how powerful you truly are!" Xanthes

promised. *"You're not the rough, you're the diamond! Let me help you shine!"*

Sylvania's black eyes snapped open. She held her breath so long it seemed that she had died. Finally, she exhaled. Her breathing was calm, but a change had come over her. She had been Sylvania, then Brandelyn, and then Sylvania again. But now, she was someone else… some*thing* else. She felt more powerful than she had in her entire life.

She sat up and looked around her room. It felt both familiar and foreign at the same time. She planted her bare feet on the wood-plank floor and felt a surge of confidence wash through every cell in her body. Up to this point, she'd had a life, but now, she had a *mission*. She rose and left her room.

She met Poppy's eyes as she walked slowly down the stairs.

"That was a short nap," Poppy said.

"It was all I needed," Sylvania said as she slipped her feet into a pair of lightweight sandals by the door. "I feel like a new woman."

"Where are you going?"

Sylvania smiled, but she knew the moment called for something more. She went to Poppy, bent down and kissed her on the forehead. "I thought I would go to market and make us something special for supper. A surprise to celebrate my homecoming."

Poppy jumped up, excited. "I'll go with you!"

Sylvania tousled Poppy's hair. "Then it wouldn't be a surprise," she said. "I'll be back soon."

"Promise?" Poppy said with some concern.

"Promise," Sylvania said. "Be a darling and set the table."

Sylvania left the door open as she walked down the path to the road that led to town. She looked back over her shoulder at Poppy and waved.

Poppy smiled and waved back, then went to the pantry to fetch plates and candles. Between her mother coming home and news from Rowan that Willa was alive somewhere out in the cosmos, Poppy felt happier than she had in a long time.

*

Opal sat cross-legged on the stone floor of her cell in Mystery, deep in a telepathic conversation with one of her counterparts for the past hour, a counterpart that, as fortune would have it, happened to be on Earth Two.

"You're sure she's safe?"

"Yes, but her family in your universe is in danger," said Opal Two. *"You have to find and stop a pilot called Elowen Koa. She's been turned by Xanthes."*

"I know who you mean," Opal One acknowledged. *"I'll alert the Provost. Please let our Willa know that we'll do everything we can to protect her family, but we can't be everywhere at once. Do you have any idea where our Elowen is?"*

"No. Xanthes's programming has created a mental shield that's hard to penetrate. She's like a ghost, fading in and out of my awareness."

"Like a Thook," Opal One said.

"What's a Thook?" Opal Two said.

"I guess you haven't met those aliens yet in your universe."

"I'll let your Willa know we spoke," Opal Two said, then broke the mental link.

Opal One left her chamber and hurried down the marble hall toward the Provost's inner sanctum. She passed a figure wearing black gloves and a black robe with the hood pulled up, which Nocturnals often did when communing with their voices so they wouldn't be distracted. As such, Opal thought nothing of it and hurried past the silent silhouette. Focused on her task, she didn't notice when the robed figure turned to follow her.

At one point, Opal thought she heard a slight shuffle of feet behind her. She glanced over her shoulder but saw no one. She figured whoever had been there must've gone down a side hall. Opal continued on her way, turned a corner and nearly ran into the same robed figure.

"Sorry, excuse me," Opal said as she tried to step around the hooded acolyte. The figure blocked her path. "What are you --"

Before Opal could finish, the mysterious Nocturnal stabbed her straight through the heart with a nano-glass needle. Opal's face registered shock and disbelief for one final heartbeat before her assailant withdrew the needle. Opal dropped to the cold marble floor as her blood pooled under her.

The Nocturnal transformed the needle back into a bead and slipped it into a pocket, then got down on one knee beside Opal's body to check her pulse and make sure she was dead. Satisfied the needle had done its job, the robed assassin slipped down the hall and melted into the shadows.

Chapter Nine:
ARGUS

"Humans used to think of history as a straight, unbroken line from the past to the present, and continuing to the future. The truth is that there have been many detours, alternate paths, dead ends, and repeating cycles that have brought us to the point we're at now. Thus, because of that outdated and myopic view, evidence of Earth's true history was ignored, buried, lost, and forgotten for millennia until the Hybrids arrived and brought us visual recordings that several extraterrestrial races had made of our history going back hundreds of thousands of years. This knowledge not only shone a light on where we came from, but also illuminated many more possibilities about where we can choose to go from here."

Excerpt from "The Winding Path: A New History of Earth"
by Habika Dzidzo – 2187

*

FIVE HUNDRED THOUSAND YEARS AGO, during the Pleistocene Age, upright hominids now known as *Homo Erectus* lived throughout Africa, Asia, and parts of Europe. They used simple stone tools, hunted for food and, at some point in their long history, they discovered how to make fire.

Although the species had thrived for well over a million years, the next few hundred thousand years would irrevocably change most of them forever because something truly unexpected, and altogether outside their experience, was about to happen. They were about to meet visitors from the stars.

The Anu, a tall, humanoid, alien race with pale, blue-tinted skin, landed their massive spaceships in the plains of Africa and the Middle East. The one hundred forty-four thousand explorers were in search of gold, an element precious to them, not for its monetary value, but because it could be used to correct a major imbalance in the climate of their home world, many light-years away in the constellation Cygnus.

They planned to aerosolize the gold and spray it high into their atmosphere in controlled amounts. Their scientists predicted that this would reflect a precise amount of sunlight into space to halt the global warming that was turning their planet into a parched desert due to fluctuations in their star.

The Anu discovered rich veins of gold in many places on the Earth and, for a while, they ignored the astonished and frightened hominids that gave the aliens a wide berth as they mined the rare element wherever they could find it. But it proved to be an arduous task, even for the Anu's advanced technology. They were simply spread too thin and the conditions on their planet were quickly getting worse. Many feared they couldn't mine enough gold in time to save their people, so large expeditions were underway to find a new, suitable home world for their people that wasn't already inhabited by an intelligent species.

Then, the Anu on Earth had an idea. Over time, they had gathered an incredible amount of knowledge about Earth's flora and fauna and recognized that their hominid neighbors, though extremely primitive by comparison, had many genetic markers that were compatible with the Anu.

They chalked this up to panspermia, the notion that genetic material had been carried to many star systems on comets, asteroids, and meteors and thus, it wasn't unusual to find that life on other planets bore certain similarities to their species.

The Anu were master geneticists. They initiated a massive program to infuse millions of *Home Erectus* subjects with Anu DNA to create an army of workers that could be taught to help the aliens mine gold far quicker than they could on their own. They knew the plan was against their laws but they were running out of time.

For six decades, which was no time at all to beings that lived for thousands of years, the Anu altered a sufficient number of *Homo Erectus* into *Homo Sapiens* to aid them in their plan. However, several groups were left untouched and, when they experienced the horror of their fellow tribemates being abducted and changed into "monsters," many of them migrated to more remote parts of Asia and Europe and it's with these groups that the story of the Sasquatch began.

As the unaltered tribes continued to evolve, they developed different skills than the newly-formed *Homo Sapiens* that served the "sky-gods." Since they retained a much deeper connection to nature, they began to perform shamanistic rituals and ingested certain plants that gave them the ability to sense other realities. Eventually, they not only became aware of alternate universes, they learned to open natural portals that would transport them from one reality to another as easily as walking through a doorway.

As more and more hominids were hunted by the Anu to be turned into modified workers, this skill became a way to escape their captors and, over time, it was passed down genetically from generation to generation until the ability became a natural trait of the evolving *Homo Erectus* people. They flourished, grew bigger and stronger and, by the time the rogue Anu explorers were recalled to their home world to face punishment for their ethical transgression, *Homo Erectus* had evolved into *Homo Giganticus*, otherwise known as Yeti, Sasquatch, Susquehannock, and by their more common name, "Bigfoot."

As the Sasquatch migrated to the rest of the world, they watched as humans evolved alongside them, but always kept their distance from their modified ancestors, often slipping into alternate realities to avoid being seen. This was especially true during those times when the more enlightened "sky-gods" took responsibility for the unintentional creation of humans and would visit Earth to teach them the secrets of agriculture, astronomy, mathematics, and bestow other knowledge that would help them develop a self-sustaining society.

The irony was that, for a long time, many humans who believed in the existence of the Sasquatch people thought they might be the "missing link" between ancient humans and modern man. It wasn't until the Hybrids arrived and shared their knowledge with Earth that mankind understood that it was the extraterrestrial Anu who were missing from the evolutionary equation.

After the Landing, the Sasquatch people felt comfortable enough to reveal themselves and share their extensive knowledge of nature with the inhabitants of Earth. It's this knowledge that allowed the Sasquatch to create Divinorum and become Masters of the craft that made the Five Levels of Mastery possible.

*

Argus had shared the secret of his people's ability to travel to parallel realities with Holly out of friendship, and Holly had promised to keep it to herself. Though Holly hadn't told anyone, she was asking Argus to use his skill to find Willa and bring her back to Earth One. Of course, that meant his secret would be exposed to Willa, anyone with her, and everyone who would wonder how Argus had managed to rescue her.

But this was Willa. Without her, Earth would be deprived of their best defense against The Archon's fleet, and Xanthes's plans to rule the Earth might succeed.

Argus could only promise Holly that he would take her request to the Elders of his tribe and ask for permission to bring Willa home. The Sasquatch entered the Port Dublin Shaddok and emerged a second later from the Shaddok in the Burren, having been teleported over one hundred fifty miles.

Argus walked the extra few miles to Poulnabrone Dolmen, an ancient structure formed from tall standing stones capped by a thirteen-foot-long slab of limestone. The Dolmen had been used by humans as a tomb once, but the location was instinctively chosen by the ancient Sasquatch people who could sense the energy of a natural portal on the desolate spot. Oddly, because of its tunnel-like appearance, the Dolmen was referred to in later years by humans as a portal tomb, long after knowledge of the interdimensional portal within had been lost.

However, Argus's people could still sense and mentally activate the portal without any effort. The Sasquatch strode to the Dolmen and scanned the barren countryside to make sure no one was watching. He stepped between the upright stones and vanished.

Argus arrived in a strange landscape on the other side of the Dolmen. While the Shaddoks transported people to various locations on Earth, the Poulnabrone Portal was connected to a planet in an otherworldly dimension. The Sasquatch people called it Shunyata in their ancient language. The name meant "emptiness" and was an apt description of the barren environment Argus found himself in.

Thirteen Portal Dolmens stood in a large circle that surrounded a massive, Stonehenge-like structure in the center. Argus's people, although ancient, didn't know who built the Dolmen Portals upon this lifeless world.

The sky was an even, pale grey, as if it was overcast, except there were no clouds. Light issued from some unseen source; a gentle illumination that barely cast any shadows. The portals and henge sat on the bedrock of a wide plain that stretched for miles in every direction and was bordered by distant, towering columns of crystallized basalt.

As far as the Sasquatch people knew, there wasn't another living thing on Shunyata other than those who briefly visited through the

Dolmens. The thirteen portals that circled the henge were connected to many different places on Earth, each serving multiple locations. All Argus had to do was hold a mental image of the Quorum Lodge to ensure that the Dolmen he came through would take him back to Port Dublin instead of to another town or continent.

Argus walked between the upright stones of the henge and stood in the center. He closed his eyes and sent a mental message to the Elders of his tribe that he had something important to discuss.

As soon as he sensed they'd received his message, Argus opened his eyes and studied the glyphs carved into the henge stones millennia ago by his people. The glyphs told the story of their journey from the ancient past to the present as the Susquehannock migrated across the globe.

There were other stories, too: tales of their connection to nature, the secrets told to them by the trees, herbs and flowering plants they considered kin, even tales of individuals the Sasquatch held in high regard for the feats they accomplished or challenges they overcame for the betterment of their tribe.

Argus's reverie was interrupted as three Elders emerged from other portals and joined him inside the henge.

The largest of them, Rhadamanthus, had snow-white fur. He hailed from the lofty peaks of the Himalayas, one of the few places left that was still gifted with a soft blanket of snow each winter.

Ts'Eme'Kwes lived in the dense forests of the American Northwest. Her tribe, the Narcoonah, revered her as a powerful medicine woman who knew everything there was to know about the flora and fauna of their domain.

Salizar, his brown fur thick like a bear's, inhabited Eastern Europe along with his people, the Chuchuna, who were one of the few Sasquatch tribes to live in a village of their own rather than in the wild.

A smile widened the white Yeti's broad face. "Good to see you, Argus. It's been far too long."

"Agreed," Argus said to Rhadamanthus, "but sad this is not social gathering. Have danger to speak of and secret I must break."

"You speak of the Takers who come through Maelstrom?" Salizar said in a thick Slavic accent.

Argus nodded his shaggy head. He understood that "Takers" was Salizar's general term for the ancient Anu and anyone else he considered a threat to his tribe.

"The whole world knows of that danger," Ts'Eme'Kwes added. "But what secret must you break?"

Argus extended his huge hands to encompass the grey landscape. "This and our way of coming here."

Rhadamanthus was suddenly solemn. "Why?"

"I told you of Willa," Argus said.

"The Hybrid with the Mark of the Takers," Salizar spat, his tone bitter as bile.

"It's not the child's fault," Ts'Eme'Kwes countered.

Salizar huffed through his wide nostrils. "Her power grows, maybe she becomes like the Takers."

Argus stepped toward Salizar, his body braced for a challenge. "Maybe first time Mark might save instead of enslave!"

Salizar puffed out his chest to return the challenge, but a warning glance from Rhadamanthus kept him silent. The Yeti turned to Argus.

"Speak of Willa."

"She went through Maelstrom. Is lost in other 'verse. Maybe can't get back, maybe in danger," Argus explained. "Need her in our 'verse to protect from new Takers. I go to get her."

Ts'Eme'Kwes understood. "Then others will know we can Slipwalk. Our secret will be out."

"Someone already knows," Rhadamanthus said, his ancient eyes fixed on Argus. "Someone asked you to do this, true?"

Argus looked down at his large, furry feet in shame. "True."

Salizar was livid. "You told outsider?"

157

"Holly, mentor of Willa. She is Cryptic! She is friend! She told no one," Argus growled.

"Yet she's asked you to do this, knowing that outsiders may find out," Ts'Eme'Kwes said.

The Divinorum Master couldn't argue the point. "I am careful. Will wait until Willa is alone. She will learn secret but she will not tell."

"You trust her?" Rhadamanthus said.

"Yes," Argus answered with unwavering conviction.

The three Elders exchanged a glance. Salizar was skeptical. Ts'Eme'Kwes seemed deep in thought. Rhadamanthus faced Argus.

"We will discuss. You will wait."

Argus nodded. The Elders left the henge and slipped through the Dolmen Portal that had transported the Yeti to Shunyata.

Argus took a large breath and forced himself to be patient. He stared out through the standing stones at the bleak landscape. Until the Elders returned, he would be the only living thing on the entire planet.

*

Sequoia, Moonstone, Selene, and the entire Nocturnal population of Mystery had gathered in shared sadness as they placed Opal's pale corpse in a marble crypt. Her body was wrapped in her acolyte robe, her lifeless expression serene as a still mountain lake.

The large, black marble cover stone, adorned with a silver crescent moon, was slid into place. Sybilline Darkwood, who kept watch over the crypts and presided over all Nocturnal death rituals, stepped forward to deliver the traditional eulogy.

"She dwells now in endless night.
She drinks from the cup of mystery.
She sleeps in the shadow of the Moon.
She knows the secrets of eternity.
She has passed through the Stygian gate.
She has journeyed to the farthest shore.

She is now at peace in spirit.
In our hearts, forevermore."

The solemn service ended. The gathering of Nocturnals dispersed. Only Sequoia, Moonstone, and Selene remained.

"A murder last year in the Contact Council chamber. A murder now in Mystery. I vow this is one mystery that shall not go unsolved," Sequoia said. She took a final look at Opal's tomb through moist eyes, then walked down the causeway that led to her chamber.

Selene turned to Moonstone. "Have you sensed any reason why Opal was killed?"

"Judging from where she was found, she was clearly on her way to see the Provost," Moonstone said. "The lateness of the hour would suggest it was something important. But this is simply common sense."

Selene nodded as she thought it through. "So, whatever Opal knew, someone couldn't risk the Provost finding out."

"Since it's been centuries since anyone has committed such crimes on Earth, both murders must be connected to the people from Xos," Moonstone continued.

"Gant's under house arrest until his banishment, so it couldn't have been him. That means one of the others... Dennik, Alarra, Gar, or even Brim, must be working for the Archon, like Koro was," Selene said.

Moonstone shifted her blind eyes toward Selene. "Or there's a spy on Earth we don't know about."

"Then, either the Archon managed to send someone covertly, like how Haldane and Gant arrived, or..." Selene didn't like the alternative.

Moonstone finished the thought for her. "The only two people who've been tortured by the Archon and escaped are Kale Ashgrove and Elowen Koa.

"But the med-tech telepaths --"

159

"They're not infallible," Moonstone cautioned. "They could have missed something. We have no way of knowing what really happened to Kale and Elowen. If Xanthes is as powerful as Willa says, then we can't be sure they weren't telepathically manipulated and forced to do her bidding."

"Opal must've figured out who the spy is. It would be the only reason to kill her," Selene said. "But how would she have known?"

"Good question," Moonstone replied. "The solution to any mystery starts with a good question. Being Nocturnals, we have access to knowledge through our counterparts in other realities. Perhaps one of Opal's voices identified the spy. Maybe one of ours can as well. Come, let's tell the Provost what we suspect. The more voices, the better."

*

Xos-Asura, Xanthes, and Uzza watched as Zaduga emerged from the potion-induced vision, his withered features more heavily lined than usual. His pale eyes flickered to the Archon, gravid with bad news before he uttered a word.

"Speak," the Archon commanded.

"My Lord, what I saw makes no sense," the Sensate began, "but I will leave it to your infinite wisdom to discern the truth of it."

"My daughter has told me your theory of alternate universes," Xos-Asura said. "If you would have us believe that impossible concept, it's a small step to accept another."

"Yes, my Lord. Impossible as it may seem, it appears that the Earth girl has physically crossed from her reality into another."

Xanthes frowned in confusion. "You're saying there's a third universe besides ours and hers?"

"Yes, my Lady. A universe in which another version of her already resides. It makes sense that she now feels twice as powerful. There are two of her, working as one," Zaduga said.

The Archon, Xanthes, and Uzza took a moment to absorb the elder Sensate's revelation. Xanthes broke the silence.

"Then, there must be a universe where I have a double," she said.

"And perhaps more than one," Zaduga confirmed.

Xanthes turned to her father, the same cold fire in her eyes. "We could build an army of my doubles before my nemesis does!"

Xos-Asura pressed Zaduga. "How can we find them?"

"Through the Maelstrom, I imagine, my Lord."

"I will send a team of my best techs to you," the Archon said. "Use your senses to help them find a way to navigate our ships from one universe to another, so my daughter may gather her army."

Zaduga bowed his head. "I live to serve, my Lord."

"And you serve to live," the Archon said. "Do this and when we crush the Alliance, I may grant the Sensate Order a planet of its own." He turned and left the chamber.

Xanthes regarded the two Sensates. "You should know, I've enslaved a second puppet on Earth in case the first one fails."

"Excellent," Zaduga said. "Your powers are becoming quite formidable."

Xanthes gave a slight bow of respect to Zaduga and followed her father out. Uzza turned to his Master, his voice low.

"We've secretly been bending Xanthes to our will, but how can we control an army of her doubles?"

"If what happens in one universe also happens in another, then perhaps our doubles have done the same to their versions of her," Zaduga said, his voice equally hushed. "We may be able to take advantage of their influence over her."

"And if her doubles are still of their own minds?"

"Then we must amend our plan. Put your thoughts to it," Zaduga ordered as he fell into a reverie. "Imagine it... a planet of our own."

"Never-ending are the Nine," Uzza said with a bow.

"Never-ending," Zaduga said with a greedy grin.

*

Lily, River, Holly, Alder, Kale, and Thorn sat at evening meal in the Nest and awaited word from Argus. Lily had served a bounty of vegetables and fruits, much of which she had grown in her garden.

"I don't understand what the Sasquatch can do to help Willa," Thorn groused, having hardly touched his plate.

"As I said, I can't tell you that," Holly reminded him.

Alder finished his meal and reached for a second helping. "Argus is a Divinorum Master. I imagine she asked him to use the brew to see if he can sense Willa's whereabouts."

"You're a Sage," Thorn said. "Why can't you?"

"We suspect that Willa's in the Archon's alternate universe," Alder said. "When I was a Nocturnal, I learned to communicate with other versions of myself in parallel realities."

"I know how it works," Thorn grumbled.

"Well, what you don't know is that I've already checked with my counterparts. Fortunately for me, but unfortunately for Willa, I don't have an alternate version of myself in the Archon's reality," Alder explained. "If I did, he's no longer alive. Or perhaps not yet born. Either way, there's no one for me to link with."

"What if Willa didn't go to fight Xanthes," Kale said as he chewed on a green bean. "What if she went through the second Maelstrom instead?"

"Why on Earth would she have done that?" Lily said.

"I don't know," Kale said. "Maybe she sensed there was something on the other side that could protect us against the invasion."

River leaned forward. "You're saying she may not be in the Archon's universe?"

Kale nodded. "We have no idea what reality the second portal connects to. While we're waiting for Argus to do... well, whatever he's going to do, I could take my ship and find out where the second Maelstrom goes."

"That's risky. It could still take you to the Archon's universe," Holly said.

"It could," Kale agreed, "but I'm willing to take that chance."

"I'll go with you," River said without hesitation.

"Me, too!" Thorn nearly shouted.

"I think we should wait to find out what Argus can do," Holly interjected.

River stood. "But you won't tell us what that is," he said. "Every moment we delay could spell greater danger for Willa."

"Just give him another hour. He should be joining us soon," Holly pleaded.

Lily touched River's arm. "Holly has always had Willa's best interests at heart. I trust her instincts. One more hour."

River gave her a reluctant nod and sat down. "One hour."

Alder finished his second helping and dabbed his mouth with a napkin. "Well, as long as we're waiting, do you have any dessert wines?"

*

As the discussion inside the Nest continued, Elowen One's mental shield prevented Holly and Alder from sensing her presence outside. She quietly attached a dozen doctored power cells to the underside of the nano-glass dwelling with molecular adhesive. The explosion would be powerful enough to obliterate the Nest and the massive oak tree supporting it and leave a smoking crater a hundred feet across.

If Willa's parents and mentors were dead, her remaining friends could be used as bargaining chips to prevent her from opposing Xanthes.

Somewhere deep within Elowen's mind, a voice screamed for her to stop, but her body refused to obey. Elowen's buried consciousness was forced to watch her traitorous hands attach the final power cell, helpless as a hostage in chains.

*

In the Nest, Holly abruptly stood, alarmed.

"What's wrong?" Lily said.

"The oak tree holding your home... it's trying to warn me..." A telepathic vision of the imminent explosion blinded Holly's senses. She reeled and River rose to steady her. "Everyone out!" she shouted.

Thorn jumped to his feet, startled and confused. "What's happening?"

"Out, now! Run!" Holly repeated.

Lily waved her hand and the door opened. They all hurried out and down the large branch that led to the ground.

Elowen was halfway up a hill that was three hundred feet away when the commotion made her look back. Her intended targets were escaping! She never really believed that Cryptics could commune with trees, but now she wondered if the oak had given her away. Elowen armed her detonator but, before she could tap the trigger, Argus's huge hand engulfed hers. He crushed the detonator along with every bone in Elowen's hand.

Elowen's scream alerted Holly and the others. They hurried up the hill where the Sasquatch's gigantic moonlit silhouette loomed over Elowen as she dropped to her knees and clutched her broken hand to her chest.

Kale was shocked to see his friend rocking back and forth in agony.

"What is this?" he demanded of Argus.

"She going to blow up Nest," Argus said, his fierce eyes still fixed on Elowen.

Alder picked up the remnants of the crushed detonator. "It appears we owe you our lives," he said to Argus. "Thank you."

Argus grunted a response.

Alder knelt on one knee and placed his index finger on Elowen's temple. She jerked away, but Argus clutched her head and held her still. Alder pressed her temple again; his raven eyes held Elowen's gaze like magnets.

"Why would you do this?" he demanded.

Elowen struggled to resist the Sage's power.

"Tell me!" Alder insisted.

Sweat poured down Elowen's face. She screamed as a thousand needles stabbed her brain, forcing her to remain silent.

Alder grabbed her face with both hands and forced his iron will through her mental shield: a steel spike against glass. The shield shattered and, utterly spent, Elowen collapsed on the grass, out cold.

The Sage withdrew his hands and felt Kale's concern. "She'll be okay. I had to break through some very powerful programming."

"Xanthes," Holly murmured.

"We should get her to the med-center," River said.

"I'll take her," Kale said.

Holly turned to Argus. He saw the question in her eyes. Argus nodded.

Lily caught the exchange. "Can you find our daughter?" she asked Argus.

"Argus can find. Bring her home."

Lily and River exhaled with relief. River glanced back at the blinking power cells attached to the Nest. "I'll call a tech squad to remove the explosives."

"Allow me," Alder said. He rose to his full height and pounded the tip of his cane against a rock. An iridescent wave of light rippled outward and the explosives vanished from under the oak.

The wind in the oak's leaves rustled a sigh and Holly felt the tree's relief.

"What did you do with the power cells?" River asked.

Alder pointed skyward. Everyone glanced up in time to see a brilliant explosion a mile over their heads. Alder waved his cane in the air and transformed the burst into a multi-colored display. Anyone who saw it from a distance would think it was fireworks.

River turned to Alder. "Thank you."

Lily laid a gentle hand on Argus's furry arm. "Please bring Willa back to us."

"I go now," the Sasquatch said with a final nod. His enormous strides took him into the surrounding forest in less than a minute. As soon as he knew no one could see him, he closed his eyes and willed a glowing portal to open in the air before him.

He stepped through, the portal closed, and the forest was once again lit only by moonlight.

A few moments after Argus disappeared, Rusalka stepped out from behind a Yew tree in his Elemental form as a large hare. His long ears were laid back and his nose twitched as he sniffed the air where the portal had been. His ruby-red eyes burned with curiosity.

"My Queen will want to know of this!" he said under his breath. He hopped toward the deepest part of the forest as fast as he could.

Chapter Ten:
SWITCH

"Murphy's Law, the idea that whatever can go wrong will go wrong, is a subset of the law of synchronicity. However, there are two sides to it. On one hand, the effect is a manifestation of ingrained negative beliefs but, on the other hand, what seems to be going wrong can often be a sign and an opportunity to take a different, and possibly better path."

"The Book of Paradox"
by Sassafras the Sage

*

ON EARTH TWO, both Willas, along with the alternate Lily and River, walked across the field toward their version of the Nest. A warm breeze carried the coconut scent of the yellow gorse flowers that lined the stone path to the oak tree that cradled the home.

Willa One glanced at the moonlit Yew forest in the distance and thought she saw movement among the trees. She squinted to get a better look, then chalked it up to nothing more than dancing shadows as the trees swayed in the wind.

As they approached the large, low branch that allowed access to the Nest, Willa One stopped to take in the breadth of the enormous oak.

"It's a little different than my tree," she said. "This branch is over there and that branch is over here and I think your tree's a little taller." She wandered around the titanic trunk to the side opposite from the path as she searched for other differences.

When she was out of sight, Willa Two felt the oak reach out with a warning vibration. "Something's not right," she told her parents and called out to her counterpart. "Willa! Come back!"

On the other side of the tree, Willa One also felt her senses flare up in response to the oak. She hurried around the trunk just in time to see a glowing portal open in the air near Willa Two.

"Behind you!" Willa One screamed.

Willa Two turned as Argus stretched his massive arms through the portal, grabbed her in his humongous hands and pulled her through.

"Argus, no!" Willa One shouted, but it was too late. The portal snapped shut before Lily's and River's horrified faces.

"What was that?" Lily Two shouted.

"It's okay. That was Argus, my Divinorum Master," Willa One said, hoping to calm her counterpart's parents. "He clearly figured out how to get me back to my universe."

"Except he took the wrong Willa!" River Two said as he stared at the empty air where the portal used to be.

"She'll be fine. Soon as they realize it's not me, they'll bring her back."

Lily and River weren't happy but they knew there was nothing to do but wait. River's com-link chimed. "Now what?" He tapped it.

"Can you all please return to Andromeda Spaceport," Commander Erebus said over the link. "We have more visitors from the other universe."

"We have a slight problem," River said. "Our daughter --"

Lily put a finger to her lips. River got the message.

"-- has gone on an important errand," he finished.

"The alternate Willa is still with you?"

"Yes."

"Then please hurry," Erebus urged them. "Our new guests are getting a bit testy."

"On our way," River said and tapped the com off.

"I can go by myself," Willa One offered.

"We promised to keep an eye on you," Lily said.

"Your daughter confirmed I'm who I say I am."

"More for your protection," River said. "After all, you're still a target."

"So are you," Willa reminded them.

"Strength in numbers," Lily Two said with the same finality Willa's One's mother used when she'd made up her mind.

"What if Argus comes back with your daughter?"

"Our Willa will find us. The people who just came through the Maelstrom will probably need to go back to your universe as well, yes?"

"Right. Of course. I bet it's Rowan," Willa said with a smirk. "It would be just like him."

Lily's mood darkened. "Rowan Ashgrove?"

Willa One nodded. "I assume there's a version of him here, too?"

Lily and River exchanged a sobering glance.

"There was," River said, before Lily could silence him.

"What are you saying?"

River sighed. No use hiding the truth now. "Rowan's father was captured by the Archon. Rowan and his brother Thorn went to rescue him."

"Kale was taken in my universe as well," Willa said, "Rowan and Thorn went looking for him, but the Resistance rescued Kale. They all made it back to Earth."

"In our universe, Elowen was the only one who came back after she escaped," Lily said. "And Rowan's ship was destroyed by the Maelstrom."

Willa was aghast. "In this universe, Kale, Rowan, and Thorn are dead?"

The answer was frozen on River's face. "Perhaps it would be best not to share that story with your Rowan."

They walked in silence the rest of the way to the transport ship that would take them up to the spaceport. Willa was sorry that Lily and River were forced to be the bearers of such awful news, but she was grateful that the Ashgrove family was alive and well in her universe. At least, she hoped they were.

*

Opal Two stood before Sequoia Two in the Provost's chamber. "Her voice is gone," she said, downcast. "I fear my counterpart is dead."

"What do your other voices say?" Sequoia gently prompted.

"They agree," the acolyte sniffed, on the verge of tears.

"So, Willa's family in that universe may not know their Elowen is compromised," the Provost reasoned.

Opal nodded and sniffled again.

Sequoia closed her eyes and stretched her Nocturnal senses as far as she could. Her counterpart voices, which included the Provost of Earth One, magnified her ability to probe multiple parallel realities.

Her senses quietly caressed the minds of Willa One's family and friends and revealed Elowen One's failed attempt to assassinate them. Sequoia Two opened her eyes.

"It appears that both our Elowen and theirs were doomed to fail," said the Provost, "yet I still sense danger." She focused on her sniffling acolyte. "I don't believe the Elowen of that universe killed your counterpart."

"Then who?"

"Xanthes," Sequoia said.

Opal was shocked. "Xanthes crossed the Maelstrom?"

Sequoia allowed her senses to paint a mental picture. "No. She has influence over someone, forced them to do her bidding."

"She's that powerful?"

The Provost's expression was grim. "And becoming more powerful every day."

"Can you see who it is, Provost?"

Sequoia Two once again pushed her senses into Willa One's universe and searched for Xanthes's secret puppet. She was suddenly struck with a dizzying jolt of energy. Her mind plunged into a churning whirlpool of pure chaos. Sequoia staggered, fell to her knees, mouth agape, eyes rolled back into her pounding skull.

"Provost!" Opal ran to her mentor and steadied her. "Provost! Can you hear me?"

Sequoia strained against the psychic onslaught and finally snapped free. She held her throbbing temples as her breath came in short gasps.

Opal Two was worried sick, her voice choked with emotion. "Provost, are you okay?"

Sequoia caught her breath, stood with Opal's help and staggered to her chair.

"The assassin's mind is protected by a powerful mental shield. I've never felt anything like it," Sequoia Two said, her head still throbbing. She clutched Opal's arm, her eyes haunted. "All my counterparts were shut out. I have no other path by which to warn Willa's family in that universe. I'm afraid they're on their own."

*

Sequoia One slowly emerged from the mental fog that remained after she unlinked from her counterpart's search for the unknown assassin. Though the combined attempt to identify Opal One's murderer had failed, at least the Provost could let Willa's family know they were still in danger, despite the fact that the Elowen of this reality had been caught.

The fact that Elowen had been brainwashed and programmed to carry out Xanthes's homicidal plan was one thing. With help and enough time, she could be deprogrammed. But the notion that

Xanthes was now powerful enough to bend someone to her will without even leaving her universe was a frightening realization.

Sequoia looked around her chamber, still half expecting to see her acolyte's eager face. Opal's absence felt like a knife through her heart. She had vowed to find the killer, but if the efforts of multiple counterparts couldn't pierce Xanthes's protective mental shield, then she'd have to find another way to uncover the second assassin's identity.

*

Rowan and Star sat in the same interrogation room where Willa One had been sequestered when she first arrived. The same two robots stood by the door, their ever-vigilant sensors trained on their new "guests."

The door opened. Erebus entered, followed by Willa One. Rowan and Star stood, all smiles.

"Willa! I knew you were alive!" Rowan said as he rounded the table.

The security robots moved with inhuman speed to block his path. Willa turned to Erebus.

"It's okay. I know them."

Erebus hesitated, then nodded. The robots stood aside and Rowan enveloped Willa in a huge hug, which Willa happily returned. They separated and Willa flashed a smile in Star's direction.

"Good to see you, sweetie," Star said.

Rowan noticed the tattoo on the back of Willa's hand. "What's this?"

"To tell me from my counterpart," she explained before she realized what that might lead to.

"Counterpart?" Rowan said.

Willa nodded to Erebus, who gestured to someone in the hallway. Rowan and Star stared at the door as Willa's alternate parents entered.

"So, you were telling the truth," River said to Erebus. "This is another universe, different from the Archon's."

Willa answered for the Commander. "Yes. I promise I'll explain everything, but first we've got to get back to our 'verse," Willa said.

"Can we get back?" Star said.

"I think so, but not through the Maelstrom. We need to go to my home…" she glanced at Lily and River. "I mean, their home."

A thought crossed Rowan's mind. "Wait. If you and your parents have doubles here, do we?" he said, gesturing at himself and Star.

Willa was at a loss. Rowan saw the look on her face and spared her.

"Never mind. I don't want to know." He turned to Erebus. "Are we free to go?"

The Commander nodded. "These two bots will escort you, to be safe. Just make sure when you get back to your universe that you prevent anyone else from going through either Maelstrom."

"Copy that," Rowan said emphatically.

*

On Earth One, Lily, River, Holly, and Alder sat in the Nest. "I think we could all use some tea," Lily remarked as she headed to the kitchen. Before she could grab the cups, the door opened again. Everyone froze as Argus ducked through the opening and practically pushed Willa Two into the room.

Lily's heart jumped for joy. "Willa!" She ran to her daughter and embraced her in a crushing hug. River and Holly joined her, nearly smothering Willa Two as Alder favored Argus with a grateful smile.

"Job well done, my friend. Now, tell us, how did you do it?" said the Sage.

Willa Two's words were muffled by the crush of her family's embrace. They all separated to let her speak.

"What was that, Little Fox?" Lily said.

"I'm not your Willa!"

"What are you talking about?" River said with a frown.

Willa Two jabbed a finger at Argus. "Your large friend took the wrong one. Your daughter is still in my universe. I'm her counterpart!"

Alder stepped forward and placed a hand on Willa Two's unruly mop of red hair. He closed his eyes and extended his sagacious senses. After a heartbeat, Alder's black eyes opened in disbelief. He withdrew his hand.

"She's telling the truth," Alder said. "This isn't our Willa."

"I don't understand," Lily said.

"Your Willa went through the first Maelstrom, but she didn't go to the Archon's 'verse," Willa Two explained as calmly as she could. "She wound up in mine. Something to do with a quirk in the physics, I think." She looked at Argus. "He grabbed me instead of her."

Everyone turned to Argus, who was looking more downcast by the minute.

"Argus make mistake?" the Sasquatch mumbled.

"That's an understatement!" Alder huffed.

Willa Two felt sorry for the furry giant. "In his defense, your daughter and I are identical. He couldn't have known."

River placed a reassuring hand on Argus's arm. "Can you take her back and get our Willa?"

"Argus make it right!" he vowed.

Alder narrowed his inky eyes at the Sasquatch. "By the way, how did you find her and bring her here from another universe so quickly?"

"That is secret," Argus grumbled as he threw a concerned look to Holly.

Alder approached the towering Sasquatch, his demeanor growing darker. "Let me get this straight. While Kale Ashgrove and his crew were held prisoner... being mercilessly tortured by the Archon, you could have gone to that universe and rescued them? You could've brought them all home safe and sound, yet you did *nothing* just to protect this secret of yours?"

The room grew cold and tense, as the Sage's mood began to physically manifest.

"Alder..." Holly cautioned, but the Sage waved her off.

"Answer me, Argus!" Alder said, his voice rising. "Could you have rescued Kale and his crew?"

Argus's eyes hid in the shadow of his heavy, furrowed brow. He hung his head and nodded almost imperceptibly. "Yes," he whispered, ashamed.

Holly stepped between Alder and Argus. "It's not his fault! His people wouldn't allow it. He barely got permission to bring Willa back."

The Sage struck the tip of his cane on the nano-glass floor. A thunderclap resounded as a literal storm began to build around them in the Nest. Flashes of lightning in the dark, swirling clouds underscored Alder's anger.

"Tell me your secret!" the Sage demanded as his power held the Sasquatch in its iron grip.

Holly's long white hair whipped in the wind along with Willa's, Lily's, and River's. She tried to reach Alder but was held back by a bubble of energy that emanated from Alder and surrounded him and the Sasquatch.

"Alder, please, I promised to keep his secret!" Holly begged.

Alder ignored her as he commanded Argus in a voice that echoed like a god from Olympus. *"Tell me your secret!"*

Argus tried to resist the Sage's power with every ounce of his formidable strength but he was no match for Alder.

"Argus can open portals to other 'verses," the Sasquatch finally said through clenched teeth.

The storm dissipated and the room returned to normal as Alder released his hold on Argus.

"Portals… just by willing it?"

Argus slumped and sat on the floor, his back against a wall, arms wrapped around his knees. He nodded, sullen and embarrassed.

"All your people can do this?" the Sage pressed.

Another hesitant nod from Argus.

"I don't believe it," the Sage said. "Tell me the truth!" He aimed his cane at the penitent Sasquatch to deliver another blast of power, but Willa Two blocked his path.

"It's true," she said, "he brought me here through just such a portal." Her eyes dared Alder to doubt her. The Sage backed off.

Holly's ice-blue eyes were colder than usual as they bore into the Sage. "How could you do that to him, Alder?"

The Sage spun to face Holly, Lily, and River. "Don't you understand? If Argus and his people can open doorways between universes, they could simply walk into the Archon's reality and bring him and Xanthes back here as prisoners! The invasion would be over before it began!"

Holly was torn between her promise to Argus and the logic of Alder's argument. She went to the Sasquatch and knelt beside him.

"He has a point, Argus," she said softly. "Let me come with you to talk to your people… explain the situation to them."

"No promise they will agree," Argus said, his voice low.

"Of course not, why should they?" Alder said. "When the Archon attacks Earth, your people can just pop off to another universe. But what about the rest of us? Do you even care what happens to us?"

Alder's bitter words pierced Argus to his soul. He pinned the Sage with a resentful stare. "Sasquatch are first people of Earth. This our home longer than yours!"

"Then defend it!" Alder shouted.

Argus pulled himself to his feet. Holly stood at his side. The Divinorum Master looked down at Alder. "Argus will go and explain to my people."

"After you bring our Willa back first, please," Lily said.

Argus nodded and looked at Willa Two. "Take you home now."

With no need to hide his secret any longer, Argus willed a portal to open inside the Nest. He gestured for Willa Two to pass through, then followed her with a final scowl at Alder. The portal closed.

River broke the silence. "Amazing."

Alder turned to Holly. "I'm sorry to have been so harsh with him, Holly, but this is a matter of life and death. Like it or not, this is war. We need every advantage we can get." The Sage walked out the door and down the branch.

Holly went to the door and called after him. "What are you going to do?"

"Call the Quorum to order," he shouted back. "They deserve to know."

The Sage moved off across the field and down the path to town. Holly stepped back inside the Nest to face Lily and River.

"What if Argus and his people refuse to help?" Lily said.

"Then we may not only have to fight a war with the Archon but, for the first time in seven hundred years, we may have one here on Earth as well," Holly said. She sat at the table, at a loss. "Please, may I have some tea?"

"Of course," Lily said as she went to the kitchen.

Holly closed her eyes, reached out with her Cryptic senses and sent a message to the Elementals in the surrounding forest. Argus's people had a long history with the Pookas, Faeries, Sylphs, and other Elementals. Perhaps they could offer an alternative to Alder's plan or, at the very least, help to convince the Sasquatch tribe to cooperate.

Rowan's ship landed in the field near the Nest on Earth-Two. Rowan, Star, Willa One, Lily Two, and River Two walked down the ramp along with the two security robots. The bots scanned the field in all directions.

"No danger detected," one of the bots announced.

"That's refreshing," Willa One said under her breath.

The bots suddenly went on alert. "An energy field is forming a hundred feet to the North," the second bot said. Both robots quickly positioned themselves between the group and the glowing portal that opened nearby.

Willa Two and Argus stepped through and the portal closed.

"Thank the stars!" Lily Two said as she and River ran to their daughter and wrapped her in a hug.

"Argus sorry for mistake," he said with a sheepish look.

Willa One hurried up to Argus. "Are my parents safe?"

Argus nodded. "I stop Elowen. Everyone safe."

River extended his hand. "Thank you for bringing our Willa back."

Argus carefully shook River's hand and turned to Willa One. "We go now."

"Rowan and Star are also from our universe," Willa one told him. "Can you take us all?"

"And my ship," Rowan added.

Argus looked at the ship and nodded. "Get on board."

Both Willas hugged like old friends.

"It's been fun… sort of," Willa One said.

"It's not every day we get to meet a counterpart in the flesh," Willa Two said.

"Wait. What about our idea to take on your Xanthes and mine together?" Willa One reminded her double.

Willa Two looked at Argus. "There may be another way of beating her."

"Maybe," Argus offered. "Others have same idea."

Willa One caught on immediately. "Of course! We can use whatever this new tech is to go to the Archon's 'verse, right?"

Willa Two kept her gaze on Argus as she waited for him to enlighten her counterpart.

"What?" Willa One prompted.

Argus shuffled his large feet. "Not new tech," he grumbled.

Rowan approached the Sasquatch. "What do you mean it's not new tech?"

"Not tech at all. Sasquatch always had ability to go from 'verse to 'verse," Argus answered.

"Naturally?" Star said, her surprise shared by the group.

"Supposed to be secret," Argus whispered.

"The Sage in your 'verse... Alder, is it? You should know he was pretty upset when he found out," Willa Two said.

Rowan felt the heat of anger rise in his face. "I think I understand why." He advanced on Argus, stabbed a finger at him. "It's your fault my father was tortured! Your fault that Elowen was forced to become an assassin! All because you wouldn't use your ability to rescue them!"

River Two gripped Rowan's arm. "Take it easy."

Rowan pulled away, fire in his eyes. He fought back his anger and headed to his ship. "Take us home!"

Willa One waved a sad goodbye to her double's family as she and Star boarded Corvus. Argus took a deep breath and reluctantly followed them. The ramp retracted and the ship lifted off the ground.

Argus opened an enormous portal in the air. Corvus and the Sasquatch slipped through. The portal closed. Willa Two and her parents headed to the Nest.

"If all Sasquatch can do that, we should talk to Ts'Eme'Kwes," River said.

Willa Two walked between Lily and River and took their hands in hers. "I have a feeling she won't be happy that we know her secret."

*

Deep within the forest on Earth One, the Elementals held an Enclave at midnight within a circle of tall Yew trees. Ashleen, the albino Pooka Queen, was attended by Rusalka, as well as Grennan, the wizened Pooka seer. Vulcanus the Salamander and Silver the Sylph were among the Faeries, Gnomes, Dryads, Leprechans, Pixies, Seelies, Elves, and Goblins. Kernunnos, the giant, elk-horned winter spirit loomed in the background of the gathering.

Rusalka spoke to the variegated gathering, his ruby eyes alight. "I tell you, the Sassies can portal without tech to other Earths, you ken me? Holly confirmed it."

"We've lived side-by-side with the First Men for thousands of years," hissed a nasty-looking goblin. "Why would we not know this?"

"If this was true, the trees would have told us," said a Dryad in a voice that sounded like the rustling of dry leaves.

"Then ask the trees," Rusalka barked. "I know what I saw!"

"Maybe you slurp to much Elderberry wine," chittered Gwyllion, a blue-hued Welsh Faerie. "Is that why your eyes are so red?"

Half the gathering joined in her self-satisfied laughter. Ashleen stepped into the center of the circle and the laughter subsided. Regardless of the differences between many tribes of Elementals, the Pooka Queen was held in great respect by all.

The white hare cleared her throat and cast her bright pink eyes around the Enclave as she waited for everyone's full attention.

"My fellow Elementals," she said with diplomatic flair, "you all know our reputation as tricksters. But we've never been liars, at least not to our kin. If Rusalka says he saw the Sassy slip through a portal of his own making then I, for one, believe we ought to take him seriously, especially if the Cryptic has said so as well. She's always been honest with us."

"But the trees would not have kept this from us!" the Dryad repeated.

"Then let's ask Graelach," Ashleen proposed.

All eyes turned toward a large oak at the outer edge of the circle. A human would have thought Graelach to be an ordinary tree. In truth, the Oak was a rare Elemental known as a Dryadus.

Regular tree nymphs, called Dryads, can, like other Elementals, take form in the physical world and then fade back into the stream of Earth's collective consciousness, called Gaia. But if a Dryad chose to remain physical for more than a thousand years, it remained in the material world, took the form of whatever type of tree the nymph used to live in, and became a Dryadus, forever rooted to the ground and enveloped in the dream world of Gaia's globe-spanning awareness.

Though included in the Enclave, a Dryadus could only be communicated with by those who had been through a Kenning. As such, Ashleen was particularly suited to draw the Dryadus out of its trance-like communion with Gaia and get Graelach to speak with the gathering.

Ashleen closed her roseate eyes and allowed her mind to connect with Graelach's roots, branches, and leaves. Much like a Cryptic, the Pooka felt the life force of the oak, sensed the life-giving water that wicked up through its roots, and basked in the gentle breeze that made its leaves dance.

Graelach awoke to Ashleen's presence. The oak's limbs swayed and creaked like an ancient sailing ship as it turned its attention to her. A powerful, telepathic voice rumbled like a deep, underground river that flooded Ashleen's consciousness.

"A single spark of the Great Light has summoned me," Graelach acknowledged.

Ashleen could practically smell the oak's ancientness as it addressed her. *"I am that spark,"* she responded with humility. *"I am Ashleen."*

"You wish to know what I know," Graelach stated.

"If you please, why haven't the trees ever told us about the Sasquatch tribe's ability to cross into other worlds?"

"Why have the trees never told you about the sun, the rain, or the wind?" Graelach said. *"These things are obvious to all and need no telling. It is simply the Sasquatch nature to Slipwalk and we had no reason to think you didn't already know."*

"I see," Ashleen said and gave the oak a respectful bow. *"Thank you."*

Graelach's branches creaked as the great tree fell back into Gaia's dream-like embrace.

Ashleen opened her eyes and took in the gathering. "Rusalka is right. The Sassies can open portals at will. Graelach called it Slipwalking. It's their nature and the trees thought we already knew about it."

"The real question," said Vulcanus the Salamander, "is why do they keep it a secret from us?"

Silver the Sylph's bell-like voice followed the Salamander's. "Yes, that is strange. We Elementals can do wondrous things. Cryptics, Nocturnals, Shapeshifters, and Sages are also adept at linking with parallel worlds or shaping time and space to their will. Why should the Sassies' ability be kept in the shadows?"

Kernunnos's booming voice resounded off the surrounding trees. "Perhaps the Susquehannock felt that if others knew their secret, they'd want to use them in the ways we're all thinking of using them now... to open doors to parallel worlds where we don't belong."

"Right," agreed Gwyllion, "it's one thing for a Nocturnal or a Sage to communicate with a counterpart. It's quite another to meet one face-to-face. Think how chaotic it would be if counterparts could come and go at will between universes. You would never know who's who. Plus, there might be more counterparts like Xanthes."

"You're suggesting the Sassies are doing everyone a favor by keeping their secret?" Rusalka said as his nose twitched in annoyance. "Have you realized this could be the best possible way to stop the invasion?"

The Enclave erupted into a cacophony of chatter as each Elemental shared their opinion as to the best course of action. Ashleen let the din continue for a few minutes and then raised her paws for silence. The gathering quieted and Ashleen once again took the diplomatic approach.

"We're merely guessing. Let's speak with Argus and hear his people's reasons."

Each head nodded agreement with her commonsense suggestion.

"I'll bring the Sassy here," Rusalka volunteered.

"You'll politely *invite* him," Ashleen corrected him. "And don't call him a Sassy to his face or he'll turn you into rabbit stew," she added. It was, of course, a joke since you couldn't kill an Elemental, at least not by ordinary means, but Rusalka got the point.

"Of course, my Queen," he said, his long ears laid back in deference to her wisdom. Rusalka hopped off through the forest as several of the Elementals flitted away on gossamer wings or vanished in a puff of Faerie dust. Kernunnos shook the sparkling dust from his bearded face and disappeared into the woods on his large, cloven hooves.

Vulcanus and the other Salamanders vanished in a ball of blue fire and the goblins and gnomes went back to their underground lairs.

Finally, only Ashleen and Grennan were left in the clearing.

"You've been unusually quiet," the Queen said to her aged Seer.

"Silence speaks volumes if one knows how to listen," said the brown-and-grey mottled hare.

"You think this path is unwise?"

"I think the path is unclear," the Seer replied. He hopped away, leaving Ashleen alone with her thoughts.

It was unusual for Grennan to be uncertain of his temporal visions, and that made Ashleen nervous. She sighed. *Time will tell,* she thought, *if we don't run out of it first.*

She turned to go and startled as she caught sight of the mysterious red fox that sometimes spied on Willa. They locked eyes for a few heartbeats, then the fox slipped off through the forest.

Ashleen was taken aback, a rare and uncomfortable feeling for the Pooka Queen. While it wasn't unusual for Elementals to take animal forms, including that of a fox, the fact that Ashleen didn't know the fox was there disturbed her. She calmed herself and reached out with her senses to the spot where the fox had been. She could tell it was a Shapeshifter, but beyond that, the fox was a complete mystery.

*

Willa One was grateful to be back in the Nest with her parents. Holly, Rowan, Star, Kale, Thorn, and Poppy partook of the sumptuous feast of exotically seasoned vegetables, plump berries, creamy puddings, savory nut cakes, and juicy melons that Lily and River had prepared in celebration of Willa's return.

Of course, Lily made Willa promise to never do anything so foolish again and, once she felt that Willa had learned her lesson, she immediately started planning the welcome-home party.

Holly filled Willa in on what had happened with Elowen in this world and everyone was captivated as Willa told them about all that had transpired on Earth Two. As Willa finished her tale, the door chimed.

Lily opened the door with a gesture and everyone turned to see Sequoia, Moonstone, and Selene. Selene exchanged a glance with Holly, who returned a slight nod: a silent agreement that neither would speak of their earlier argument.

Willa leapt to her feet. "Provost! I didn't know you were coming."

Sequoia took in the festive mood of the gathering and hesitated. "I apologize for interrupting."

"Nonsense," Lily said with her usual charm. "Please come in. Join us."

Willa's senses flared a warning as the trio entered. "You have bad news."

Sequoia struggled to keep her composure. She reached up and wiped a tear from her eye. That simple gesture shocked Willa more deeply than if the Provost had changed into an Aldebaran dragon.

At a nod from Sequoia, Selene took over the task of delivering the message. "Our acolyte, Opal Deserette, has been killed... murdered, in fact."

The gathering froze. River was the first to find his voice. "Another murder? But, that means..."

"Elowen wasn't the only one doing the Archon's bidding," Moonstone said.

Sequoia recovered her composure. "I tried to sense who it is, but the murderer is protected by a very powerful mental shield." The Provost's dark eyes shifted to Willa. "I was hoping..."

Sadness and anger welled up in Willa. Unable to speak, she simply nodded as Holly placed a comforting hand on her shoulder.

"We'll convene the Quorum at first light," Holly said to the Provost. "If the three of you will join us, perhaps together we can pierce that bubble."

"We'll be there," Sequoia vowed, "but we must be mindful that, if Xanthes and the assassin learn of this, they'll do everything in their power to stop us." She turned and, along with Selene and Moonstone, left the Nest.

Holly faced the gathering. "We'll need a particularly potent draft of Divinorum, perhaps double the number of Talus leaves."

"Isn't that dangerous?" Poppy said.

"So is the killer," Willa answered.

Lily faced Holly and bristled. "This is our daughter you're experimenting with!"

"I know, and I'm sorry, but we must take the chance," Holly said. She turned to Willa. "Are you up for this?"

Willa fixed Lily and Holly with her golden gaze. "Try and stop me."

Chapter Eleven:
PRISONER OF THE MIND

"Here's the truth about power that Twenty-First Century humans failed to understand: If you need a weapon to get what you need, then you actually believe you're powerless without it. A weapon doesn't make one powerful, it only proves that one is weak. It takes no power to destroy or try to force your will upon others. Anyone can destroy or threaten, but to create something takes real power. That creation will then contain power and attract what one truly needs like a magnet."

"The Book of Paradox"
by Sassafras the Sage

*

ONE THOUSAND NEW ATTACK SHIPS sat on the five-mile-diameter circle of concrete that surrounded the factory complex on the outskirts of Arcana on Xos. A genetically-engineered army of thousands of Splicers swarmed over the black starships like ants, attaching powerful energy and projectile weapons to the shield plates on the hull.

The Splicers were gaunt and grey with black, insect-like eyes: manufactured abominations, programmed to blindly serve the Empire, devoid of any will of their own.

Xos-Asura and Xanthes observed the final preparations on monitors within the central factory tower.

"Once we've secured Earth, we shall set up factories and use their tech to create a larger, more powerful fleet," Xos-Asura explained to his daughter. "Then we take the next world in the Alliance, secure it, and repeat the process. If we do this with every planet, they will never be able to stop us."

"What about my doubles?" Xanthes said, eager to explore that path.

The Archon pointed to one of the attack ships. Xanthes magnified the view by tapping the monitor and noticed that the ship was slightly different than the others. It was the Archon's ship, Thrall, based on Kale's original ship Sagittarius, with a sentient computer loyal to Xos-Asura. It had redundant Q-jump engines, powerful shield plating, and an impressive array of energy weapons.

"I programmed my ship's computer to obey you for the duration of your mission. Take it through the Maelstrom and search for your doubles," said Xos-Asura. "The interior has been stripped to a minimum to expand the cargo hold. It will be stocked with Q-jump engine cores, shield plating, and weapons. Have each of your doubles build a ship outfitted with Alliance tech and return here. Together, you will lead the attack on Earth."

"May I offer them the same plan for each of their universes," Xanthes said.

"You may," the Archon said. "But before you go..." He turned as Uzza entered the tower chamber with a hand-held injector. "Hold out your hand," the Archon commanded Xanthes.

She did so and Uzza tapped her wrist with the injector. It released a hiss of pressurized air.

Xanthes was insulted. "A tracker?"

"I want to be able to tell *my* daughter from your doubles when the time comes to eliminate them," Xos-Asura said. "Gives new meaning to the term 'double-cross,' wouldn't you say?"

"You surprise me, Father."

"You didn't think we'd actually allow your doubles to hold onto power, did you?"

"Of course not. I meant I'm surprised to find you have a sense of humor."

The corners of the Archon's razor-thin lips curled into a sadistic smile.

*

Willa and Poppy sat on the bed in Willa's room. Everyone from the party had gone and Lily and River were downstairs, talking softly before the fire-lit hearth.

"Are you sure you should go through with this?" Poppy said.

"Opal was a friend. I'd do it for you."

"Mom was missing for a year, then I thought you were dead," Poppy said softly. "You only just got back from that other 'verse. I'd hate to lose you again is all I'm saying."

Willa held Poppy's hand. "I'm really sorry about that. Listen, my powers have grown a lot, even with the little time I've been at Mystery. I think I can handle this, especially with the Quorum backing me up."

"If you say so," Poppy relented.

"Speaking of your Mom, how's she doing?"

"Good, really good. She's happy, just like she used to be before she became a Nocturnal. It's odd but, being someone else helped her to be more of herself."

Willa weighed an idea, reluctant to give it voice.

Poppy frowned. "I know that look," she said. "You're about to suggest something I'm not going to like."

"Just hear me out, okay?"

Poppy nodded, though her frown remained.

"Sylvania was pregnant with you when she trained to become a Cryptic. That predictive sense you use to win at Hexes is because of that, right?"

"I think so," Poppy said. "Why?"

"I could use my powers to enhance your ability. You could predict the Archon's plans, give us an edge."

Poppy felt a chill as she met Willa's eager gaze. "No. No way."

"But --"

"No! Can't Holly, Selene, or Alder do that? Why do you need me?"

"Yes, they can and so can I, but we need every advantage we can get. You and I could do it together, like a team," Willa pressed.

"Look, I get it," Poppy admitted, "but I'm human, not a Hybrid. What if I can't handle it? What if I become like my mother before she went away? Detached. Cold. Distant. Hexes is just a game. What you're asking..." Poppy shook her head.

"Okay, okay. Sorry. It was just a thought," Willa said, disappointed.

Poppy got down off the bed. "I should get home."

Willa nodded and forced a smile. "See you tomorrow? Maybe play a game of Hexes?"

"After the Quorum? You're trying to flush out a murderer. I'll understand if you're not up to it."

"I'd be grateful for the distraction," Willa said. "Anything to feel normal again, if only for a few hours."

Poppy understood. "Okay. I promise to go easy on you," she teased.

"Are you kidding? I'll beat you blindfolded, even with your so-called secret talent," Willa said as she flashed a broad smile.

Poppy returned the smile. "You're on. I'll be there after mid-day meal."

The nano-glass staircase spiraled Poppy down to the first floor. Willa heard her say goodnight to Lily and River before she left. Willa tapped the wall over her bed. A section turned transparent and she watched Poppy head down the main branch and walk off toward town.

Willa glanced up at the Sentinel moon as it sped across the sky. Its cratered eye gazed back down at her in rebuke for the wound she inflicted upon it. Willa tapped her window closed, waved her light to its dimmest setting, and went to bed. She closed her eyes but she knew she'd get very little sleep tonight.

*

Five thousand light-years away on the planet Sed, Gant sat alone in a domed nano-glass dwelling situated in a small clearing amid a thick grove of tall Talus trees. Thin as bamboo, with spiky red leaves, they surrounded the meager encampment and hid it from prying eyes.

Sed was a backwater world beyond the borders of Alliance territory. The Subappu, the race of aliens that inhabited Sed, had agreed to allow Gant to begin his banishment on their home world until the Alliance could figure out how to send him back through the Maelstrom to his universe, along with Dennik and the other members of the Resistance. Ever since Willa returned and briefed the Alliance on her time in Earth Two's parallel universe, both Maelstroms had been quarantined.

The Subappu looked like squat kettle drums that walked on eight retractable rubbery legs and surveyed their surroundings from the tops of eight flexible eye-stalks. Gant's secluded location was more for his benefit than the locals because the squishy aliens gave him nightmares. While the Subappu weren't officially Alliance members, a mutually beneficial trade agreement existed between them and the Alliance because dried Talus leaves were one of the primary ingredients of Divinorum. The rare plant thrived on very few worlds within the Alliance, but grew in abundance on Sed.

In return, the Alliance provided the Subappu with a wide variety of foods that were inaccessible to them since the Subappu weren't a space-faring race. They had agreed to harbor Gant for the time being in exchange for a substantial increase in garlic, burdock root, and peppermint imports, which the Subappu couldn't seem to get enough of. So, in addition to the fact that their appearance gave

Gant night sweats, the inhabitants also reeked of the stinking garlic bulbs. The smell pervaded the air and made Gant nauseous.

While the nano-glass dome provided whatever he needed in the way of tables, chairs, and a bed, and was stocked with various foodstuffs that would last for months, the dwelling was sterile in its simplicity. He had a Luminaria to communicate with Dennik and Alarra on Earth. And though he was free to go wherever he wished on Sed, he felt like a prisoner. As long as the Maelstrom remained off-limits, there was nothing he could do to help the Resistance overthrow Xos-Asura and take his place.

The Alliance had provided Gant with a breathing mask that filtered out the scent of garlic or any other foreign substance in the planet's atmosphere. Gant sighed. *Long as I'm stuck here*, he thought, *I might as well see if there's anything these creatures can do to help with my plan.*

He placed the mask over his nose and mouth along with a pair of nano-glass goggles that kept his eyes from stinging and left the domed enclosure. He walked down the narrow path through the dense grove of Talus trees toward the main causeway that would take him to the nearby Subappu town of Sed'mok.

Before he was halfway down the path, a dark-blue Subappu waddled toward him on its eight springy legs. Gant pulled the translator from his pocket, but before he could ask what the rubbery, spider-like alien wanted, it collapsed like a deck of cards and shifted into Variabilis.

Gant was momentarily startled, then his face lit up with hope. "Please tell me you're here to take me back to Earth."

"Not unless you want to spend the rest of your life in confinement," the Shapeshifter said. "I'm here to get the truth out of you."

"What are you talking about?" Gant said.

"You conveniently forgot to tell anyone that Koro was your brother."

"I didn't know he was spying on the Resistance for the Archon," Gant protested. "Besides, with everything that happened, it didn't seem wise to mention that we were family."

"Why should I believe you?" said Variabilis.

Gant studied the Shapeshifter's lethal gaze and thought it might be time to take a different approach.

"You're right," Gant conceded. "I haven't been completely honest."

"I'm listening," the Shapeshifter said.

"I will help the Alliance and the League to defeat Xos-Asura. That much is true," Gant began. "But when he and his witch of a daughter are dead, I plan to become Archon."

"The Alliance won't replace one despot with another," Variabilis assured him.

"I don't want to oppress the people of Xos, I want to free them from a thousand years of tyranny!"

Variabilis wasn't swayed by Gant's patriotic passion. "I don't trust you."

"Then give me a chance to earn your trust."

"How?"

"I don't know," Gant admitted. "First, I have to find a way back into the Alliance's good graces."

"Good luck with that," the Shapeshifter said with undisguised sarcasm.

"You may not trust me," Gant said, "but never underestimate me. I'll think of something."

*

Elowen One was, quite literally, in a dark place. Cyclopean walls of dark grey stone lined the claustrophobic passages that twisted and turned in an endless maze. Strange symbols were carved into the walls. They seemed important, but Elowen couldn't make sense of them, nor could she remember how she wound up in the serpentine labyrinth.

What little light there was shone down from a thick mist that cloaked the tops of the towering walls. The light was devoid of warmth and cast no shadows.

She wandered down the dimly-lit paths in a dreamlike fog, her thoughts cocooned in cotton. Elowen stopped in a hub where six paths crossed. She was uncertain about which route to take. She slowly became aware of a froth of whispers that drew her attention to one path.

Her legs carried her forward though she didn't recall making a conscious decision to move. As she walked, a small voice in the deep recesses of her mind grew louder with each step.

Where am I? How did I get here? What's happening to me?

The desperation in the voice was palpable. It seemed to Elowen's dulled senses that some distant part of her was struggling to break free from a dark and terrifying prison.

The whispers began to coalesce into a single phrase as Elowen moved farther down the corridor.

"Remember. Remember. Remember who you are."

Her head began to throb as the voices penetrated deeper into her mind but, hard as she tried, Elowen couldn't stop herself from moving forward.

She arrived in a circular, dead-end chamber. The arcane glyphs on the walls began to glow with golden light as the voices cut into her brain like surgical knives.

"Remember who you are!"

Elowen screamed in agony and dropped to her knees. The walls exploded as Xanthes's mental shielding was wrenched from her mind.

"REMEMBER!"

With a jolt, Elowen was back in the Archon's torture chamber, strapped to a steel chair, needles penetrating her skull and piercing her brain. She was drenched in sweat as she brought every last ounce of strength to bear to resist her grey-faced tormentor.

"REMEMBER!"

The voice coursed through her blood like a transfusion of energy. Elowen tore through her steel restraints like they were tinfoil. Her hands shot out, clutched the torturer's neck and crushed the life out of him.

Elowen ripped the needles from her skull and stood over the dead body.

"I KNOW WHO I AM!" she shouted with all her might.

The torture chamber shattered like glass. Elowen's eyes snapped open. She found herself lying on a bed. Alder and two med-tech telepaths stared down at her, relief in their eyes.

"Where the hell am I?" Elowen demanded.

Alder smiled. "You're on Earth. You're safe... and you're yourself again."

The memory of her attempted assassination flooded into her mind and out of her eyes in a waterfall of tears. She buried her face in her hands as she sobbed, horrified by her behavior. "What have I done?"

Alder gently took her hands in his as the med-techs left. "You've done nothing," he said softly.

"I'm so ashamed," Elowen cried.

"Listen to me. It's not your fault," said the Sage. "There's no way you could've resisted."

"I should've tried harder!"

Kale's voice drew her attention to the door. "Believe him, Elowen."

"Captain! You're alive... or is this just another part of the nightmare?"

Kale went to her bedside. "You don't remember seeing me before when they repaired your eye?"

Elowen relaxed, allowed the memory to return. "It's still a little hazy."

Kale turned to Alder. "She's really herself this time?"

The Sage nodded. "Xanthes's mental shield has been shattered. Elowen's mind is hers and hers alone."

"There's talk of Xanthes being able to control others while still in her universe," Kale said. "What's to stop her from trying again with Elowen?"

Elowen looked at the Sage as she shared Kale's concern. Alder gave her a reassuring smile.

"With your permission, I can shield your mind as Xanthes did."

Elowen hesitated. "I don't know. Too many people have been mucking around in my brain as it is."

"I promise it won't hurt," Alder said, "and that you'll be in full control. It's just a precaution and completely your choice."

Elowen looked to Kale, who nodded his assurance. She took a deep breath and let it out. "Okay. I never want to hear her horrible voice in my head ever again." She locked eyes with Alder. "Let's do this."

*

Rose and Lilac Larkspur, the porcelain-pale Cryptic twins, fixed their lavender eyes on the dark, hooded figure that stood on the moonlit path a few yards ahead. They had been out in the fields, gathering Midnight Marigolds for the special tea they brewed each month for the med-techs in Port Dublin. Daylight Marigolds were vibrant yellow and symbolized the sun, but the bio-engineered midnight variety were bright blue and associated with the mysteries of the two Moons.

Thus, it wasn't surprising to see a Nocturnal out at night, plucking a basket of Midnights for some of their more esoteric rituals. Before she died of a mysterious disease, their mother, Laurel Larkspur, had told them stories of how the blue Marigolds, when ground and mixed with other flowers and herbs, allowed Nocturnals to dive more deeply into their meditations and sometimes, brought them into contact with the Inbetween, the thin-as-a-soap-bubble borderline of energy that separated one parallel reality from another.

It was said that an unusual race of Elementals, called a Kachinas by humans in North America, or Dakini by other Elementals, inhabited the Inbetween.

Rose and Lilac used to love hearing the stories and, although they were only Cryptics, they often asked each Nocturnal, Shapeshifter, or Sage they met to share what they would with them. Most declined and warned that the Kachinas were not to be sought out. Now and then, one would pass on a tidbit of information that occupied Rose's and Lilac's imagination for days. They made a pact that when they achieved the Second Level themselves, they would spend their time exploring the Inbetween and discover the Kachinas' deepest secrets.

Thus, the eager twins were excited to happen upon the lone Nocturnal on the path, since it was far more likely that, out here where no one else would hear their conversation, the cloaked figure might be willing to share a tale or two.

"A fine night," Rose said as they approached the stranger.

"May we speak with you?" Lilac added hopefully.

No sooner did Rose and Lilac step within arm's length of the silent figure than a gloved hand lashed out with a gleaming silver blade and sliced both of their heads off in a single swipe.

The Nocturnal sheathed the short sword, turned and walked down the path. The twins' blood pooled in the dirt, speckled with blue flecks of Marigold petals as they fell like sapphire snow.

*

The next morning, Willa arrived at the Quorum Lodge to find nearly everyone already there. Holly was deep in whispered repartee with Argus as both hovered over the cauldron of Divinorum that boiled in the hearth.

Eridani Ginko, the Nocturnal, held court with Shapeshifters Encantado and Moshi, while Alder conferred with Selene, Sequoia, and Moonstone.

"Ah, the guest of honor," Moshi said when he noticed Willa enter.

Holly turned to see her pupil and smiled. "Soon as Rose and Lilac arrive, we'll get started," she said, then turned her attention back to the Divinorum.

"They're never late," Eridani commented.

"True," Encantado agreed. He walked over to the Luminaria that floated in the corner and tapped a sequence on the surface of the sphere. It remained transparent. The Shapeshifter tried again. After a moment, he found himself staring into the electronic eyes of a security robot.

"State your identity," the robot demanded.

Everyone in the Lodge turned to look at the communication sphere as Encantado responded.

"Encantado, a member of the Northern Quorum of Port Dublin."

"Identity confirmed," the robot replied in its no-nonsense tone.

"I'm trying to contact the Larkspur twins," said the Shapeshifter.

"I regret being the bearer of bad news," the robot said with programmed empathy. "Rose and Lilac Larkspur are dead."

Holly's voice sounded small in the stunned silence that filled the Lodge. "What happened?"

"They were murdered last night in the fields outside of town. Please remain at the Lodge for the next hour. Someone wants to speak with all of you," the robot said and cut the link.

"Four murders now," Sequoia said, her voice hushed. "This is unbearable."

"Was he suggesting that one of us had something to do with their deaths?" Selene remarked, slightly ruffled.

"I'm sure it's just routine," Holly said to keep a lid on Selene's temper.

Eridani turned to the gathering. "We should attempt to discover the killer before Security arrives." After a moment, everyone nodded their agreement.

"Is the Divinorum ready?" Holly said to Argus.

"Ready."

"We just found out that two of our friends were murdered," Moshi said. "Shouldn't we wait --"

"What? Wait until the killer strikes again?" Willa raged.

"She's right," Alder said. "This can't wait. I don't mean to be cold-hearted, but Sequoia and Moonstone can take the twins' places. We owe it to them to try!"

Willa plunked herself down on the floor in the center of the ritual circle, determined to find and capture the killer. The Quorum slowly took their places around the ring as Argus dipped the tiny golden cup in the bubbling brew and handed it to Willa.

*

Poppy emerged from her bedroom as she yawned and wiped the sleep from her eyes. She noticed that the table wasn't set for morning meal and assumed her mother was still asleep. She shuffled through the living room to get plates from the kitchen and stopped, puzzled to see Sylvania in a chair, still as a statue in her dark robe, staring at the last of the glowing embers in the fireplace.

"You got home late last night, Mother," Poppy muttered. "Haven't you slept?"

Sylvania didn't answer or move an inch.

Puzzled, Poppy walked around in front of her mother, only to see that Sylvania's cheeks were wet with tears. She noticed a few small, blue flower petals stuck to her mother's robe. A section of her hem was damp with what appeared to be blood.

Poppy was afraid that something had caused her mother to revert to her former state of detachment. "Mother? Are you okay?"

Sylvania's moist eyes slowly found Poppy as though she was waking from a dream. "Poppy... oh, sweetheart..." She reached out her hand and Poppy took it, growing more worried by the second.

"Mom, what happened?"

"I was out in the fields last night, picking Midnight Marigolds and..." a horrifying memory choked her words off.

Poppy gripped Sylvania's hand harder, as though she might be ripped from her grasp any second. "Mother, please, you're scaring me."

"I'm sorry, my darling. It's just that... I was on my way home when I came upon the Larkspur twins. You remember them, don't you?"

Poppy nodded, unable to speak. Sylvania wiped at her swollen eyes and continued.

"I found them on the path. They'd been picking Marigolds, too. I've always thought they looked like porcelain dolls, don't you think so?"

"Mother?"

"They were both... they were both dead."

"What?" Poppy's mind spun when she realized the blood on her mother's robe was likely theirs. "How?"

"They were murdered, Poppy."

"Murdered? Are you sure?"

Sylvania stood and moved away as she tried to block the grisly memory of the twins' detached heads in a pool of blood. "I'm quite sure." She turned back to Poppy. "I forgot my com-link, so I ran to town and told Security. That's why I was so late getting home."

"And you've been sitting here all night?"

Sylvania nodded, went to the kitchen, took plates from the cupboard and started to set the table. Poppy stared at her in disbelief.

"Mom. What are you doing?"

"You need to eat. I'll make breakfast."

She headed back toward the kitchen. Poppy stopped her.

"Why don't you change out of that robe and I'll make breakfast for both of us," she said softly.

Sylvania gave Poppy a sad smile and nodded. She bent down, kissed Poppy's forehead and went to the staircase. Poppy noticed small smears of blood on the wooden stairs as her mother climbed to her bedroom.

*

Rather than the endless blue plain that she was used to seeing in her Divinorum visions, Willa found herself in a circular iron chamber. She stood in the center of a ring of copper witch-glyphs inlaid in the floor that reflected the firelight from the torches that circled the room.

Xanthes, Uzza, Zaduga, and the hooded assassin occupied the four quarters of the chamber, their eyes locked on Willa with unyielding malice.

Xanthes's voice was dark silk. "Welcome to my world."

"I know I'm not really here," Willa said.

"Of course not," said the Archon's heir. "Neither are we here in the flesh. This is only a mental construct. But your consciousness will remain here, unable to reconnect with your body until I allow it. So, when I enslave your mind, you'll become another one of my puppets."

"Elowen's been freed from your control," Willa shot back. "Just as I will be!"

Willa focused, tried to end the vision, but couldn't.

Xanthes smiled, a cat toying with a mouse. "You see?" She gestured to the assassin whose face was hidden in the shadow of the hood. "We knew you'd try to find out who killed your friends. It was only a matter of time before you took the bait."

Willa advanced on the assassin but was stopped by an energy field that surrounded the ring of glyphs. Xanthes laughed at Willa's failed attempt. Willa ignored her and stabbed a finger at the killer. "Who are you?"

The assassin remained a silent silhouette.

Xanthes clicked her tongue. "Where are my manners," she purred. She gestured to her Sensate mentors. "This is Zaduga and this is Uzza. They're called Sensates, the equivalent of your world's Sages I suppose, although far more powerful."

"We'll see about that," Willa countered. She summoned all her strength and sent a blast of energy out from her mental body in all directions. She strained as hard as she could to break free from her prison, but Zaduga and Uzza held the field in place. Willa gave up, her energy spent.

"You're a lot like me in your own, naive way," Xanthes said.

Willa smiled. "Good. Then when I kick your ass, you'll only have yourself to blame."

Xanthes laughed. "This is going to be fun." Xanthes leapt through the energy field, delivered a roundhouse punch to Willa's jaw and landed outside the field on the opposite side of the ring.

Willa recovered, took a swing at Xanthes. Her fist was stopped dead by the field, just inches from Xanthes's wicked grin.

"There's one difference between us," Willa said as she nursed her throbbing knuckles.

"What's that?"

"I'm not afraid to fight fair."

"Nice try," Xanthes said. She swung her fist through the field again and knocked Willa into the energy wall.

Willa staggered to her feet, fists up and waited for the next attack. "Come on!"

"I'm just warming you up," Xanthes said. "My assassin is the main event."

Willa turned as the hooded killer pulled a silver sword from its sheath and swung it through the field. Willa ducked as the blade whipped through the air, less than an inch above her head.

Xanthes was impressed. "You have excellent reflexes, but they won't save you for long."

"I'm not here alone," Willa said as she rose to her feet.

"You mean your Quorum? Yes, I can feel them pumping energy into you to back you up," Xanthes said. "It won't help."

The assassin brought the sword down. Willa dodged left, then right as the hooded figure tried to strike her again and again. The killer thrust the blade straight at Willa's heart. She clamped her palms together on either side of the sword, trapping it, and pulled the weapon through the field along with the assassin.

Willa put all her strength into a wicked right cross that dropped the killer to the floor. She yanked the hood back to expose her foe, but the robe was empty.

Xanthes laughed at Willa's surprise. "You didn't think I'd risk revealing my puppet's identity, did you?"

Willa grabbed the sword and tried to force the tip through the field toward Xanthes. The Archon's daughter stood her ground, confident that the Sensates would reinforce Willa's prison.

Willa closed her eyes and tapped into the energy that flowed to her from the Quorum.

*

In the Lodge, Holly and the others could sense that Willa needed more power. They stretched themselves to the limit and poured energy into Willa's body in the center of the circle.

*

Willa's mental form felt the Quorum's flood of energy reinforce her resolve. Her eyes glowed with preternatural light. She pushed the blade through the field and into Xanthes's ethereal heart. Xanthes screamed. Her mental body vanished along with her Sensates' apparitions. The field disappeared as did the Assassin's empty robe. However, the sword remained in Willa's grip.

She stood in the iron chamber, puzzled as to why she was still there. She closed her eyes and willed herself back to her body. "Wake up. Snap out of it!" Willa's eyes opened. The dark metal walls still surrounded her. "Now what?"

*

In the Lodge, the Quorum members emerged from their trances, except for Willa.

"Willa?" Holly whispered. Willa's eyes remained shut.

Argus reached out and gently shook Willa's body. There was no reaction.

Alder's senses flared up. He looked at each person in the circle. "I sensed that someone nearby was feeding energy to Xanthes instead of Willa!"

"Who?" Moshi demanded.

"I can't tell," the Sage said. "The assassin's mental shield is far stronger than the one that protected Elowen."

*

Willa attempted to return to the real world several times without success. She paced around the chamber as she searched for any clue she could use to escape. She finally focused on the copper glyphs in the floor. She had no idea what they symbolized but, as the only things besides the sword and the torches in the otherwise empty room, she hoped they might hold the key to her freedom.

She sat on the floor in the center of the ring of glyphs. That's what she'd always done in the Lodge. Xanthes was a parallel counterpart, so she reasoned the glyphs would work the same way that the Mastery symbols did on Earth.

She looked at each of the copper shapes but nothing seemed to jump out at her. Willa decided to take a different approach and began to ask herself a series of logical questions.

Xanthes and her minions have gone, Willa mused, *so why is this illusion still here? If I'm the only one left, I must be creating it,* she reasoned. *Maybe that's the real trap. Xanthes distracted me with the fight, made it seem like I won, and all the time it was about conditioning my mind to accept this room as a real place. But I know it's not real, so why can't I leave?*

Willa absent-mindedly traced a finger over one of the glyphs as she continued to ponder the conundrum.

Maybe Xanthes knows that I don't want to be the one everyone's counting on. So, maybe I don't really want to leave this place. But I also don't want her and the Archon to attack Earth. And why didn't the sword disappear when they did? Maybe she thinks I'll use it on myself if I can't find any other way out. Then I'd be doing her dirty work for her, wouldn't I? But if these symbols can help me figure out how to escape, then why leave them for me to use. The sword and the symbols. Maybe the sword is my wish to end this and the symbols are my wish to go back and save my home, my family, my friends.

Willa ran every possible scenario she could think of through her mind. She wondered if her counterparts could shed any light on the situation. Willa was shocked to realize she couldn't hear the voices at all. The constant background whispers were gone! *My mind must be locked in some sort of bubble, like the mental shields Xanthes used to hide Elowen and the assassin,* she thought. *I'm truly on my own!*

She thought back to her Cryptic and Nocturnal training. Was there anything that Holly, Sequoia, Moonstone, or even Selene said to her that could help her now?

A portion of the Nocturnal mantra bubbled up from somewhere deep in her mind:

All secrets are shrouded in darkness. But I do not live in the darkness, the darkness lives within me.

"Okay," Willa said out loud, "if I'm creating this chamber, then it's coming from a dark place within me. Xanthes was right. We're more alike than I was willing to admit." Willa took a breath and allowed another memory to rise to the surface. "Holly taught me that I can't change what doesn't belong to me. So, to change this place, I have to own it. I need to make it mine. I need to own the darkness within me. I may not be able to connect to my voices," she continued, "but Xanthes is also my counterpart. This place was created by both of us. I don't need the other voices. I only need hers."

The sword vanished. Willa stood in the center of the ring of symbols. She held them in her gaze for several heartbeats, then closed her eyes.

"Speak to me, Xanthes. I am you and you are me. These symbols are yours and they are mine. Your darkness may live within me, but my light also lives within you. Show me the way home!"

*

Xanthes staggered in her stone chamber on Xos. She fell to her knees inside the symbol ring as Willa's voice shouted in her mind.

"Show me the way home!"

Xanthes struggled against her counterpart's command, shocked by its intensity. "No!"

Uzza rushed in at her cry. "My Lady?"

"SHOW ME!" Willa's voice demanded.

Xanthes hand shot out against her will and covered one of the copper glyphs.

Uzza knelt before her. "What's happening?"

"It's her!" Xanthes cried out. "She's in my head!" She pivoted and slapped her palm on a second symbol.

*

The second glyph that Xanthes had touched in her stone sanctuary glowed like fire in the iron chamber along with the first symbol Willa had mentally forced her to reveal. Willa continued to exert her power over Xanthes and was rewarded as a third symbol burst with golden light. The three illuminated glyphs formed an equilateral triangle of energy that encompassed Willa. She touched

206

the three symbols in the same order Xanthes had done. The iron chamber vanished.

Willa gasped as her mind reconnected with her body in the Quorum Lodge. She opened her eyes.

"Willa!" Holly cried out.

Willa focused on Holly as her disorientation faded. "I'm okay," she assured her mentor.

"What happened?" Sequoia said.

"Did you learn the killer's identity?" Alder added, his senses alert and ready for action.

"No," Willa admitted, "but I created a stronger bond with Xanthes."

"Stronger?" Encantado said with concern.

"It allowed me to control her and escape from her mental trap."

"Still, that sounds dangerous," Moonstone said.

Willa offered a crooked smile. "What's the old saying? Keep your friends close, but keep your enemy closer. I'm not afraid of Xanthes anymore."

"That may be," Alder said, "but while we were sending you energy, the assassin's focus must've wavered. I determined it's someone nearby, someone close." Alder scanned the gathering. "Maybe even someone in this room."

Before anyone could react to Alder's accusation, the Lodge doors swung open. Three security robots entered and stood in a triangle around the Quorum members. "Please remain where you are," one of the bots ordered.

Willa frowned at the familiarity. *Triangles,* she thought. *The Maelstrom's locations, Xanthes's glyphs, and now this. What's the 'verse trying to tell me?*

As she pondered the mystery, another person entered the Lodge. A shock of surprise shot through the Quorum. Willa stood and turned, mouth agape, as she beheld a being she thought she'd never see in her lifetime.

The tall, stately woman was transparent as a ghost, similar to Belladonna the Banshee, but surrounded by an ethereal blue glow that radiated pure power. She floated just above the floor; her gossamer robe and long, white locks undulated in a slow-motion wind that issued from some unseen realm. The effect underscored her otherworldly nature. The woman spoke in a voice that shimmered in the air and caused ripples in time.

"My name is Amakeeri," said the Wraith. "Now, where shall we begin?"

Chapter Twelve:
AMAKEERI

"Back in the twentieth and twenty-first centuries, humanity began to compile reports of people who had been pronounced clinically dead for several minutes, yet were able to be resuscitated, often simply coming back to life on their own. These anomalous events were referred to as "Near-Death Experiences" or NDE's.

Eventually, similar patterns were observed across the reports that superseded culture, gender, social standing, or the religious beliefs of those who had an NDE. Descriptions of a "tunnel of light," or meeting relatives who had crossed over long ago, or going through some type of life review along with feelings of bliss, were often dismissed by skeptics as hallucinations generated by a dying brain.

In time, additional research and scientific experimentation provided some intriguing evidence for the reality of an afterlife. Of course, with the arrival of the Hybrids and the advanced knowledge they brought to Earth, they proved beyond a shadow of a doubt that we not only survive after physical death, but that by using various mental techniques, it was possible to communicate with the spirits of those who had passed into the great beyond."

Excerpt from "The New Book of the Dead"
by Rabbi Aster Zeff: 2109 – 2217

*

"You're a Wraith!" Willa blurted before she could stop herself.

Amakeeri's laugh reminded Willa of crystal wind chimes. "What gave it away?"

Willa felt foolish and blushed, which was very obvious in a face as fair as hers, and that made her blush even more.

The Wraith waved her embarrassment away with a flourish of her left hand. A glint of light reflected from the tiny diamond sigil set into the clear quartz ring that adorned her thumb. "That was mild compared to the reactions I usually get." Amakeeri cast her ghostly gaze around the gathering. "So... which one of you is the murderer?"

The Quorum's reactions ranged from bemused to outraged, the latter being Selene's stock and trade.

"Who do you think you're talking --"

Amakeeri cut Selene off with a look that could freeze fire.

"Relax, it's no one in this room," the Wraith said.

"My senses don't lie," Alder protested.

"You thought the assassin's guard was down, but it was yours. The idea that one of you might be the killer was fed to you by the assassin to sow discord among you," Amakeeri said. "Do you feel the same way now?"

Alder extended his senses. "No. The feeling's gone."

The tension evaporated from the Lodge as everyone exhaled. Holly turned to Amakeeri, puzzled.

"Then why are you here?"

"Because you're all going to help me catch the killer," the Wraith said with absolute conviction.

"How catch?" Argus said, mesmerized by the pale specter.

Amakeeri gestured to Willa. "With our lovely piece of bait."

At first flushed, Willa now turned almost as pale as the Wraith. "What?"

"Well, you are who the assassin really wants, after all," Amakeeri said. "So, let's make it easy for them."

Holly's hackles went up. "You can't be serious!"

"Do any of you have a better idea to flush them out?"

Glances were exchanged around the room. All eyes landed back on Amakeeri.

"I didn't think so," the Wraith said.

Alder stood and straightened his vest. "Forgive me if I'm not as familiar with the powers of a Wraith as I ought to be, but aren't you supposed to be a Master of time, space, and spirit?"

Amakeeri regarded the Sage with infinite patience. "Your point being?"

"Can't you simply sense who the killer is?"

"An excellent question. Would anyone here care to enlighten Master Redwood? Raise your hands if you know the answer. Come on don't be shy. No one?" Amakeeri released an ethereal sigh that sounded like faint panpipes and turned back to Alder.

"I suppose it's not fair of me to expect a Sage to know what you haven't experienced yet. How can I explain this in a way you'll all understand?"

"No need to be condescending," Moshi fumed.

"Oh, I do apologize," the Wraith said with great sincerity, "it's been so long since I've been physical, I forget how fragile your egos are."

"And there you go again," Moshi added.

Amakeeri ignored the Shapeshifter and gathered her thoughts. "As you might already know, being a Wraith means I'm not exactly a spirit, nor am I exactly physical. I'm a combination of the two, a bridge between two dimensions."

"Like a Banshee," Willa said.

"Well, sort of, except that a Banshee is stuck on the bridge and I'm on both ends of it at the same time. Does that make sense?"

Willa and several others nodded while Argus and Moshi shook their heads.

"Anyway," Amakeeri continued, "physical beings have a personality while spirits only have an identity."

"What's the difference?" Eridani said.

"Identity is the essence of who you are. Personality is a mask composed of beliefs. In physical reality, your identity wears the mask and is limited by what the personality chooses to believe. In spirit, the mask comes off. You become your true self."

"So, you're different as a Wraith than you were as a living person," Willa said.

"Much different," Amakeeri acknowledged, "but still not as different as a spirit."

"Probably just as annoying, though," Selene said under her breath.

"Almost as annoying as you," the Wraith countered. "If you become a Wraith, it will definitely be an improvement. That is what you wish, is it not?"

"I... I don't know what you're..." Selene sputtered.

"That much, my senses can see," Amakeeri said. "In fact, I may grant your wish."

Selene was at a loss for words, a state completely unfamiliar to her. "What?"

"I'll get back to that in a minute. You asked me to explain why I can't sense the killer."

"Please, do continue," Alder said.

"As I was saying, spirits only have an essential identity and, while each identity is distinct, they're more alike than different. Spirits have shed the beliefs of their personalities, which may have harbored fears, doubts or misguided ambitions. They've let go of the past and live only in the present."

Willa suddenly grasped why Amakeeri couldn't identify the assassin. "You're saying you can extend your senses into the spirit realm, but in that reality, the killer is no longer a killer."

"Exactly! Whatever a person was in life, whatever experiences they may have had, are preserved within the spirit, but it's not evident on the surface. So, just as a Cryptic can't experience what it is to be a Nocturnal until you are one, in order to see more deeply into a spirit's earthly experiences, I'd have to be dead too. Fully dead."

"Okay, we understand," Selene said, "but what did you mean you could grant my wish?"

"There are only seven of us in the world. We need an eighth," said the Wraith. "I can help you get through the next levels of Mastery faster than you would advance on your own."

"Wait a minute," Willa said. "An analysis of both Maelstroms' energy patterns showed that they may be the result of a Sage transforming into a Wraith."

"Oh, that's just a myth," Amakeeri assured her. Willa nodded and was about to let it go when the Wraith finished her statement. "It's not an accident at all."

A chill ran through Willa's veins. "What are you saying?"

Amakeeri smiled as though delivering welcome news. "I'm saying, dear girl, that we Wraiths are creating the Maelstroms on purpose."

*

Dennik, Alarra, Gar, and Brim sat at a table in the Stargazer Inn nursing drinks.

"How long are they going to keep us on Earth?" Gar grumbled over his cider. "We can't even get a decent drink on this planet!"

"They're only trying to protect us, Gar," Alarra said. "We don't want to wind up in the wrong universe."

"Seems to me that's where we are now," said the old soldier.

Dennik clapped Gar on the shoulder. "I'm worried about what's happening with our comrades back home as well. We can't even get a message to them. For all they know, we could be dead."

"Willa said they're doing everything they can," Brim said. "Besides, it's not so bad here."

Star brought them four fresh cups of cider. "How are you all doin'? You hungry or just drownin' your sorrows?"

SHARDS OF A SHATTERED MIRROR

Gar wrinkled his nose at the fresh cider. "Don't you have anything stronger?"

"Elderberry wine," she offered.

"Pah! Stuff's so sweet it makes me gag," Gar said with a sour face.

Star sat in an empty chair and lowered her voice. "Well, I've got a few bottles of Batch Twenty-Seven that's been preserved in my private stasis locker for the past three hundred years. Handed down from my father. I make it available to special customers like yourselves." She jerked a thumb over her shoulder at the original Stargazer who was tending bar. "Just don't tell my boss."

Brim looked around at Stargazer's multiple doppelgangers. "Aren't you the same person?"

"Hey, she's not the boss of me," Star said.

"But you just said --"

Gar cut Brim off. "This world can drive a man to drink. Bring us a bottle of your Batch Twenty-Seven."

Star gave him a nod and a wink and left the table.

Dennik smiled and shook his head. "Listen, I'll go check in with the Council, see if they've made any progress."

Alarra placed her hand on his. "While you're at it, why don't you use one of those Lumineria devices to see how Gant's holding up."

"I still don't trust him," Gar said as he pushed his cider over to Brim.

"You and Variabilis seem to agree on that," Dennik said.

"The Shapeshifter? Not sure I trust him either. Someone who can become anyone or anything..." Gar picked up his knife and tapped the table with it. "For all we know, he could be this table." He stuck the point of the knife in the tabletop.

Alarra's expression was clear: *Really?*

Gar shrugged it off. "Just checking."

Star returned with a non-descript bottle and four glasses. She poured a round of the caramel-colored whiskey.

Gar picked up his glass, sniffed it, then took a cautious sip. The sudden fire in his throat made him cough and blink tears away. "Now, that's a drink!" he rasped.

"Enjoy," Star said and went to attend to other customers.

Dennik, Alarra, and Brim took small sips and had the same reaction.

Brim coughed and gulped his cider to quench the burn. "I'll stick to this."

Dennik cleared his throat and stood. "I'll be back soon." He gave Alarra a quick kiss, patted Brim on the shoulder, and handed Gar his glass of whiskey. "If we could dump a few thousand gallons of this in the Archon's water supply, we could knock his army on their asses without firing a shot."

Gar raised his glass. "Sounds like a plan."

Dennik smiled at his comrade and left the Inn.

Gar took another sip and stoically endured the burn. "At least this makes being stuck on this planet tolerable."

Alarra laughed. "Drink enough of it, and you won't remember being here at all."

"I'll drink to that," he said and clinked her glass. He knocked the rest of his whiskey back, ignored the tears that rolled down his cheeks, and poured himself another as Alarra and Brim looked on, astonished at the old soldier's stamina.

*

Night on the planet Sed added an extra layer of strangeness to an already alien world. Gant sat outside his dome dwelling and gazed up at the deep purple sky. Aside from the unfamiliar constellations, a titanic ring drew an arc across the heavens, flanked by several small moons.

Gant had seen images of Saturn's rings on his tablet when he was confined to his quarters on Earth, but to witness the rings of Sed from the planet's surface was both breathtaking and disorienting. It seemed like the ring of rocks, dust, and ice particles could come crashing down to the ground any second.

The Luminaria in his dwelling chimed and he went inside, grateful for anything that would turn his attention away from this alien gulag.

Dennik's smiling face appeared in the floating crystal globe. "Gant."

"Dennik. It's good to see you. Does this mean we've found a way home?"

"I'm sorry. Not yet, but the Council has assured me it's being given top priority," Dennik said.

"That's what all bureaucracies say when they have no clue how to solve a problem," Gant said, disappointed. "I need to get off this rock."

"I know," Dennik said, "but the next planet outside the Alliance that's fit for humans is more than fifty thousand light-years away. Just sit tight. I'll see if I can speed up the process."

"I appreciate it," Gant said, resigned to his fate for the moment.

The Luminaria became transparent as Dennik signed off. Gant exhaled his frustration. "Time for plan B."

He donned his filter mask and goggles and left the dome. Gant did his best to ignore the disturbing sky and made his way down the path between the crimson Talus trees.

*

"What are you talking about?" Willa shouted at Amakeeri. "Why the bloody hell would the Wraith create the Maelstroms on purpose?"

"You destroyed an entire planet!" Sequoia said, her ire rising. "You nearly killed a million people!"

"We knew no one would die," the Wraith assured the stunned Quorum. "We knew Willa would use her powers to give you time to rescue everyone."

"You knew?" Alder said with disbelief.

"Hello. Wraith. Master of space, time, and spirit," Amakeeri reminded him. "When it comes to the physical universe, we can see farther up the timeline than any of you. Well, except maybe for Willa. Besides, we helped."

"Even if that's true," Selene broke in, "you still haven't said *why* you did it."

"I can't tell any of you that just yet. Let's just say it's necessary for the safety of the Alliance."

"That's convenient," Alder said. "Why should we believe you?"

"I don't mean to be rude," Amakeeri said, "but you really have no other choice."

Eridani wrinkled her nose. "For someone who doesn't mean to be rude, you do it an awful lot."

"If it makes you feel better, please accept my apology," the Wraith said.

"You're about to create a third Maelstrom, aren't you?" Willa said.

"Yes, and we must create even more."

Holly was aghast. "More?"

The Wraith nodded. "I'm afraid so. We need a total of eight."

"That's why you need another Wraith, isn't it?" Willa said. "There are seven of you and you can only create one Maelstrom each."

Amakeeri nodded. "Belladonna Bloodroot would have been one of us, but you know what happened to her. Even we can't change her into a Wraith now, nor even reverse time to make her a Sage again. It's been too long and would cause havoc in the timeline to erase three hundred years of history."

"Three hundred years!" Willa blurted. "According to Alarra, that's when the first Maelstrom appeared. Belladonna's transformation into a Banshee must have created the rupture, along with the bubble that limits the Empire's expansion."

"Yes," Amakeeri acknowledged. "But that was an accident. It took us a while to figure out how to do what she did on purpose." The Wraith gestured to Selene. "You desire to become one of us and we need you to complete our plan."

Willa locked eyes with Holly, who realized what her apprentice was about to do. She shook her head. "Willa, no."

Despite Holly's plea, Willa turned back to the Wraith. "I'll do it."

Selene stood up and stepped between Willa and Amakeeri. "No! You promised to help me become a Wraith! This is my path, not yours!"

"I have the Mark," Willa countered. "I can go through the Levels of Mastery faster than you can!"

"I applaud your bravery, Willa," Amakeeri said, "but you have a different path. It has to be Selene. I'm sorry."

The Nocturnal flashed a haughty look of victory at Willa, who grudgingly backed down.

"Tell me what I need to do," Willa said to Amakeeri.

"All in good time, my dear," said the Wraith. "All in good time."

*

Xanthes went over the controls of the Archon's flagship, *Thrall*, one last time as Uzza looked on.

"The safest course through the Maelstrom has been laid in, my Lady," Uzza said.

"You're certain it will take me to a 'verse parallel to our own instead of Willa's?"

"According to Zaduga's insights, the appearance of the second Maelstrom in her universe altered our portal's path," Uzza assured her. "It should take you to your double's universe just as it took the Earth girl to her double's reality."

"And reversing course will return me and my double to this reality, yes?"

Uzza nodded. "Zaduga has sensed that the Earth girl is back in her own universe. We assume she went back through the second Maelstrom, my Lady. We know of no other way she could have returned."

"You assume?" Xanthes kept a tone of command in her voice, though she was less than confident about the plan's chances for success. Several unpleasant thoughts bounced around in her skull.

What if she couldn't get back? What if her double planned to double-cross her? What if she wound up in an entirely different universe instead?

Uzza took her silent concerns for displeasure at his answer. "I apologize, my Lady. The physics of the Maelstrom are still mostly a mystery. Zaduga has called upon all of his powers to learn this much. That, plus the intel from the Earther's damaged ship is all we have to go on," the Sensate babbled. "But, if it worked for the Earth girl --"

"Why are you reluctant to speak her name?" Xanthes said.

Uzza hesitated for fear of upsetting her further.

Xanthes sighed. She decided that a softer approach would work better than intimidation. "It's alright, Uzza. Just tell me what you're afraid of," she coaxed.

"To name a thing is to form a connection with it, my Lady. After your experience with her in the mind bubble, I thought it best to tread lightly so she doesn't sense our plan."

Xanthes nodded. "A wise precaution. Very well, from now on, we'll refer to her as the Earth girl."

Uzza relaxed, relieved his response had pleased Xanthes. "Very good, my Lady."

Xanthes checked her readouts one last time. "I'm ready to depart."

Uzza bowed his head. "May the Elder Gods guide you on your journey. We eagerly await your return."

Xanthes didn't believe the Elder Gods were real but nodded at the traditional sentiment as she brought the engines online. "Tell my father I'll see him soon."

"I live to serve, my Lady." Uzza moved to the airlock.

"Don't we all," Xanthes replied, distracted by the ship's startup protocols.

Uzza raised an eyebrow at her unorthodox response and left the ship. The airlock doors sealed and the cabin pressurized with a hiss.

Uzza stood a hundred feet away on the concrete tarmac as he watched the *Thrall* rise off the ground on its levitation thrusters. The main engines glowed to full power and the starship shot upward toward the stratosphere at breathtaking speed.

Once Xanthes reached orbit, she looked at the view screen to see the concrete-and-steel-clad surface of Xos far below her. With a final glance at her readouts, she spoke to the ship's computer.

"Plot a course to the Maelstrom," she ordered.

"Course plotted," Thrall answered in the Archon's cold voice.

A reminder from my father that he's always watching, she mused. "Execute."

A hum of power rose in the Q-jump engines and the ship vaulted to the stars.

*

Sed'mok was a bustling city by Subappu standards, although, with a population of only thirty thousand, most people in the Alliance would consider it to be nothing more than a sleepy village.

As befitted the Subappu physique, most of the stone and Talus-wood buildings were large, open-plan rotundas with personal chambers that surrounded central, circular meeting rooms where the denizens would gather to talk or eat.

The Subappu's rubbery legs were also their feeding tubes and so food, which tended to be mushy or liquefied, was poured into shallow cavities cut into thick wood or stone slabs set on the ground where the aliens could easily vacuum it up.

Above each of their eight legs, and just under each of their eight eye stalks, prehensile tentacles with delicate hands ringed their circular bodies. Due to a large tympanic membrane inside their thick, disc-shaped bodies, the Subappu language was a staccato series of percussive beats and, when several were having a conversation, they sounded like a symphony of steel drums, cymbals, bongos, and booming kettledrums.

The Alliance had provided Gant with a translation device but, not being active members, the translator wasn't programmed with the most up-to-date lexicon. Thus, Gant's translations sounded somewhat stiff and formal to the Subappu, which many of the aliens found polite and charmingly old-fashioned, so they usually didn't bother to correct him. Gant felt a little lost and waved one of the denizens down.

"You possess the directions that would lead me to the Organizer who makes decisions?" Gant's translator said in stilted Subappunese.

The alien's response began with the soft brush of a cymbal, which Gant's translator didn't decode, but that he had begun to recognize as a lighthearted chuckle. The tri-gendered Subappu pointed one of its tentacles toward a cobblestone path that led uptown. Gant's device decoded a short run of beats as "That way."

"Thank you," Gant's translator said with a single thump of a timpani.

The towering Subappu went on its way as Gant followed the path through town. The cobbled street was very wide to accommodate the average ten-foot diameter of the adult inhabitants, so Gant had no trouble navigating past the shops and market stalls that lined both sides of the thoroughfare. Here and there, other alien species who were visiting Sed would glance at Gant, then continue to barter with the Subappu shop owners for a variety of exotic goods.

Gant came to a large rotunda at the end of the street. The twenty-foot-high walls were cut and polished stone slabs that supported heavy Talus-wood beams. The impressive structure was capped by a slate-shingled roof that surrounded a tall chimney in the center. Wisps of wood smoke rose into the deep purple sky.

Gant entered the wide foyer and was greeted by a relatively small, six-foot-tall Subappu with pale violet skin, which Gant recognized as a youth of about twenty.

The assistant's thrumming translated as: "Greetings, friend of the people. How may I help you?"

Gant spoke into the mic on his device. "I am in appreciation to have a beneficial exchange with the Organizer," it drummed.

A couple of the assistant's eyes blinked at the odd phrasing, but it replied politely. "Please give me a moment to see if *thumpity-thump* is available."

Since the tri-gendered aliens didn't have a word for "he" or "she" or names that fit the Earthly model, the translator simply repeated the Subappu's drum beats.

The assistant ambled through a wide door that led to another chamber. Gant chose the opportunity to look around. The walls of the foyer were painted with a single mural that depicted several scenes throughout the civilization's history, from primitive round rafts to massive trading ships, to the construction of enormous artificial islands and bridges in the shallow seas that surrounded the interconnected villages of the present.

The young Subappu returned. "The Organizer will see you in the Great Room," it said with a gentle wave of three tentacles, which was the polite way to direct an honored guest.

"Thank you," Gant's device thumped. He went down the indicated hallway and emerged into an enormous, high-ceilinged chamber with a crackling, circular hearth in the center.

Expertly-carved statues of previous Organizers were displayed around the room's circumference. If it wasn't for the various colors that indicated the differing ages and life-cycles of the immortalized

Subappu chiefs, Gant wouldn't have been able to tell the statues apart.

He gazed at the fire in the hearth, took a chance, and removed his filter mask in the hope he would smell something other than garlic. He inhaled and was rewarded with the comforting aroma of wood smoke. But there was another scent in the air. Gant cautiously took a sniff. His eyebrows rose in surprise.

"Peppermint?"

Gant turned to see the Organizer as it padded into the Great Room on its eight cylindrical legs like a rubbery spider. It was all black, an indication of great age and wisdom but, at only seven feet in height, it wasn't much taller than its youthful assistant. Despite its advanced age, its eight violet eyes were bright and clear. They blinked the Subappu equivalent of a smile.

"Greetings, friend of the people. I expected you would pay me a visit at some point."

"Greetings," Gant's translator drummed. "I am in appreciation to share thoughts on a matter of importance."

"Of course," the Organizer said. "Would you like a bowl of Talus tea? I believe it's compatible with your species."

"Another time, perhaps," Gant said politely.

The Organizer gestured to a bench near the hearth. Gant sat on the polished wood surface as the Subappu perched on a large stool that looked something like a squishy orange marshmallow. An Earth human would have smiled at what appeared to be a giant spider squatting on a Halloween pumpkin.

"How may I help you?" the Organizer began.

"The clan of many clans," the translator began, giving its best attempt at the word 'Alliance' in Subappunese, "gave to me a book about Sed, but I desire to learn of the things that are not within its pages."

"That could take a lifetime," the Organizer said lightheartedly.

"I don't need to learn about all things," Gant rephrased, "just the things that can help me. You know that the clan of many clans will soon fight a battle with a powerful enemy, yes?"

"Yes," the spider thumped.

"I want to stop the enemy chief," Gant continued. "Do your people have anything that can help us do that?"

"We do not belong to the clan of clans," the Organizer said. "It is not for us to fight your battles."

Gant took a leap. "But you are hiding a secret, aren't you?"

The Organizer made a faint thrumming sound for several seconds as it pondered Gant's implication. "Why would you think that?"

"I have studied your history, mostly because there is not much else for me to do while I am here," Gant confessed. "Your people have been asked to join the clan of clans many times, but you have always refused. In my experience, that means you either know something, or have something you do not want to share with them. If you joined, you would have to reveal everything about your world."

The Organizer's tentacles twitched, uncomfortable with Gant's assessment. However, it was common knowledge in the Alliance that the Subappu never lied. "That is true," the Organizer finally admitted. "But that doesn't mean I must tell you our secrets." The Organizer rose off of his perch. *Thumpity rat-a-tat bang:* "This meeting is over."

Gant knew he'd hit a sensitive nerve. He stood and politely bowed. "I apologize if I've given offense. Thank you for your time. I'll see myself out." Gant left the chamber as five of the Organizer's eyes watched him go.

As he passed through the hall that led to the entry chamber, Gant noticed a small, tubular air duct high up in the stone wall. Acting on a hunch, he tapped the control panel on his translator and set it to record. He reached up and pushed the device as deep into the air duct as he could, then continued on his way.

Gant entered the foyer where the Organizer's assistant was working. It blinked a smile at him. *Thump thumpity pop pop?*

Without his translator, Gant thought the safest response would be to smile and bow. The gesture seemed to satisfy the assistant and Gant left quickly to avoid further conversation.

*

Once back in his quarters, Gant opened one of the three large containers of supplies the Alliance had sent with him to make his exile more tolerable. As he'd hoped, there was a backup translator stored next to the medical kit and other emergency equipment. He removed the device from its protective cover and matched its frequency to the translator he'd hidden in the air duct. Gant was rewarded with a series of percussive thumps that were quickly translated:

"Based on the information provided by the clan of clans, our guest comes from a world where suspicion is a way of life," the Organizer's voice said.

"He must not discover our secret," thumped an unidentified Subappu. *"We must find a way to satisfy his suspicions without revealing the truth."*

"But it's one of our most sacred doctrines that our people do not tell falsehoods," the Organizer said.

"All the more reason he'll believe us."

"I cannot violate our principles, even to protect that secret," the Organizer thumped with conviction.

"Then give him a different secret," said the unknown Subappu.

"It would still need to be something we normally wouldn't share with outsiders," the Organizer said.

"As long as it satisfies his curiosity," said the stranger.

"Very well. I'll take care of it."

"See that you do," the stranger curtly thumped. *"We must protect our discovery at all costs!"*

Gant heard the unknown Subappu shuffle off as the Organizer called out to his assistant.

"Send word to our guest that I'd like to speak with him."

"Right away," the assistant said with a crisp *Thump pop boom!*

Gant wondered what secret they would feed him in place of the one that really mattered. He welcomed the challenge. Subterfuge gave Gant purpose and, for the first time since he had arrived on Sed, he felt more like himself.

*

Poppy arrived home from morning market to find her mother donning a fresh Nocturnal robe.

"Morning, Mom. You're going out? I was just going to make breakfast."

"I'm sorry, sweetheart, I've eaten. But please sit for a minute. I want to talk to you about something."

Poppy put the fruit and vegetables in the stasis cupboard in the kitchen and went to the living room. She sat on the couch, her mouth fixed in a straight line.

Sylvania sat next to her and rested a hand on her daughter's. "It's okay, Poppy."

"Sorry. I've just come to expect bad news."

"I know, and I regret that," her mother said. "But despite all that's happened, you've been so strong... stronger than me. I'm very proud of you."

"Thanks, but I wasn't that strong," Poppy said, still tense. "What news are you going to give me today?"

"Only that I've decided to continue my training."

This was the last thing Poppy expected to hear. "You mean as a Nocturnal?"

Sylvania nodded. "And continue to become a Shapeshifter and a Sage."

"But..."

"I know, I know," Sylvania said. "It's harder for a human. But the calling is stronger within me than it's ever been."

"Why?"

"A combination of things. I think being Brandelyn for a year... being someone other than me... opened up more possibilities in my mind. And there are other things... the murders for one. I just feel that, if the Archon does attack Earth, I want to do my part."

Poppy sat quietly as she took it all in.

Sylvania rubbed Poppy's back. "Are you okay?"

"Yes. Actually, I'm relieved. I thought maybe you were going to leave again."

"I'm not going anywhere... well, except to Mystery. I need to talk with the Provost."

Poppy lapsed into silence once again.

"What is it, Poppy?"

"Willa asked if she could help me develop my senses so I could predict the Archon's plans."

Sylvania was surprised but nodded her agreement. "I see the wisdom of it, not only to help protect Earth but also to keep yourself safe."

"So, you think it's a good idea."

"We can talk more about it later," Sylvania said, "if you want."

Poppy felt the tension melt from her shoulders. "Okay. I'd like that."

Sylvania kissed Poppy on the cheek and headed to the door. "I promise to be home for evening meal if you'd be willing to prepare those delicious vegetables you got, maybe with those Verulian spices you like so much."

Poppy smiled. "Deal. And Mom..."

"I'll say hello to Willa for you if I see her," Sylvania said.

"Remind her that she owes me a game of Hexes and that, no matter how powerful she may become, I'll still kick her butt."

*

Willa sat in her meditation chamber in Mystery and mentally communed with her five primary counterpart voices while she waited for Amakeeri's plan to unfold.

"That's a terrible plan," said Willa Two, *"if anything goes wrong…"*

"I agree," added Willa Three. *"There are too many variables."*

"Willa broke free from Xanthes's mind prison," the elder counterpart named WIllow pointed out. *"If she can do that, she can handle the assassin."*

"My question," said Willa Five, the Shapeshifter nicknamed LoLo, *"is why none of this has happened in any of our 'verses. If it had, one of us would know the assassin's identity by now."*

"Good question," Willow said. *"There seem to be more differences than similarities between our 'verses. Shouldn't it be the other way around?"*

Willa One's silver door chimed.

"We'll continue this later," she said and shunted the voices back to indistinct whispers. Willa opened the door, surprised to find Sequoia standing in the hall. "Provost! Please come in."

Sequoia entered and shut the door. She remained standing for a moment, her expression dark.

"Is everything okay?" Willa said.

Sequoia sat on the single seat at the desk as Willa took a spot on her bed.

"Despite what Amakeeri said, I still get the feeling that the assassin is one of the Quorum members," Sequoia said, her voice low.

"Why would the Wraith lie about that?"

"Perhaps to throw the killer off, get them to drop their guard."

Willa pondered the notion. "But Amakeeri also said the assassin planted that idea in Alder's mind to make us suspect each other. Why would the killer do that?"

"Mental tactics," the Provost said. "Throw suspicion on yourself, then have it discounted. After that, no one looks at you twice."

"I suppose," Willa said, uncertain. "I mean no disrespect, Provost, but if that's true, shouldn't I be wary of you, too?"

Sequoia stood. "You're right, of course. I shouldn't have come, but I felt you needed to be aware of my suspicion."

"Yet you can't tell me who you suspect."

Sequoia shook her head. "It's puzzling how strong the assassin's mental shield is. Unless…"

"Unless Xanthes isn't the only one protecting the assassin," Willa said. "But that would mean there's more than one spy on Earth, or…"

"Or Elowen's still under Xanthes's control, although I find that harder to believe. Alder and the med-techs were very thorough in deprogramming her," Sequoia added.

"Do you think Xanthes reached out to her own counterparts in other 'verses to strengthen the shield?" Willa wondered.

The Provost shook her head. "It's possible, but it doesn't feel that way."

Willa nodded. "Then that brings us back to the first possibility. Someone else on Earth is blocking our attempts to sense the killer."

"Our list of possible suspects just became impossibly long."

"Plus, there's another mystery," Willa said. "I was communing with my voices. None of them have had this experience in their realities. Don't you find that odd?"

Sequoia nodded. "That does seem unusual. What do you make of it?"

"You're asking me? *You're* the Provost."

"And *you're* the one with the Mark who's gone through a Kenning, yet you're as much in the dark as I am. Doesn't *that* strike you as odd? Who among us could block your senses to such a degree?"

A flash of insight exploded in Willa's mind. "The Wraith?"

229

Sequoia's eyes narrowed. "Indeed."

"But why would Amakeeri want to shield the assassin? She's the one who came up with a plan to flush the killer out."

"Unless Amakeeri herself is the killer and she's trying to frame someone else for the murders," Sequoia said.

Willa threw her a suspicious glance. "Forgive me, Provost, but making me doubt the Wraith's intentions sounds like something the assassin would say."

Sequoia nodded. "Of course, you're right. I apologize. What would the Wraith have to gain from the murders?"

Willa pondered the question. "Unless..."

"Unless?" the Provost prompted.

"Amakeeri refused to tell us why, or even how the Wraiths are creating the Maelstroms. Is it possible the murders are some sort of, I don't know, ritual sacrifice or something... that the deaths are somehow necessary to create the portals?"

"That's quite a stretch," Sequoia said.

"You're right. It's crazy." Willa stood and paced around the room. "All my abilities and yet I've never felt so blind!"

The door chimed. Willa opened it to find Malvania Moonstone's blank eyes staring at her. The Divinorum Master gave a slight bow of her head.

"Good morning, Willa."

"Good morning, Master Moonstone," Willa said and returned the bow. She knew Malvania could sense the gesture even if she couldn't see it and hoped she hadn't overheard Willa's remark about being blind.

"I'm sorry to interrupt, Provost," Moonstone said, slightly irked as she entered the chamber, "but you have a visitor who insists on speaking with you right away."

Sylvania stepped inside, her hood raised.

"Well, now it's a party," Willa remarked.

"Please forgive my rudeness, Provost," Sylvania said, her head bowed. "I meant no disrespect."

"What's so urgent?" Sequoia said.

"I wish to continue my training immediately if I may be allowed," Sylvania said.

Willa, Sequoia, and Moonstone were equally surprised. "You're certain?" the Provost queried. "You had quite a difficult time of it before."

"I'm not the person I was back then, Provost. Please allow me to try again. I promise not to disappoint, despite my lack of Hybrid genes."

Sequoia placed a hand on Sylvania's shoulder and offered a gentle smile. "You were never a disappointment. Yes, of course you may continue your training. Come, let's talk in my chamber." Sequoia glanced at Willa. "We can continue this conversation later if you wish."

Willa nodded as Sylvania turned to her. "Poppy sends her love and has accepted your offer to train her."

Willa was surprised for a second time. "She has?"

"Oh, and she's challenged you to a game of Hexes, which she insists she'll win."

Willa smiled. "She didn't put it that politely, though, did she?"

"No. She said she'll kick your butt."

"We'll see about that."

Sylvania left with Moonstone and Sequoia. Willa shut her door, reclined on her bed, and continued to ponder other possibilities that might allow her to pierce the assassin's mental shield.

*

Sequoia, Sylvania, and Moonstone walked down the corridor in silence as they headed to the Provost's chamber: three hooded figures intermittently lit by the cool pools of blue light from the Ye Ming Zhu stones set in the black marble walls.

A focused telepathic message was secretly sent by one of them to Xanthes: *The shield bubble is holding. Willa cannot sense that I'm your assassin, my Lady, nor that I've planted a suggestion in her mind to suspect someone close to her."*

*

Xanthes's ship floated in space a hundred klicks away from the Maelstrom's churning maw. She sat in her pilot's seat, her eyes closed as she received the telepathic report.

"Excellent. I shall return soon. Keep the Earth girl focused."

"Should I not kill her when she's alone?" the assassin mentally replied.

"No," Xanthes commanded. *"My plans for her have changed."*

Xanthes ended the telepathic exchange, powered up her engines and dove into the swirling portal.

Chapter Thirteen:
SECRETS

"It has been said that all questions contain their own answers. What is meant by this is that, if one's consciousness didn't contain the answer, then one couldn't have conceived of the question in the first place. This holistic view proposes that cause and effect exist in an entangled state, and that both occur simultaneously. It is only from our space-time perspective that one appears to come before the other.

The point of framing a question is to take one through a process to discover the answer that was within one all along. This leads to the notion that the true purpose of life is not to find answers but to experience the process itself. It is through the process that one changes, grows, and expands one's awareness. In other words, as has often been said, the journey itself is the destination."

"The Book of Paradox"
by Sassafras the Sage

*

Gant opened the door to his quarters and admitted the Organizer's assistant. He grabbed his backup translator as the assistant gestured toward Gant's Luminaria and peppered him with a series of vocal thumps.

"Your communication device appears to be malfunctioning," the assistant said.

"Yes," Gant lied, having deliberately switched it off. "I'm sorry you had to come all this way in person."

"It's my duty and my pleasure," the assistant said with practiced politeness.

"What can I do for you?" Gant said, feigning ignorance.

"The Organizer requests your presence. If you're available now, I would be happy to escort you."

Gant closed his door. "Very well. But before we leave, I'd like to make you an offer."

Thump thump pop-poppity bump: "I don't understand."

Gant sat in a chair and gestured to one of the supply containers, which was about the right height to be a seat for the Subappu. The assistant hesitated, then thought it would be impolite to refuse, so it sat down. It adjusted itself to be more comfortable on the container's hard nano-glass surface and turned four of its eyestalks toward Gant.

"I've been studying your civilization and its trade agreements with the clan of clans," Gant began. "Some of the items your people requested are very interesting. For example, I know about your love of garlic…"

"Oh, yes," the assistant thumped with enthusiasm. "It's quite delicious."

"The list contains various spices along with vanilla, strawberry and chocolate extracts. I was a bit surprised by one item, though. Peppermint." The word translated as *bong-bang* in Subappunese.

There was a slight hesitation before the assistant responded. "Is that not a common flavor on Earth?"

"Yes, but when I passed Sed'Mok's market stalls, I smelled all the items on the list except peppermint. The aroma was only in one place… the Organizer's chamber. I'm curious as to why."

The assistant squirmed and made a low sound that betrayed its nervousness. "It's not my place to discuss --"

"It's okay. I'm not one of you. You can speak freely here. The conversation won't leave this room, I promise," Gant assured the young Subappu.

"But if the Organizer asks what we spoke about, I must tell him."

"Tell him we talked about spices. That's the truth, yes?"

The translator made a clicking noise that Gant had come to learn was the sound a Subappu made when thinking things over. He gambled that the gullibility that often accompanied the young of many species would get the assistant to lower its guard.

When he felt the timing was right, Gant gave the assistant a gentle push. "So... peppermint?"

"I'm not sure how to explain... there's no single Subappu word for it..."

"Just keep it simple," Gant suggested.

The assistant lifted itself off the container and paced around the room to quell its nervousness. "It gives a certain kind of pleasure. The kind of pleasure one wants more of. After a while, one must have even more of the pleasure, then more and more. It's never enough."

"The word for it in my language is addiction." Gant's translator turned the word "addiction" into *thrum-boom-boom-bang-pop-pop-pop*, which was Subappunese for "a state of unending desire." *So, the Organizer has a drug problem,* Gant thought. *I can use that.* "Thank you. You've been very helpful," Gant said.

"I have?" the assistant thumped, still nervous.

"Oh, yes. As a guest of your people, it's always a good thing to learn more about one's hosts, don't you agree?"

"I suppose that's true," the young Subappu said, relaxing a bit. "Shall we go now?"

"By all means," Gant agreed with a smile. "But I might have more questions for you later."

"I'm happy to answer as best I can," the Subappu thumped.

"Well, to make sure you're happy, I'd like to pay for your help and your time."

"That's not necessary. It's my duty and my pleasure to --"

"I'd like to pay you in peppermint."

The assistant stopped in mid-thump. All eight eyes focused on Gant.

Bong-bang? "Peppermint?"

The translator resumed its series of clicks. Gant knew the Subappu was considering it.

"How much peppermint?" the assistant asked.

I've got him! Gant thought as his smile widened. "I can ask my friends to send as much as you want."

"And you won't tell the Organizer?"

"Not a word," Gant promised. "Are we agreed?"

Thump! "Yes!"

Gant stood. "Then let's not keep the Organizer waiting." As they walked out the door, Gant thought how appropriate it was that the word 'agreed' was ninety percent 'greed.'

*

Holly and Argus stood before Rhadamanthus, Ts'Eme'Kwes, and Salizar in the barren, grey landscape of Shunyata.

"Many Susquehannock agree to reveal our secret," said Rhadamanthus, "and many do not agree."

"Then Alder is right," Argus growled in disgust. "Cowards will Slipwalk to other realities to escape attack. Earth is home! We must help defend!"

Holly placed a hand on the Sasquatch's arm to calm him. "The last thing I want is to cause a rift between you and your people, Argus."

"Not care!" Argus boomed. "Not want to side with cowards! I will protect home! Who will protect with me?"

"You cannot make decision on your own!" Salizar shouted back in his thick, Slavic accent.

"Argus can! Argus will! Argus has!" The Sasquatch stomped toward the dolmen that would transport him back to Port Dublin. "Holly and I go now."

"Wait!" Ts'Eme'Kwes said.

Argus and Holly stopped and looked back.

"I, too, will fight for Earth," she vowed.

"As will I," Rhadamanthus added.

"Most of my people are not decided," Salizar protested. "You cannot expose secret if they say no!"

"Then we will convince them to say yes," Ts'Eme'Kwes said.

Argus grunted in agreement and, along with Holly, vanished through the dolmen portal.

*

Xos-Asura Two, the Archon of the second Xos universe, was in the middle of his third torturous interrogation of Kale Ashgrove's counterpart and was relishing every moment of it. The Archon sipped an alcoholic drink, then gently pushed the twentieth extraction needle into Kale Two's skull and shivered in delight at his victim's scream. He waited until Kale nearly passed out, then threw his drink in Kale's bloody, battered face to shock him back to consciousness.

"You've thoughtfully provided me with all the information my techs need to replicate your star-drive engine. Now, if you'd be so kind as to explain the computer interface that controls the ship?"

Kale mumbled incoherently through his swollen lips.

"I'm sorry," Archon Two said, "I didn't quite catch that."

Kale Two summoned what little strength he had left to raise his head. He glared at his tormentor through two black eyes. "I said go to hell," he croaked from his parched lips.

"I've heard you talk about this 'hell' before. What exactly is it?"

"A place of eternal pain and suffering," Kale rasped.

"But we're already there," the Archon laughed. "I'm the one providing the pain and you're the one doing the suffering. Now, you're trying my patience." Xos-Asura Two jiggled one of the needles. Kale screamed through clenched teeth and promptly passed out.

The Archon held Kale's slack face in his talon-like hands and sighed. "And we were having such a nice chat."

"My Lord," squeaked a shrill voice to one side.

The Archon glanced over at Eschavek Ren Two, his personal attaché. The diminutive purple alien seemed more agitated than usual.

"I asked to not be disturbed. Unless you'd rather take his place in the chair?"

Eschavek swallowed and licked his lips. "My Lord, your daughter is here with... with..."

"What in the name of the Elder Gods is wrong with you?" the Archon snapped.

"Perhaps it would be best if she showed you herself, my Lord."

"Fine. Send her in."

Eschavek Two couldn't scurry from the torture chamber fast enough.

Xos-Asura Two turned to the unconscious Kale. "I suppose we'll have to continue our little talk another time."

The sound of armored footsteps drew the Archon's attention to the entrance. His daughter, Xibalba, led four guards into the room. They flanked her exact double. The Archon's pale eyes blinked in confusion. "What sorcery is this?"

"Father," Xibalba said, "this... duplicate was captured as her ship approached Xos. She claims to be, well, me from another universe."

"My name is Xanthes. *I am* from another universe. I can prove it."

Xos-Asura Two approached Xanthes and examined her closely from every angle. "This must be a ploy by one of the other Overlords," he said. "Probably Vorga if I had to guess. His gen-techs must've created this clone intending to replace you."

"That would mean someone smuggled my DNA to his camp," Xibalba said. "It would be my pleasure to find and kill the traitor."

"I'm not a clone!" Xanthes said, incensed. She turned to Xibalba. "You saw my ship. Have you seen another like it anywhere on Xos?"

Xibalba glanced at Kale. "It does bear a resemblance to the stranger's tech."

Xanthes pointed at Kale, still out cold. "Tech which I will gladly share with you so that together, we may conquer not only the stranger's planet, but every world within the Alliance he comes from," Xanthes boasted.

"He did mention something about an Alliance in one of our talks," the Archon said. "How many worlds are we talking about?"

"Over a hundred," Xanthes said with a gleam in her eyes.

The Archon's suspicion was countered by just enough greed to kindle his curiosity. He turned to the guards and gestured at Kale. "Put him back in his cell." To Xanthes he said, "Shall we retire to my chamber? My daughter and I would love to hear more about this other universe of yours."

*

Gant sat on the bench in the Subappu meeting chamber, his backup translator in hand, as the Organizer sat on its orange perch across from him. Gant politely waited for the alien to start the conversation.

Pop-pop thumpity-thump rat-a-tat bang. "I apologize for ending our previous conversation so abruptly."

"I take no offense," Gant's translator said in Subappunese.

The Organizer cleared its vocal canal. "I have decided to address your concerns by sharing the secret you suspect my people are keeping."

Gant gave a slight bow of his head. "I'm honored."

"However, if turns out to be of no use in the battle with your enemy, you must agree to keep it a secret as well."

"I have no problem with that," Gant assured the octopod.

"Very well," the Organizer said. "The reason that Sed refuses to join the clan of clans is because we wish to retain control over the export of Talus leaves."

Gant was quiet for several moments as he pretended to ponder the information. He hoped that the silence would make the Organizer nervous enough to keep talking.

"You see," the Subappu continued, right on cue, "we know that the Hybrids use it in their Divinorum ritual and, well, with more and more Hybrids choosing the Path of Mastery, we could soon run short. Our people rely on a continued supply of Talus for our own special needs."

"And what would those special needs be?" Gant said.

"It's a very private part of our birthing process," the Organizer admitted. It was clear from how the Subappu's eyestalks twitched that this was an uncomfortable subject. Nevertheless, the Organizer pressed on. "Without a sufficient supply of Talus, our birthrate would drop to a dangerous level."

"I understand," Gant said.

Gant could see the Organizer visibly relax once it believed it had gotten its message across. It was time to go for the jugular, assuming the Subappu had one, of course.

"I think you have other secrets as well," Gant said.

The Organizer blinked. "Well, yes, of course, but --"

"Like your need for peppermint."

The Organizer froze; all eight eyes locked onto Gant. "I don't know what you --"

"I thought your people didn't lie."

"I'm not! I mean, I really don't understand what that has to do with --"

Gant pressed his advantage. "The secret you shared about Talus... I'm sure that's true, but it's not the real secret, is it? Not the most important secret... the one that could help the clan of clans in the fight against the Archon."

The Organizer was dead silent.

"Tell me what it is," Gant said to the spider.

Bang! "No!"

"If I tell the clan of clans that peppermint is creating addicts among your people, they won't export it to you anymore."

"A-d-d-i-i-i-x-x-x?" It was the closest the Organizer could come to repeating the words "addicts."

"It means it puts your body in a state of unending desire. You'll do anything to get it. You want more and more and, without it, you feel pain and weakness that grows stronger and stronger until you eat peppermint again," Gant explained as simply as he could.

The Organizer's eyestalks nearly retracted into its body. "You wouldn't tell --"

"I won't if you tell me the real secret. And if I think it can help to win the battle against the Archon, I promise to make up a story so that no one will know it came from the Subappu."

The Organizer thrummed again as Gant patiently waited.

"I must discuss this with the Organizers of the other clans," the alien said.

Gant stood and bowed. "I'm sure you'll make the right choice." Gant smiled to himself as he left the chamber, certain that his gamble was about to give him a one-way ticket back to the Alliance.

*

The Archon of the second Xos universe sipped a rare wine from a fluted glass as he chatted with Xanthes and his daughter in his private chamber.

"So, your father, my counterpart as you call him, is also Archon in your universe," Xos-Asura Two said as he absorbed what Xanthes had told him.

"Probably in several universes," Xanthes said, counting on his ego to keep him interested.

"Yet you and I have different names," Xibalba said to Xanthes.

"It appears some things are the same and some are not," Xanthes said. "If everything was identical, how would you know you were in a different universe?"

"Fair point," Xibalba yielded. "But this Willa person is also one of our counterparts?"

"Yes. She has doubles that are like her, just as we likely have doubles that see things more our way," Xanthes said.

"How do we find more of them... more of us?"

The Archon set his glass down. "Neither of you are going anywhere until my techs study your ship," he said to Xanthes.

"Of course, my Lord. Whatever you need. I live to serve."

"A wonderful phrase," the Archon said. "I'll decree that all my subjects use it."

"One question," Xibalba added. "Why is it that the Maelstrom's bubble limits our Empire to twenty worlds, yet this so-called Alliance is free to travel to over a hundred?"

Xanthes hadn't pondered that puzzle and suddenly felt the pressure of Xibalba's and her father's icy gazes. They had the look of two predators sizing up their prey.

Is this how my subjects see me? she wondered.

Xanthes's keen survival instinct kicked in. The bond that Willa had forged between them gave Xanthes access to some of Willa's knowledge. The answer came in a flash.

"The Maelstroms were created in her universe," Xanthes replied.

"There's more than one?" the Archon said.

"I believe so. They act as portals to other universes, but her universe is the hub." Her hosts' blank stares told her she wasn't getting through to them. "Think of it like a tree… the branches and leaves all stem from the same trunk but they only stretch so far."

The Archon and Xibalba exchanged a puzzled glance.

"What's a tree?" Xibalba said with a knitted brow.

Xanthes realized she was seeing things from Willa's point of view. There were no trees on her version of Xos either, yet she could now clearly envision the lush forests that covered vast areas on Earth.

She struggled to explain the concept. "It's an organic life form. It grows randomly in the exposed soil of Willa's planet. Trees can grow as tall as this tower. They draw water up through their roots, convert sunlight into energy and carbon dioxide into oxygen. They're mostly green."

Xos-Asura two and Xibalba strained to picture what Xanthes had described.

"An organic version of an oxygen-and-water-generating factory?" Xibalba said with amazement.

"Sort of, I guess," Xanthes replied. "I've heard stories that Xos also had such trees before our people arrived."

"It sounds disgustingly unpredictable," the Archon said. "No wonder our predecessors converted Xos into the organized, efficient world it is today."

Xanthes nodded. "Yes, of course." She didn't dare voice it, but she was troubled by the fact that she not only accessed Willa's knowledge but also felt her affinity for trees. Xanthes quickly buried the feelings so they couldn't weaken her resolve. She would need to meditate later and place filters in her mind to block such an emotion in the future.

"You said you had spies on Earth that you mentally control," the Archon broached. "Why go through all this? Why don't you have them simply kill the Earth girl?"

"I tried that but she foiled my plan. She used her counterpart connection with me to strengthen the bond between us. She knew what I was thinking, and forced me to do things against my will.

243

But it can work both ways. Killing her isn't the solution," Xanthes said. She looked at Xibalba. "When we connect with our Xos counterparts, we'll have the power to turn her. Our greatest weapon against Earth will be Willa herself!"

*

Gant followed the Organizer through the cobbled streets of Sed'Mok as they wound their way toward the wide, central plaza that surrounded the Subappu's sacred Temple of Time.

Gant was impressed by the towering circular structure of stone and wood. It reminded him of a hologram he saw back on Earth of an ancient temple in the area known as China.

The temple was unusual in many ways, the most noticeable being it was three stories tall, whereas every other building in the village was a single story.

Two wide ramps hugged the interior walls. One spiraled clockwise and one went counter-clockwise up to the second and third levels. Several Subappu of various ages and hues went about their business in the enormous temple, though Gant noticed slight gestures of respect in their tentacles as the Organizer passed by. He also caught a few strange looks from their eyestalks.

"You are the first off-world being to enter the Temple of Time," the Organizer told Gant. "If not for the fact that some of the other Organizers have a… taste for peppermint, they wouldn't have agreed to grant you access."

"I appreciate their wisdom," Gant's translator drummed.

The Organizer led his guest to a third ramp, hidden behind a thick stone wall, that went down below the ground floor. Gant and the Subappu descended three stories until the ramp brought them to a large wood door carved with unusual glyphs.

The Organizer's delicate tentacle-hands tapped a complex code of glyphs and the heavy door slid to one side with barely a sound. They entered a large airlock chamber and waited until the first door closed before the Organizer tapped an equally complex code on a second door.

The inner door slid open. Beyond it was a massive laboratory of steel, glass and ceramic, huge as a warehouse and brightly lit by hundreds of luminescent beads set into the high ceiling.

Gant was transfixed. The lab was populated by dozens of Subappu, each working at a highly advanced computer station or assembling some exotic piece of alien technology.

The workers stopped and stared at Gant with all eight of their eyes as the Organizer led him down the central aisle. Gant could see the Organizer gesturing to all of them that Gant's presence was allowed. They relaxed but remained curious.

"Your culture is far more advanced than the clan of clans believes you to be," Gant said. His pulse raced as he took in row after row of sophisticated devices he couldn't identify.

"We estimate that this technology is at least one hundred years ahead of the tech used by the clan of clans," the Organizer replied. Gant's translator even supplied a hint of pride in the statement.

"So even if the enemy chief copies Alliance tech, this tech could still defeat him," Gant surmised.

"Yes," came the deep thump.

"You also have ships with engines that jump?"

Another affirmative thump needed no translation. "Our ships only jump to stars that do not belong to the clan of clans. If we happen to come across one of their exploration ships, we do not show ourselves on screen and say our ship is from a different planet they haven't heard of."

Gant frowned. "I thought Subappu didn't lie."

"It's not a lie," the Organizer said. "All this tech and weaponry comes from another world, from a clan called *drum, drum, drum, thump, gong.*"

Gant's device failed to translate the name but it hardly mattered.

245

"A ship from their world crashed on Sed three years ago," the Organizer explained. "We've been studying and replicating its technology in secret since then."

Gant's mind was already plotting how to introduce the Subappu's "borrowed" tech to the Alliance without spilling their secret. Of course, Gant knew that one secret led to another. The Organizer may have been forced to tell Gant about the alien ship and its high-tech weapons, but the Subappu didn't say *why* they wanted to keep it a secret from the Alliance. They could trade this tech for just about anything the Alliance had to offer. The reason for not doing so must be extremely important. Gant decided not to press the issue for now. The time would come for another discussion, perhaps after giving the Organizer a generous "gift" of peppermint.

"I will leave it to you to think of a plausible story to tell the clan of clans as to how you acquired this tech," the Organizer said.

Gant smiled. "You mean you'll leave the lying to me."

Thump, said the Subappu, which by now Gant understood as "Yes," even without his translator.

Gant looked around the lab. Most of the workers had gone back to their tasks, the novelty of Gant's presence having worn off. "I need to know what all these devices do."

"Where would you like to begin?" the Organizer said, his eight eyes looking in as many directions.

Gant focused on a long rack that held hundreds of large, shiny black tubes about ten feet long and two feet in diameter. He pointed at them, careful that his gesture was polite. "Let's start with those."

*

Thirteen hundred light-years from Earth, the Orion Nebula shone like a jewel in the heavens. The titanic cloud of gas was home to nearly three thousand stars, born in phases over the past three million years.

Something new was being born in the stellar nursery. A swirling portal erupted amid the cocoon of hydrogen and atomized dust. It began to vacuum hundreds of thousands of tons of gas into its voracious maw, along with a sizeable section of a protoplanetary disk, thus condemning the nascent star system to form fewer planets in its future.

The third Maelstrom flared to life in an incandescent blast of superheated plasma that sent a shockwave outward at close to the speed of light and rippled the very fabric of space-time.

*

Willa was in mediation in her chamber in Mystery. In her mind, she was inside a grey, nondescript room with her double from Earth Two.

"Where are we?" Willa Two asked.

"A mental construct, sort of like the one Xanthes trapped me in, but without the 'evil lair' look," said Willa. "We need to talk."

"Why here?" Willa Two asked.

"I discovered in my last encounter with Xanthes that neither she nor anyone else can hear us in this place unless we mentally invite them. Listen, I have an idea of how I can expose the assassin, but I need you to enlist someone in your 'verse for my plan to work."

"In my 'verse? Who?" wondered Willa Two.

Before Willa One could answer, her senses were rattled and her thoughts scrambled by an overwhelming wave of energy. She reeled from the impact as the sensation flowed through her to Willa Two. Both of them held their throbbing temples as the wave slowly passed.

"The third Maelstrom!" they said in unison.

"Five more to go," said Willa One. "I'm running out of time."

"To do what?"

"To stop the Wraiths from completing their task, whatever it is."

"Amakeeri didn't tell you?" Willa Two pressed.

Willa shook her head. "Not beyond her general assurance that it's in the Alliance's best interest."

"And you don't trust her..."

"I'm not sure. She's hard to read. Something about it just feels wrong. Have you ever met a Wraith in your 'verse?"

"No, and I'm not sure I want to," said Willa Two with a shiver.

Willa One collected her thoughts. "Never mind that for now. I need you to go to Mystery right away."

"Okay. Who am I looking for?"

*

Kale sat at the table under the flower-covered arbor at Ashgrove cottage as he counseled his sons, Rowan and Thorn.

"The Sasquatch are allowed to keep their secrets if they so wish. We must respect their decision."

"They allowed you and your crew to be tortured! They left Thorn and me in the dark for a year without a father, and all the while they could've brought you home!" Rowan said in anger.

"It was bad enough when Mother went missing," Thorn added, equally upset. "But to find out that Argus could've saved you and yet did nothing... it's not right!"

"Listen to me, both of you. It's my fault I wound up in the Maelstrom. My fault that my ship was destroyed. My fault that my crew was captured and tortured and..." Kale took a moment to push down the horrifying memory of witnessing the cold-blooded murder of most of his crew at the Archon's command. "It's my fault and no one else's that you were left alone, understand?" he said, still choked with emotion.

Rowan and Thorn were shaken, unused to seeing their father so bereft.

"You were looking for Mother," Rowan said. "We don't blame you for leaving."

Kale lowered his head, lost in dour thoughts.

"I think we should go back to Shan," Thorn suggested. "I still think they're not telling us something about Mother's disappearance."

"We went over her ship's trail a dozen times, Thorn," Kale said. "She never made it to Shan. There's nothing to find there. It's a dead end."

"We can't give up!" Thorn protested. "Mother's out there somewhere, I just know it! We can't abandon her!"

Kale pounded his fist on the table. "She's gone, Thorn! Do you understand? She's gone! It's just us now and you need to let her go!"

Thorn stood, eyes welling, rigid with anger. He stormed off.

Rowan placed a calming hand on Kale's arm. "Are you saying that to convince us, or to convince yourself, Father?"

Kale shook his head, at a loss. He gripped Rowan's hand, his eyes flooded with tears of regret.

*

Thorn fumed in silence in his hammock as night fell.

Kale gently knocked on the wood door frame to Thorn's open-air bower. "May I come in?"

Thorn's eyes flickered to his father for a moment, then fixed on the arbor's ceiling of thick ivy, hanging vines and purple flowers. He crossed his arms and remained sullen.

Kale sighed and entered. He took a chair in the corner opposite from the hammock and joined his son in silence. A warm breeze wafted between the intermittent posts that supported the pergola's roof and slowly lifted the tension from the air.

"I'm sorry I snapped at you," Kale said. "I haven't given up hope that your mother's still alive somewhere among the stars."

Thorn listened as his anger cooled, but he stayed silent.

Kale felt his way through the next words before he spoke them. "We'll go to Shan, you, Rowan, and me. You can ask the Shan'ti whatever you want."

Thorn sat up and swung his legs over the side of the hammock. "Really?"

Kale nodded. "You and your brother were too young to go with me before. You deserve a chance to seek your mother out now that you're older. I just don't want you to be disappointed if we don't find the answers you're hoping for."

Thorn jumped down and went to Kale, who stood to accept his son's grateful hug.

"Thank you, Father."

Kale held Thorn close and hoped that his son's resolve would give him the courage to take up the search for Celandine anew. They parted, Thorn brimming with excitement.

"I have one request," Thorn said. "I want to ask Willa to join us. Her abilities could make all the difference in our search."

Kale saw the wisdom of it and nodded. He was rewarded with a smile big enough to split Thorn's face in two.

"I'll go tell Rowan!"

Thorn ran down the hall to the main room. Kale sat back down and gazed out through the arbor posts at the spray of stars that crusted the velvet night. He closed his eyes and softly sang an old sea shanty to himself.

"The moon on the ocean was dimmed by a ripple,
affording a checkered delight.
The gay jolly tars passed a word for the tipple,
and the toast, for t'was Saturday night.
Some sweetheart or wife he loved as his life,
each drank and wished he could hail her.
But the standing toast that pleased the most
was to the wind that blows,

to the ship that goes,
and to the lass that loves a sailor."

Kale wiped a tear from his eye. "If you're out there, my love, I promise I'll find you, or die trying."

Chapter Fourteen:
ASSASSIN

"When it was demonstrably proven beyond a shadow of a doubt that the spirit realm was real and that our consciousness lived on in another form after physical death, the human race found itself in an unprecedented ethical and legal dilemma: If there really was no death, was there such a thing as murder? Ultimately, after much heated debate, it was agreed, regardless of the fact that we continue, that each person's life is purposeful and sacred, and no one but the person living that life has the right to end it.

Ironically, three unexpected things resulted from this decision: The elimination of the death sentence, the decriminalization of attempted suicide, and the establishment of many new rehabilitation and counseling services to deal with, and eliminate the causes of, homicide and suicide. Thus, a new age began in which many troubled people found new purpose in their lives and became productive members of society."

"The Paradigm Shift"
by Dr. Quillian Walda

*

SYLVANIA SAT IN A STATE OF REPOSE, deep in meditation within her private chamber in Mystery. The Divinorum initiations she'd undergone when she first entered the monastery had allowed her to develop some tentative connections to her counterparts in parallel universes. The changes in her psyche from her time as Brandelyn, along with her success at resisting Xanthes's attempt to influence her mind, had strengthened not only her resolve to continue her training, but also her ability to connect more powerfully with her dopplegangers.

Of course, she had also been deeply affected by her discovery of the Larkspur twins' murders, and the numbing shock that fogged her mind at witnessing such a horrifying, bloody nightmare. Perhaps the humans of an earlier age, used to unbridled brutality, wouldn't have reacted quite so intensely at finding two decapitated bodies, but Sylvania was the product of a new era. Like most humans and Hybrids on Earth, as well as most beings throughout the Alliance, she found the idea of murder almost incomprehensible.

A tap at her door pulled her mind away from the grim memory and back into the room. She rose and placed her palm on the door's silver surface to open it. Willa stood in the hall, its soft blue light making her red hair appear black.

"Doyenne Rousseau."

It took a moment for Sylvania to recognize her unexpected guest. "Willa! Please, come in."

The door closed as Sylvania offered the only chair in the room. Willa politely declined with a wave of her hand. "I apologize if I'm interrupting your meditation."

"Not at all. What can I do for you?" Sylvania asked.

"Can you tell me anything more about what you remember when you found Rose and Lilac?"

Sylvania was immediately thrust back into the grisly memory. "I'd rather not revisit that."

"It's important," Willa pressed.

"Why? You think there's something I forgot to tell Security?"

"Let's just say your memory may have a few gaps in it," Willa suggested.

Sylvania's eyes narrowed to black slits. "What are you implying?"

"I mean no disrespect, Doyenne. But I've fought Xanthes often enough to recognize her mental fingerprints in others that she's touched."

"You think she's controlling me? That she made me murder those poor women? I would remember!" Sylvania cried.

"Not necessarily," Willa countered. "She's powerful and extremely cunning. It wouldn't be beyond her ability to wipe your memory."

Sylvania sat and gathered her courage. "You're right. Xanthes recently attempted a telepathic attack. But she didn't succeed, I swear!"

"How can you be sure?"

"I think that Brandelyn, the alternate personality that the Thook implanted in my mind, changed my neural pathways, even after I became myself again," Sylvania said.

Willa thought it through. "So, in a sense, you're now both Sylvania and Brandelyn."

"Yes, exactly! The dual aspects of my personality make it harder for her to get a telepathic lock on either one. That's why I was able to fight her off. But please don't tell the Provost. If she suspects that I'm under Xanthes's control..."

"I won't," Willa promised. "And I apologize for questioning you. I had to be sure."

"Of what?"

"That you're not the assassin," Willa said.

"So, you believe me?" Sylvania hoped.

"It took me a while to sense it and work through it, but when you, Moonstone, and the Provost were in my chamber, someone planted a suggestion in my mind to make me suspect you. I doubt you would have incriminated yourself."

Sylvania was shaken to her core. "But... but that means..."

"Yes," Willa said. "Either Moonstone or the Provost is the killer."

"It's hard to believe either of them would succumb to Xanthes's influence," Sylvania said in the hope that there might be another suspect.

"Xanthes grows stronger with each passing day. In time, even I may not be able to resist her," Willa admitted.

"That's a sobering thought. So, how do we tell which one it is?"

"You're going to help us find out," Willa said.

"Us?"

Willa palmed the door open. A hooded Nocturnal entered.

Sylvania caught a glimpse of the face under the hood. She stood, her mind a swirl of confusion. "This is a trick!"

"No trick," Willa said.

"How is this possible?"

"The 'how' I'll tell you later. It's the 'why' that's part of our plan," Willa said.

*

The Isle of Man, where Holly had reluctantly given Selene charge over Willa's Nocturnal training, was situated in the Irish Sea between Ireland and Britain, and when most of the world's ice melted and the oceans rose, the island's dry land was reduced by half. Cyclopean blocks of stone had been formed into walls that held back the rising tides around some of the coastal habitations, like Castletown in the south, but the sea had claimed the lion's share of the island's coastal real estate hundreds of years ago.

Many of the quaint, ancient buildings of Castletown survived within the sea wall's protective borders, but they amounted to no more than a small village, about three kilometers from end to end. The town that was home to locals and visited by tourists in past centuries was now only inhabited by a strange mix of humans,

Hybrids, aliens, and even a few Elementals involved in divining the secrets of the spirit realm by various means.

In one building that used to be a popular pub, Sages experimented with different recipes for Divinorum as they searched for the elusive formula that would have transformed the unfortunate Belladonna Bloodroot into a Wraith in a heartbeat.

A nearby cathedral functioned as a library, where specially-constructed Luminaria spheres peered into parallel realities and recorded alternate histories.

In the center of it all was Castle Rushen, a cluster of square, gray-stone towers, set on a high berm and surrounded by an octagonal wall with guard stations and parapets. The three-legged Manx triskelion, the ancient symbol of the island, was carved on a stone plaque above the castle's north gate. The ancient castle served as the gathering place for the seven existing Wraiths and, although the village denizens often served the Wraiths' needs, none dared enter the main rooms where the ethereal beings held court, and none dared to reveal the location of the Wraiths' gathering place to the outside world.

Inside the castle walls, Amakeeri addressed her fellow Wraiths in the chamber known as The Hall of History. There was a large hearth at one end, set into a tall stone wall and lined with ancient brick. Spirit flames flickered within and bathed the room in cool, blue light. Stout, triangular wood trusses supported the ceiling. There were no chairs, benches, or tables in the room as the semi-transparent Wraiths never sat.

"The third Maelstrom has opened," Amakeeri announced to the members of the Septet. She focused on two of her fellow Wraiths, a female named Devashka and a male called Ethaniel. "You've done well. The three portals are stable." She gestured to another male Wraith. "We'll need your portal soon, Yojiro."

"All the portals will amount to nothing if we don't have an eighth," Yojiro complained.

"You know I have a candidate," Amakeeri reminded him.

"Selene is unqualified," Devashka chimed in. "She's headstrong and impatient."

"What about Alder Redwood," Ethaniel said. "He's an accomplished Sage."

"With an ego that dwarfs Jupiter," Devashka said. "It's a shame we can't allow the child to become one of us."

"We've all seen her timeline," Amakeeri said, "and the Seers in the village have confirmed it. Willa must become a Wraith on her own or all is lost."

A very thin female Wraith named Viviana spoke up. "Belladonna created the original Maelstrom and there are seven of us. You're the strongest among us," she said to Amakeeri. "Are you sure you can't be the eighth and also perform the crystallization?"

"I appreciate your vote of confidence," Amakeeri said with a slight smile of gratitude, "but opening the final Maelstrom and crystallizing the Merkabah is beyond even my powers. We need another Wraith or it might not be stable."

The Wraiths all nodded in agreement, except Devashka.

"The child doesn't suspect why we're creating the Maelstroms, does she?"

"No. Her mind is focused on finding the assassin, as it should be," Amakeeri said. "Now, to other business. When will the next batch of Divinorum Indigo be ready?"

"In three days." Viviana said.

Amakeeri nodded her approval. "Excellent. I must inform the Dakini of our progress."

"Are you certain we can rely on the Space-Dancers to do their part when the time comes?" Devashka asked. "They can be more mercurial than Pookas."

"They've assured me that there's room for Earth and the nearby systems in the Inbetween," Amakeeri said. "Unfortunately, the rest of the Alliance is on its own."

*

257

Sequoia and Moonstone were deep in conversation in the Provost's chamber when Sylvania entered in haste, flustered.

"Provost, I beg your pardon for coming to you unannounced at this hour."

"Has something happened?" Sequoia said.

"I just had a very disturbing conversation with Willa. I think she suspects me of being the killer!"

"What? That's nonsense," the Provost countered. "I'll speak to her."

"Thank you. If she spreads that false rumor to the other Nocturnals --"

"Where is she now?" Moonstone inquired.

"Right here," Willa said as she entered. She glared at Sylvania. "I knew I'd send you running to the Provost, pretending to be innocent!"

"I *am* innocent!" Sylvania protested.

Sequoia stepped between them. "This is a serious charge, Willa. What proof do you have?"

"The proof is lying in a coma on Andromeda Spaceport!" Willa said.

"What are you talking about? What proof?" Sequoia demanded.

"Opal's alive!" Willa shouted.

"Impossible!" said Moonstone. "We were all at her burial."

"I discovered that the medical robots were able to revive her. She's in an induced coma. Her burial was staged to keep her safe from the assassin while she recovered," Willa explained. She stabbed a finger at Sylvania. "They'll wake her tomorrow, and she'll confirm it was you who attacked her!"

The room was dead silent.

Moonstone cleared her throat. "You've seen Opal yourself?"

"I have."

"How did you find out?" Sequoia said.

"After the burial, I could still sense Opal's life force."

The Provost nodded. "None of us could. Your senses have indeed grown strong."

Willa continued. "I tracked her to the spaceport and confronted Security. I used my powers and forced them to admit the truth."

Moonstone glanced at Sylvania as she approached Sequoia. "Provost, if Willa's suspicions are true, we should at least take precautions until your acolyte awakens."

"But I'm innocent!" Sylvania cried.

"Then you have nothing to fear," Sequoia said as she tapped a button on her console. A security robot emerged from a secret alcove in the wall. "Please confine Doyenne Rousseau to her quarters," she ordered.

"Yes, Provost," answered the bot.

Sylvania looked at Willa, her heart crushed. She walked from the chamber ahead of the robot like a person destined for death.

"Thank you for bringing this to our attention," Sequoia said to Willa.

Willa bowed her head and left.

Moonstone turned to Sequoia. "Do you believe her?"

Sequoia was silent for a moment as she digested what Willa told them. "I prefer to reserve judgment until I speak with my acolyte."

"Yes, of course," Moonstone agreed. "With your permission, I shall leave to meditate on the matter myself."

Sequoia nodded. Once Moonstone left, the Provost tapped a sequence on her Luminaria. Within moments, Commander Erebus appeared in the crystal globe.

"Good evening, Provost. To what do I owe the unexpected pleasure?"

"I need to discuss a matter of the utmost importance," Sequoia said. "But not here. I'll be at the station within the hour."

*

A Security robot led Sequoia down one of Andromeda Spaceport's corridors to a medical isolation ward that was off limits to most station personnel. Erebus had granted the Provost special access to visit her acolyte once she confronted the Commander about Opal's presence.

Sequoia reached the double airlock doors that quarantined the ward from the rest of the spaceport. The robot transmitted the access code and the doors parted.

"Please wait here," Sequoia said.

"As you wish, Provost," the robot replied.

Sequoia passed through the airlock. The doors sealed behind her and she made her way to Opal's recovery room. Opal was on a magnetic healing bed, eyes closed, as various tubes delivered nutrients to her body. A readout indicated her comatose state, but her heartbeat and respiration were near normal. She'd be awakened in less than a day and, presumably, able to identify her attacker.

"I'm sorry, child," the Provost said as she pulled a thin hypo-spray from a pocket in her robe. She was about to inject the dark liquid into her acolyte's nutrient tube when Opal's eyes snapped open. One hand shot out and grabbed Sequoia's wrist as the other hand snatched the injector from her.

Sequoia stepped back in shock as Opal sat up. The door to Opal's room opened. Two Security robots entered, followed by Willa and Commander Erebus. The robots clamped their flexible hands around both of Sequoia's arms, pinning her in place.

"What is this?" she cried out. "I demand you let me go!"

"You're in no position to demand anything," Erebus said as he took the injector from Opal, who was now on her feet. Erebus injected a small amount of serum from the hypo-spray into a port in one robot's torso. "Analyze," she commanded.

The robot responded within seconds. "Distilled foxglove serum, also known as digitalis."

"Poison to stop Opal's heart," Willa commented.

"I never thought you would be the assassin," Erebus said sadly.

"She's not," Willa said. She walked up to Sequoia and locked eyes with her. Willa reached out with her senses and scanned the Provost. "You're not Sequoia."

Willa snatched the injector from Erebus and held the hypo against the assassin's neck. "Who are you?"

Erebus and Opal were shocked but held their tongues.

The assassin glared at Willa and shifted into her true form.

"Malvania Moonstone!" the Commander said, truly surprised.

"How is it no one knows you're a Shapeshifter?" Willa demanded.

Moonstone remained silent.

Willa pressed the injector against her neck a lot harder. "Talk!"

"I belong to a secret society of Shapeshifters called the Colloquium," Moonstone said. "We don't officially exist." Moonstone turned her attention to Opal. "How are you still alive? I couldn't have failed. I felt the life force leave your body!"

"You didn't fail," Willa said. "Opal is dead."

Moonstone blinked her milk-white eyes. "I don't understand."

"Willa brought me here from a parallel Earth. I'm Opal's counterpart," said Opal Two with a satisfied smile.

"That's impossible!" Moonstone said.

"I'm beginning to believe that nothing is truly impossible," Willa said.

Erebus gestured to the robots. "Escort her to holding."

The robots marched Moonstone out of the room.

"Alder can help her," Willa said. "He was able to break Xanthes's hold on Elowen."

"The Provost... I'm not sure if it was the real one or not... told me you suspected Doyenne Rousseau of being the killer," Erebus said, slightly confused.

"Part of our plan to put the real killer at ease," Willa explained.

Erebus glanced at Opal Two. "You're really from a parallel universe? Did you come through the Maelstrom?"

"No," Opal said and glanced at Willa.

Willa handed the injector to Erebus and took a seat. "Argus gave me permission to fill you in, Commander."

"Argus? Your Divinorum Master? What's he got to do with this?"

Willa's tone spoke volumes, summed up in a single word: "Everything."

*

Dennik, Alarra, Brim, and Gar were present with Brahma Kamal in his chambers as they all listened to Gant on Brahma's Luminaria. Gant fed them a story about an alien smuggler outside the Alliance who had powerful weapons to trade.

"Alliance tech is certainly more advanced than what the League possesses," Gant said, "but we all know the Archon is copying it as we speak. The devices the smuggler is willing to sell are a hundred years ahead of anything I've seen in the Alliance. This tech would practically guarantee our victory over the Archon's fleet. You've got to convince the Tribunal to end my banishment so I can bring the weapons to Earth."

"Don't take this the wrong way," Brahma said, "but, why should they? Variabilis said you admitted that you want to take the Archon's place. How can we trust that you'd be a beneficent ruler?"

Gant was prepared for that possibility. "I told the Shapeshifter the truth. Besides, the smuggler will only deal with me. The Subappu are too primitive to use the tech, and he won't set foot in Alliance territory because, frankly, the weapons are illegal under your laws. He's afraid the Alliance would simply confiscate them without paying."

"Laws can be suspended if we go to war. Regarding your situation, we could simply drop the smuggler's payment off on Sed and bring the weapons back to Earth without you," Brahma reasoned.

"I thought you wanted to help the Resistance," Gar said, his temper rising. "If you hold those weapons hostage, the Resistance suffers as much as the Alliance. Maybe more!"

Gant struggled to remain calm. "You don't understand. This tech is beyond anything any of you has ever seen. It comes from somewhere outside Alliance territory. It would take your scientists months to figure it out. The smuggler has shown me how it all works, but it's too difficult to explain. I need to work hand-in-hand with your technicians to make the weapons operational. Their power cores require perfect alignment and the controls aren't conventional. Even one mistake could be disastrous."

"I can't promise the Tribunal will reverse their decision," Brahma said, "but I'll do my best to explain the situation."

"Do what you have to," Gant said, "but we're running out of time. The Archon won't hesitate to attack as soon as his fleet is ready."

The Luminaria went clear. Brahma looked to Dennik, Alarra, Gar, and Brim. "Any ideas?"

"I'm with Variabilis. I don't trust Gant," Gar grumbled.

"Well, at least you and the Shapeshifter are of one mind on that," Dennik said, "but what choice do we have?"

Brim threw a thought into the ring. "Couldn't the Alliance just go to Sed and force Gant to show your technicians how the weapons work?"

Dennik and Alarra were shocked at their son's suggestion, but Gar slapped Brim on the back and grinned. "Spoken like a member of the League!"

Brahma shook his head. "Unfortunately, no. Sed isn't an Alliance world. It could cause a diplomatic nightmare."

"Maybe we should bring Willa in on this," said Brim. "She might think of something we can't."

"That poor girl has enough on her plate," Alarra said.

Brim persisted. "She broke free from Xanthes's mental attack. She found her way back home from another universe when everyone said it was impossible. She discovered the assassin's identity. If Gant has weapons that can help us defeat the Archon once and for all, then we should at least consult with her. She's not only one of the most powerful people in the Alliance, she's also someone we trust."

Brahma looked around the table. Dennik, Alarra, and Gar nodded their agreement. Dennik regarded Brim with parental pride. "You'll make a great Resistance leader someday, my son."

"I agree," Alarra said. "But let's hope it won't be necessary."

Dennik nodded and turned to Brim. "Please ask Willa to join us when she's able."

Brim nodded and smiled at the prospect of seeing Willa again.

Alarra caught the look and whispered, "You're attracted to her, aren't you?"

His mother's comment made him slightly uncomfortable, but Brim shrugged it off. "What's not to like?"

Dennik noticed that Brahma's thoughts were a thousand light-years away. "Is something wrong?"

"The Tribunal hasn't reversed a decision in the past one hundred seventy years," Brahma said. "And it certainly wasn't for someone accused of murder. Besides, Magister Oringa will likely view Gant's proposal as extortion."

"You have to understand the world we come from," Dennik said. "Desperation is a way of life under the Archon's rule. You do what you must to survive."

"Gant's life isn't in danger on Sed," Brahma pointed out.

"If what he said about the tech is true, it could be the difference between victory and defeat," Dennik pressed. "If the Tribunal can't see that, then all our lives are in danger."

Despite his misgivings, Brahma knew Dennik was right. "We need a demonstration of these advanced weapons before we see the Tribunal."

Dennik stared at Brahma. "Before 'we' see the Tribunal?"

Brahma smiled. "If you think I'm going on my own, you're out of your mind. Like you said, Gant is from your universe. You'll explain his behavior better than I can."

Dennik nodded but wondered if he was in over his head. Leading the Resistance was one thing, pleading a case before the Tribunal that could change the fate of the entire Alliance was quite another.

Brahma caught Dennik's hesitation. "Don't worry, I'm sure you'll know what to say when the time comes."

"And if the Tribunal says no?"

"Then I'm sure you'll know what to do," Brahma said. "Just don't tell me."

Dennik understood: If he took matters into his own hands against the wishes of the Tribunal, he, Alarra, Brim, and Gar would be entirely on their own, operating outside Alliance law. The goodwill and trust they'd worked so hard to forge would be destroyed. Brahma couldn't appear to have any knowledge of their actions.

"Let's hope it doesn't come to that," Dennik said.

"Let's hope," Brahma agreed.

Chapter Fifteen:
THE ANU-HET

"Graft a branch from one type of fruit tree, say apples, onto the rootstock of another type of fruit tree, then save the seeds of the apples produced by that tree and plant them. You won't get apples on the next tree; you'll get whatever fruit that the rootstock was meant to bear. When planting seeds, one must always be aware of what the rootstock was that bore those seeds."

"The Galactic Gardener"
by Dr. Amber Oakley, Research Director
Botanical Institute of North America
2145 - 2176

*

XANTHES AND XIBALBA EXITED from the third Maelstrom into a new parallel universe. Their starship remained just beyond the vortex's gravity well as they took sensor readings.

"Judging by the shift in the positions of several stars, we're definitely in a different universe than mine or yours," Xibalba said as she scanned the readouts.

"That means the second Maelstrom leads to a third alternate reality," Xanthes noted. "I'm beginning to see a pattern here. Thrall..."

"My Lady?" answered the computer.

"Are there any ships on long-range sensors?"

A heartbeat later: "Five cargo vessels, a scout ship and what appears to be a space station, although there's no similar configuration in my data banks."

"Nobody of importance," Xanthes remarked. "Calculate the difference in position for this realty's version of our solar system and set a course for Xos."

The computer was silent for a tenth of a second. "Course laid in, my Lady."

"Jump," she ordered.

The stars on the view screen coalesced into a spectral ring, and a moment later, the ship was in orbit around Xos's single, large moon.

Xanthes and Xibalba were surprised to find two short-range ships waiting for them at the exact coordinates where they arrived. The com snapped on with an incoming message.

"The Archon welcomes you to Xos. Please allow us to escort you to the landing dock," said one of the pilots.

Xibalba cut the com-link. "The moon should've blocked their sensors. How did they know we were coming and where we'd show up?"

"They must have more advanced tech than we do," Xanthes surmised. "Too late to turn back now."

"And why are they so... hospitable?" Xibalba added. She didn't trust people who were too polite. It usually meant they wanted something – most likely something you didn't want to give.

Another message from the lead escort ship sounded over the com. "We mean you no harm. Our weapons are offline. Please allow us to escort you to Xos. The Archon is expecting you."

"We're here to find our counterpart," Xanthes said to Xibalba, "so we might as well cooperate. For now."

"Agreed," said Xibalba. She switched the com-link back on. "Very well, but if we sense the slightest deception, we'll blow your ships to dust."

"We would expect nothing less," the escort replied.

"Follow them in, Thrall," Xanthes ordered.

"Yes, my Lady."

Thrall glided forward and followed the escort ships as they descended toward the surface of Xos Three.

*

Brahma and Dennik had arrived on Sed, their translation devices in hand. The Subappu assistant escorted them to an open expanse at the edge of a salt flat. While Brahma was familiar with the spider-like denizens, most of the aliens Dennik had met since coming to Earth had been somewhat humanoid. He was mildly disturbed by the Subappu's eight-legged gate and multiple eyestalks.

"Bumpity-bump," said the assistant: "We have arrived."

"What is this place?" Dennik asked.

"It used to be a large lake," the assistant explained. "The climate changed long ago and it dried up."

Brahma and Dennik offered their thanks. The assistant clearly didn't enjoy the arid salt flat and hurried back toward town. Dennik and Brahma looked around at the featureless plain as they waited for Gant to arrive.

"I don't like this," Dennik grumbled. "It's too open."

"Spoken like someone who's lived in tunnels his entire life. The Subappu that escorted us here... did it smell like peppermint to you?" Brahma asked Dennik.

"I thought you said they smelled like garlic," Dennik said.

"Most of the time, yes." Brahma squinted at a distant dust cloud. He could just make out a vehicle approaching from the horizon. "Ah, here comes Gant now."

The distance was difficult to gauge on the plain, and it took another five minutes for Gant to drive up in a large, flat truck with eight enormous wheels. One of the ten-foot-long black tubes Gant had first seen in the Subappu's lab was mounted horizontally on a gimbal on the flatbed of the vehicle.

Gant jumped down from the driver's perch, which was built to accommodate a large octopod rather than a human. He clasped Dennik on the forearm in greeting and bowed to Brahma. "It's good to see you both. Thank you for coming."

Dennik gestured toward the black cylinder. "That's one of the weapons? It looks more like a packing tube. You sure the weapon didn't fall out somewhere back there?"

Gant took Dennik's skepticism in stride. "It's like nothing you've ever seen. Would you like a demonstration?"

"We didn't travel five thousand light-years to have breakfast," Brahma said.

Gant climbed back up on the vehicle and swiveled one end of the tube to face a rock outcrop a thousand yards away. "I explained to the Organizer - that's the head of the village where you arrived - that we needed complete privacy. It assured me we wouldn't be disturbed here. The Subappu don't come here much because the salt dries them out." Gant touched a few places in a specific pattern on the tube's surface as he prepped the device, although Dennik and Brahma didn't see any specific controls.

"How can you tell what you're doing?" Dennik asked.

"The controls operate a bit like your Luminaria. The weapon recognizes patterns of touch instead of normal controls," Gant explained. "It takes time and practice to learn the patterns."

Dennik nodded. "I see why you need to teach the Alliance techs in person."

Brahma was impressed. "It's more like playing a musical instrument than firing a weapon."

"Yes, I suppose it is," Gant agreed. "Please stand over there, my friends."

Dennik and Brahma moved to the side of the vehicle as Gant tapped out a final pattern on the weapon's obsidian skin. A ring of bright blue lights glowed beneath one section, rendering it translucent. An etheric blue glow formed inside the tube as a deep, bone-shaking hum vibrated the sand around the truck.

Gant touched the weapon once more. There was a loud THUMP from the heart of the tube. The distant outcrop was instantly atomized in a blinding bubble of blue light. A one-hundred-foot diameter crater five stories deep was scooped out of the salt flat, and a mushroom cloud of salt and dust rose high into the air.

Dennik and Brahma were speechless. Gant tapped a pattern that put the weapon to sleep and jumped down off the flatbed.

"What did I tell you? And this is one of the smaller weapons," Gant said like a hawker selling his wares.

"There was no visible energy beam... no projectile. What destroyed the outcrop?" Dennik said in mild shock.

"It's a subspace weapon," Gant said. "It focuses energy from another dimension like a lens and rips apart the atomic structure of any physical object. At least, that's what the smuggler told me. You think the Archon's fleet can withstand this kind of power?"

"You weren't exaggerating, I'll give you that," Brahma said. "Alright, I'll talk to the Tribunal. No promises but, if anything could make them pardon you, it would be this."

Gant smiled as the three of them watched the dust cloud blow away across the plain. His plan was unfolding perfectly.

*

Willa and Amakeeri were on top of the main tower at Castle Rushen, the Wraith headquarters on the Isle of Man. The night was warm with a slight breeze, but Willa felt a chill as she glanced at the moon through Amakeeri's diaphanous body.

"I'm honored that you'd trust me with the location of your lodge," Willa said.

Amakeeri let out a faint wind-chime chuckle. "With your powers, you would've found it sooner or later. By the way, congratulations on exposing Xanthes's puppet."

"You knew I would," Willa said.

"Yes, but I didn't know how. I could only sense the probability was very high."

"So, your mastery of time, space, and spirit isn't absolute?" Willa replied.

"Oh, heavens, no," said the Wraith. "With so many parallel realities and probable outcomes, we can only sense which path is most likely to unfold in our universe, but that's usually sufficient. All I had to do was set things in motion in a certain way to make one outcome more probable than the others."

"Can you see if the Alliance will defeat the Archon?"

"Unfortunately, there are still too many probable paths, even for a Wraith to follow," Amakeeri said with mild frustration. "However, we know that something important is about to change. We can't say yet whether or not it's in our favor."

Willa extended her senses, just enough to read the Wraith's energy field. An image of the Maelstrom flashed in Willa's mind. "The Maelstroms that you and the other Wraiths are creating... they're your failsafe, aren't they?"

Amakeeri was taken aback by Willa's insight. "I sometimes forget how powerful you are. You must keep that between us. If you share that information with anyone else, you could alter the outcome we're attempting to manifest."

"Which is?"

"Victory for the Alliance, of course," Amakeeri assured her.

"Of course," Willa parroted, though her tone carried a hint of skepticism.

"You don't trust us?"

"I trust you'll serve your own interests, like everyone else," Willa said. "Where your interests overlap those of the Alliance, there's no problem. It's the hidden agenda that concerns me."

Amakeeri studied Willa with her senses for several heartbeats. Willa could feel the Wraith's telepathic probing and allowed her to continue. Amakeeri stopped and assessed what she had gathered from Willa's mind.

"Find what you were looking for?" Willa asked.

"Although I'll train Selene in the ways of the Wraith, I do hope you'll continue on the path of Mastery and become a Wraith yourself one day. The Mark would make you the most powerful among us," Amakeeri said.

Willa turned her senses inward and reflected on the comment. "I can't be any more certain than you at the moment, but I sense I may walk a different path in the future."

Amakeeri was genuinely surprised as she felt the faint vibration of Willa's inner vision. "The Anu-Het? Could it be?" she whispered with uncharacteristic reverence.

"The what?"

Amakeeri weighed the consequences of revealing more and decided to continue. "What do you know of Hybrid history?"

Willa shrugged. "What Holly and other teachers have told me. What most everyone knows, I guess. Why? Is there more to the story?"

"There is," said the Wraith. "Much more."

*

After landing near the Citadel on Xos Three, Xanthes and Xibalba were escorted off their ship and led to the Archon's iron tower.

"I wonder how different this version of Father will be from ours," Xanthes said to Xibalba, her voice low.

"This Citadel is nearly the same. How different can he be?" Xibalba responded as they entered the circular lift and rose up the tower's central shaft.

Xibalba's question was answered the moment they entered the Archon's chamber at the top of the tower.

One of the escort guards signaled them to stop a few yards from the Archon's throne. He took the stunned expressions on their faces for awe as he made his proclamation.

"Bow before our glorious Archon, Lady Xos-Xanthia!"

Xanthes's and Xibalba's counterpart stood with a smile and open arms. "No need for ceremony. I bid you welcome, my sisters!"

*

Amakeeri led Willa down a narrow spiral staircase of stone that led to the Hall of History. The Wraith floated down the stairway like a feather while Willa nearly tripped on the cracked, time-worn steps.

"I apologize," Amakeeri said. "We haven't needed to repair the stones since Wraiths rarely touch the ground."

"No problem," Willa said as she took greater care to avoid further pitfalls.

They arrived in the Hall, and Amakeeri glided over to a floor-to-ceiling stone pillar at the far end opposite the hearth. It was covered with ancient glyphs Willa couldn't read.

"I've never seen writing like that," Willa remarked. "What culture created it?"

"We don't know. But it's not writing, the glyphs are musical notes," explained the Wraith. She passed her ghostly hand over several glyphs in a specific sequence. A deep tone issued from each one, producing a musical code. The pillar split in two and the upper half rose into the vaulted ceiling. A large Luminaria, black as obsidian, rested in a shallow depression in the pillar's lower half.

"This is the Akasha Stone," Amakeeri explained. "It's the only repository of our complete Hybrid history, past, present, and future."

"Future history? Isn't that an oxymoron?"

"I could say it's a non-temporal holographic nexus of parallel probabilities, but 'future history' rolls off the tongue more easily," the Wraith said with a smile. She reached toward the Akasha sphere and slid her phantom hand inside the jet-black stone. After a moment, she pulled her hand back.

"I programmed the Akasha to show you the whole story in simplified images. Otherwise, you'd be here for days," said the Wraith. "Place your palm on the stone and open your mind."

Willa sensed no subterfuge. She reached out, gently laid her palm on the stone's smooth, cool surface and relaxed. The Akasha glowed a deep blue, and an azure energy bubble expanded to contain Willa. Within seconds, she fell into an open-eyed-trance as the Akasha unspooled pictures in her mind, accompanied by Amakeeri's voice.

"As you already know," began the Wraith, "an extraterrestrial race called the Anu arrived on Earth more than three hundred thousand years ago."

Willa saw the Anu's giant saucer-ships land in the African veldt. Primitive proto-humans cowered among the trees and rock outcrops as they peered at dozens of nine-foot-tall, blue-skinned humanoids who disembarked from the gleaming discs.

Another series of images unfolded in Willa's mind as Amakeeri described the scene. "The Anu came to Earth to mine minerals that would help them correct an imbalance in their planet's climate, but the task was too great for the small band of aliens. As master geneticists, their solution was to engineer an army of workers by splicing their genes into the hominids that evolved on Earth to create *homo sapiens*. Those humans became *Hybrid Zero*. Once they had what they needed, the Anu returned to their home- world and left humans to their own devices."

The scene shifted to a future vision of Earth that was technologically advanced, but environmentally on the verge of collapse. Polluted air, deforested landscapes, and dead oceans surrounded decaying cities.

"Over time, Earth humans created many technological marvels. Driven by their greed for wealth and power, they became blind to the damage they were causing the planet. The climate shifted, the ecosystems on land and in the oceans collapsed, and Earth became uninhabitable."

Willa watched as humans began to mutate into small beings with large eyes and leathery, grey skin.

"Humans went underground and, over time, were forced to genetically mutate themselves to survive the harsh environment. They lost the ability to procreate. They tried cloning and other experiments, but no matter what they did, they knew they were a dying race."

Like an army of ants, the diminutive beings began to manufacture saucer-like spaceships and a large, ring-like portal in one of their enormous underground bases. The portal flared to life and formed a tunnel of energy. Their ships entered the tunnel.

"In a last, desperate attempt to preserve their race, the mutated humans used their advanced technology to go back to a time before the destruction."

Willa was riveted as scenes of "alien abductions" took place before her eyes.

"The 'Greys' – now known as 'Whelks' to all of us – began to extract DNA from their ancestors to create the Hybrids that would allow their culture to continue."

Willa saw five different types of Hybrids born in liquid-filled tanks onboard spaceships. They ranged in phases from the withered Greys to those that appeared almost human, like Willa herself.

"Hybrids were created in five phases, each phase becoming more and more human. But as their genetic program progressed, many of the original Anu traits also came to the forefront, making Hybrids more than human."

Images of the Landing, where Hybrid ships arrived on Earth and revealed themselves to twenty-first-century humans, played across Willa's vision. Time raced forward until Willa saw an image of herself. For a moment, she thought she was gazing into a mirror until a double helix of DNA superimposed over her body. The DNA then transformed into a triple helix as Amakeeri continued.

"With the creation of Hybrids, the timeline was altered and Earth became the sixth Hybrid race. But because the genetic marker of the original Anu race has unfolded within your DNA, you, Willa, have become the seed of a seventh Hybrid race that we Wraith call the Anu-Het."

Willa watched her reflection transform into a tall, slender being with piercing, almond-shaped black eyes, blue-tinted skin, and long dark hair.

"The Anu-Het will be born with the combined abilities of all the levels of Mastery. Your descendants will be an entirely new Hybrid species that will spread to the farthest reaches of space and transform the galaxy into an indestructible new Alliance where peace and prosperity will reign for a hundred thousand years."

The blue bubble of the Akasha field retracted into the stone. Willa snapped from her trance and stared at Amakeeri, who gazed at Willa with an almost spiritual reverence.

"I knew you were meant for something greater than merely becoming a Wraith, but I had no idea until now..." Amakeeri collected herself. "This probable future, not yet set in stone, is why you're so important, Willa, and why our plan to repel the Archon's attack must succeed. If we fail, the new future will be one of darkness instead of light."

*

Poppy sat in the grass next to the Hexes game field as Willa joined her. "Ready to have your butt kicked?" Poppy challenged as she stood.

"The game will have to wait. It's time to start your training," Willa said. "So, I'll be kicking your butt."

"How's Master Moonstone?" Poppy asked.

"Alder says her deprogramming is coming along."

"Clever of you and mom to expose her. For a while there, I thought my mother --"

"I know, but she thwarted Xanthes's telepathic attack. Sylvania's more powerful than she knows," Willa assured her friend. "She's evolving as a Nocturnal, and I wouldn't be surprised if she made it all the way to Sage."

"But she's human," Poppy said.

"And so are you," Willa said, "but look what you can do."

"Being able to sense which hex will come up is a parlor trick next to your abilities," Poppy grumped.

"Like I said, your 'trick' can become so much more. Shall we begin?"

Poppy's nod was laced with self-doubt, but she promised herself that she'd give it her all. "What's first?"

Willa went to the game control panel and activated the field. The hexagonal grid of various colors glowed to life. She gestured to Poppy to take a position. Poppy chose to start on a blue hex.

Willa's hand hovered over the start button. "Ready?"

Poppy took a deep breath, locked her gaze with Willa's and nodded.

Willa tapped the button; a countdown from six began, and a chime sounded as it reached zero.

Poppy jumped into the air toward a nearby hex as the colors changed underneath her. The hex shifted from green to white a split second before she landed on it. Willa let the game run for twenty more rounds. Poppy jumped from hex to hex and never landed on a black hex, which would have eliminated her. The scoreboard kept track of the shifting probabilities until Willa tapped the stop button. Poppy landed on a gold hex and won the game even though the board calculated her chances of winning at nearly zero.

Willa walked out onto the game field. "How do you know which way to jump?"

Poppy shrugged. "It's just a feeling."

"Describe it," Willa pressed.

Poppy closed her eyes, analyzed the memory. "It's hard to put into words. It's like the whole playing field fades away. It becomes unreal, except for the hex I should jump to next. That stays sharp."

Willa glanced at the scoreboard. "It's like your brain is calculating thousands of probable outcomes and eliminating the paths that don't lead to a win. Your ability could really help, Poppy. We just need to change your data input to search for the path that leads to victory against the Archon. That's your new golden hex."

"The game's relatively simple, Willa. What you're talking about, I mean, can a human mind process that much data?"

"That's where I come in. I can create a mental space for both of us, enhance your processing ability," Willa said.

"You mean a telepathic link?"

Willa nodded. "We just need to be on the same wavelength, is all. It may take some practice, but it shouldn't be too hard. After all, we're close friends. We already think alike in lots of ways."

Opal Two waved to Willa as she approached the game field, still wrapped in her Nocturnal robe. "Hi. Your mom said you'd be here."

"Poppy, this is Opal… Opal, Poppy," Willa said.

Poppy extended her hand, but Opal bowed instead. They laughed.

"Sorry," Opal said. "Nocturnal habit."

"You're the Opal from the other universe, right?" Poppy said.

"Yes, which is why I'm here." She faced Willa. "Any chance your furry friend can take me back to my 'verse sometime soon?" Opal's smile fell flat as she glanced at Poppy. "Oh! I'm sorry, that's still a secret!"

"It's okay," Willa assured her. "I told Poppy about what Argus's people can do. Poppy's my best friend. We have no secrets. Well, none that really matter, anyway."

Poppy puffed out her chest, just shy of a challenge. "That's right. Best friends." Poppy deflated a bit. "Wait a minute, what secrets haven't you told me?"

"Later. Right now, we need all the friends we can get." Willa turned to Opal. "How would you feel about sticking around for a while? We could still use your help."

"They'll be wondering what happened back in my 'verse," Opal said.

"I'll send Argus with a note," Willa offered.

Opal nodded and glanced at the playing field. "We don't have this game in my 'verse. Can you teach me how to play?"

Poppy winked at Willa and threw Opal a mischievous smile. "Be happy to."

*

Xos-Xanthia was sequestered in her lush, private chamber with Xanthes and Xibalba. They sat in three chairs arranged in a triangle around a low, polished stone table inlaid with gems.

"How did you know we were coming?" Xanthes asked, her tone tainted with suspicion.

"Our Seers have been probing parallel realities for over a hundred years. They predicted your arrival about a year ago," Xanthia explained. "Of course, we couldn't be absolutely certain you'd show up, but here you are."

"So, you already know our plan," Xibala said.

"Oh, yes, it's brilliant! I would have sought you out myself long before this, but it took some time to arrange my ascension to the throne, so you see, I've been rather busy."

Xanthes and Xibalba eyed each other as Xanthia's meaning sank in. *She killed her father and took his place!*

Xos-Xanthia poured a golden liqueur from a crystal cruet into three cordial glasses and handed two to her guests. She raised her glass.

"The thrill of conquest!"

Xanthes and Xibalba mirrored their host.

"The thrill of conquest," they parroted together.

They all took a languid sip of the rich liquid.

"It's delicious," Xanthes said. "What is it?"

"Fermented glandular secretions of the Arbogast were-beast," Xanthia replied with regal nonchalance.

Xibalba's smile faded. Xanthes looked like she was going to be sick.

Xanthia doubled over with laughter. "You should see your faces. I'm joking. It's a rare liqueur made from a fruit that grows once a decade. It's called Zapota."

"You have an interesting sense of humor," Xanthes said flatly. "Shall we get to business?"

"What's the point of being Archon if you don't savor it now and then?" Xanthia remarked. Xanthes and Xibalba were unamused. "Oh, very well, I didn't think the two of you would be so dour." She downed the rest of her Zapota, set the glass on the table, and regarded them both, her fingers steepled. "To business, then. How many ships will your plan require?"

Xanthes mirrored the Archon's haughty affectation. "How many do you have?"

*

That night, Willa sat between Poppy and Opal Two at the dining table in the Nest. Lily and River had prepared several bowls of seasoned vegetables, many of which were fragrant with herbs from Lily's garden.

"Thank you for helping our daughter expose the killer," River said to Opal. "That took a lot of courage."

"But why haven't you returned to your universe?" Lily posed. "Don't get me wrong, we're delighted to have you as our guest, but won't your family miss you?"

"I have an older sister," Opal said. "Her name's Dahlia. Our parents died when I was eight."

Lily took Opal's hand in hers. "I'm so sorry."

"It's okay. We have no other relatives, but Dahlia did a good job raising me on her own... most of the time, anyway."

"Where's your sister now?" River said.

"She's a research scientist stationed in the Trappist system. She doesn't get home that often," Opal said somewhat wistfully. "Anyway, Willa told me that Argus contacted her and told her where I am."

"I didn't know our Opal that well," Willa said, "but your life sounds very different from hers."

"Isn't that common for parallel realities?" Poppy said. "I mean aren't there usually a lot of differences between them?"

"I suppose," Willa mused, "but my counterparts feel more alike than not."

"If that's true, maybe it has to do with the Mark," River said with a mouthful of sage-roasted potatoes. "Maybe it imparts similar characteristics in each version of you."

Willa tossed the thought around. "Maybe. I don't know."

The door chime sounded. Lily gestured for it to iris open, and Brim entered with a smile.

"Brim... please join us," River said as he made space at the table.

"I ate. Thank you. I hope I'm not disturbing you."

"Nonsense," Lily said. "Please sit, have some juice at least." She poured him a tall glass of apricot nectar as Brim took a seat that faced Willa. "I believe you know Poppy, and this is Willa's new friend, Opal."

Brim nodded to both girls then turned his gaze back to Willa.

"So, what brings you here?" asked River.

"I... we... my mother and father and I, um, and Gar, of course, we need Willa's help." He mentally kicked himself for his clumsy answer. He sipped the juice to wet his dry throat.

"What is it?" Willa said.

"You remember Gant..."

Willa hesitated as her senses went on alert. "Yes, of course."

"Well, it seems he's come into possession of some very advanced weapons," Brim said. He shifted in his seat, unsure if he should be revealing the information to Willa's family and friends.

Willa sensed his unease. "It's okay, Brim. You can talk freely here."

Brim flashed a self-conscious smile. "Sorry, of course. Caution is a way of life in the League."

"I understand. Please go on," Willa encouraged him.

"Anyway, it seems the only way the Resistance and the Alliance will get to use those weapons against the Archon's fleet is if the Tribunal ends Gant's banishment. Father and Brahma Kamal are petitioning them to grant his release as we speak."

"There's no way the Tribunal would pardon him for murder!" Lily said. "I'm shocked that Brahma would even consider such a thing!"

"I don't know," River countered. "These are desperate times. If Gant's weapons can defeat the Archon's fleet --"

"How did he come by these weapons?" Lily interrupted. "I thought Sed had no advanced technology."

"A smuggler from outside the Alliance who trades with the Subappu for spices and other goods," Brim explained.

Willa leaned forward. "You want to know if I can sense what the Alliance should do... if they should accept Gant's offer."

"Yes," Brim said.

Willa swept her eyes around the table. Lily subtly shook her head, River furrowed his brow with concern, Brim gazed at Willa with hope, Poppy held her breath, and Opal stared expectantly with her all-black eyes. Willa was silent for several heartbeats, then locked eyes with Brim. "Give me tonight. I'll come to you with an answer in the morning," she promised.

Brim nodded and stood. "Thank you for your hospitality," he said to Lily and River. The doorway opened as he walked toward it and closed behind him as he made his way down the main branch.

"I don't like this," Lily said.

"It'll be okay, Mom," Willa said with a smile as she rested her arms on Poppy's and Opal's shoulders. "I'm not alone anymore."

*

Later that night, after Lily and River had gone to bed, Willa, Poppy, and Opal sat in a triangular formation on the floor in Willa's room. A Luminaria floated in the air between them and cast mesmerizing patterns of light that ushered them into a deep meditation.

Willa spoke softly, focused on her friends' eyes. "Let yourselves feel the energy that connects us. Let go of where you think you are, and allow your minds to pass through the door to the space I'm creating in my thoughts. Breathe deeply, let go of the reality you know. We breathe as one, we feel as one, we come together as one."

They all closed their eyes. When they opened them, they were sitting in a space that existed only in Willa's imagination. The circular chamber was white, ringed by golden glyphs set into the floor, and lit by an ethereal glow that suffused the room: Willa's benign version of the mental chamber where Xanthes had trapped her.

Poppy and Opal glanced at their surroundings.

"It looks so real!" Poppy said.

Opal ran her palm over the cool, white floor. "It feels real, too."

"In the realm of the mind, thoughts are things," Willa said. She snapped her fingers. Three of the floor glyphs floated up into the air. With a wave of her hand, one of the glyphs – a ring of circles – moved and hovered over Poppy's head.

"The glyph of probability," Willa announced.

Another wave of her hand positioned an asterisk-like symbol over Opal's head.

"The glyph of connection," Willa said.

A subtle gesture brought a circle with a central dot over Willa's own head.

"The glyph of insight," she proclaimed.

With a final gesture, the three glyphs were joined by a triangle of light, and each symbol shot an energy beam downward through the tops of each girl's head. Poppy and Opal gasped as the energy flowed through them.

Willa's voice reverberated within the chamber. "Each of our abilities will expand and link us together. We are three. We are one. Apart or together, we will always be connected. We are more than counterparts. We will know each other's hearts, minds, and spirits. We are now, and forevermore, a Trinity."

The mental chamber vanished in an incandescent flash of light. Willa, Poppy, and Opal opened their eyes to find themselves back in Willa's room in the Nest.

Poppy was the first to find her voice. "What just happened?"

"We just formed an unbreakable bond," Willa said. "I flowed some of the energy I received from the Elemental Kenning to each of you. Your abilities have been amplified and will continue to grow. As a Trinity, we're now capable of withstanding Xanthes's mental attacks."

Opal nodded as she explored her expanded powers. "My counterparts' voices… there aren't only five. There are fifty! Yet I can hear each one clearly. The wealth of knowledge is staggering."

Poppy's mind exploded with waves of probability. She saw pathways as glowing lines of light, some fading away while others brightened. "Wow! I can actually see probable pathways and outcomes being calculated in my brain. It's… making me dizzy."

"You'll get used to it," Willa promised.

"What did the insight symbol do for you?" Opal asked.

Willa focused. "I can see Xanthes's thoughts more clearly, without being detected by her." Willa froze in shock.

"What?" Poppy said as she felt Willa's rush of fear.

Willa tried to make sense of what she saw in her mind's eye. "She's found two of her alternate universe counterparts! She's going to form her own Trinity!"

Opal's joy was ripped from her. "Then this was for nothing?"

Willa shook her head and inhaled her resolve. "No, not for nothing. If we hadn't done this, she could have overwhelmed us. We have to remember that what happens in our reality will likely happen in hers, too."

"So, now what?" Poppy wondered.

"So now we keep practicing. We get stronger. We search for the best possible outcome and we stay on track," Willa said with renewed conviction. "We watch each other's backs."

"Reminds me of something from an old story Mom read to me once," Poppy said with a wistful smile. "One for all and all for one."

"Unus pro omnibus, omnes pro uno," Opal said.

Willa and Poppy threw her a puzzled look.

Opal shrugged and smiled. "Apparently, one of my new counterparts knows ancient Latin."

Poppy's stomach growled. "Anybody for a midnight snack?"

"Yes! I'm starving," Opal said.

Willa rubbed her stomach. "Uh, oh. I think when we connected our hearts, minds, and spirits, our stomachs got connected too."

The girls' moods brightened as their laughter filled the room.

Chapter Sixteen:
CURRENTS

"There are many currents in the ocean of existence. Every person has their own flow. Sometimes, the currents bring us together. Sometimes, they pull us apart. The thing to remember is that our flow knows where we need to go. At first, it may seem we've landed or been stranded upon a foreign shore. But sooner or later, we discover something familiar in the midst of the strange, a hint of home in a place where we never thought to find it. In that moment, all questions answer themselves."

Excerpt from "Way of the Wanderer"
by Ash'kara Ak'wasi

*

THE NEXT DAY, Willa stood between Dennik and Brahma as they faced Oringa Kala in the Tribunal chamber.

"I know this goes against every instinct," Willa began.

"Not to mention our laws and thousands of years of tradition," Oringa added.

"I understand," Willa agreed. "But with all due respect, my senses tell me it's crucial that you allow Gant passage to Earth along with the new weapons."

"No slight to your senses, Willa, but it will take more than a feeling to convince the other Magisters to reverse the decision."

"Are *you* convinced?" Brahma asked Oringa.

"Not entirely," admitted the Nommos. "Regardless of how promising those mysterious weapons may be, I can't help but suspect that there's something Gant isn't telling us."

"I remind the Tribunal that he did believe he was saving my life," Dennik said. "But if you suspect he might have yet another a hidden agenda, we can keep a close eye on him."

"True," Brahma agreed. "We only need him to teach our techs how to operate the weapons. If he's allowed to come to Earth, his freedom can still be restricted."

"I can sense Gant's hunger for power," Willa said. "If we manage to defeat the Archon, we already know that Gant wants to take his place. For the time being, his interests align with those of the Alliance, so he poses no immediate threat."

"I'll discuss this with the other Magisters," Oringa said. "You'll have your answer soon." Oringa stood and entered his chambers.

Willa, Dennik, and Brahma made their way to the exit.

"Can you sense what the Tribunal will decide?" Dennik asked Willa.

"The answer will be no."

Dennik and Brahma stopped.

"You're certain?" Brahma pressed. "Why?"

"The decision has to be unanimous," she said. "I ken one of the Magisters has his own agenda."

"Who?" Dennik demanded.

"I'm not sure. The Nommos are hard to read, even for me. But they must all strongly believe they're doing the right thing. That makes it tougher to sense who it is."

Dennik and Brahma exchanged a glance. They knew that if Willa was right, Dennik would have to resort to subterfuge to get the weapons that the Resistance and the Alliance desperately needed.

"That will be dangerous," Willa said, as if the others had spoken aloud, "but it may be the only way."

Dennik and Brahma were taken aback. Willa faced them squarely. "Unlike the Nommos, you're easy to read. Count me in."

"Your parents would never allow it," Brahma retorted.

"Believe me, I'd love to be left out of all of this, but I've come to accept that I have a part to play to protect the Alliance," Willa said. "My parents will understand."

*

Malvania Moonstone awoke in a hospital room in the medical sector of Andromeda Spaceport. Hyacinth and another telepathic med-tech flanked her as Alder stood at the foot of her bed. The telepaths scanned Moonstone's mind and nodded to the Sage.

"She's clear," said Hyacinth.

He nodded his thanks, and the med-techs left him alone with the blind Nocturnal.

"How are you feeling?" he asked.

It took a moment for Moonstone to recognize his voice. "Alder?"

"Yes, Malvania."

She tried to sit up. Pain stabbed through her brain. She cried out and collapsed back onto her pillow.

"Take it easy," Alder cautioned. "You've been through a lot."

The horrifying memories of the murders came crashing back into Malvania's mind. "What have I done!"

Alder moved to her bedside. "You weren't yourself."

"That little witch seized control of my mind like I was a novice. How could I have been so weak!"

"Xanthes has grown very powerful. If she gets her claws into anyone else's psyche, I may not be able to break them free," Alder said.

Tears rolled down Moonstone's cheeks. Her gnarled hands covered her stricken face as images of Opal's, Rose's, and Lilac's ghastly murders forced their way back into her memory. "Oh! Those poor girls!"

Alder pulled up a chair, sat, and gently pulled Moonstone's hands away from her face. He held then in his own hands to calm her. "Malvania… why haven't you told anyone you're a Shapeshifter?"

Grey irises and black pupils suddenly replaced Moonstone's milky blind eyes. She held Alder in her gaze. "Because then I'd have to leave Mystery. The Provost, the students, they've become my family, my home."

"You told Willa that you're a member of a secret society called the Colloquium," Alder said. "Where's that located?"

"On the planet Cimarron," she admitted. "The ones I told… you think they'd be willing to keep my secret?" she pleaded.

"I'll see to it," Alder said as he squeezed her hand.

Malvania let out a sigh. "Thank you."

Alder patted her hand and stood. "Get some rest. I'll look in on you later."

Malvania nodded and shifted her eyes back to alabaster orbs as Alder left. Even though Xanthes was responsible for forcing her to commit those grisly murders, the three victims' faces were seared into her memory. Malvania knew they'd haunt her for the rest of her life.

*

Willa sat with Dennik, Alarra, Brim, and Gar in their quarters. "As I suspected, the Tribunal refused to commute Gant's sentence, so the question is, how can the Alliance learn to use the weapons without his training?"

"We could deal with the smuggler directly," Dennik suggested.

Gar nodded in agreement. "And we've got to get enough of those weapons to arm the League as well. 'Course, we don't know when we'll be able to go back through that blasted Maelstrom!"

"What if Gant won't take us to the smuggler?" Brim said.

289

"We could put a tracker on him," Alarra said. "He's got to contact the smuggler at some point."

"Right!" agreed Gar. "We grab the smuggler and leave Gant in the spiders' web!"

Brim turned to Willa. "What do you think of that plan?"

Willa stared at the table in a trance.

"Willa?" Brim gently prodded.

She looked up at them, unsettled. "It won't work."

Dennik held her gaze. "Why not?"

"I'm not sure there is a smuggler," she said.

"You're saying Gant lied? What a surprise," Gar huffed. "He didn't tell us he was Koro's brother, he didn't tell us he wanted to sit on the Archon's throne, and now, according to Willa, he probably lied about the smuggler to force the Alliance to bring him to Earth. Why do we still trust him?"

"We're don't," Dennik said, "but we need him to think we do for now."

Gar wasn't pleased but he knew it was useless to argue when Dennik's mind was made up. "If there's no smuggler, how'd he come by the weapons?"

"I don't know yet," Willa said, "but I have an idea how to bring Gant and the weapons to Earth without breaking the law."

*

That evening, after Willa explained her plan to her new cohorts, she made her way through the nearest Shaddok and walked across the flower-filled field toward her home. She was only a few hundred feet from the Nest when Thorn came running up to her.

"Willa! I need to talk to you."

"Everyone wants my opinion lately," Willa joked.

"What?"

"Nothing. Why are you in such a hurry?"

"Father, Rowan, and I are going to look for Mom. We want you to come with us," Thorn said, still a bit breathless.

"You have new information about what happened to your mother?"

"No," Thorn admitted. He sat down on the grass. Willa joined him. "Father may be right. Mom may be dead. But I'll never stop looking until I know for sure. I was hoping, you know, with your abilities…"

Willa rested her hand on Thorn's shoulder. "That I might sense what happened to Celandine."

Thorn wiped at a tear. "Will you come with us?"

"When are you leaving?"

"It'll take three days to get our flight plan approved by the Contact Council since Shan isn't part of the Alliance."

"You're going to Shan?" Willa's eyes glazed over as a vision flooded her senses. She was suddenly alone in the field. The night was eerily silent. The ancient moon was partially eclipsed by the cratered eye of the Sentinel moon as it cast its malevolent gaze down upon Willa.

A rustling in the field, like something heavy slithering over dry, dead grass, grew louder. Willa stood and searched for the sound. A second crackling from another direction joined it. The tapping of staccato footsteps issued from behind her: a third unseen entity.

Willa sharpened her senses as three hulking silhouettes rose from the ground in a triangle formation around her: A large salamander, an enormous snake, and a giant spider glared at her, the pale moons reflected in their glistening, black eyes.

"Willa!"

Willa snapped from her vision.

Thorn looked up at her, his face etched with worry. "I called your name over and over. What happened to you?"

Willa remained standing. She gazed out over the moonlit field as though the visionary creatures might return. "I had a vision."

Thorn stood alongside her. "What did you see?"

Willa looked deep into Thorn's eyes. "That I'm going with you to find your mother. There's something I need to do first. I'll come find you in three days."

Thorn crushed Willa in a hug, overwhelmed with gratitude. "Thank you!" He pulled back, and kissed her full on the lips. The weight Willa had been carrying on her shoulders for so long evaporated in the heat of his passion. She held him tight and felt their bond deepen, as though their hearts had reached out and cupped each other in a deep, loving embrace.

Thorn backed up a few steps, let out a victory yell, and ran towards home.

Willa watched Thorn go. She brought her fingers gently to her lips and felt the lingering warmth of his kiss. For a moment, she was thirteen again: just a girl, kissed by a boy for the very first time. Had that only been a year ago? It felt like an eternity had passed since she was forced to become the bloody savior of the galaxy!

But right now, this night was theirs and theirs alone. She felt her heart swell and, without a care in the world, she turned toward home.

A rustle in the distant grass made her freeze. "Not again," she said. Fearing that the vision, and the monsters, were upon her again, she spun around, expecting the worst. Then, her eyes caught the culprit.

The fox had returned. Its ruddy fur and white chest shone in the moonlight, its golden eyes full of secrets.

"Who are you!" Willa shouted. "What do you want? Why are you watching me?" She walked toward the animal, extending her senses, and, as usual, the fox trotted off through the field and melted into the night.

"Why can't I sense you?" she said, more to herself than the fox. Miffed, Willa turned her back on the vulpine stalker and crunched through the grass toward home.

*

Three days later on Sed, Willa, Dennik, Alarra, Brim, and Gar, along with Gant, had loaded hundreds of the alien weapons into the hold of a used cargo ship that Alder borrowed from his old friend, "Fig" Rigoletto. The Sage sat in the pilot's seat as he went through the pre-flight checklist.

Dennik secured the last weapon and went forward to the pilot's cabin. "The Cargo's secure," he informed Alder. "It's all on you now."

"Relax, my friend. It'll work like a charm. Come to think of it, it is a charm," Alder said with his usual bluster. "Excuse me." He squeezed past Dennik and walked to the cargo hold, staff in hand. Dennik followed, his expression doubtful.

Gant turned to the Sage, slightly nervous. "I still don't understand how you think a disguise will fool anyone."

"It's far more than a disguise. Just stand perfectly still. It won't hurt a bit," Alder assured him.

Gant took a deep breath and exhaled. Alder lifted his staff and drew a circle in the air with its glowing tip. Gant's face, body, and clothing began to shift in increments like flipping through the pages of a book filled with illustrations. Gant's wide brow narrowed; his nose elongated; his mouth widened. His eyes went from green to blue to brown and settled on grey; his hair went from black to salt-and-pepper. Gant's utilitarian garb changed into a well-worn pilot's uniform.

With a final flourish of his staff, Alder conjured a large mirror that hovered in the air before the transmogrified Gant.

"I've heard that the Archon's Sensates have witching powers, but nothing like this!" Gant said as he studied his new reflection. "You're sure no one will know it's me?"

"The change isn't merely cosmetic," Alder explained. "Your fingerprints, your retinal scan, and your DNA will read as a completely different person. You are now the smuggler you lied to us about."

"Sorry about that," Gant said without a hint of regret. "It was all I could think of."

"You still haven't told us where the weapons actually came from," Dennik reminded him.

"That will need to remain my secret," Gant said. "I made a promise."

"And you always keep your promises, right?" Gar said sarcastically.

"A promise?" Dennik said. "To who? You said the spiders weren't involved."

"None of your business," Gant shot back.

"You lie like most people breathe," Gar said with a sneer.

"I didn't lie about the weapons, did I?" Gant countered, his temper rising.

"This is no time to argue," Alarra interrupted.

"Right you are, my love," Dennik said. He threw a scathing look at Gant as he went aft to raise the cargo ramp.

Alder headed back toward the pilot's cabin. "We lift in three minutes."

Everyone took their seats and buckled in as the ship's engines hummed to life. Brim sat next to Willa.

"This was a brilliant plan."

"I have my moments," she said with a smile.

The cabin shuddered as its anti-gravity thrusters floated the ship off the Subappu landing pad and into the violet sky. Within seconds, they were speeding through the velvet void of space.

*

On Xos Three, Xanthia led her alternate universe counterparts to the observation window that overlooked her starship factories. A rush of adrenaline coursed through Xanthes and Xibalba as they beheld row after row of ships on the tarmac below.

"Ten thousand ships, weapons-ready and hardened against the worst that the Maelstrom can throw at them," Xanthia boasted.

"Between our combined fleets, that's twenty thousand ships!" Xanthes said, barely able to contain her excitement.

"No Resistance, no Alliance, will be able to stand against us. The spoils of three universes will be ours!" Xibalba added, equally thrilled. "We're an unbeatable Triad!"

Xos-Xanthia went over to a small, pink-skinned alien servant who held a tray with three glasses and the bottle of Zapota. She poured each of them a drink and raised her glass. "Perhaps now, you're willing to savor the moment?"

Xanthes and Xibalba raised their glasses.

"To the Triad," Xanthia said.

"The Triad," Xanthes repeated.

"The Triad," Xibalba joined in.

They drank the golden liquid in unison, even as each of them secretly plotted how, when victory was assured, they would betray and kill the other two.

*

The next day, Willa arrived at Andromeda Spaceport and headed to the docking bay that held *Sagittarius,* Kale's ship. She was accompanied by Lily, River, Poppy, and Opal, who came to see her off.

The inner bay doors parted, and Thorn ran to greet them. Kale, Rowan, and Elowen were at the ship's ramp, loading the last of their supplies.

Thorn gave Willa a quick hug, then turned to Lily and River. "Thank you for allowing Willa to come."

"Like I could stop a force of nature," Lily said, her tone tinged with concern. "Still, I hope she's able to help you find your mother."

"I'll be okay," Willa said to her parents. "Please tell the Provost I'll continue my training when I return." She faced Poppy and Opal. "Keep practicing like I showed you."

Opal tapped her head and pointed to Willa. "You'll know if we don't."

Willa hugged them all in turn. "I'll see you all soon. That's a promise." She turned and walked to the *Sagittarius* with Thorn. She kept a brave face for her parents and friends, but as images of the monsters from her vision flashed through her mind, Willa knew she was about to face her greatest challenge so far.

To be continued in:

Shards of a Shattered Mirror
BOOK THREE: SHAPESHIFTER

CAST OF CHARACTERS

HYBRIDS

WILLA HILLICRISSING - Our hero, a strong-willed fourteen-year-old Hybrid girl with a rare genetic "Mark" that gives her special, amplified abilities far beyond her years and training.

LILY HILLICRISSING - Willa's mother, a wise and caring soul with a love of growing things, along with a fierce protective nature where her daughter's wellbeing is concerned.

RIVER HILLICRISSING - Willa's father, a gentle man who exudes warmth and assurance but relies on a no-nonsense attitude when the circumstances call for a level head.

HOLLY COTTON - Willa's Cryptic mentor, and a member of the Northern Quorum, who loves her apprentice as though she was her own daughter, and does her best to focus Willa's stubborn nature toward her study of Mastery.

KALE ASHGROVE - An explorer who was rescued by Dennik of the Resistance after being captured and tortured by the Archon of Xos. Father of Thorn and Rowan, he searches the stars for Celandine, his missing wife, every chance he gets.

THORN ASHGROVE - Kale's youngest son and Willa's boyfriend, insecure due to the loss of his family after his mother went missing and his father was captured by the Archon. He is impetuous and jealous of any boys who might vie for Willa's affections.

ROWAN ASHGROVE - Kale's oldest son, studying to become a First Contact Specialist, is somewhat more level-headed than his younger brother, but is prone to taking dangerous risks to protect his family.

CELANDINE ASHGROVE - Kale's wife and Thorn's and Rowan's missing mother, mysteriously lost without a trace on a diplomatic mission to Shan, an alien world beyond the border of Alliance territory.

ALDER REDWOOD - A flamboyant Sage and another Quorum member, given to eccentric behavior that belies his power and wisdom, and who, when he realized Willa's full potential, chose to become one of her mentors.

SELENE NYMPHAEA - A Nocturnal and a Quorum member with a hidden agenda who forces Willa to use her abilities to search for a lost formula that could transform Selene into a powerful Wraith like her Great-Grandmother, Belladonna Bloodroot.

SEQUOIA AUGUST MOON - The Provost of Mystery, the training lodge of the Nocturnals.

MALVANIA MOONSTONE - The Divinorum Master of Mystery, a blind Nocturnal.

OPAL DESERETTE - A Nocturnal in training and Sequoia's apprentice.

ERIDANI GINKO - A Nocturnal in the Quorum who keenly and

silently watches events unfold and only speaks when she has something important to say.

ROSE LARKSPUR - A Cryptic within the Quorum who possesses strong empathic abilities and whose mere touch brings a soothing calm to tense situations.

LILAC LARKSPUR - Rose's identical twin in the Quorum with identical Cryptic abilities.

BRAHMA KAMAL - The monk-like head of the First Contact Council, who has served in the position for years due to his deep wisdom, sacred respect for all life, and, as reflected by his ice-blue eyes, the soothing demeanor of a placid mountain lake.

VARIABILIS - A reclusive Shapeshifter who suffered the loss of his wife and daughter in a tragic accident, and has hidden away in a remote stone tower until events forced him back into society to protect his friends and the Alliance.

QUINLAT - An elder female Shapeshifter on the planet Cimarron, former mentor to Variabilis, and the leader of a secret society known as the Colloquium.

ENCANTADO - A brooding Shapeshifter in the Quorum known for his terse, impatient encounters with people, and who prefers decisive plans and physical action more than talk.

MOSHI - Another Shapeshifter in the Northern Quorum, more thoughtful than Encantado, prone to sarcastic comments, but quick with praise when praise is due.

SYBILLINE DARKWOOD - A Nocturnal who oversees Mystery's death and burial rituals.

STARGAZER & STAR - A Shapeshifter, often simply called Star, who can split herself into multiple copies to run the Stargazer Inn as both owner and staff.

JACARANDA FLORUS - Head astronomer of the Interstellar Alliance on Earth, a fact marked by an eight-pointed star tattoo on her shaved head.

ELOWEN KOA - Kale's former pilot, captured and tortured by the Archon's minions to give up the secret of Earth's advanced technology.

COMMANDER IVY EREBUS - Head of Andromeda Spaceport, the Interstellar Alliance's embassy in orbit around Earth. The spaceport also serves as a training ground for pilots and First Contact Specialists as well as containing a wide array of science labs.

CAPTAIN BRYONY BRACKEN - Head of Earth's rescue squad, assigned to patrol the solar system and maintain security.

CAPTAIN YARROW - Commanded one of the rescue squad ships destroyed over Saturn by Haldane's stealth weaponry.

HYACINTH – A telepathic med-tech who works on Andromeda Spaceport.

HUMANS

POPPY ROUSSEAU - Willa's best friend and playful confidante, who has a propensity for blunt talk and a psychic gift she uses to level the playing field between humans and Hybrids.

SYLVANIA ROUSSEAU - Poppy's mother, a rare human Nocturnal, often withdrawn and secretly struggling against Xanthes's telepathic intrusions that threaten her sanity and Poppy's life.

BRANDELYN ESPERANZA – Sylvania's alternate identity on the planet Tavanna.

ANDER GARZA - An astronomer on Andromeda Spaceport, and Jacaranda's colleague.

CAPTAIN SORREL - Commanded one of the rescue squad ships destroyed over Saturn by Haldane's stealth weaponry.

FIGUERO "FIG" RIGOLETTO – A starship designer at the Mitsuyama Starship factory in Italy and personal friend of both Kale Ashgrove and Alder Redwood.

DARIA DOS SANTOS – A Portuguese woman who rents submarines and other conveyances to tourists in her home town of Sintra.

ZEV BUKOWSKI – A tech-engineer who maintains ships on Andromeda Spaceport.

THE BLACK LEAGUE

DENNIK - A Captain in the Black League, the Resistance movement attempting to overthrow the Archon's tyrannical reign over the Empire's enslaved worlds.

ALARRA - Dennik's wife, another member of the Resistance, sequestered in the tunnels of a dark moon orbiting a rogue gas giant planet, with a warm heart and a firm resolve to defeat their Overlord enemies.

BRIM - Dennik's and Alarra's teenage son, eager to join the Resistance, and play his part in fighting the Archon, but is somewhat headstrong and impatient to grow up and be taken seriously.

GAR - A seasoned, grizzled old soldier, always ready for an argument or a fight, who lost an eye in battle but still acts as Dennik's right-hand-man while also mentoring Brim in the ways of the Resistance.

KORO - A Resistance pilot and secretly, an undercover spy for the Archon.

DARVA VAL AT'N - Founder of the Black League and the Resistance movement against the Overlords' occupation of Xos and the other enslaved worlds of the Empire. Darva died in a failed strike against the Archon's Citadel fifty years ago.

KARA VAL AT'N - Darva's daughter, who inherited her mother's mantle as leader of the Resistance after Darva's death. Kara commands the Black League with cool assurance despite her secret doubts about their ability to defeat the Empire.

JONNA - Kara's right hand, Jonna keeps the League's secret moon base running efficiently and ensures that supplies keep flowing via raids on the Empire's cargo ships.

VODNIK - A tall, imposing figure who guards the entrance to the League's communications chamber and other sensitive areas within the moon base, making it impossible for any spies to send a secret message to the Overlords.

OVERLORDS, SENSATES & SERVANTS

XOS-ASURA - The cadaverous, grey-skinned Archon of the Overlords, who rules the Empire's twenty enslaved worlds with an iron grip and plans to use intel from Kale's captured crew to breach the electromagnetic anomaly known as the Maelstrom in order to conquer Earth and use its advanced technology to defeat the Interstellar Alliance.

ARCHONS TWO & THREE – The Overlords of two alternate universes.

XANTHES - The seventeen-year-old Overlord of the Eastern Block on Xos and the Archon's daughter, who has the same Anu genetics as Willa and exhibits similar abilities that she refers to as her "witching" powers.

XIBALBA – Xanthes's counterpart on Xos Two.

XOS-XANTHIA – Another of Xanthes's counterparts, and Archon of Xos Three.

UZZA - Xanthes's aged mentor who instructs her on perfecting her powers and thus, belongs to a rare and powerful group known as the Sensates, the Xoshi equivalent of Earth's Sages.

ZADUGA – Head of the Sensate order, a powerful wizard equal to an Alliance Sage, with plans to control Xanthes and rule the Empire.

KALVIA - Xanthes's mother, who secretly aided the Resistance and was killed by Xanthes for her betrayal of the Empire.

GANT - One of the Archon's former guards who, after he declared he had a brother hiding in the Resistance, was commissioned as a spy and sent to Earth to discover the Alliance's weaknesses.

HALDANE - One of the Archon's most loyal and experienced pilots, who takes Gant to Earth in his stealth ship.

SPLICERS – Mindless, genetically-engineered soldiers and workers created to serve the Archon's Empire.

SASQUATCH

ARGUS - The Quorum's eight-foot-tall Divinorum master presents a gruff exterior but has a huge heart and an appetite to match.

RHADAMANTHUS – A powerful Yeti from the Himalayan region.

TS'EME'KWES – A female Sasquatch of the American Northwest.

SALIZAR – A skeptical and argumentative Sasquatch with a Slavic accent.

ELEMENTALS

RUSALKA - A shape-shifting Pooka who usually takes the form of a large hare with red eyes and who, through trickery, is responsible for turning Belladonna into a Banshee.

ASHLEEN - Queen of the Pookas, also usually in the form of a hare with white fur and bright pink eyes, who performed a Kenning on Willa to amplify her powers in the hope of staving off the coming invasion.

GRENNAN - Another Pooka, somewhat older than Ashleen and Rusalka, referred to as a "Seer" who has the gift of perceiving past and future parallel realities and sensing dangerous shifts in time.

KERNUNNOS - A very ancient forest spirit, bigger than Argus, with a strange, bearded elk-like face, hoofed feet, and enormous antlers. His penchant for rewarding the good and punishing the bad formed the original seed for the story that eventually evolved into the concept of Santa Claus.

SILVER - A small, flying, faery-like Sylph that offers her insights at Elemental gatherings called Enclaves.

VULCANUS - An ancient Salamander Elemental that looks similar to a sleek amphibian but appears shrouded in blue flames.

GWYLLION – A blue Welsh Faery who likes to tease her fellow Elementals.

GRAELACH – A large oak tree that used to be a Tree Nymph, and who can communicate with other elementals.

BANSHEE

BELLADONNA BLOODROOT - Once a Sage, Belladonna tried to transform into a Wraith. Tricked by the Elemental, Rusalka, she turned instead into a mournful, wandering spirit stuck between life and death.

WRAITHS

AMAKEERI – A wry Wraith with a secret plan to protect Earth from the Archon's attack.

DEVASHKA, YOJIRO, VIVIANA & ETHANIEL - Four of Amakeeri's fellow Wraiths.

ALIENS

BRAELAN - A young Shinzai, and friend of Poppy's, with a skin of scarlet scales and a long tail, often competes against Poppy in the prediction game called Hexes.

DOONA SET - A diminutive alien from the planet Tet, initially served as the Archon's attaché until he no longer proved useful and was killed.

YADRA JEET - Another alien from Tet who also functioned as the Archon's lead Tech.

ESCHAVEK REN - Also from Tet, a planet where genders can shift from male to female and back again, Eschavek served as an attaché to the Archon.

SANJA VET – A violet alien from Tet, also served as a lead tech.

SOONASH - An alien from Takanni, with pea-green skin and a single, yellow eye, a lead Empire Technician.

WHELKS - Small, thin beings with huge black, bug-like eyes, known in the twenty-first century as the Greys, and responsible for genetically engineering the Hybrids that eventually arrived on Earth during the Landing.

THE ANU – The ancient extraterrestrial race of tall humanoids with blue-tinted skin who spliced their genetics into *Homo Erectus* to create *Homo Sapiens*.

THE THOOK – An alien race with uncanny telepathic abilities that cause anyone not looking directly at them to forget that any encounter took place.

THANNIK – A Thook friend of Sylvania's who helps arrange her disappearance.

THORASTA – A Thook Mind Master.

THE SUBAPPU – Large spider-like aliens on the planet Sed where Gant was banished.

THE NOMMOS - Amphibious beings from the Sirius star system, home of the Interstellar Alliance Tribunal, where Gant is sentenced for Haldane's murder.

ORINGA KALA – Head Magistrate of the Sirius Tribunal, tasked with sentencing Gant.

OANNU & YADROON – Oringa's fellow Tribunal Magistrates.

SHAROON – A Nommos med-tech on Andromeda Spaceport who works with Doctor Policarpo.

DR. VELIKA POLICARPO – Chief med-tech on Andromeda Spaceport and ex-lover of the Shapeshifter Variabilis.

CHATTERBOX – A lemon-yellow alien tech on Andromeda Spaceport who earned the nickname "Chatterbox" due to his penchant for spreading gossip.

VAS-BASSO – A four-limbed, four-eyed controller in the Andromeda Spaceport operations center.

SENTIENT COMPUTERS

OCULARIS - The Artificial Intelligence that operates Andromeda Spaceport and sees to the needs of the station's thousands of workers and visitors.

CORVUS - Rowan Ashgrove's ship, the first sentient computer to greet the Resistance members when Kale and his sons were reunited after his escape from the Archon.

RIGEL - River Hillicrissing's ship, used in pursuit of Rowan and Thorn during their attempt to rescue their father, Kale.

SAGITTARIUS - Kale's starship, damaged by the Maelstrom. A new *Sagittarius* was designed and built by Fig Rigoletto.

STARLING - Captain Yarrow's rescue ship, destroyed over Saturn's moon Titan by a missile from Haldane's stealth vessel.

THRALL - The Archon's new computer and ship, built with tech from Kale's damaged ship, *Sagittarius*.

ABOUT THE AUTHOR

DARRYL ANKA is a writer-director-producer at Zia Films LLC (ziafilms.com), a film production company he owns with his producing partner and wife, Erica Jordan. He has an extensive background in miniature effects, storyboards and set design and has worked on some of the biggest sci-fi and action films over the past thirty years, such as *Star Trek II: The Wrath of Khan, Iron Man* and *Pirates of the Caribbean: At World's End.* His film resumé can be viewed under "Darryl Anka" on the Internet Movie Database (imdb.com).

He is also an internationally known public speaker on UFOs and metaphysical topics. Over twenty books of his seminars have been published in the United States and Japan and recordings of his talks have been sold to thousands of people around the globe by April Rochelle, his partner at Bashar Communications, Inc. (bashar.org)

Information about new books and other projects can be found on his personal website (darrylanka.com). Darryl is always working on new films, scripts and novels. He lives in Woodland Hills, California, a suburb of Los Angeles.